Arrival

NEW HORIZONS:

ARRIVAL

° ° ° ° ° ° ° °

W. Ross White

MBP Press
Kelowna

An MBP Press Book

Library and Archives Canada Cataloguing in Publication

White, W. Ross, author
Arrival / W. Ross White.

(New horizons)
Issued in print and electronic formats.
ISBN 978-0-9940265-4-5 (pbk.).--ISBN 978-0-9940265-5-2 (html)

I. Title. II. Series: White, W. Ross. New horizons.

PS8645.H5475A77 2015 C813'.6 C2015-900285-0
C2015-900286-9

This book is a work of fiction. Names, characters, places, and incidents either are products of the author's imagination or are used fictitiously. Any resemblance to actual persons, living or dead, or actual events is purely coincidental.

Cover Image Credit: NASA, ESA, H. Teplitz and M. Rafelski (IPAC/Caltech), A. Koekemoer (STScI), R. Windhorst (Arizona State University), and Z. Levay (STScI)

Connect with Ross and learn more about his work
at: www.wrosswhite.com and www.newhoizonmission.com

Thanks and Acknowledgements

Carl Sagan
Gene Roddenberry
NASA and the New Horizons spacecraft
Neil deGrasse Tyson of Star Talk
Michael Shermer of The Skeptics Society
Bill Nye of The Planetary Society
Kiki Sanford, Justin Jackson, and Blair Bazdarich
of This Week In Science
Dan Carlin of Hardcore History and Common Sense
Phillip Adams of the Australian Broadcasting Corporation's
Late Night Live
Seth Shostak of Search for Extraterrestrial Intelligence
Molly Bentley of Big Picture Science
Fraser Cain of Universe Today
Pamela Gay of AstronomyCast
Phil Plait of Bad Astronomy
Bob McDonald of the Canadian Broadcasting Corporation's
Quirks and Quarks
Leora Dahl of Okanagan College
Dale Donovan of Okanagan College
John Pugsley of Okanagan College
Manuela Ungureanu of UBC – Okanagan
Zach Walsh of UBC – Okanagan
James Paley

Joyce Kunzelman

NEW HORIZONS

W. Ross White

"It's just a ride,
and we can change it anytime we want.
It's only a choice.
No effort, no work, no job, no savings of money.
A choice, right now, between fear and love.
The eyes of fear want you to put bigger locks on your door,
buy guns, close yourself off.
The eyes of love, instead, see all of us as one.
Here's what we can do to change the world, right now,
to a better ride:
Take all that money that we spend on weapons and defense each year
and instead spend it feeding and clothing and
educating the poor of the world,
which it would many times over –
not one human being excluded –
and we could explore space, together,
both inner and outer,
forever, in peace."

- Bill Hicks

Part Three:

ARRIVAL

"Every period of human development has had its own
particular type of human conflict –
its own variety of problems that, apparently,
could be settled only by force.
And each time, frustratingly enough, force
never really settled the problem.
Instead, it persisted through a series of conflicts,
then vanished of itself, – what's the expression, –
ah, yes 'not with a bang, but with a whimper,'
as the economic and social environment changed.
And then, new problems,
and a new series of wars.

\- *Isaac Asimov's 'I, Robot'*

Prologue

Earth year: 2323

After a twenty year burn, the Generational Starship 'New Horizon' cut its ion engines and silently slid into shallower waters of the cosmic ocean. After a century and a half of anticipation, they finally left the deep ocean of the interstellar void, and arrived on the shores of an alien star system.

It had been ten years since the crew first detected indications that they were entering a new star system. It was at this point that they'd entered the stellar bow shock zone, where light pressure and high energy radiation from the Sigma Draconis star began to be the dominant force, as opposed to the more general galactic cosmic rays which dominated the radiation environment of interstellar space. It was the same standard by which over two hundred years ago the Voyager space probes had been deemed to have officially reached interstellar space, officially marking the beginning of humans beings as an interstellar civilization in the process. There was a direct line between the spirit with which Voyager I and II were launched, and the spirit of the G.S.S. New Horizon.

For the first few years they made their way through their new system's equivalent of the Oort Cloud, a spherical halo of comets of all shapes and sizes. While the total mass of the icy cloud was about three times that of the ship's target planet, the gargantuan volume which they occupied meant that they hardly ever came into contact with each other. When they did, one would sometimes begin slowly tumbling down into the gravity well of the star, and more often than not they would get swallowed up by the binary outer gas giants.

Except for the exceptionally lucky ones, most comets which fell in from the Oort cloud would, over hundreds and hundreds of orbits (if they were even that lucky), inevitably chance an encounter with this two planet system and find their final resting place.

Once past this system's Kuiper Belt region of the outer star system, the ship passed two massive gas giants eternally dancing around each other in the distant cold of the system. One was a more massive Jupiter type of planet, and the other was a super Neptune, an icy giant with a mass somewhere between that of Saturn and Jupiter. A plethora of rocky moons of all shapes, sizes, and compositions found their celestial homes in orbit around one of these titans of the system. The New Horizon's crew could only take a quick look with their eyes and telescopes as they sailed past the system and manoeuvred themselves ahead of the more massive planet.

Sailing ahead of the larger ball of gas allowed the New Horizon to slow itself down by being pulled back towards it, a manoeuver known as gravity braking. Other kinds of ships back in their home star system had been engineered to be able to brake atmospherically through friction while flying through a gas giant's atmosphere, but a ship like the New Horizon was never designed to fly through any kind of planetary atmosphere whatsoever. It was in fact remarkably fragile in this respect. Gravity braking ahead of the system's most massive planet allowed them to bleed tremendous amounts of kinetic energy and dramatically fell their orbit down into the inner solar system.

Far distant from their gas giant rendezvous, the crew watched mesmerized as they had a similar fly-by encounter with a super-Earth type planet near the orbit of what would have been the asteroid belt in the Sol System. For a couple decades now, the crew had had the chance to study the Haven system and they'd discovered that this planet was four times as massive as the Earth and double the density which meant that the gravity at the surface was more than two and a half times what a human was used to. If this alone didn't make the planet seem inhospitable enough, observations revealed an intense magnetic field and rampant volcanism and tectonic activity. All the crew could see with the naked eye as they passed the planet for another gravitational braking maneuver was the thick toxic yellow and green atmosphere, which would have been reminiscent of Venus to their ancestors who had originally left their home star system.

Closer in than the orbit of Haven itself (which was roughly equivalent to Earth's), was a hot ice giant, a planet of the same approximate mass and composition as Uranus and Neptune, but in an orbit as close to the star as that of Mercury. Future Haven astronomers would later surmise that the giant's original location had been somewhere between the orbits of the double gas giant system and the super-Earth, but had been flung inward towards the star through unstable three body interactions with the outer giants. All any individual human could ever see was a snapshot of the body's excruciatingly slow death as its orbit gradually decayed in the solar atmosphere towards its inevitably fiery and unceremonious death, when it would be ripped apart and swallowed by its star.

The ship arrived at Haven and successfully manoeuvred into a stable orbit around the planet. Six satellites were launched in rapid succession out of the tube they had been carefully installed in so long ago. Each began only a few meters across on any given side, but once launched from the ship, they beautifully unfurled into a structure easily three times larger than their original size, exposing the entire suite of their instruments to the planet, including everything any of the crew on the ship or on any planet could ever need. They were a real time communications network and were full spectrum light detectors, able to turn those eyes down onto the planet for study, or back out to the depths of space.

The crew cautiously celebrated that the initial studies didn't indicate any reason why this planet would be uninhabitable for them. So far it didn't look like they would have to resupply and begin yet another multi-generational journey to yet another star, or worse back home. The satellites moved into their proper orbits, and immediately began studying Haven in far greater detail than the ship could on approach with its own instruments. Their first job was to find the first landing site for the crew after studying the planet's climate and geography. The rest would be up to the crew itself…

Haven Year: 0

Chapter 1

"Hello? Do you know who you are? Where you are? ...*What* you are?" He was asked after opening his eyes.

"Give me a second..." Wiremu asked as he looked up to the ceiling for a few moments as he tried to remember. "Yes. My name is Wiremu Tynes... this is supposed to be the New Horizon."

"It is." his interrogator confirmed. "Do you remember what you are?"

"...What I am?" It struck him as such an absurd question, but then he remembered. "Oh right, uh... I'm a simulant."

"Yes. Does everything feel right to you? Were all of your memories properly integrated? There was an... incident along the way which involved you; we were worried you may have been adversely affected."

"I think I'm all here... I seem to have all of the memories I should expect to have.... everything that was available up until a few weeks before the launch anyways..." He was now remembering that the original Wiremu Tynes, of whom he was a simulation, must be long dead now. He was a sophisticated mechanoid, who was running a sophisticated personality simulation program on the quantum computer brain in his head. The intended effect, was to create the illusion both to himself and to others, that he was in fact the person he was a replication of. "We've made it to the Sigma Draconis system then? We really... we really actually made it?"

"Don't sound so surprised." the human said with an edge which bordered on a snarl. "We're in orbit around Haven right now."

"Hot damn!!" Wiremu excitedly exclaimed, but then his heart sank (or whatever the equivalent feeling should be characterized as, for a being such as himself). "Wait, why didn't you wake us up earlier? We wanted to see the approach and everything; we were supposed to help you navigate into the system!" Wiremu was the ship's original captain, and he was disappointed that he'd missed the most interesting space flight aspect of their mission. From his decades with the Peacekeepers and the Trade Corps, he'd been so intimately familiar with the Sol System. Part of the whole point of him participating in this ultimate Hail Mary pass was to get the chance to navigate through an entirely new and alien star system. He'd been so looking forward to it... or more accurately the original him had been so looking forward to it. But if he wasn't Wiremu, then why should their arrival matter to him at all? It was already confusing him.

"To be honest, we... just forgot. We were too busy with all of the work required for the most critical part of our journey. I suppose it just didn't seem important enough to remember."

That didn't sit well with Wiremu. He didn't like the idea that the expressed wishes of he and the other mission founders could be so easily and remorselessly 'forgotten.' He could only wonder what other explicit instructions they'd left which had also been ignored. He scrutinized this other person in the room who appeared to be so carelessly masking his disdain. He had black hair which came down to the bottom of his ears, a brown Arab complexion, angular nose, and beady black eyes which had yet to look away.

"So who are *you* then?" Wiremu asked.

"My name is Asari. I am the current patriarch."

--- --- ---

Sadhika awoke sitting in a chair with an unfamiliar individual sitting across a table from her in an unfamiliar room.

"Hello. My name is Halley Bowland. What's yours?" The tone was friendly enough, if cautious.

"Sadhika," she answered reflexively without having to think about it, "Sadhika Sengupta"

"Good! And... you know *where* you are?" Halley gently asked.

"Well, I'm not familiar with this room in particular but... I should be somewhere on the New Horizon generational starship, and on close approach to Haven if our instructions were correctly followed."

"They weren't... I'm sorry. I protested, but... they waited until we'd already achieved orbit around Haven to wake you up."

"Oh." Sadhika didn't quite know what to make of that. "Wait, so we actually *made* it? That's incredible! You mean to tell me that we're actually in orbit around Haven *right now*? I want to see!" she declared as she energetically stood up.

"Soon, I promise." Her new friend told her. He was a tall man of physical substance, but he was remarkably pale with freckles and medium length auburn hair which framed his oval face and appeared to have begun receding. "Last question I have to ask you Sadhika. Do you know... *what* you are?" He scrutinized her response with intense blue-green eyes.

It was only after he asked that she remembered. Now she immediately recalled helping Neil come up with the waking protocol in the first place, and the need to specifically remind them of what they were for them to remember. "Yes of course. I do now... I'm a simulant; a *simulation* of the original Sadhika Sengupta. I understand this on an... intellectual level, but somehow it's... it's somehow hard to believe. Nothing about my... my experience suggests that I'm anything other than myself. I mean... her."

"I sympathize with your confusion, believe me... but that'll come later."

"So this is... this is the first time that *I've* been conscious. Me, the simulant... and not her?"

"That's right. You didn't leave specific instructions as to who should wake who. We thought it best to wake you all individually in one on one interviews with the senior staff. *I'm* the current captain."

--- --- ---

In-Su opened his eyes suddenly, and with instantaneous alertness. He was in a barren room with grey walls. The entire ceiling emitted the light which brightened his surroundings, and he figured it must be an opaque surface uniformly backlit from behind. He was sitting across from a woman of about thirty who had long straight black hair. She looked at him as though she were studying him with her big black eyes. Like himself, she had a touch of yellow to her skin tone, but her face was flatter and more angular than his, which was much rounder with narrower eyes and unlike hers his black hair was cut short.

"Greetings," he offered.

"Hello," she answered back a little sheepishly at first, and then with her fog of reservation burning away in the light of intense curiosity, she softly asked: "what's your name?"

"Kim In-Su. What's yours?" He asked reflexively.

"Aset," she replied. "I'm the Matriarch." After a pause she asked, "do you know where you are?"

After considering it for a few moments, In-Su replied: "I *should* be on the New Horizon, which *should* be in the Sigma Draconis star system if I've been awoken."

"Correct. So you know… *what* you are."

"I'm a… simulant." It wasn't a revelation per se; it was not a truth for which he had initially believed something false in its place. It simply… hadn't crossed his mind since he'd woken up which was, now that he thought about it, the first time he'd *ever* been conscious at all since he'd been… well born, and just a few minutes ago.

"How does that make you feel?" she asked, as though she'd followed along with him in his internal train of thought.

"I don't know. In a way it means that I'm dead. The person who I think I am, the *real* me… is long dead. And yet here I am. It's… it's quite a thought."

"I bet…" Aset seemed entranced by his predicament. "I can only imagine what that must feel like."

--- --- ---

"Hello, my name is Søren, this is Ishtar… may I ask what your name is?" The speaker had white skin, but the woman beside him had a shade of skin which was even darker than Neil's own. True to his name the man who'd called himself Søren had a decidedly Nordic appearance with his tall frame, blond hair, blue eyes, and narrow nose. The woman beside him on the other hand had short cut curly black hair over top of her round face, flat nose, and prominent cheekbones.

"Neil… Neil Sagan." He tilted his head to the side in reflection for a moment. "We're in the Haven star system aren't we?"

"Actually, we're in orbit around Haven already," Ishtar answered.

Neil stood up and looked around. He then started moving his body about as though he were checking to see that everything worked as it was supposed to and as he remembered. "Orbit hunh? Well you've already gotten that part wrong... not very encouraging I have to say." He looked at Søren and Ishtar expectantly for several moments. "Yes I know I'm a sim by the way," he finally said with a bit of a chuckle.

"I'm sorry um, Neil," Ishtar offered with a smile. She seemed amused by him and his attitude. "I'm head of flight operations and I oversaw our orbital insertion. The truth is... we just forgot. It just didn't seem that important or necessary. I mean, we'd been training for it our whole lives." Neil started jumping up and down as high as he could, and getting some good vertical distance too. "We were so busy plotting and analyzing our braking manoeuvers that we just never got around to it; before we realized it we'd already forgotten about you."

"Truth is we... we just didn't think of you that often at all," Søren added. "I mean we think about the um, originals of you four, but... not so much about you simulants."

"Well," Neil said as he came up behind them and put his hands on their shoulders, "now we're all that's left of either."

Chapter 2

"So..." Wiremu asked leadingly, "you said there was an incident. Did we miss anything?"

"I'd say you have," Asari answered. "There's been a... sort of schism on the ship." He ineffectively tried to demonstrate the schism with hand gestures.

"Schism?" Wiremu stood; it was instinct. He was informed of a threat and he was instantly on alert.

"Oh no, it's not any kind of... immediate threat of the moment or anything, but it is something you need to be aware of. One of the original wildcard crew members violated mission protocols and instead of creating naturally blended children, he instead created two successive clones of himself and passed them off as his son and grandson. It is... suggested, that he created the original clones as some sort of vanity project, to create differentiated incarnations of himself. Since his death there have been two more successive clones created, one knowingly raised as the son of the other. Together they are collectively known as the Bowland experiments. The last living one is Halley Bowland, and today he is the captain." There was obvious but checked venom in his voice as he stated that particular fact.

"There was an incident involving the original clones. The younger one tried to hijack the ship using you sims as his muscle. He wanted to take the ship to a nearer planet where a different colony ship was already headed so that we would arrive within his own lifetime. Before he could succeed though, he was killed by his older clone-father. It was then that everyone in general found out about the clandestine cloning program. There was a... disagreement over the circumstances of that death, and the... appropriateness of creating any further clones. There has since grown over time a sort of... political factioning on the ship."

--- --- ---

"All of your best laid plans... and yet you somehow missed so much," Halley informed Sadhika.

"What are you talking about?" Sadhika asked. She leaned forward in concern. They were sure they'd thought of everything, what could he possibly mean? What could have happened?

"You really thought that you could just package the parts of humanity you liked and excise the rest... but it turned out that humanity doesn't work that way. Everything you tried to leave behind on Earth re-emerged in the crew. The natural human behavioural spectrum re-expressed itself en-route, and the worst part is that because you tried to shield us from all of humanity's darkness, we were completely unprepared to deal with it, totally ill-equipped to see what was happening right in front of our eyes...

"I don't understand..."

"One of the original crewmembers was a man named Markus Bowland, and if you'd had adequate psychological screening, he probably wouldn't have made it onboard in the first place. As evidence, me. I am the fourth clone incarnation of Markus Bowland. Johannes was the first and Markus raised him as his son, and when the time came he created his second clone Tycho, and raised him as his grandson. All he changed were their appearances, and just enough to avoid raising any suspicions. He wanted to explore different ways he himself might have turned out if he'd been raised with different... emphases."

Sadhika's jaw dropped. She knew it was possible to create such clones; she had after all founded the largest biotechnology company back on Earth before they'd left, but it was a flagrant violation of some very fundamental principles of the mission.

"Another thing you failed to account for was deviance, antisocial compulsions which seemingly came out of nowhere. Of the first ship born generation, one turned out to be a pedophile. The story goes that he resisted his urges for a long time, but when he couldn't anymore he indulged himself with enthusiasm. One of his victims was the Tyco clone, and it led him down a very dark path. He wound up brutally murdering the man who tortured him, and then tried to redirect the ship to a nearer planet where another colony mission was already headed, all so he could have an outside chance of getting off of the ship in his seventies... You have to understand, his was a tragic story with a tragic end. He was killed by Johannes, the man who'd raised him as his son, before he could permanently derail the mission. Tycho reprogrammed you and the other sims in his hijacking effort, and that's why we're interviewing you individually now to check and see if you're all working as you're supposed to, if you've been properly restored.

"Everything came out publicly in a truth and reconciliation process which followed," the man explained. "Johannes was convinced that he, his progenitor, and his clone-son all deserved another chance to get it right, and to prove that there was not something fundamentally wrong with their genome and who they were on a fundamental level. He asked Dhika Sengupta, the granddaughter of your own progenitor and the woman I call my grandmother, to impregnate herself with a new third clone. She agreed, and he soon after killed himself to avoid any contamination of the new clone with any vestiges of previous incarnations.

"My father... was a saint. He and I had no changes made whatsoever and are effectively identical twins of the original Markus Bowland. My father Herschel did everything right, he followed all of the rules, and did everything he could to ingratiate himself to those who felt he should never have been born in the first place, but they would never accept him. His efforts made him a celebrated hero to half of the ship, and forever an unforgivable pariah to the rest, through no fault or action of his own. His very existence was a lightning rod which drove a wedge between the two ever crystallizing opposing sides. He wanted to be captain or patriarch when the opportunities came up but they always found a way to block him.

"I still wonder sometimes why he created me... amidst all that. All I know is that I had to watch him do everything right, and never get any credit or respect for it. I had to watch him bend over backwards to make them happy and end up with *nothing* to show for it. I myself was just barely able to squeak out a victory when my time came, and they still suggest that I am somehow illegitimate to sit as captain."

"That's um… quite a story," Sadhika offered, not really sure what else to say. "We were expecting all the excitement of the journey to start at *this* point. Here we were feeling guilty for subjecting you to all of the boredom…"

"Well most of the time there was most certainly that, and since it was your progenitors who planned the mission and not you… I'll try not to hold any of it against you personally."

--- --- ---

"I'm curious about what the journey has done to the crew… problems on extremely long duration space flights have been known to happen. We tried to do everything we could to mitigate any problems we could foresee though," In-Su offered.

"Such hubris... to think you could anticipate so much." Aset answered.

"Well," In-Su uttered in a rare display of defensiveness, "I think we did pretty well considering! You *are* finally *here* are you not?"

"We are… a divided crew. What you didn't account for, was a re-expression of the natural human dichotomy."

In-Su appeared confused. "What do you mean?"

"There is a... natural balance in the human psyche, between conservatism and progressivism, between socialism and libertarianism, between the part of us urging us to aggress, to dare, to risk, to change… and the urge to do none of those things and to stick with what has worked since before anyone can remember." Aset offered thoughtfully. "I've heard it described as being comparable in an evolutionary sense, to the urge to venture out among the stars, and the urge to retreat back into the jungle. You loaded up a ship with assertive and progressive forward thinking people, I can only assume in the belief that you could indeed take just that part of humanity with you.

"The truth is though… left alone for any length of time, any human population will inevitably reach a behavioural equilibrium of sorts, with progressivism and conservatism back in balance."

"Why?" In-Su asked. It was after all his favourite question.

Aset sighed. "Because they are both effective strategies, which speak to a very deep dichotomy in the human heart, and thus it's a tale as old as humanity itself. One strategy is based on what is best for the group as a whole, and the other is based on what is best for the individual. It is an eternal conflict because humans are fundamentally social animals, with both social *and* individual priorities. Each serves the other, but each is also limited by the other."

"I think I understand." In-Su offered.

"You loaded up this ship with ambitious and independent minded people. It is my belief that all of the conflict that has happened since has been a result of that natural dichotomy re-expressing itself and the more conservative group loyalty element re-establishing *it*self."

"And what side do *you* identify with?" he asked.

She looked away and considered the question for a few moments. "Like everyone, I incorporate elements of both."

"Tell me, is there... *open* conflict on the ship, or just harmless malcontent and political dissatisfaction?"

"Well, it's not a... shooting war or anything if that's what you mean. It's more like... open and unabashed contempt. The patriarch and I... my husband and I, find the cloning program an abomination which should never have been allowed to continue after Midway."

"I'm sorry, Midway?"

"It's what we call the events of about eighty years ago when one of the clones went crazy and tried to change the course of the ship after killing a couple people. It was Asari and I's parents and predecessors who were able to successfully block a later clone Herschel from becoming captain through politics alone... but Asari and I were unable to block *his* clone-son Halley. He's much worse, so much more... aggressive and willful than his predecessor."

"I see." There was much that he didn't understand. What clones was she talking about? And of what significance were these Herschel and Halley she spoke of?

"I must admit I'm curious about you too. Not just you, but all of you simulants. I've read all about the real you, all of you. They were very impressive human beings, how do you feel about being just a copy of them, yet so perfect a copy?"

"Well that's just it... I don't *feel* like a copy. I woke up believing that I *am* Kim In-Su. I never considered that I was anything else until you mentioned it. However differently I'm constituted... *I* don't perceive any difference in my constitution."

--- --- ---

"Ok well this is boring now, I want to see the rest of the ship; I want to see Haven out of a window! We worked so hard to get here! Hell I chose this planet in the first place! Did you know that?" Neil asked proudly and with excitement.

"I'm afraid I can't do that, Neil." Søren somberly informed him.

"Why not?" Neil asked in frustration.

"We have to wait until we get the signal that all four of you are ready."

"Says who?"

"The captain, the matriarch, and the patriarch."

"Now you listen to me. I am one of the original founders of this mission. We instituted the very system by which you govern yourself today. I am *ordering* you to let me see out of a *fucking* window right *now!*" He wasn't really angry; he was just anxious and generally excitable. He was also testing them to see how they'd react to a direct order.

"Again, I'm sorry but I can't do that."

Deeply frustrated, Neil asked again: "Why not?"

Seemingly with equal frustration Søren declared: "because you are *not* Neil Sagan!"

Neil whirled around from facing the door with daggers in his eyes. Now he really *was* angry, and quite contemptuous of the reasoning. He sat back down in his chair and declared in an even, almost threatening voice, "No, but I'm all that's left. And there is a *lot* left."

"I know," Ishtar said as she put her hand on his to comfort him. "We all know that. This is just a protocol *we* wrote, okay? It's part of why we didn't wake you when your progenitors dictated. They left us instructions as though you were them but only frozen and in need of waking up. They came from a world with many simulants, but we on the other hand... well, none of *us* has ever met one."

"We just wanted to check you out first is all," Søren offered. "There was an incident with you sims eighty or so years ago, and we're interviewing you one on one just to make sure that your programming was properly restored. And besides, we just... well, we wanted to at least *meet* you before handing complete control of our entire world over to you mechanoids, even if you *are* modelled on our founders."

Chapter 3

"We've made some… modifications and adjustments to the ship," Søren explained, as he and Ishtar led the Neil Sagan simulant down one of the four struts between the habitat ring and the non-rotating engineering section. The gravity effect of the rotating outer ring decreased steadily as they climbed down the access tube running along the interior of the strut. "You all said that you wanted to be brought to a window so you could see the planet, but if you really want the best possible view, nothing really compares to the bubble."

"The bubble?" Neil asked as he pushed himself out of the access tube and floated into the forward section of the long corridor. The far end of it where the mighty ion engines were located was so distant that he couldn't see all the way to the end; the corridor seemed to go on forever.

"Yeah, when it was originally built they did it just for the novelty of a large zero gravity gymnasium and a great place to look out at the stars," Søren continued as he, and then Ishtar, also emerged into the larger central corridor. "But when we entered the system and started doing our fly-bys and braking manoeuvers, it sure didn't take us long to realize what a great place it was to see those planets up close. The field of view it grants is truly amazing, really unlike anything possible anywhere else on the ship."

"Again, *really* wish you'd have woken us up when you were supposed to, we all would have really loved to have seen that, bubble or no bubble," Neil chastised them resentfully.

"Right. Again… sorry about that." Søren offered. "In any case, now that you're awake it's by far the best possible place for you to look down on the planet from the ship."

"You know, beyond just the view it allows, it's a pretty impressive engineering achievement too," Ishtar suggested as Søren pushed off against the foot and hand holds embedded in the walls, and then made his way towards the access hatch.

"Oh?" Neil asked with a raised eyebrow, now more interested.

"Oh yes, it's a transparent synthetic material which we can inflate or deflate on command," Ishtar explained. "We were always worried about interstellar debris out in the void, but here in orbit it's relatively safe so we've been leaving it inflated all of the time since so many people want to come in and have a good look at the planet. At the moment we've cleared it out so you four can have it all to yourselves though."

"If this doesn't wow you, well..." Søren predicted as he opened the hatch for Neil, "*nothing* will." Using his hands and feet Søren thrust himself through the portal off of the edges of the hatch, inviting the other two to follow.

Within the void of the zero gravity bubble, there were two ways one could move about. One way, was to deploy the filament network which consisted of thin cables strung up in such a way that within the bubble there was a geometric grid of three meter wire mesh cubes. When deployed, one could push and pull themselves around these fibers while still having reasonable mobility about the space. If this filament network was retracted, one could also grab from behind the entry hatch before entering, a compressed air canister with which one could puff themselves about the space freely and without any obstruction.

Neil enthusiastically thrust himself into the large void, but had not been warned about the filament network being deployed. He unexpectedly clipped his shoulder on one of the threads and the encounter threw his body into a moderate spin, which was only made worse by his initial attempts to mitigate the rotation. After flailing through a few more encounters with the filaments, he finally reached the far end of the sphere, and was caught and pulled to a stop by Wiremu and Sadhika. Although the three of them were old friends, their simulant incarnations were only now meeting for the first time.

"Easy there big guy," Sadhika cooed as she and Wiremu steadied his body, "and look..."

Neil followed her hand to see the massive expanse of the planet hanging in space beneath them. All three were speechless as they took in the unbelievable natural beauty laid out before them. The colours were so forceful, and the resolution so infinitely sharp, that it seemed to them like they could almost reach out and touch the green, yellow, and brown continents, or run their fingers through the deep blue ocean's surface as they flew past.

As they began to fly into the current night side of the planet, Sadhika turned to her handler and asked: "How thin is the material of this bubble again Halley?" The original Sadhika Sengupta had been a born engineer who always wanted to understand everything and to know how everything worked. In her pre New Horizon life, she had applied those natural capacities to biotechnology, and had founded the largest and most successful biotech company Earth had ever known at the time of their launch.

"Only two centimeters," Halley answered, "with an overall diameter of about fifty meters." It was pretty impressive considering that the vacuum of space was trying to suck the ship's entire atmosphere out through just that thin layer of transparent material. Søren and Ishtar made their way over to Halley who was floating several meters to the left of the three simulants, while Asari minded Wiremu from several meters to their right.

It was then that In-Su appeared with Aset in tow, carefully making his way into the bubble. He was methodically pulling himself along one filament at a time, instinctively trying to avoid the same kind of embarrassing entrance which Neil's enthusiasm had preceded him with.

"This is really it isn't it?" he asked the three people who he perceived as his old friends.

"It's too bad you missed the dayside In-Su…" Neil lamented. "Oh well, just give it some time. We'll wait until we swing back around again"

"So that's really Haven down there?" In-Su seemed mesmerized as he looked down on the planet's dark night. "There's something eerie about how dark it is, the great emptiness of it…"

"There's no lights of civilization…" Wiremu remarked. He remembered how much evidence one could see of Earth's civilization while looking down on its night side from orbit. "It really *is* a totally virgin world isn't it… It's one thing to talk about it-"

"But another thing to see it with your own eyes," Sadhika finished his thought for him.

"There... also isn't any light from any moon," Ishtar added. "Earth had a large and highly reflective moon did it not? That would have often added a lot of ambient light to the night side too."

"No moons at all?" Neil the astronomer and astrophysicist asked.

"No large planetary moons, no," Søren answered; he had a similar scientific background. "There are plenty around the outer planets, but Haven only has the two small moons which seem to just be captured asteroids."

"Hmm, like Mars..." Neil replied, seemingly lost in thought. "Any risk of them coming down anytime soon?" he asked.

"We ran an analysis a while ago and no, not really. One is in a high enough orbit that it'll essentially stay there forever, and although the other one *will* come down, it won't be for another six or seven thousand years or so. We've already drawn up plans to build a large ion engine onto its side and boost it up to a higher and safer orbit, but... at the moment it's pretty low on our to-do list given how far into the future the danger is."

"How much damage would it do if it came down?" Wiremu asked.

"Damage?" Halley asked. "Total. It may only be a captured asteroid but it's pretty massive all the same."

"Understood."

"That utter darkness must make for some amazing stargazing from the surface..." Neil remarked as he gazed down at the planet. He imagined lying on his back in a field at night, looking up at the stars as he'd been so fond of doing back on Earth. "So, what *is* this system's overall planetary configuration?"

"Rather interesting actually," Søren said, getting interested in the astronomical conversation. "In the outer reaches there's a binary system between a large but ordinary class I gas giant and an unexpectedly massive ice giant. There's also another more typically massed ice giant in a slowly decaying orbit in close around the star. Maybe most interesting of all though, is a sort of... super-massive Venus roughly where the Sol System's asteroid belt was."

"Crazy..." Neil answered in absorbed contemplation. It was exactly as they'd predicted based on the observations they'd made of the system from Earth, and it was greatly satisfying to be able to test their predictions and know for sure how precisely they'd nailed it. "And did we get all of the atmospheric compositions right?" he asked.

"Looks that way from what we've been able to tell so far, I mean all of our spectroscopic readings are still the same as they were when you left Earth."

"I still wonder where all of the ices came from..." Neil wondered out loud.

"I was wondering the same thing myself!" Søren exclaimed with a touch of pride. He was obviously warming to the mechanoid.

"How is Earth?" Sadhika asked. "When did you receive your last transmission from them? Have you transmitted your arrival yet?"

"We have, but-" Aset tried to answer, and then looked over at her husband Asari.

"Wait," Sadhika interrupted her, "I'm sorry, but who are you? In fact could you introduce everyone? We've each only met one or two of you at this point."

"Of course, my apologies. I'm Matriarch Aset, this is my husband Patriarch Asari, over there is Captain Halley, his wife Ishtar, and his first officer Søren."

"Thank you," Sadhika said while she and the other simulants put faces to the names they'd heard about after waking up. "Now what were you going to say about Earth?"

"I was going to say, that yes we've transmitted our arrival, but... well, Earth went dark a long time ago. The last laser transmission we received from them was ninety-two years ago... and we don't know why. We were expecting one eighty years ago, right in the middle of the Midway incident, but it never came. We've left at least one telescope pointed at Earth continuously ever since, but... no message has ever come."

"I see..." she answered. She looked around at the other three simulants and none of them seemed to know what to make of it. It was an eerie mystery. "Well in that case, we should probably send messages to the other two colony planets. They probably won't be receptive, but... we should at least try and give them the option of opening a dialogue with us if they want to, especially with Earth having gone dark."

"I'll see to it," Halley stated officiously.

"Have you studied the spectrum of Earth and the Sol System?" Neil asked Søren, "did you see any clues as to what might have happened to them?"

"I'm afraid not..." he answered to his new friend, "the planet was studied as closely as possible after the missing transmission but nothing came up. Now we're out of range to study the planet specifically and... the spectrum of Sol itself doesn't offer any insights either I'm afraid."

Meanwhile, In-Su had resumed looking down on the planet. "That's *really* Haven down there..." he repeated in wonderment. They were here, what did Earth matter now? Let the earthlings worry about the Earth he thought, now they had their own planet to worry about.

"All that work..." Wiremu said as he joined In-Su in looking back down on the planet.

"All that planning..." Neil added.

"All that *money*..." Sadhika joked with a bit of a laugh. An incredibly wealthy woman, the original Sadhika Sengupta had been the mission's primary financier.

"All that faith..." In-Su finally added after a few moments of sombre silence. The other three nodded in understanding.

Aset, now having gone over to float beside her husband, stated: "Mission protocol dictates, that the matriarch, patriarch, and captain, retain primary authority over the ship, while you four assume command of all planetary operations. I assume this is still acceptable to all parties involved?"

Being perfectly acquainted with *all* of the mission protocols and in most cases being programmed with the memory of having personally written them in the first place, all four simulants nodded along with Asari.

"Look everyone, um..." Neil interjected, "can we just have a minute to ourselves before we get down to business? We haven't had any chance just to talk amongst ourselves since we woke up."

"Oh. Oh, sure." Halley answered. "Come on everyone, let's give them the room. We'll be right outside." With that, all five of their chaperones made their way through the hatch and Søren closed it behind them. The four simulants floated in silence for several moments, looking down at the dark side of the planet.

"So um… hi," Neil said with a bit of an ironic droll, "nice to meet you?" The other three chuckled a little awkwardly.

"It's a weird feeling," Sadhika offered, "to be me and yet so clearly not me, to be something else… anyone else getting that?" The other three nodded.

"It's like, existential déjà vu or something." Neil offered with a chuckle.

"You joke," Wiremu observed, "but you're probably not too far off. I remember *being* Wiremu Tynes… but I'm *not* him. I have his memories, but…"

"But what little you've already experienced around here in just this brief time," In-Su offered in explanation, "is coloured in such a way that makes our programmed memories feel somehow in black and white."

"Exactly…" Wiremu confirmed.

"Well you'd better not let *them* hear you say that," Sadhika suggested with a gesture to the airlock. "They already seem a little reticent to hand any authority over to us. They're following protocol for now but I don't like how reluctantly they seem to be doing it."

"It's probably too late," Wiremu speculated. "You really think they haven't been listening to everything we've been saying in here?" he asked. All four suddenly felt very exposed and vulnerable, floating in this thin transparent bubble hundreds of kilometers above an alien planet on the first day of their lives.

They remained alone in the bubble for the next two hours. They watched mesmerised as they flew more than a full orbit around the planet, allowing them to see the entire side which was currently lit up by the sun. Sometimes they'd just watch in awe, but often they'd be pointing features out to each other. All along though, they never lost the excitement of little children captivated by a new toy.

Chapter 4

The next day, Neil was sparring with Armina Shostak in an exercise room. He was anxious to fully feel out his shiny new body, and wanted to push some of its limits to see what it really felt like. He was curious to know if there would be anything which would betray the reality of his new mechanoid incarnation as opposed to the biological one he so clearly remembered being so intimate with. It was a natural effort for him, he was the simulation of a man who had always enjoyed testing limits and exploring boundaries both physical and intellectual, but most of all theoretical.

Without holding back, he attempted a five strike hand and foot combination, but the woman easily deflected it. He felt safe to try as hard as he could both because his body was limited to human capability, but more importantly because Armina Shostak was the ship's 'keeper of combat.' In one sense it was just another educational specialty among the crew, and no different than a specialty in astrophysics or ecology. On the other hand, it was distinctly unlike any other vocation on the ship. It was mandatory education for the ship's head of security and while she was not the only one so trained, she was a natural, and she excelled far beyond the rest as a superior fighter and tactician.

Exactly like his old biological one, his new simulant body was bulkier and more muscular than the thinner woman he was sparring with, though she herself had a powerfully firm and toned athletic musculature. She was about as tall as he was too; they were both almost two meters tall. Unlike his own short and curly black hair, hers was long and bright red, matching her pale freckled skin and intense, piercing blue eyes. He'd noticed when he first met her that her own hair had a natural curl to it as well, but it was now obscured since she'd tightly wound it up to spar with him.

The educational curriculum for a keeper of combat specialty was both academic and practical. She'd been required to study military history and battle tactics throughout all recorded history, from small localized battles to international total war. She was also trained in personal hand to hand combat, with a complete mastery of a wide variety of weapons and martial arts schools and techniques. The small exercise gymnasium they were in was much as Neil remembered it. The pale blue mats on the ground had significantly faded, but so too had the brown and green floor to ceiling panels which encircled them.

"Not bad," Neil offered. He himself was not only a brilliant astrophysicist, but he was also similarly skilled in personal combat, and had studied a variety of martial arts. Having a position known as the 'keeper of combat' was in fact his idea in the first place so many years ago. The military history and tactical element was not some-thing he himself was expert in, but he'd always imagined it would be a great compliment to the personal and physical aspects of martial arts training.

"So you're the legendary Neil Sagan, hunh?" the woman said with a smirk, getting more comfortable being around him now that they'd exchanged a few blows. Neil grinned, feigned a few hand strikes, and then went in for a leg sweep. Armina leapt over his long swee-ping leg and while he was still off balance, reached out with her foot and pulled in the knee he was still carrying his weight on. He collapsed backwards and fell flat on his back. His arms and legs went out spread eagle and he laughed out loud as he lay there without trying to get up.

"You're very good!" he exclaimed.

She was standing over him and looking down with an amused look on her face. Let alone fighting him, she'd been apprehensive about even meeting him, but she was pleasantly surprised about how funny and good natured he seemed to be. She backed away as he nimbly climbed to his feet. He was grinning as he wiped the corner of his mouth and bushy black moustache with his right fist, and then got into his standard go-to boxing stance before starting to bounce about in anticipation of the next strikes.

"How does it feel?" Armina asked. "Does it feel like you remember your human body feeling? Like you'd expect it to?"

"Oh yeah, it's amazing! I know this body is physically capable of more... I know its real capacities are limited for the sake of an accurate simulation, but I could swear I feel better than ever, stronger and healthier than I ever did before; right now I feel like I could take on the whole world! Ha! Take on *this* world, I guess that's the whole point isn't it!"

"Hasn't seemed to let you get the better of *me* yet," Armina said with a taunting wink. Neil attempted a triple combination but the woman ducked and bobbed all three of the strikes.

"You are fast..." he remarked in marvel, "I'll give you that."

Armina attempted a similar brief combination on Neil. He was able to avoid all three, but it took a great deal of attention and concentration. When she soon after attempted a series of kicks and punches, Neil was able to grab her right leg in his left arm, and land a hard blow to her midsection with his right knee. He then in one swift motion kicked her remaining left knee up and pushed her over with his right hand on her chest, swinging her body back and over. She hit her back hard on the mat they were exercising on, and it knocked the wind out of her.

He got on top of her and held her wrists down with her arms spread out. He was smiling with a wild kind of excitement. For a moment she thought he might try to kiss her, and she had no idea how she was supposed to react to that. She found him attractive enough, but it was completely unexpected. Not only was he technically her superior, he technically wasn't even human! The moment passed though, and she didn't have to find out. His grin turned to a knowing smile and he got up and released her.

"Tell me..." she said as she sat up on the mat and caught her breath. Neil made his way over to the weapons rack and pulled down a long staff. He held it behind his back and started repeatedly swinging his torso back and forth from left to right. "Are you really Neil Sagan?"

He erupted with a full throated laugh. "What exactly do you mean? You'll need to ask a more specific question I'm afraid, if you're hoping for an answer that actually means anything."

"Well... in introductory philosophy, I remember being presented with something they called the transporter dilemma. One part of it was the idea of walking into a transportation chamber back on Earth, and then walking out of a similar chamber on Haven."

"Go on..."

"The question was, would it really matter if instead of a transportation system, the first chamber was instead an annihilator, and the second chamber really some kind of perfect duplicator? That way the you that walks out of the second chamber, as far as it knows, is the real you. You feel like you, you have all of your memories..."

"And what did you think when you were posed the question?" He'd heard of the thought experiment, but philosophy wasn't an area of expertise for him.

"Some people in my class thought it wouldn't matter, but I had a deep sense that whatever walked out of that second chamber... it wouldn't be *me*. Whatever came out the other side, the real me that went into that first chamber... was still dead."

"Yes," Neil offered, "but there *would* be a *new* you that came out the other end right? And that new you might not be the original, but it would still be *a* you."

"I suppose..."

"No Armina... in the sense that you're getting at, in the *numerical* sense, I am definitely not Neil Sagan. I am definitely not the physically original being of that designation who actually lived all of those experiences I have memories of."

Neil came over and sat on the mat beside her, still holding the staff. "Let me ask *you* something though. Given that whatever walked out of the second chamber wouldn't be whatever walked into the first, what *would* it be? I mean, if it *was* so perfect a replica that even itself couldn't tell the difference? What if, say... the two chambers were right beside each other, the first one failed to annihilate you, and you were both knocked out in the duplication process? What if you were both then later woken up together and were *never told* which one of you had been the original? How could you tell?"

"I don't know..."

"Maybe more importantly Armina, would it even really matter at that point which was which?"

"It would seem to."

"Yes, it would *seem* to... but it *wouldn't*. It might bother both of you to not know for sure, but you'd get over it, and then you'd go off and live your own respective lives, and gradually differentiate into different people over time as you lived different lives and had different experiences.

"For all intents and purposes Armina, I *am* Neil Sagan, but no I am not the Neil Sagan of a few weeks before the actual launch of the New Horizon. He had a whole other life once the ship was underway... a life that will forever be just his and his alone, a life that I have no memory or experience of. *That* part, is all his and his alone. Just like all this," he waved his hand around to gesture the totality of his new existence, "is all me, not the man I was a simulation of, but *me* me. At one point, and for a brief moment in time, we may have been basically and essentially the same person, and me just a duplication of him, but ever *since* that moment we've certainly diverged. As I was left in storage, he lived out the rest of his life and became a person that I will never know and never become. Likewise from the moment I was woken up, I started becoming a person he never was and could never be."

Neil pushed himself up off the ground with the staff he was still holding, and then held his hand out to Armina. She took it and was helped up to her feet. Neil handed her the staff weapon and then headed back over to the weapons rack to grab a blunt wooden broadsword for himself.

"The way I see it... for one brief moment, I was as close as possible to being a full duplication of Neil Sagan; at one point in time we were effectively the same person. Going forward from that point though, we both evolve on our own time into different unique beings; he into whatever man he became on this ship, and me into whatever man I will become down on that planet."

The wooden sword and staff repeatedly made sharp clacking sounds as Neil and Armina traded attacks and parries.

"Kind of like the clones..." Armina offered as she lobbed a few jabs with the tip of her staff, probing his defence style.

"How so? And what clones?" The woman struck and made him defend, and then swung the other end of the staff around and landed a strike on his thigh. "Nice..." he commented as the pain made him wince a little.

"They didn't tell you? Halley is a clone of one of the original crew who left Earth. Unbeknownst to anyone else his son and grandson were actually his clones... Later on after everyone found out and they were both dead, Halley's father Herschel was created and then later on Halley was also created as Herschel's son. They're all clones of the same man though."

"I see... and how is that like my situation?" he asked. He was disturbed to hear all of this but it was something he'd have to investigate once he was done here.

"Well it's not, not really, except for the concept of having the same starting point as another being, and then becoming different from each other over time as you have different lived experiences. The distinction being that their identical starting point was as identical embryos."

"Sure, I guess from a certain point of view it could be seen as analogous to that." They continued through a series of strikes and parries as they probed each other's styles with their respective weapons.

"Why just a simulation?" she asked. "Why not make something... *better* than a human?"

"What do you mean by better?" Neil asked, amused by the question.

"I don't know... smarter I guess."

"I don't think you'd like the answer very much" he said as they continued to fight without either landing any significant blows.

"Try me."

"Because humans only know how to define intelligence in terms of *human* intelligence, and in terms of the kinds of intelligence displayed by the humans who impress them. They can only break it down into different specific capabilities and then build machines which can do those individual things far better than a human can. They can build machines that can think faster and complete tasks more efficiently than a human can, but humans can't create anything more intelligent than a human because they can't conceive of what that notion even means.

"I am personally the height of human engineering and artificial intelligence; a reasonable approximation of a human being. Humanity's greatest possible accomplishment of all time, is just to create something equal to themselves; me." He winked as he said it. He revelled referring to himself, personally, as the apex of all creation.

"But there's nowhere else to go. I believe it to be a metaphysical impossibility for any being to create something superior to themselves, nor anything which could itself create anything superior to them. Humans can create machines that can do specific things better than they themselves can do, but they cannot create something superior to a human being because to a human, a human being is the height of all creation, the be all and end all. It's a nonsense proposition to create a 'better than human' human. Being human is an intersection of a lot of different factors, and anything which exceeds humanity on any of those factors is no longer thought of as human."

"You're right, I *don't* like that answer." She was distracted and he hit her, harder than he'd meant to, and right across the side of her face. She went down on her right knee and fist, cradling her jaw with her other hand.

"Oh shit I'm sorry, it got away from me... you alright?"

"I'm *fine*" she said as she swung the staff around and pulled both of his legs out from under him, causing him to fall flat on his back. This time she clamoured on top of *him* and held *his* hands out at arms lengths by his wrists. He smiled up at her and she smiled back.

She couldn't remember ever having this much fun sparring with anyone else on the ship. Not only did nobody else seem to get it, but nobody else ever trained as hard as she did so there was never any real competition for her. Without knowing why, she kissed him. For the moment she'd forgotten that he wasn't human and when she did remember, she found that she really didn't care. He was funny, charming, and attractive. She liked him, and that seemed reason enough.

Neil kissed her back and felt her body up and down. She wasn't really his usual type, but she had an attractiveness that transcended that sort of thing. Despite himself he started laughing, disrupting the kiss and bringing an end to it.

"What's so funny?" she asked, almost offended.

"Nothing, nothing, I'm sorry, I just had the thought of it having been a hundred and sixty year dry spell for me," he said with a chuckle.

She looked at him sideways and then sat up with a smile on her face. *"Dry spell,* aren't you a one day old *virgin?"* They both had a good laugh together over the idea as Neil nodded up and down since he had to admit that she was right about that.

"You said you'd change as a person over time..." Armina reflected once their laughter had died down, "but you won't ever age, will you?"

"No..." Neil answered thoughtfully. "Someday I'll just stop working and effectively die, but... no, I won't ever physically appear to age the way a person would... the way *you* will. It's the kind of thing that sounds like a blessing but might actually turn out to be more like a curse. It is after all... the ultimate proof of my inhumanity. I'll never get to live out a natural human life, and the longer I survive the more obviously inhuman it'll make me. So I'll let *you* decide which of us is better off in that respect."

Chapter 5

After walking alone through the corridors of the ship for a while, Sadhika decided that she needed more information about what had happened on the ship, and what had given rise to such obvious political tensions within it. She figured that since she'd already had a one on one encounter with the captain Halley and that they'd seemed to have established a bit of a rapport, she'd seek him out first to get a better understanding. She asked the ship where she could find him, and it informed her that he was currently in the dining hall.

When she entered, it felt as familiar to her as it should have if she'd personally overseen the design and construction of every part of the ship, including the dining hall. As far as it seemed to her, she had. She could clearly remember a lot of the initial construction process, but her simulation finalization had taken place sometime before the ship had actually been completed and launched. Still, to her it felt as though she'd just been in this room the other day.

It was midafternoon on the ship's now twenty-sixish hour clock, and there weren't many people in the large room, certainly not as many as there would have been if it was a regularly scheduled meal time. The room was a large open space on the ship, and second in size only to the arboretum which took up a full third of the habitat ring's total volume which was half a kilometer wide, two hundred meter deep, and twenty-four meters high with eight floors. The dining hall was designed to be able to accommodate the full three hundred maximum capacity of the ship at once if need be, but there was rarely any need to actually shoehorn everyone so uncomfortably into the room at once. Whatever the occasion, a skeleton crew usually had to be maintained elsewhere on the ship regardless of whatever else was going on.

The room was large enough to clearly show the curvature of the habitat ring in the floor and the ceiling. It was on the bottom level which meant that a series of windows could be, and were, embedded in the floor. Through most of the journey they were only portals into empty blackness since the dining hall lights which were usually fully illuminating the room washed out the view of the stars. Now that they were in orbit around Haven though, the portals periodically allowed a clear and brilliant view of the planet down beneath their feet, as the ring section of the ship slowly circled around to simulate gravity.

Rectangular tables were neatly arranged up and down the room in rows, with the exception of the round central table which was reserved for the captain, matriarch, patriarch, and department heads. She… or rather, the original she and her cohorts, hadn't wanted the typical hidden away captain's table. They'd wanted to foster more of a family feel to everything than just the feel of a crew on a ship. As she went over to join Halley and Søren who were sitting alone at the captain's table, she passed one of the spiral staircases leading up to the second level balconies which looked down on the main area below.

She was wearing the same standard coveralls which most of the crew wore the majority of the time. They were functional enough and rather quite comfortable, but it probably explained why neither of the men immediately noticed her when she entered the room. Not only was she wearing the same coveralls as everyone else, but she was wearing the greys, the most common colour which Halley and Søren were also wearing Some of the other people in the room were also wearing the few different colours which indicated that they belonged to specific departments.

Beyond that though, there were quite a few West Asian women onboard (exactly as many as there were of the other four ethnicities), and to look at her in passing she really didn't stand out much from the crowd with her straight nose, wide eyes, brown skin and long dark hair. The only difference was that she was fully of Indian descent as opposed to the homogenized West Asian ethnicity which existed on the ship today. Five such homogenized ethnicities were preserved onboard for the sake of genetic variability once they landed. Besides the West Asian, there were also the East Asian, African, Australasian, American, and European ethnicities.

They were preserved through carefully creating appropriately matched zygotes from preserved or digitized genomes as opposed to any kind of social controls over whom one could and couldn't mate with. People simply had children to replace themselves through blending their own gametes with those of an appropriately match genome. Although this scheme was preserved on the ship while en route, once on the planet they would not have the sophisticated genetics laboratories and equipment available on the New Horizon. Once a settlement was established on the planet, the colonists would simply reproduce the old fashioned way, with the benefit of the enhanced genetic diversity which had been so carefully preserved on the ship.

When he did notice her, Halley waved his hand to invite her to come and join them. As she approached, he and Søren exchanged some last words as he stood to leave. "Master Sengupta," he acknowledged with a nod as he left to give them some privacy. It was an old title which her progenitor had earned before the New Horizon had ever even been a concrete idea. She was heartened to find that Søren was acknowledging her so. So far the human crew seemed generally accepting of the sims.

"What can I do for you Sadhika?" Halley asked. "Are you hungry? Can I get you some lunch? Wait... do you even *get* hungry? Can you even eat?" He'd never had to wonder such a thing before.

"Yes Halley, I can eat," she answered as she pulled a chair out and sat down. "I can eat if only for the enjoyment of the tastes and smells, or... even just for fitting in. Most of it goes right through me after an appropriate interval, but there are certain things I really do need to extract from food from time to time, like hydrogen for the compact fusion reactor which powers me. There are also other raw materials I need to extract from food to manufacture things I need to make me go... I rarely actually *need* to eat, but I certainly can, and as often as I like."

"And presumably without ever putting on any weight, lucky you!" Halley remarked with a smirk.

"Quite true..." she hadn't actually considered that part. "My physical dimensions will never change for any reason." Halley was scrutinizing her; he was still waiting for an answer to his original question of what it was that she wanted.

"I need some information from you Halley, I need you to fill me in on what's happened here, why there's so much bad blood on the ship."

"Ah... of course," Halley said as he took a sip of his drink. "Let me tell you a story Sadhika, let me take you back, oh... thirty years ago, to the election for the captain who preceded me. My father Herschel, the clone who raised me as my father was in the running. He was an ideal, and... perfectly valid candidate. He was remarkably competent and had an impeccable record.

"His only flaw, was a state of being beyond his control; he was a clone, and this alone was enough to condemn him in many people's eyes. They could only ever see him as something unnatural... their fear of him made them see his lineage as an abomination which most certainly should have stopped at his predecessor. No amount of good deeds, no amount of service to the ship, the crew, or the mission, could ever redeem him in their eyes. His very existence was con-sidered unforgivable; and doubly so, for his 'son.' Me.

"His opponent was well-liked; she too was quite suited to the job. She was of a humble background, and she too worked hard her whole life at cultivating relationships on the ship. Both candidates were thoroughly qualified and there was no extraordinary or particular reason to vote for either. But the election became about the clones; they *made* it, about the clones. They *made* it into a referendum on whether or not Herschel had redeemed the cloning program or not, and whether or not the Bowland Experiments should be allowed to continue at all."

"Who?" Sadhika asked. "Who made it about that?"

"Aset and Asari's parents!" Halley explained in a surge of anger which he immediately checked and suppressed. "Specifically, Aset's father and Asari's mother. By marriage, Aset and Asari are both the great grandchildren of the first clone Johannes, and the great great grandchildren of Markus Bowland who started it all in the first place. No they're not clones themselves, nor are they in any way *genetically* linked to any of them, but they deeply resent the historical asso-ciations they *do* have with them. I *think*, that they all so vigorously oppose the clones as a way of distancing themselves from their own links to them. Me thinks they doth protest too much…"

"I see."

"I've actually done some poking around about it, since you ask… The serious resistance to the cloning program seems to have started with two women. One was former Matriarch Maharet, and the other a woman named Kirana. *She* was the son of Johannes and the brother of Tycho. She found out that her brother and father were clones of the man she'd known as her grandfather at the same time as everyone else did, *and* at the same time as she was finding out that there were plans to make yet another clone… it must have all really gotten to her.

"Kirana's children… Aset and Asari's father and mother respectively, came to hate my father and later on myself especially, and they were sure to pass that hatred down to Aset and Asari as well. They were taught that they needed to not just be against us, but to be *seen* to be against us, and to avoid being… contaminated with the same stain."

"My *father*, on the other hand, had been taught his whole life about loyalty, about forgiveness, and about honour. When he was young, he took it upon himself to redeem the existence of all of the clones, and to validate the decision to create him. He wanted to become the model crew member, and maybe someday even captain or patriarch. All he wanted his whole life was to serve, to be appreciated, and to feel an ever elusive sense of acceptance. This was *his* response to the stress of being the living embodiment of all political conflict on the ship."

"But he lost the election?" Sadhika asked.

"That's right. He told me that something died in him when that happened… he'd spent almost fifty years trying to prove himself worthwhile, but that night he realized that no matter what he did, it could never happen. When he lost the election, it wasn't just a matter of being electorally defeated. He was *personally* impugned and rejected.

"Mathematically it was clear that many of the people on the ship who had told him they would vote for him in the secret ballot had instead voted against him. It broke the poor man's spirit. To his death he never spoke ill of any of those who had so casually lied and stabbed him in the back, nor did he ever confront of condemn those who had. He just didn't have an angry or spiteful bone in his body. He was truly good to the core... those who knew him before I was born told me that when he lost the election something seemed to have broken in him, his spirit seemed to slump and he was never the same again. He existed, he spoke, and he... did the work that was required of him. He faithfully served the ship and did his duty to the very end until his death a few years ago, but there was no more spark left in his eyes. His heart had been permanently broken."

Halley went quiet for a moment in reflection. He looked down through one of the windows as the ship flew through the night-day boundary and the landscape lit up beneath their feet. "A whole lifetime spent being the bigger and better man, of letting it all roll off of his back, only ever earned him more hatred. Losing the election finally made him completely deaf to all of the cries of outrage when he announced his intentions to have another clone-son; me."

"But why?" Sadhika asked in confused frustration, "Don't get me wrong Halley, I'm not suggesting that there's something wrong with you or that you don't have any right to exist or anything, but... but why do that? Why go through it all over again if he'd already seen for himself that nothing could ever make the rest of the crew okay with it?" Sadhika just couldn't understand.

"Well, in part because it wasn't the *whole* crew who was against him! From the beginning and to this day, the crew is pretty evenly split between those who would condemn it all and those who would accept it. Many came to see it as a legitimately interesting biopsycho-social experiment, one which could never get past any academic ethics boards back on Earth! Having gone this far already, many found it a shame to simply abandon the whole project altogether, if only on the grounds of intellectual curiosity and scientific study.

"The more vocal the opposition became, the more the pro side justified itself, the more it became about our right to do what we wanted to do as a matter of principle, and it just spiraled and spiraled from there. There's been a kind of bitter... *resonance* between the two sides, the opposition just keeps pushing harder, and supporters keep pushing back even harder in defence. When my father announced his intention to make me, the anti-clone faction were absolutely livid but politically there was nothing they could do stop it because between the three leaders, only the patriarch of the day was willing to outright condemn it."

"And how did *you* respond to all of this Halley? How do *you* feel about Aset and Asari and... and about all of their people's attitudes towards you?" Sadhika asked cautiously and somewhat afraid of the answer.

"Fierce indignation." he answered coldly. "What *I* learned, was that they would never accept me no matter what, no matter how good I was. I learned to be angry, to be aggressive, and I developed a burning desire to *take* all of the things which my father had deserved to be given but was denied. I decided that if they wouldn't accept my father, I was better off becoming his opposite, better off being the very embodiment of their nightmare, and to make all of their worst fears about us come true. I decided to make them all *wish* that they'd given my father everything he was due, everything he'd *earned*.

"It became me and my people against Aset and Asari's people every day, and for a long time now. We took every opportunity to oppose them, but we never broke the rules or pushed things too far. The more their responses to us were excessive and disproportionate, the more people came over to *our* side in response to their unfairness and belligerence.

"It just so happened that in the last six years, all three leadership positions came up. Their cruelty had won me enough support to win the captaincy, but unfortunately they still had enough support to squeak out victories as the matriarch and patriarch despite every possible effort from me and mine. Since that time Aset and Asari were married, and many of the crew have been uncomfortable with the idea of a married couple monopolizing two thirds of all the political power on the ship. This increasingly unpopular imbalance of power has made even more of the crew sympathetic to us."

"What a mess..." Sadhika exclaimed in overwhelmed dismay.

"Indeed...." Halley replied with a knowing smile as he took another drink from his glass.

Chapter 6

"Aset? Am I interrupting?" Wiremu asked after the door opened onto the aeroponics bay. When it did, his nose had been delightfully confronted by the myriad scents.

"Not at all Wiremu, come on in," she replied invitingly before returning her primary attention back to her work. Everyone onboard was required to sign up for all the different duties required on the ship, and Aset opted as often as she could for tending to their gardens. Her formal education hadn't been in ecology or any related field, but she seemed to have a natural aptitude for nursing the plants, and she found the work relaxing. On a ship where everything else could seem so sterile, she enjoyed being able to watch things grow and develop organically.

She enjoyed the arboretum too, but didn't have any interest in working there. To her the ship's living forest all seemed like so much… managed chaos. All those plants and trees all fighting each other over finite resources and competing for a greater share of the artificial sun's good graces… It was all too reminiscent of the political situation on the ship for her liking, too much like the psychology and political science she had studied in her tertiary and quaternary education.

The aeroponics bay was different though; it was all so neatly ordered and controlled. Row after row of engineered plants growing out of long planters filled with nothing but air and dispersed nutrient water. It seemed to her about as organized and orderly as any organic system *could* be, very *unlike* the political situation on the ship.

The aeroponics bay was an essential supplement to the arboretum in their food production. Many things were grown in the arboretum, but usually things which required more room to grow and things which grew on trees or in bushes. Anything smaller which could be grown individually was for the most part grown here instead, and without any of the arboretum's limitations due to the efforts of trying to preserve the simulation of a natural space.

"Quite the array of smells in here isn't it? It's wonderful!" Wiremu admired as he came over. Most odorous were the herbs and spices, but also evident were the small number of flowers grown for research projects and in private gardens.

"Mmmm…" Aset agreed, and then almost as an afterthought and without looking away from her work she asked, "can you really even smell it?"

"What do you mean?" Wiremu asked probingly. He thought he had a general idea of what she'd meant, but he wanted a more explicit question before offering an explicit answer.

Now she turned away from her work to face him fully. "I mean, if you're only a simulation, isn't some machinery in you just registering particular aerosols, and then informing your brain of their presence? Or can you actually *smell*? Do you actually have the *sensation* of smelling?"

"What's the difference?" Wiremu further questioned.

"The difference?" Aset balked incredulously. "I'd say there's a *big* difference! I'm a real person, with thoughts and dreams and a vivid experience of the world around me! I see you in front of me, there's a visceral *phenomenon* to my vision, I don't just register the fact that you're there!"

"I see the world vividly too Aset, the smells in here bring up different things for me, they elicit… emotional reactions." As far as he could tell of his own experience, he was telling the truth.

"Un hunh…" Aset replied skeptically. "Can you prove it?"

Wiremu laughed, "can *you*?" Aset seemed taken aback. "I'll tell you what," Wiremu continued, "you figure out how to prove to *me*, that *you* have an internal phenomenological experience, and I'll take the same test, alright? At the end of the day your body and systems work the same way mine do, *you* detect a particular aerosol, that detection is registered in *your* brain, and *then* your brain constructs an experience of that detection. As far as I know it does anyways." He was trying to tease her in a playful way; he certainly didn't want to incite an actual confrontation about any of this.

Aset didn't seem bothered, but her interest did seem to be carried. "But it could easily be the case that you're just programmed to *claim* that you have the internal experiences I'm talking about."

"Again, the same thing could just as easily be said about *you*!" Wiremu countered.

"You could just be programmed to *believe* that you have that phenomenological experience even though you don't," she argued further, "how would you even know the difference!?"

"Ditto!! How would *you* know the difference if *your* brain were orchestrated the same way!? *You'd* be just as fooled as *I'd* be!"

Aset sighed heavily with exasperation, and although being a good sport about it, she gave up. "Stalemate I guess," she concluded as she threw some trimmings into the bucket at her feet. One way or another they would be recycled like everything else on the ship inevitably was.

"So what can I do for you Wiremu?"

"Well first of all, you can call me Wii."

"Noted," she remarked as she continued to pick at the plants in front of her.

"And I… was hoping you could tell me about your side of what's going on on the ship."

Aset let out a long and heavy sigh. "You and the others wrote the mission protocols right?" Another soft rustle as she threw more plant material into the bucket.

"That's right."

"Well at its core, that's what it's really all about. *We*, think that the mission protocols were and are there for a reason. We, think that they should have been observed, and should still be observed. *They*, openly and remorselessly flout the rules, and do whatever the fuck they want."

"I see." It hadn't been framed in quite that way for him before. When stated that bluntly, he found himself quite sympathetic to their perspective.

"The original clones were understandable, if not condonable. One lone nut took it upon himself to violate some of the most fundamental mission protocols. Well sure, we recognize that sometimes… sometimes disturbed people do unexpected things. You might even say that on a ship like this, in the situation we're in, some anomalous things like that were bound to happen. Head of genetics goes rogue and creates clones of himself, one man out of nowhere anomalously turns out to be a pedophile... hell we can even understand how the two factors in conjunction with each other could lead to murder and hijacking. The *point* is, that none of these things were conspiratory or colluding in nature, just... bad apples acting badly." She moved over to the next row, opened the seal on the aerosolizing chamber, and lifted up the lid. She began methodically plucking matured potatoes off of the hanging roots which were now exposed.

"Some blamed you, er... I mean the original yous, for all that happened... but I didn't. They claimed it was your hubris and lack of planning for the human community part of the mission that led to it, but I don't think so. I think it was just some stuff that happened, a few items that *did* happen on a long list of things that *could* have happened despite anyone's best efforts or best laid plans."

"But?" Wiremu asked, he knew she was headed somewhere with this.

"But everything changed at Midway," she stated purposefully as she dropped one potato after another into a different and larger bucket. "After Midway it became a conspiracy. Multiple people began conspiring to openly violate the mission protocols. They made another clone in full view of everyone, and in open defiance of the rules." She turned to face Wiremu and pointed an accusatory potato at him. "Were we supposed to just let them get away with it?? Were we supposed to just be okay with the rules not mattering anymore? If they could so easily get away with breaking *those* rules then how were we supposed to decide which rules we were still supposed to follow? If they could break those rules without consequence, then why bother having any rules at *all*!!?" She was yelling at Wiremu; she was angry.

Wiremu didn't answer, and she calmed down somewhat. She dropped the potato in question into the bucket with the others and turned back to pluck some more.

"They'll tell you all sorts of lies Wii... they'll make up all kinds of justifications for what they did. They'll hide behind concepts like intellectual curiosity and vague notions of freedom, but it's all just a screen. It's all just a way for them to justify breaking the rules they wish to break, and making us out to be the bad guys for trying to enforce those rules, the rules *you* instituted and left for us to follow. *We're* the loyalists. *We're* the ones who tried to make sure the ship followed your designs. *We* never lost our faith in the founders. *They* did."

Chapter 7

Kim In-Su was walking through the arboretum which his progenitor had created. The man had originally modelled it on the temperate coastal rainforests of his native Korean homeland, but he'd also drawn heavily on the rainforests of the north-western coast of North America. A lot of work had gone into making the artificial oasis feel natural and wild, but to those who came from Earth its artificiality was always quite apparent. In-Su imagined that to people born on the ship, people for whom this was their one and only remnant of actual nature, it must seem quite wild.

He observed that it did seem to be a more mature forest than it had been when it was originally constructed all those years ago. The original plants and trees had matured, and were now competing for the light coming from the sky with their later generations of offspring. He smiled to himself as he considered the similarity of his own position as one of the originals, now in a sort of competition with the later generations.

It was his way; he was always looking for connections and threads through things which others couldn't see or didn't care to. Though his training was in linguistics and he spoke many languages, his true love was poetry and his own collections had been as world renowned as his novels were when the New Horizon had left Earth. Of the four sims and the four humans they were based on, In-Su was the soul of their quartet, their conscience. The others had big vision; they saw the sweep of history, the epic scope of the mission, and the majestic infinitudes of the universe, but In-Su saw the small. He saw the fine grain of existence, the space between the atoms, and the fine threads that connected everything around him. He saw poetry everywhere.

He looked up at the sky and warmed his face in the sun's rays. It was a massive and powerful photon emitting array which slowly moved across the digitally projected blue sky, but it felt good. When deactivated or in night mode, the surface of the artificial sky was transparent, and through it one could see the non-rotating central section of the ship, at the front of which was the zero gravity bubble he'd enjoyed so much. Beyond that one saw the interior surface of the opposite side of the habitat ring. Beyond that still, now that they were in orbit around Haven, one could also occasionally see the planet below them slowly pass in and out of view.

But at the moment it was late afternoon, and the sun was shining. In-Su strolled down the winding path through the trees and dense underbrush which all served the ancient reciprocal relationship between plants and animals, each providing air for the other and each greedily consuming the other's waste products.

"In-Su?"

He turned around to see an old East Asian woman sitting at a picnic table in a small clearing off of the main path beside one of the small streams which served to irrigate the simulated forest. It was a woman he hadn't met before, and he noticed that she wasn't wearing the usual coveralls. Instead she was wearing a comfortable looking purple sun dress with yellow flower prints on it, and what appeared to be a faded yellow straw hat with a wide brim.

"You *are* Kim In-Su, right?" she asked in a clear and confident voice.

"Effectively," he said. At that point he really hadn't given much thought as to what relationship he had with the original being of that designation. It didn't seem that important to him. He tended to live in the moment, and nothing of his experience betrayed that he was anything other than what he felt like – Kim In-Su.

"Would you like to join me for a sit-down on this fine afternoon?" she asked.

He remarked on what an odd thing it was to say in a place where every afternoon, while pleasant, was always exactly as fine as the last one or the next. While he didn't know who she was, she appeared to have been waiting for him and she'd peaked his curiosity as to what she might have to say or ask.

"Certainly, and you are?" he asked as he sat himself down on the bench facing her. He noticed that she'd removed her sandals and her feet were on the grass. He followed suit and took his own socks and shoes off. The cool green grass felt wonderful on the soles of his feet and between his toes. He took a moment to notice how sweetly the grass smelled after narrowing his senses down on it from the myriad of other scents around him.

"Kim Bao," she answered with a smile. "I'm your great granddaughter," she said with a further widening smile through the shadow cast on her face by her hat.

"Is that so?" In-Su asked with a reciprocating smile.

"Mm humh," she confirmed. "And by blood too," she added, "not just by marriage." The clarification was necessary because children born on the ship were usually only genetically related to one of the people they knew as their parents. They were the product of one of their parent's gametes being blended with those of another of the same ethnicity out of the ship's five. It meant that for every member of the original crew, today there was only a single parent child thread which constituted their genetic descendance.

"Well, I'm very happy to meet you Bao."

"And I you... I was hoping to run into you and meet you before planetary operations got under way. I didn't want to go through the bother of trying to find you though; I figured it was only a matter of time before you found your way here. You did design it, didn't you?"

"Indeed, but this is just a garden! Are you as excited as I am to see our wild new planet?" he asked.

The woman let out a hearty laugh. "I'm ninety-two years old In-Su! It scares me half to death to think of something that open and wild! I've lived my whole life on this ship, with every comfort and every aspect of my life completely managed and controlled, with limits to my physical world that I can reach out and touch at all times... I'm in no hurry at all to leave my comfort and security for some great unknown, certainly not at my age. I'm not ashamed to admit that the idea is actually pretty scary... There are others though, even some who are much younger than me for whom it elicits a real paralyzing fear.... Mine is nowhere near as severe, but... I do feel it to some degree in my own way."

"I see," In-Su remarked. He didn't know what to say. "I don't understand though, you've come this far, and now you don't want to see what it was all *for*?"

"You misunderstand," she answered. "To you the ship is just a vehicle, only a means to an end. You boarded it on Earth, and now you wake up after the long journey ready to take on what is for you, the whole point of the trip: the planet below. Try to see it from my perspective though. I was *born* on this ship. I've lived twice as many years on it as you had years on before you left. To me it's more than just a vehicle; it isn't just a means to an end. To me this ship is... it's my home. More than that though, it's my whole world. From my perspective the interior of this ship may as well be the entire universe."

"Right," In-Su acknowledged. That he could understand.

"Being born when I was... for me the possibility of living long enough to see the arrival was a fifty fifty proposition. I figured I was as likely to die before we got here as I was to live to see it. I made peace long ago with the reality that the planet so far off in the distance was never to be *my* home; it was never *my* destination. This ship is. I'm not like the young ones born more recently who've been itching their whole lives to escape our humble home. They've had to live their whole lives with the heavy weight of their destiny, anxious to begin the ultimate struggle of their lives. I'm too old for any of that now. No, I'll be one of the ones to stay on the ship with the good medical facilities, and I'll help maintain its systems as long as my body will allow."

In-Su smiled; he understood. The ship *was* her existence, and she hungered for no other.

"Maybe someday... years from now, if I'm still around and kicking I'll make the trip. Maybe when the colony is fully established and up and running, and they can assure me it's safe and secure, maybe *then* I'll make the pilgrimage down... if only to honour the memory of all those poor souls who never even had the chance, the ones who never really had any choice about anything whatsoever."

"What do you mean?" He was immediately curious about those she was referring to who she claimed had no choices at all.

"We call them the children of the void, it's... an expression that's come into common usage to refer to those who were born after the launch, but never had any hope of ever seeing Haven." Bao answered. "They were the people who lived their entire existence in the empty void between the stars… and who knew their whole lives that this was their inescapable fate. It wasn't a fate they could ever have chosen for themselves, nor could they ever have the ability to choose any other kind of life.

"The clone who they say went crazy and hijacked the ship all those years ago? I knew him… he was my primary school teacher. He was the *ultimate* child of the void. His madness didn't come out of nowhere In-Su… and it wasn't his fault."

"Go on…"

"Your people… the original crew who originally boarded the ship? Sure they had to live the rest of their lives here, but for them it was a completely informed choice. They all had their own reasons to come aboard in the first place, informed by ideals and principles they believed in. They had a chance to see the ship first, to meet a lot of the other original crew and meet with you founders! They had a choice… and they could hope that it would amount to something someday when they were long dead and gone.

"Even the current crew didn't have it as bad as the children of the void though… no we might not've had any choice in the situation we were born into, and no we weren't able to make any meaningful choices about what we do with our lives or what kind of life we wanted for ourselves, but at least we had *hope*. At least for *us* there was the hope that someday our lot in life could change, at least for us there was hope of someday getting off of the ship if we *wanted* to. For us there's always been the promise of something *more*. *We* always knew that at the end of our imposed existence there would be a new kind of freedom waiting for us, and a whole world for us to explore and tame."

"I think I understand," In-Su offered. He believed that he was now beginning to see what human element Aset had so chastised him for neglecting when he'd first woken up. He was beginning to understand the cruel existential nightmare to which he and the others had subjected the people Bao described as the 'children of the void.' It made sense to him how it might drive some mad, or at least be a contributing factor for someone who suffered additional injustices.

"We… had hope," she explained, "and *they*… had choice. But the children of the void had neither, and it broke the spirits of many of the generations who raised me. Please don't misunderstand me, most people it didn't bother at all since humans generally adapt pretty readily to whatever life they're born into. Some people it only made deeply unhappy, but others it devastated so much that it made them lash out. Of those who did, some only became self-destructive… but others wound up taking it out on the ship and crew."

Chapter 8

"What the hell??" Neil exclaimed incredulously. He and the other three sims were in one of the two suites they'd been assigned while still on the ship. Like in the dining hall, this and the other suite had large round windows in the floor through which the planet occasionally migrated past.

"What?" In-Su asked.

"I died!"

"Of course you did; we all died."

"No," Neil sighed in frustration, "I mean... I died early like, way before we even launched, before my simulation was even complete!" They were conferring together about what they'd learned on their own over the last day or two, and reviewing the ship's records on medium and large scrolls.

Scrolls were the standard video display devices used on the ship and on Earth when they'd left. They consisted of two long and narrow posts which when pulled apart, unrolled a flexible screen which went rigid once extended out to the desired length. It displayed whatever one wished on the side facing the user, and the same image or another altogether on the opposite side.

"It says here... that it happened when the ship's fusion core was originally fired up and they were testing the core, engines and artificial magnetosphere. There was a problem and the core went into an over-regeneration cycle and it was gonna detonate. Apparently I went over to the ship to manually disconnect the power relays and got irradiated in the process..."

"Hot damn! You're heroic!" Wiremu exaggeratingly exclaimed with a laugh. Neil widened his eyes as if to say 'apparent*ly*!"

"But that means that... there's nothing missing. He had no experience of his own, no life that I don't have any memory of... He never had a long life on the ship after we were all put on ice the way all of yours did. I'm more like a... resurrection than whatever it is all of you are."

"And what are we?" Wiremu asked.

"It's almost like we are them getting a second chance... at a second life," Sadhika offered. "It's almost like, with the exception of Neil of course, we... I mean *they* had their life on the ship, but now they're getting a second chance at an entirely different life after the point at which we were simulated. I mean they, after the point at which *they* were simulated."

"Okay," Neil dropped his fully deployed half meters diameter large scroll down onto his lap in frustration. "So how long are we going to let that confuse us?"

"What do you mean?" she asked.

"We all know that we're not the same... beings as those we were modeled on," Neil answered. "*They* certainly all know, and they generally don't seem too keen on letting *us* forget it either."

"We were programmed to think of ourselves as the continuation of them..." In-Su offered, "it would be kind of silly to keep trying to force ourselves to continually clarify the distinction."

"It's also not entirely appropriate to claim that we *are* them," Wiremu warned. "There are obvious ways in which we are clearly *not* them."

"No," Neil countered, "but it would be equally inappropriate, I think, to pretend that we're totally unrelated, or... totally disassociated!"

"We are one identity... with two incarnations." In-Su offered thoughtfully. "From this point forward, to refer to the identity of Kim In-Su, one must necessarily refer to two different incarnations of that identity. However, one must also necessarily refer to us collectively as a unified... *incorporated* identity. I belong as much to the identity of Kim In-Su, as does the long dead human who also shares that identity, and as much as I myself am *not* that dead human."

"Damn right..." Neil stated, almost satisfied. "So... we?" he said with a chortle and the others chuckled a bit. "I'll tell you what, from now on I'm just going to say 'I' to refer to both of us, but you are all free to understand that I implicitly mean 'we.'"

"Understood." Sadhika said with a playfully feigned seriousness and gently puckered lips as she nodded her head in agreement along with the others.

Satisfied for now, Neil picked up his scroll again and resumed reviewing the biographical material. Having discovered that there was little of himself which he couldn't remember and didn't already know, he shifted his focus to reports of what had happened on the ship to the other sim's progenitors, as well as to all of the other factors which had led to the current mess they'd woken up into.

He could operate the scroll and all of the other technology on the ship by thought control as effectively as the human crew could, but for him and the other sims, the transmitting technology was simply built into their mechanoid physiology. This was in contrast with the Brainchip system which the human crew had implanted into their brains when they were around thirteen years old. What were referred to collectively as the Brainchip were in fact three transmitters each about the size of a grain of rice, embedded into different key sections of the cerebral cortex. They analyzed the activity of the user's brain, interpreted the signals, and broadcasted demands to technological devices around them.

For the rare oddity when the Brainchip system went down, or for children too young to have had them implanted yet, everything could also be operated by touch and voice commands. Most of the people on the ship were so comfortable with the Brainchips and so used to using them though, that reaching out with their mind to control the technological world around them was entirely as natural and unremarkable as physically reaching out with their hands to operate anything. In fact, actually having to physically manipulate technology was for them something unusual, something quaint, and something which usually only the children had to muddle through.

The Brainchip in humans, and the analogous technology in the sims, allowed them to open doors, navigate computer interfaces, dictate text, and send messages all with only a thought. It was exclusively a brain out system though, meaning that information could only travel from the brain to a computer, but not from a computer directly into the brain. This limitation in the technology necessitated the use of devices such as the EAR (Enhanced Auditory Rebroadcaster), and the PANE (Personal Area Network Eyes).

The EARs were tiny devices implanted into the auditory canals around the same time as the Brainchip. They could record sounds as well as play them in such a way that only the user could hear them. There were also two kinds of PANE devices; there were the more useful glasses with screens similar in functionality to the scrolls, going from transparent to any display configuration with a thought. The PANE glasses were typically used for things like filmmaking and documenting, and had embedded within them high resolution multi-spectral cameras and better microphones than the EARs. Also available though, were the PANE lenses; contact lenses which could display things discretely to just the user, but which had no microphone and only a basic lower resolution camera to facilitate a heads up display. The PANE lenses were for more discrete personal use.

While the sims in principle could have had all of this technology built into them, the purpose of their creation was to recreate as faithfully as possible the original beings upon which they were based, *not* to improve upon them. While it would have been quite easy technologically to just adjust their visual system to be able to view whatever they wished without the aid of such devices, or to turn their head itself into a sophisticated audio/video capture device far superior to the PANEs, this would have defeated the true purpose of their being. As a result they needed to use the various audio and video devices as much as any of the human crew did and for the same reasons.

"Well this is disturbing…" In-Su remarked.

"What?"

"Someone, some… child of the void, describes the mission as a 'worst case scenario religion," In-Su explained.

"Children of the void?" Sadhika asked.

"Something one of the… well my great granddaughter actually, something she told me…" the simulated man answered. "That's what they call the people born after we launched, but soon enough after that they had no hope whatsoever of ever seeing Haven. She said that those who launched had a choice, and that those born more recently had hope, but those in the middle had neither and they call *them* the children of the void.

"One of them here suggests that the religions of Earth were miserable because they were false, but that their *redeeming* quality, at least more recently in a historical context, was that one was free to leave them if they were able to realize that they were false."

"And how is the New Horizon mission supposed to be a worst case scenario of that?" Neil asked.

"According to this person, because the mission was true... because it really was worthwhile and it wasn't possible to discover the error of it. It had an undeniable merit and reality to it, and even worse they say... one could never leave it, one could never escape it. It imposed a technically worthwhile existence, while leaving one neither free to renounce it nor choose any other. The injustice they say, was the absence of injustice, in an unjust situation. It totally forbade any of them from having any possible sense of control over their own lives..."

"Boy we really did some damage here didn't we..." Wiremu lamented. "How did this happen? How did we get so much so wrong? This place feels like a powder keg..." he observed. "I'm left hoping that from here on out everyone will just be too busy to be so much at each other's throats anymore, but I'm still very concerned."

They had already conferred with each other about what they'd learned from the members of the crew they'd spoken with. They were all aware of the fundamental dichotomy on the ship and what the real problem with it was; that neither side of the conflict was clearly in the wrong. Certainly neither side had all of the virtue, but likewise neither side could be fairly said to have a monopoly on all of the blame either.

"Okay," Neil exclaimed half in frustration and half in irritation, "let me see if I've got this, I want to make sure I've got all of this straight." The other three nodded. They too wanted to make sure that they had a firm grasp on what the narrative at this point.

"So, this Markus Bowland character, who none of us ever met, was a wildcard member of the crew who got a last minute promotion to be the head of Genetics. Then, because he has issues I can't even fathom, when they go to him to create what is supposed to be his son and later his grandson, he instead creates clones of himself as some kind of bizarre vanity project. He gets into his head the idea of raising them differently from himself to see how they turn out, and by extension how he himself could have turned out if he'd lived a different life."

"Correct." Sadhika confirmed.

"And while all of *this* is going on, another member of the first ship born generation anomalously turns out to be a pedophile and out of nowhere starts raping boys on the ship, *including* this Markus' clone-grandson Tycho."

"Right."

"Then," Neil continued, "between finding out that he's a clone, Earth mysteriously going dark, and the whole 'children of the void' thing, this Tycho character goes all wonko. He brutally murders his rapist and soon after, hijacks the ship using *us* in a kind of... hack 'slave mode' as his muscle. He tries to redirect the ship to a planet where a different generational colony ship was already headed, but one which the ship could theoretically arrive at in his lifetime. Tycho then winds up getting killed by his clone-father Johannes before he can fully carry out his plan."

"Correct."

"Then," Neil chuckled angrily, "and this is the part I *really* can't understand, this Johannes, for *some reason,* decides that he can't just let it all end with that, and makes yet *another* clone before killing himself."

"That's right," Sadhika responded. "That clone was the one they call Herschel, and he later created Halley as his own son. Their creation is what really created the rift that we see on the ship now... Aset and Asari's people think they have no right to exist and that none of them should have ever been created in the first place. Halley thinks that his father's inherent goodness should have been enough for everyone to accept him, and now he's super bitter that so many never did."

"Boy we really *did* do some damage here didn't we..." Wiremu remarked despondently. "What a mess..."

Chapter 9

One week ago…

Immediately upon arriving in orbit around Haven, the New Horizon launched five drone satellite platforms in rapid succession out of the same launch tube. Once released, the drones spread out and assumed a formation in orbit which provided a relay network between the mother ship, and with any location on the planet. Through successive orbits, the satellites would pass over every part of the planet over and over, building up comprehensive models of its features. They generated data on important elements like ocean depth, atmospheric concentrations, weather mapping, and high resolution imaging of the entire planet's surface.

Another five identical such drone remained dormant in the same launch tube. They served as back up spares in case any of the primary units irreparably malfunctioned or were somehow destroyed. On a long enough timeline and if they were not needed as replacements, there was also the possibility of attaching liquid rockets and ion engines to them. So equipped, they could be sent off to explore other parts of their new home star system. This was a distant concern, but the mission by its very nature always thought and imagined very far into the distant future.

As the sophisticated devices silently slid into their orbits, they began to unfurl like spring flowers. The parts of the devices which started out as their exterior, wrapped in on themselves and became the interior spine of their new configuration. Large multi-spectral solar panels, which generated tremendous amounts of energy since they captured a wide swath of the star's light instead of a single narrow wavelength, unfurled into long spectacular arrays.

As the structures continued to unpack themselves, two telescopes telescopically emerged, and extended into eight meter wide low energy light observing dishes, and twelve meter long reflecting tubes which captured more rebellious high energy light. Lengths, optics, and reflecting profiles of both could be changed and adjusted remotely, allowing them with equal effectiveness to observe the planet below in fine detail, as well as to turn their focus back further into the dark skies in which they lived.

The probes also had omnidirectional gamma ray detectors which allowed a constant monitoring of the most dangerous high energy light in the environment. This could be in the form of cosmic rays which proliferated through all of the cosmos, or the occasional radiation spikes violently burst from the star which they were orbiting along with the planet.

--- --- ---

"This is when the fun part starts right?" Sadhika asked the other sims while they were waiting for all of the relevant humans to arrive in the conference room. The room wasn't that big, but it was large enough to house a long rectangular table identical to those in the dining hall, and set up lengthwise in front of a wall sized screen.

The team was anxious to begin the work they'd travelled so far for. They were here for the first descent mission briefing; it was now that they were to select a landing site and review the descent procedures. After having to orient themselves to all of the petty grudges and posturing on the ship, they were keenly looking forward to getting on with what they considered to be the real business at hand.

Neil chuckled at Sadhika's remark, and then asked: "are we early or are they late?"

As though his question had summoned it, the door opened and in walked a woman none of them had met before. "Oh," she exclaimed as she looked around the room and realized that she was the first human to arrive. She'd had a confident air about her when she strolled through the door, but now she seemed decidedly self-conscious as she asked: "Oh, am I early?"

"We were just asking the same thing," Neil answered, deliberately keeping her off balance for his own amusement.

"Oh." There was every reason for her to ask Neil to clarify what he'd meant but she declined to pursue it for fear that it wouldn't lead anywhere terribly helpful. She had large brown eyes and remarkably dark brown hair which had a natural loose curl to it. The colour of her hair and eyes, in conjunction with her remarkably yet naturally red lips, accentuated the pale lightness of her skin and gave her a look of striking visual contrast.

"Um, hello everyone," she awkwardly offered, "I'm Blair Bentley. I'm the... head of biology? I'll be part of your second descent team."

"Of course," Sadhika offered kindly, "I'm Sadhika, this is Wiremu, Neil, and... In-Su."

Blair let out a little giggle despite herself. "I... yeah, I know who you are," she said with an admiring smile.

At that moment, as Blair headed for a seat, Armina Shostak entered as well, followed soon after by Halley, Soren, and Ishtar. After Neil and Armina exchanged furtive and knowing smiles at each other, Neil said to the other sims: "guys this is Armina, the woman I was telling you about?"

Sadhika eyed Neil suspiciously as all the new arrivals exchanged greetings and pleasantries with the sims and with each other. She saw the way they'd looked at each other and she knew what Neil was like. She was only thinking about the inappropriateness of their fraternizing with the crew in general; the interspecies element, if that was even the right word, didn't even occur to her.

A slender man with short black hair and dark brown skin and eyes walked in a minute or so later, and Halley introduced him as Huli Koroba, their head of atmospherics. As he and the sims greeted each other, Asari and Aset finally arrived and they were all ready to get started.

"Okay," Asari stated with a characteristic lack of emotion in his voice, "Haven." With a thought he brought up a large high resolution image of the rotating planet on the wall screen. It was spinning much faster than the actual planet, completing a full revolution once every five seconds or so. Asari's educational specialties focused on planetary sciences and he'd been studying Haven his whole life as they approached it.

"Average diameter is twelve thousand, six hundred and ninety-eight kilometers, mass is six point eight times ten to the power or twenty-four kilograms, and… it had a density of a little greater than Earth's but roughly equal to it, about five and a half grams per cubic centimeter. It has a comparable magnetic field to Earth which itself can tell us a few things. It makes it likely that the planet has a comparable internal structure to Earth but we'll need to do a lot of seismological observations on the surface to know for sure. We also have the thermal sensors on the satellites confirming that the planet is geologically active and that's another line of evidence suggesting the same thing.

"Um…" he uttered as he looked back down at his scroll, "the planet's orbit is a little further out from the sun than the Earth's was, and has an average distance from the sun of about a hundred and fifty million kilometers. Its days are twenty-five point seven earth hours long which we've already adjusted to on the ship, and its years are approximately three hundred and forty-five Haven days long. Spectrum of light which penetrates the atmosphere is again, similar to Earth… it only has two small captured asteroids for moons, and… it has an axis tilt only eight point two degrees off. Any questions so far?"

Wiremu raised his hand and asked: "have you been able to tell yet what impact the lesser tilt has on the climate?"

"Huli?" Asari asked.

"Two primary factors," Huli answered. "Compared to Earth, there is far more dramatic latitudinal gradation, and the seasonal variability at any given latitude is far reduced. Basically the planet is more climactically consistent year round. The sub-equatorial regions where we'll probably want to put our colonies is temperate year round; it never reaches freezing in the winter and never gets hotter than oh… thirty-five or so, but the polar regions basically stay in a year round winter deep freeze with total ice cover."

"And what is the current season on the planet?" Wiremu asked.

"Well like I said the seasons are a lot less pronounced, but for all intents and purposes it's basically late spring in what we're calling the northern hemisphere… and obviously late fall in the south."

"Okay." This seemed to satisfy the original captain for now.

"I have what may be a more… esoteric question," In-Su stated.

"How are we to adjust our time keeping to the longer day? I understand that the crew has already adjusted to it, but... are we just equating that twenty-five point seven hour day to twenty-four hours and adjusting the length of what we call hours and minutes, or..."

"For now we're planning on keeping our time units and just having the twenty-sixth hour have only forty-two minutes," Asari answered. "It may seem confusing, but it's the *least* confusing solution we've been able to come up with so far. That reminds me..." He picked up his scroll off of the table and looked through the data for a specific piece of information using thought commands. "Right... the year is actually three hundred and forty-seven *point eight two* days long, so eventually we'll have to figure out some sort of complicated leap year system to keep our calendars accurate. I consider that a pretty distant concern at this point though."

"Quite reasonably," In-Su agreed. "Thank you Asari."

"As I said, the planet's density is about the same as Earth's and while it's slightly smaller in diameter, the decreased gravity at the surface shouldn't be detectable without sensitive instruments; we didn't adjust the ship's simulated gravity to prepare us for it or anything." He looked around at all of the faces and everyone seemed to be following without any questions.

"So," Asari said, now directly addressing Wiremu, "you've got your choice of quiet a few potential landing and colony sites which we've identified based on fundamental parameters and requirements." The rotating globe on the wall screen flattened out to reveal the entire surface of the planet at once with pie sections cut out of the top and bottom so as to reasonably preserve the map's accuracy.

On the left of the map was a large super continent which looked like several haggard and misshapen entities all haphazardly crushed together. The bulk of this continent was roughly between about fifty degrees latitude both north and south. It contained mountain ranges and high plateaus, inland seas, and many large islands off of the mainland. It looked like someone had taken Asia, Australasia, Africa, and Europe, and chaotically smushed them all together in a hurry. Various regions betrayed their local climates in their colours, desert yellow, lush green, barren brown, and snow-capped white.

On the right side of the map was an irregular cigar shaped land mass. Its bottom edge lay near the planet's equator and at its fattest in the middle it stretched almost up to the tropic of cancer. At this point, a large island appeared in the process of being slowly torn away from the main continental mass, revealing a wide sea strait between the massive island and the main continent. A significant mountain range could be seen from the north north west of the flat continent diagonally down to its south south east.

This continent too displayed all of the colours of the other, but it was smaller, and the geography was less varied and complicated. The large continent on the left had coastlines that appeared to be shattered with countless small and large islands. It was littered with inland seas and large fingered lakes.

"The satellites have been scanning since we arrived," Asari reported, "and we've been able to tell a lot. Look," he directed as he zoomed in on what appeared to be vast grassland plains on the left jumble of a continent. Clearly visible was a herd of tens of thousands of grazing animals. Without a sense of scale though, it was hard to tell how big the animals were until Asari zoomed in further and now, only half a dozen animals were visible on the whole wall, and a scale ruler appeared in the top right hand side of the image. It revealed that the greeny gold skinned animals were each several meters long from their multi horned head to the tip of their fat stubby tails.

"Those are the only animals we've been able to see so far with our orbital telescopes," Blair piped up. "They appear to have two big primary back legs that they run or hop around on and two arms on the front that they use for grasping and just moving around. At this distance we could be wrong of course, but the colour to their skin makes them look like they might be scaled."

"That's amazing..." Sadhika softly exclaimed in wonderment. Like a giant kangaroo..."

"Sure, if you crossed one with some kinda dinosaur!" Neil exclaimed.

"Show them the jungle," Blair suggested. Asari complied and the image zoomed out, crossed over half of the continent, zoomed back in, and began panning over the lush green canopy. "*That's* what *I'm* really excited to study," she said. "If they're anything like the jungles that were left on Earth, and they probably are, they've gotta be just positively *thick* with interesting life." She was practically salivating at the prospect.

"Spectroscopy of the atmosphere shows a perfectly appropriate atmospheric composition," Huli reported. "As for any potential diseases..."

"We'll need physical samples of the air from the environment you want to bring humans down to for the first time," Blair informed, "but the shuttle's air filters will probably give us the most information if they're just left to filter the atmosphere and analyze what they trap. We can study those results remotely from the ship. In reality though, and don't get me wrong, I know we have to take every precaution anyways... but on Earth it was hard enough for a bacteria or virus to jump between even similar species. Even if life here has an identical DNA system, I think the odds of infections readily crossing species is quite slim."

"Understood." Wiremu stated. "What else can you tell me about the climate Huli?"

"Well," he said, sitting up straight, "Although it's less variable, it's a somewhat cooler planet overall. It has, as Asari explained, roughly the same diameter, mass, and gravity, but it's a little further out from the sun than Earth was."

"What about tectonic activity?" Neil asked.

"Well active, obviously, as Asari said." Ishtar answered. "So far that's all we can tell you. We're getting ready to launch the drone seismology landers this afternoon," Ishtar added. As the head of flight operations, her responsibilities included supervising the launch of their robotic landers. "They'll be strategically placed around the planet so we'll be able to detect and triangulate seismic activity everywhere across the globe, but..."

"But seismology is slow by nature," Asari concluded for her. "It will take centuries if not millennia to build up enough data to have an accurate model."

"Anyways Wiremu," Ishtar spoke up again, "we can land just about anywhere you want to in the wide sub-equatorial regions wherever you can find a flat spot, we've outlined a couple dozen good choices for you, each has its own particular benefits and interesting things nearby." She had obviously accepted the sims as the new incarnations of the original mission founders. "We just need to send down a runway drone once you pick a spot."

"Asari," Wiremu asked, "can you zoom in on that... breakaway island at the top of the continent you had on the right there?"

Issuing the commands with his thoughts, Asari zoomed the image out from the close up on the jungle canopy to reveal most of the whole planet, and then back down onto the spot Wiremu had described.

"Zoom in on the um, uh... western entrance to those straits between the island and the mainland, please." Asari complied. "How wide *is* that strait there?"

"Oh... about a hundred kilometers on average," he estimated.

"Perfect," a pleased Wiremu stated. "Are there any good sites some-what... interior to that strait's entrance on the continent's mainland? I'd like our colony site to be near the water and that island is a good natural breakwater." The large island was narrow and wide, and had a thick mountain spine capped with snow.

"Umm... yeah," Ishtar confirmed as she approached the screen and pointed to a particular location. After Asari zoomed in more on the specified area, she pointed to a more specific spot.

"Here," she said, "there's a sort of... boundary zone between the grasslands closer to the water, and the jungle further inland. The whole region is several dozens of meters above sea level and runs up against high cliffs on the coast, so... flooding should never be a problem. A couple dozen kilometers away where the ground's lower there's a river feeding into the ocean which would well suit our needs too... It's a good site," she offered encouragingly. "Actually one of the better ones I'd say," she added.

"Both shuttles are fully operational," Ishtar continued, "you can take one and make your first descent whenever you're ready," she informed the ship's original captain. "We've been making preliminary plans based on you leaving tomorrow morning, but... nothing's cast in stone yet."

"The heat shield is perfect after all this time?" Wiremu asked. "I don't want to have come all this way just to burn up on our very first re-entry."

"Entry." Neil reflexively corrected.

"What?" Wiremu asked, somewhat irritated.

"Well it'll... it'll only be re-entry the *second* time we do it," Neil explained. "If it's our first time ever going down to the planet, then...

it'll just be 'entry.'" Wiremu smiled and nodded his approval that yes, he was of course right.

"Yes, the heat shield is perfect." Halley answered, sounding a little insulted at the idea that he wasn't adequately doing his job. "As soon as we made orbit I had crews out there completely refurbishing it."

"Good." Wiremu stated. "And thank you." he added somewhat apologetically.

"Okay," Ishtar said, "site Alpha... eleven it is then. I'll launch the paving drone for you right away. The site looks like it's on an ancient sea bed so it should be a nice hard surface for us. The drones should have a pristine runway for you by morning. That work for you?"

Wiremu looked at his fellow sims and they all subtly nodded their approval. They were all anxious to get on with what they had come all this way to do.

Chapter 10

The airlock opened and one by one the four simulants passed through the portal and boarded the shuttle. Like the bubble, it was located off of the central non-rotating zero gravity section of the ship. Halley and Søren watched respectfully from either side of the airlock as the four passed through.

"Good luck then," Halley offered somewhat somberly.

"Yeah, don't fuck it up," Søren said with a grin. "We've only got two of these things after all…" He rapped his knuckles against the hull of the shuttle.

Wiremu harrumphed. "We ain't come this far…" he said as he passed the two humans and they closed the airlock behind him. They certainly hadn't come this far only to crash and be destroyed in the midst of their final triumph.

"Alright everyone," Wiremu said with authority as he joined the other simulants in the rear compartment and lead them forward to the flight deck, one hand or foot hold at a time. "Strap in."

All four made their way past the large and empty rear section of the shuttle which doubled as either passenger space or fuel tanks depending on the need at any given time. They would be gliding down empty but for the return trip the tanks would be filled with liquefied hydrogen and oxygen, separated and condensed out of the planet's atmosphere by the shuttle's systems.

As the bulkhead isolating the flight deck closed behind them, Wiremu took the left captain's seat, Sadhika took the co-pilot seat on his right, and they both buckled up their harnesses. Neil and In-Su pulled down the sideways mounted seats off of the wall behind Wiremu and Sadhika, then worked their bodies into the rear seats which faced each other, and harnessed themselves up.

"I hate to ask Wii, but uh… you *are* qualified for this right?" Neil asked from behind Sadhika. "I mean, your *progenitor* was an expert pilot, but um… how can you be sure that those skills transferred over in the simulation process? Maybe you just *think* you can pilot this thing, but we're *really* just on our way to our fiery deaths?" He was trying to add some humour to what was actually a very serious question.

"I appreciate your vote of confidence Neil," Wiremu said without looking away from the consoles in front of him, through which he was conducting the pre-flight checklists by thought. "But rest assured that when my simulation was created, the original Wiremu's experience was grafted onto the most sophisticated artificial intelligence piloting program in existence at the time. This makes my capacities beyond his or the shuttle's own autopilot, which could easily pull this landing off on its own without breaking an electronic sweat. Does that satisfy you?" he asked sarcastically but with good humour.

"I suppose so…" Neil answered, feigning residual misgivings.

"Fantastic." Wiremu answered while preserving an air of false irritation. "Mission control we are ready on our end, we are requesting permission to launch."

"Acknowledged Shuttle One," Ishtar answered from the bridge. As the head of flight operations she was overseeing their departure and descent. "You are go for launch. Good Luck." She didn't know what else to say.

"Thank you Ishtar, Shuttle One out," and with that Wiremu switched off the line.

"It *is* a big moment," In-Su offered. "Maybe somebody should say something?" he offered.

"Like what?" Neil asked him.

"Well actually, nothing comes to mind now that I think about it," In-Su admitted.

"How bout… let's go?" Sadhika offered.

"Works for me," Neil said.

After unlocking the grapples and magnetic seals which held it firmly in place, gentle jets pushed the shuttle off of its mother ship and away from its docking port. It manoeuvered itself safely away from the large rotating habitat ring which went around and around the long cylinder of the non-rotating central engineering section which housed the fusion reactor powering the ship, the many required fuel pods, and the four powerful ion engines which had brought them so far.

Once at a safe distance, the shuttle positioned itself upside down and with its nose pointed in the opposite direction to that of their orbit. A ten second burn from their main engines slowed them sufficiently that they began to fall out of their orbit, and further and further down into the thicker and thicker atmosphere of the planet out of its negligible density at the height which the New Horizon sailed through the sky.

After completing their de-orbiting burn, the small craft flipped up and somersaulted so that its nose pointed around to face the direction of their now decaying orbit. By the time they began hitting the first real wisps of atmosphere, they were already in their proper orientation, with their nose up and the heat shielding of the shuttle's entire underside facing their direction of motion through the ever thickening atmosphere.

The obscene kinetic energies of their orbital velocity began to gradually bleed away into heat energy as violent plasma flares erupted from underneath the shuttle. The layers of heat shield material between the violent inferno and the simulants inside, were gradually ablated away by the superheated atmosphere plasma sanding it off. This was the most dangerous part of their descent and for all intents and purposes, it was *the* dangerous part. Any tiny imperfection in the heat shield would incinerate the entire shuttle nearly instantaneously.

"We're through," Wiremu declared and informed mission control once they were finally through the violent burning phase of their descent and the regular flight surfaces of the shuttle became usable again. The flight deck and mission control back on the ship both erupted with cheers. They had survived this phase and that was worth celebration, but no one was forgetting the danger that still lay ahead.

Wiremu began conducting long lazy s-curves to bleed off the still considerable kinetic energy of their air speed. They were flying over a rocky coast line still quite a ways below them, and the landscape was distinctly blue out the windows on one side of the shuttle, and distinctly green out the other.

"Ok," Wiremu reported back to the ship, "The runway just popped up on the HUD… no visual yet though.

"Understood."

The drone satellite system was not the only trick up the New Horizon's launch tubes. There were a variety of different industry drones which could be launched, descended ballistically, and then softly landed with rockets. Much like the satellites, from their initial compact launch and descent configuration, once on the surface they unfurled to reveal all of their functional elements.

The paving drone was the first the ship had launched down to the planet, and it had only been deployed after Wiremu had chosen their landing site. It contained within itself (or had the ability to create from available raw materials) everything necessary to lay down a minimum three kilometer long runway, given appropriate terrain and materials. It was yet another display of their home planet's amazing technological sophistication in autonomous programming and engineering.

"Okay, I got it now." It was a clear day. There were some clouds but they were sparse and the day was well lit and ever more beautiful the closer they descended upon it. Wiremu had spotted the runway constructed by the drone in the jungle a few kilometers from the coast. Just as he had pointed out the day before, it was right at the mouth of the strait's inlet and several dozen meters above sea level. He'd wanted their colony site to be right in the jungle for easy access to its game and lumber, as well as having close and easy access to a relatively calm part of the ocean which would provide maritime access to the rest of the planet.

"We are now on final approach," Wiremu reported to Ishtar up on the ship as he deployed the landing gear, and then turned to his friends who were with him on the flight deck. "Hang in there guys, in theory the worst part is behind us."

Using regular flight surfaces, Wiremu glided the shuttle down towards the runway carved out of the jungle. All of his commands were issued by thought, and to look at him he only appeared to be firmly gripping the sides of the console in front of him, and looking out through the window and ahead of them in deep concentration.

With unparalleled skill, he came down just ahead of the trees at the beginning of the runway, and with a not insignificant bump and jostling about, the rear wheels settled firmly onto the runway surface. Then all that was felt was the sudden deceleration from the parachutes deploying behind them, and the last great bump as the nose landing gear came down onto the tarmac and the electromagnetic brakes in the wheels were finally added to the decelerating force of the parachutes.

The shuttle finally came to a complete stop and there was a sudden and unexpectedly conspicuous silence. They'd spent over a century and a half in motion, and now they were finally at rest.

"Lady and gentlemen... welcome to Haven." The words ignited cheers in the shuttle and in orbit, and were remembered for generations.

Chapter 11

After In-Su got out of the way, Wiremu opened the hatch behind his seat which provided direct access between the flight deck and the outside world. The gullwing door swung from the floor up to sit parallel to the ground above the height of their heads. He took a deep breath in through his nose to smell the air. It was deeply satisfying, as though the scent itself was a trophy for all of their hard work.

"Good, there's oxygen on this planet..." Wiremu stated as the interesting smelling air swept up his nose and past him to fill the shuttle's flight deck.

"What?" Sadhika asked, confused.

Wiremu laughed to himself, and then left the shuttle without an explanation. The other three looked at each other a little bewildered, and then unstrapped themselves from their seats and followed him out.

Somewhat anticlimactically, they stepped down the stairs which extended out when the door opened, and onto the dark greenish brown tarmac the drone had created for them. Only a few meters beyond the wing though, was a tall forbidding wall of dark greenery. It had an upper canopy that varied between twenty and thirty meters in height, with what appeared to be broad green leaves all competing to get over each other and into the sun of the perpetual temperate summer.

With the noises of the shuttle winding and settling down, the simulants stood in silence. The sounds of the jungle became audible once they listened, just a whisper at first but then as they attuned their ears to it, it became a complex cacophony. It was the sound of an alien jungle with as of yet unexplored native insects and animals, and maybe more. There was a shrill whistle at regular intervals of about twenty seconds, and a low grunt sound which cycled every second or so from various directions, and apparently amplified by hundreds of thousands of whatever was emitting the sound. These were the only discernible and individually distinguishable sounds; the rest was a mad roaring jumble.

"Would you listen to that..." In-Su said in wonderment, "even during the day." The density of the canopy declined the nearer one looked to the floor of the jungle, where there was sparse shrubbery and endless trunks of the trees which fought for light far above, some seeming to be strangled by a brown vine which appeared to be producing large bluish-purple fruit.

Sadhika put on her PANE glasses and with a thought fed the camera's ultraviolet scanner through the main optics. "Wow, those fruit are really bright in UV... like flowers to bees on Earth..."

"I'd hate to see the bees." Neil said dryly and the other three laughed cathartically.

"Okay," Wiremu said in an officious voice, "we have to stay the night to give the shuttle enough time to separate out of the atmosphere all the fuel we'll need to get back to orbit. I suggest we just set up camp right here on this runway... I don't know about the rest of you, but I certainly don't want to spend the night in the middle of the totally unexplored alien jungle, simulant or not." The other three nodded, still smiling.

The captain tilted his head to one side, and slowly breathed in through his nose. "You smell that?" he asked the others. "Like... sweet cinnamon."

While the other three were looking around and trying to zero in on the smell he was talking about, Wiremu was instantly transported back to his childhood or at least, to the childhood he was programmed to be able to remember. It was a cold winter's day, and his mother had made cinnamon buns for breakfast. The resolution of the memory was so crisp that he was taken aback for a moment. He wasn't expecting such a thing.

Sensing something wrong, Neil placed his hand on the man's shoulder and asked: "you alright?"

"I just had a memory... a flashback to something from Wiremu's childhood… triggered by that scent. Cinnamon buns…"

"Oh yeah, sure, now I know what you mean," Neil offered with further sniffs. "Just part of the programming, my friend," he said with a smile. "A deep relationship between scent and memory is very important to humans, so like everything else they incorporated it into us as much as they could."

"Was it a happy memory?" In-Su asked.

"Oh yes…" Wiremu said distantly, "warmth, family, comfort food…" he added with a grin. "Except now I have a serious craving for cinnamon buns!" The other three laughed and allowed their focus to wander back to various curiosities about their new environment.

Getting back to business, Wiremu put his own PANEs on and put a communication request through to the ship above, and Ishtar answered. As directed by his thoughts, her image appeared on the top left hand quadrant of both lenses.

"We're standing on the surface Ishtar, and everything looks good." Wiremu could hear some cheers in the background. Certainly they were watching them very closely from orbit but a silent bird's eye view could only tell them so much. "Please launch the First Descent Module," he requested. "Uh… right over there please," he said as he pointed to the near end of the new runway, ahead of where the shuttle had come to a stop. "As snugly against the end of the runway as the program will allow, please."

"Yes sir, anything else we can do for you?" Ishtar asked, hoping to be able to help further.

"Not at the moment. Try to be patient," he offered sympathetically, "we know you'd all rather be here instead of us," he added, looking up at them as he did and giving them a wave.

"Yes sir, have fun."

"Acknowledged."

The First Descent Module raced out of its launch tube with the tunnel's magnetic accelerators. There were many of these descent modules, each of them able to immediately provide different capabilities down on the surface. Most were designed with very specific purposes such as refining and smelting platforms or other industrial capacities, and there were even ones which unfurled into air, land, and water vehicles. The First Descent Module served multiple functions, but was primarily designed just for this first night when the simulants had to spend the night on the alien planet's surface before being able to return to the ship the next day. It contained an inflatable habitat with four beds and some food, along with instruments and storage vessels which would allow them to analyze the planet from the surface in addition to taking samples back to the New Horizon.

Later on, once a settlement was up and running and the FDM's primary function was no longer needed, it would become the runway's flight control station for incoming shuttles and aircraft. It had scanners which could confirm that the runway was clear, it housed emergency supplies, and could serve as an emergency shelter for whatever situations might call for one.

The module's heat shield descended and formed a protective ablative umbrella which burned through the atmosphere in a similar way to that of the shuttle, with wisps of plasma beneath it early on, and later a raging fireball entirely engulfing the module during its most volatile phase. Sufficiently slowed by the burning, it reached the bulk of the atmosphere and began to tumble in free fall at its terminal velocity. A series of control jet bursts righted the module so that it fell straight up and down, and then tilted itself to glide in the direction of the simulant team instead of straight down.

When in the vicinity and at the appropriate height, the module launched the 'halo' from which it suspended itself after a set of three parachutes deployed out of the halo and pulled the whole apparatus up to a slower descent speed. A hundred meters from the ground, the parachutes were released and a set of rocket nozzles fired downward from the halo, slowing its descent until the module was gently set down at the end of the runway exactly where Wiremu had intended.

"Perfect," Wiremu stated with satisfaction, and then led the other three over to it.

When he came within a few meters of the module it came into range of his Brainchip and Wiremu ordered the initial start up to its full landed configuration. Out of one side the habitat began to inflate. It was windowless but the material it was made of could resist anything from a sharp knife to the vacuum of space. It was a nontransparent predecessor material to that with which the crew built the ship's zero gravity bubble. Along the other side of the module was a bank of sensors, cameras, and instrument surfaces for them to exploit from inside the habitat or elsewhere from their scrolls.

"First things first." Sadhika stated decidedly as she walked over to the wall cut out of the jungle by the runway drone, and touched the trunk of a tree which had its large leaves far above her head. She held her hand to it for several moments as though she were trying to determine something about it by feel. She then reached down and grabbed a dark green leaf off of one of the sparse plants on the floor of the jungle just beyond the runway. Returning to the module, she pulled out a tray and lifted its lid. She laid the leaf down onto the tray and pressed the lid firmly back down on the leaf, and then pushed the shelf back into the body of the module. She opened the main tall narrow door and pulled out a large scroll, then closed it again. Turning around and sitting down, she leaned back against the inflated outside wall to run the analysis on her scroll.

"What are you looking at?" Neil asked.

"Oh, just the first ever analysis of life on an alien world..."

"Careful with that first ever talk... you know as well as I do that the other two missions have probably themselves landed at this point."

"Fuck that!" Wiremu exclaimed, despite himself. "We ain't come *this far*," he declared, "they were far less prepared and we can't point to any evidence at all that they actually made it to their planets, that their planets were appropriate, or that they successfully landed. We had far better odds of success than them from the outset, *and* we've been *lucky* at every step we've needed to be so far, so... let's just stow all that 'are we or aren't we first' talk." In-Su and Neil chuckled. He was absolutely right, but his sudden and excited irritation amused them.

Sadhika leaned her head back and looked up into the sky. Looking distant, and seemingly more just to herself than to the other three, she said: "I just made... the most important human discovery... that has *ever* been made since we first discovered that there was life anywhere in the universe other than Earth."

"What have you found?" In-Su asked.

"It's the same as Earth, the... the DNA system is the same, can you believe it!? That means that there is either a... a common panspermic source or... or a natural convergence! Either thought is, well..." she seemed too excited to be able to finish her own thought.

"...unimaginable." In-Su thoughtfully answered for her.

"Right!" she exclaimed. "It's the most important... most *exciting* human discovery in a quarter millennium!!"

"And you're not even human..." In-Su remarked. Sadhika calmed a bit and thought about this. He was right. It was humans who made this discovery possible, but it was her, a simulation of a once living human, who had made the actual discovery. The issue had its roots in the very beginning of the space age, the question of whether cheaper robotic probes should explore space or whether fragile and expensive human missions should be prioritized.

"What does that mean?" Sadhika was left to wonder if this moment was some sort of handing of a torch over from life to its simulated creation, or if she was herself only an incredibly sophisticated instrument, and her role no different than the genetic scanner which had informed her of the experimental results. Or was she a ghost of one of the original mission founders, a vain echo or impression left on the mission so that the original Sadhika Sengupta could in some remote way be a part of the big moment? She was the focal point of one of the most pivotal moments in all of human history. Was she truly a part of the moment as a person? Or was she just fortunate enough to be some kind of witness or spectator to it? Could she really just be an instrument, only created to make this moment possible for other beings, the true architects of the mission and her existence?

"I don't know." In-Su replied, as though he were answering all of the questions in her head. In reality he was only answering her first spoken question. Internally though, he was asking himself all of the same questions Sadhika was asking herself.

"It means..." Neil offered, "that nobody can tell the story of humans anymore, without telling *our* story too. *That's* what it means."

Chapter 12

The four walked together through the cool jungle in the late afternoon, carefully making their way around the bushes and trees while trying not to trip on the labyrinth of vines and roots on the jungle floor. The place was positively thick with life. The sights and sounds were overwhelming, and small bugs and critters of every size, shape, and colour seemed to be everywhere to be seen.

"Here," Neil pointed out, "more of those… blue-purple fruits."

"Well if they're anything like fruit on Earth," Sadhika commented as she moved in to take a closer look, "they have seeds which are dispersed after the fruit's eaten. It's the only reason to commit so much of their resources to making something like that." She carefully snipped one of the fruit off of the vine which connected it to the main dark stalk. After taking her back pack off, she carefully placed the bulbous blue-purple mass into the bag she'd rested on the ground. "Hopefully these are edible for the humans…" she commented as much to herself as to the other three.

"That's funny," she further remarked as she inspected the plants closer. "There are flowers…" she said as she sifted through the mass of the plant. "But they're just dull grey. I bet…" taking her PANEs out of her grey coveralls, she put them on and thought them to ultraviolet again. "Yeah… just what I thought, these are very bright in the ultraviolet guys… they don't need to be bright in the spectrum of light visual to humans, just to the pollinators they're trying to attract. They could even be specifically trying to avoid predation of the flowers by whatever other animal they're trying to attract to eat the fruit... or anything else for that matter."

"Speaking of pollinators…" In-Su said to attract the attention of the others. The bright red insect was hard to miss. It was the size of a grasshopper, but it was an efficient hoverer. He carefully followed it over to another bush and vine system like the one Sadhika had been investigating. Sure enough it started flitting from one flower to the next, just like any number of insects on Earth. Now that they were attuned to their presence, they could see that the creatures were all around them as they periodically buzzed in and out of sight.

"Careful In-Su…" Sadhika warned. "That bright red marking is probably a warning signal to *some*thing."

"So… what, you're afraid it'll sting him?" Neil asked with a smile. "Simulant, remember?"

"Of course…" Sadhika shook her head, trying to keep that in her active consciousness. "That doesn't make us invincible though," she said as she came over to In-Su and carefully finessed the insect into a sample jar which she then placed in In-Su's back pack.

"No, but it does make us pretty invulnerable to biological attacks like whatever that thing might sting us with," Neil countered. "That is after all why we're here in the first place, to scout ahead for the humans and put ourselves at risk before them. We're here to make sure it's safe for the human crew to descend. Of course," Neil further considered, "our programming would only know to simulate an adverse reaction if exposed to a *known* toxin…"

"Oh right, that reminds me…" Wiremu took off his own back pack and removed an air sampling apparatus. It was his responsibility to take air and water samples from the different areas they explored for later analysis. He inserted a hard plastic vial into the palm sized apparatus and after a few moments of humming it had compressed to several times normal pressure a sample of the local atmosphere. Wiremu placed the vial into its protective storage zipper book, placed it and the machine back into his bag, and then slung it over his back again. "Let's keep moving," Wiremu suggested, "we've still got a lot of ground to cover."

They walked on and continued to make their way through the temperate jungle. "It must be a thin soil in this area," In-Su observed as they walked. "The tree's roots can't just go down further when they grow because they run into the bedrock… they have to go out exploring sideways. Normally there'd be a lot more growing at different layers of the jungle in a place like this… but the trees have figured out how to starve most everything else out."

"You're right," Neil informed him, "This whole area is sitting on a flat granite slab." While they walked Neil and Sadhika were both looking on medium scrolls tied in to all of the ship's telescopes and sensors, networked satellites, and all of the other sensors and devices on the shuttle and the FDM, all useably compiled at their fingertips.

"There should be a clearing… about half a kilometer ahead," Neil reported.

"I see it," Wiremu answered, and they all moved towards what lay beyond. They were working their way towards the cliffs overlooking the ocean straits which Wiremu had selected their landing site based on. They were all anxious to see the great ocean stretching out before them. Although the landing strip was a far more open space than any place had been on the ship, they were all still anxious to see the relaxing infinitudes of the ocean seeming to stretch on forever before them. They were looking forward to being able to send up to the ship a live video feed of what the crew had to look forward to: an open sky and an endless horizon. Finally, after their long troublesome journey on a claustrophobic ship, they had finally reached a new horizon.

"So… guys, I've been looking over the results from the genetic scanner on the FDM," Sadhika said as she read her scroll. "It's definitely the same DNA *system*… but the base pairs don't match. I won't be able to say exactly what's going on without further analysis in the bio-lab back on the ship, but there doesn't appear to be any adenine or thymine… there's cytosine and guanine but there seems to be a different base pair set substituted for adenine and thymine! That's incredible! It also means that a whole other set of amino acids are at play based on the different DNA system… there's only about forty percent overlap with the amino acids used by life on Earth…" she looked up around her at all of the plant life and remembered the initial animal life they'd come across so far. "At least it appears to be that way in just the one sample I've analyzed so far… but at the genetic level all life on Earth uses all of the same genetic tools and ingredients. There's no reason to think it would be any different here."

"And what does that mean?" Neil asked. He was an astrophysicist and while he understood the way DNA coded for chains of amino acids, which then built up into proteins which do and make up everything else in the body, biology was sufficiently distant from his areas of specialty that he didn't really understand the implications of what she was saying.

"Well, on Earth there are twenty-two amino acids which all life on Earth uses to make proteins out of, but there are many more that *could* be used for... well, for a whole other planetary biome like this one. It's just a... a different set of chemical building blocks used to build a similar structure."

"And... what does *that* mean?"

"Well, it doesn't-" Sadhika sighed heavily in exasperation. "It doesn't *mean* anything; it's just... *really* interesting!!" she said as they continued walking through the jungle. "It might inform the question of whether or not there's a connection between the life here on Haven and the life back on Earth. It doesn't... it doesn't *say* anything definitive in and of itself, but... but it's a piece of the puzzle!"

"Wait, shh, shh, shh... Look at that..." Wiremu said as he motioned for them all to get down and be quiet. He pointed to something moving towards them in the branches above.

From where they were it was difficult to make out what it was but it became more apparent as it moved towards them. It looked rather like a greeny-brown octopus but with only four arms, and it was moving forward by swinging its rear two limbs down, around, and up to its next grip point and then repeating, back arms to front, over and over again. A few dozen meters from the sims it paused, held its head-like central projection down while suspended upside down, and looked around with its two black eyes. After arching its arms in preparation, it jumped several meters away to a lower and further off branch, and then continued swinging off into the jungle, its head moving to follow it overhead as it went.

As they watched it recede behind them, they then heard a lot more noise coming from the direction the first one had originally come from. When they turned back around to look, they saw several thousand of these creatures approaching them and appearing to make the whole jungle shudder as they passed through in one colossal mass. They seemed to be following the first, as though it was leading them; either that or the rest were trying to catch it for some reason. It took several minutes for them all to pass overhead, and the simulants could only watch in dumbfounded amazement as they did.

"Okay… well that was weird." Neil stated a couple moments after the last stragglers had made their way past them and were themselves finally receding deeper into the jungle.

"They looked like…" In-Su started.

"Octopus, yeah. Cephalopod-like in any case," Sadhika answered for him. "You know it's interesting, we… we always thought that the ones on Earth had the potential to evolve in that direction, but… they never did."

Then, just when they thought the excitement was over, a creature began leaping through the trees, appearing to be on the trail of the herd which had just passed them by overhead. It was easily twice the size of any of the other animals at about a meter and a half long, and it used its slender body and long legs to spring itself from one branch to the next, periodically hissing out a long forked tongue. It paused momentarily over the heads of the sims, seeming to be investigating them, but with a flick of its tongue it carried on with its pursuit. It appeared to have scaled skin with a black and dark brown camouflage pattern. Eventually it too disappeared off into the distance.

"That was so cool…" Sadhika whispered to the others. "I can't wait to study them more closely."

"It looked reptilian," Wiremu observed.

"Yeah… but neither of those species could possibly be cold blooded, not keeping up an activity level like that. Like I said, I can't *wait* to study them all in much more detail."

"Well at least we have great images to show the other biologists on the ship, I recorded the whole thing with my PANEs," Neil informed the others.

"All very interesting," Wiremu agreed, "but shall we?" he asked as he gestured in the direction of the edge of the jungle. They could already just barely hear the sounds of the shore at this point, but Wiremu was already concerned about how soon the night would be upon them. He led the way and the others followed. Before long they came to the edge of the jungle where the trees got sparser and sparser until they completely gave way to open grasslands which extended over a kilometer to the cliffs beyond.

Finally they crossed the grassland and came to the edge of the cliff. They looked down the several dozen meters to the ocean below, and out to the horizon. There was a large island out there beyond the waters of the straits, but it was far enough away that it couldn't be seen from where they were. All they could see was wide open ocean out to the horizon. The four stood together in silence and savoured the moment, the afternoon sunshine, the view and the breeze, the sounds of the waves crashing below, and the salty smell of the fresh ocean air.

After a few minutes, Sadhika broke the silence. "We need to examine the ocean life as soon as possible. All the important first evolutions of life on Earth all happened in the ocean… it probably happened the same way here too."

"So I have a question," In-Su said, "how do we decide which animals are okay to kill?" he asked. "Frankly I don't have much objection to a fish being killed to study or to eat for example, but what about those creatures back there? How do we deem and declare whether or not they are to be considered a food source?"

"We need more study," Neil offered.

"And how do we do that?" In-Su asked, "capture and imprison one so we can study it?"

"Better than killing it outright, I should think." Wiremu flatly declared. Nobody could deny the wisdom of his answer. "Besides, killing or capturing alien fish or weird four armed tree octopus things is way out of our current mission profile anyways. We leave that for the human crew landing tomorrow… we don't get to have *all* the fun I'm afraid. Come on," he said as he motioned for them to follow him. "It's starting to get dark and we have significant ground to cover to get back to the landing strip." He led them back into the jungle and towards the shuttle.

"It kinda looks like a cross between a panda bear and a… and a fucking *dinosaur*!" Neil commented to the others as they lay down to hide. They'd accidentally snuck up on a large muscular animal picking and pawing at something on the ground. Neil was still taking video and with a thought zoomed his PANEs in for a closer look. "Whatever it is, it sure looks dangerous…" He added as he settled down with the others on the ground.

"Problem is," Sadhika offered, "there's no way to know whether it's a scavenger that'll be afraid of us and run away, or an apex predator that'll charge us at first sight."

"I think we're about to find out..." Wiremu said as they felt a breeze brush past them in the direction of the beast. They had all noticed that the large animal was equipped with a prominent wet nose rhinarium.

"Wait," In-Su asked, "we're simulants, do we even... would it even *want* to?"

"Part of our simulation," Sadhika informed him, "is to *smell* like humans too. Humans communicate a lot more than you'd think with pheromones. And yes while we certainly wouldn't make a very satisfying meal for it, we're far from invulnerable. We could easily be terribly damaged beyond repair if it tried to eat us, or trampled us... or for that matter if it just gored us with that ominous looking horn."

"Quiet." Wiremu ordered with irritation. The large animal lifted its head and actively sniffed the air. It was significantly bigger than even the size of a large bear, and when it turned around to face them the four could clearly see its flat face and rounded ears.

Like the animal which had been chasing the herd through the trees, this large beast also had scaled skin but with panda patterned black and dark green camouflage. It had a single but large and menacing horn protruding out of its head, and a long thick tail. As Neil had observed, it really did look like some kind of terrifying cross between a large bear and a small dinosaur. The beast let out a noise which was something between a whimper and a growl, and then turned and wandered off, seemingly in some mixture of confusion and frustration.

"Guess it doesn't like strangers, hunh?" Neil suggested.

"Or it's gone to get its friends..." Wiremu further suggested with a chill.

"*Or* it was only a youngling, and it's gone to find its parents" In-Su offered. All four shuddered at the thought.

Wiremu was looking over to where the large animal had been before wandering off. "I bet you a loonie... that it was eating one of those tree octopus things. I want to go check it out."

While the other three stayed hidden, Wiremu cautiously stood up and made his way over to the spot where the animal had been eating something. Sure enough, it was a half-eaten tree octopus thing. Wiremu motioned the other three over with his hand. "Would you like to do the honours Sadhika?" Wiremu asked.

The simulated woman sighed as she turned In-Su around, unzipped his back pack, and pulled a cylindrical sample container out along with a pair of metal tongs. She pulled the lid off, then knelt down and picked up the animal with the tongs. She then gently placed what was left of the carcass in the sample container along with the tongs themselves, and sealed the lid. "Okay then, sample gotten, and no killing."

"Wonderful. Now let's get moving," Wiremu ordered without any ambiguity. By this point it was getting quite dark and there was still significant ground for them to cover before they returned to the relative safety of the shuttle and FDM back at the landing strip.

Chapter 13

Hello, Sadhika. If you're listening to this, a lot has had to go right already, and we're both very lucky. I don't really know what to say… I can't imagine what questions you might have, either very few or… or far too many to count I would imagine.

You are there for only one reason: because I can't be. Don't believe the story about needing any of you for the first descent team; there were other ways. I would have given anything to be there instead of you, but instead I gave everything I had in my life to make sure that you could be there, instead of me. You are not me though, you can never be me, and I can never see what you see… and that makes me sad. It makes me happier though to know that you'll be there, seeing and experiencing things for me.

I want to make it clear that you don't owe me anything, and I'm not going to lay a bunch of burdens on you as your creator. You were programmed to be as faithful a simulation of me as possible; I told your programmers things about myself that I never told another living soul, and they were the best simulators in the whole system. You are not me, but you are nonetheless a version of me, a new version of me… a new iteration of us. The way I see it you and I are now joint owners of a shared Sadhika identity.

Follow your instincts, for they are my instincts. Follow your heart, for it is my heart. Live for us, and experience this world and adventure for the both of us. Be significant Sadhika, be extraordinary… outshine my star.

The sun had gone down. It was their first night on the strange alien world, which was in some ways strangely familiar. The last vestiges of light had only recently evaporated and their new starscape was now in its full glory. Sadhika Sengupta, or at least whatever was left of her, was lying on her back on the shuttle runway some distance from the shuttle and the First Descent Module. She was processing, reflecting on the day that had been, a day so long in the making…

She pushed closed the scroll on which she'd been watching the message left to her by her originator. Her eyes were teared up; she'd found the messaged deeply emotionally moving. It was a message left for her by a long dead figure who was something much more profound and intimate to her than any parent could possibly be.

She felt a tinge of sadness for the woman; the original Sadhika couldn't be here to enjoy all of the benefits of all of her own hard work. She found herself likewise comforted though, that she could in a way experience and enjoy it for her. That's why she, her simulant, was really here in the first place. Her role, she now understood, was to experience this great moment in human history on behalf of her human progenitor. She was her witness.

"Would you look at that…" Neil said in wonderment, nearly tripping over Sadhika as he approached her with an undeviating absorption with the sky above him. "It's so…"

"Alien." Sadhika offered. Neil only nodded in agreement, and then got down to join her on the ground. He put his head down right beside hers but in the inverted orientation, with his feet out in the opposite direction from her own.

"I've spent my whole life looking up… I've practically memorized Earth's night sky, now I have to start all over again… what a treat!"

"What do you see?" Sadhika asked.

"Oh a jumble… I usually orient based on constellations, but… for now it's still just a jumble of stars."

"Well we'll have to invent some then… there," she pointed to the south east, about halfway between the horizon and zenith. There's four stars that seem to roughly form an upright ellipse, with a bright star ahead of it, and two fairly bright ones trailing it? It's the New Horizon…"

"Alright, alright… and see there," Neil pointed to the north, closer to the zenith, "there's four stars that make kind of a box, and a few stars you could *call* its legs, and two bright stars forming a horn, it's that big beast we saw in the jungle today!"

Sadhika laughed. This was fun. "Hmm… and look there," she pointed straight up, "just off the zenith, four particularly bright stars just hanging out together…"

"What about em?"

"They're us... they're the simulants," she answered, turning her head over to look at him.

"I like it," he answered without removing his gaze from the sky.

For several minutes the two fell into silence, lost in their respective thoughts and the endlessly fascinating starscape. On Earth light pollution always interfered with this kind of viewing of the night sky unless one got far enough away from the lights of civilization. Here however, there were no artificial lights whatsoever, and no moon. It was an amazingly deep dark which allowed an amazingly bright and detailed view of the celestial sphere.

"Have you checked on the shuttle?" Sadhika finally broke the silence to ask.

"Yup," he answered, "On my way over. The fuel tanks are almost at sixty percent already, so... we should be ready to leave by morning."

Sadhika chuckled and feigned a whine in her voice. "Aww, but we just got here!"

Neil smiled in the dark. "Were you able to do some more detailed research on those samples we got?"

"Yes," she answered. "We'll need to analyze them with the ship's equipment to be able to do it properly, but the FDMs equipment was able to code the DNA of all of the samples we obtained."

"And?"

"Well first of all, it's a phenomenal discovery in and of itself to find that they operate on something we recognize as DNA at all! Let's not let *that* get old! Beyond that though, it only gets more interesting. Like I said earlier today, they use two DNA base pairs of the four we use but also use two different ones that we don't. That means that we share no genes at all with life on this planet."

"They, not we," Neil corrected her.

"Whatever," she said irritatedly.

"Sorry, go on."

"*Humans,* share more genetic material with other Earth organism the closer they're related to them in an evolutionary sense, but there's a basic amount of genes shared by all life on Earth. They share something like seven percent DNA with bacteria, it's the most basic and fundamental stuff like 'how to make and use DNA in the first place' and 'how to make a cell,' and it's all based on the same four DNA base pair tools. Since life here has a different set of building blocks, there's not one iota of overlap between life on Earth and life here. However, there is the same genetic overlap with the life I've analyzed here as there is with all life on Earth. There's something like twenty-six percent genetic overlap between the insect we caught and the tree squid thing, eighteen percent between the insect and the plant I plucked a leaf off of."

"Especially given that," Neil commented, "I find it odd that they're somewhat familiar looking animals at all… I always figured that people who thought that alien life would resemble Earth life in any way whatsoever just suffered from a lack of imagination and after-the-fact explaining. Why still four limbs instead of six or eight, aren't more better? Why still body plans and classes of life that we understand or recognize at all?"

"Convergence… evolution is essentially an exercise in engineering. Under radically different conditions of gravity or atmosphere I too would expect to see much more exotic life, but conditions here are so similar to those on Earth that I would expect to find a lot of similar solutions to similar problems. I mean, even on Earth things like flight and eyes, evolved independently a remarkable number of times. The problems were the same, the limitations and available solutions were the same, so the end product solutions were remarkably similar. To see light on Earth, you need some sort of eye within a certain range of parameters. Likewise to fly through Earth's atmosphere you need wings, again within a certain restricted range of required mechanical parameters.

"Same thing goes for limbs. In a higher gravity environment, six legs might make sense for a slow moving animal that can just barely make it to its feet in any case, but in this kind of gravity environment four seems to simply be ideal if you're not built to stand on two. Animals on Earth don't have four limbs just because that's just the way life *is* on Earth, they tend to have four because evolution has determined that to be most efficient given the surface conditions that exist on Earth. Nothing is wasted in evolution and nothing is superfluous. Each limb we have represents tremendous resources to grow, and tremendous risk of getting damaged. A deep wound, a broken bone, or a mangled joint on an animal's limb usually means certain death. The more limbs you have, the more opportunities there are for that sort of thing. I guess what I'm saying is... there's nothing for animal life to gain by having more than four limbs which would offset the inherent costs and risks of just having them in the first place. I mean, you certainly couldn't run any faster on six legs than you could on four, they'd just get in each other's way."

"But that's not necessarily accurate," Neil retorted a little defensively. "I mean, all the four limbed animals you describe, could easily just have only four because they originally evolved from a tetrapod in the first place, and it would have been too radical a change for evolution to allow the addition of extra limbs along the way. Besides, there's certainly life on Earth with more than four limbs, arachnids have *eight* legs for example... arthropods can have a whole *whack* of legs!"

"You're right," she answered, "but I think your point about the arthropods serves my argument more than yours. If *they* could evolve any number of extra limbs, then why couldn't tetrapods?"

"Oh come on, arthropods can do it because they're segmented, they can evolve by just adding new discrete segments to their bodies which have legs or don't. Tetrapods are more holistic though, they can't just develop a whole new segment to their body when their environment calls for it."

"True, but I still think that if there had been any significant advantage to more than four limbs that outweighed the inherent risks and costs, a new superclass of hexapods could have come along and supplanted the tetrapods or co-existed on the planet with them. If there was a significant advantage to extra limbs I'm sure... I'm sure life would have found a way."

"Hmm... well, I'm skeptical that new limbs could just evolve on the fly without any architectural antecedent. It just doesn't work that way. There'd need to be a whole other class of animals developing from a simple form, like a... like a six finned fish or something..."

"You're right of course, but what I'm saying, is that if there was a significant advantage to six or more legs, that simple form would have established itself, developed, and soon *supplanted* the four leggers. Evolution... has a sort of gravity; similar challenges engender similar solutions over and over and over again in evolutionary history. Need to see? You build an eye. Need to fly?

You build wings. Need to get around efficiently on land as an animal of sig-nificant size in one gee? Use two or four legs depending on your size and mobility requirements…"

"But even if you're right that four legs is just the most efficient for running or whatever, why not… why not four legs and two arms then?"

"What? You mean like, like a centaur?"

"Sure! Why not!?"

Sadhika just started laughing. "I don't know Neil, why not indeed… I was just suggesting that there are certain solutions that evolutionarily speaking are 'fallen' into once you're in the neighborhood. A rhinoceros can't just grow wings and fly, its way out of range, but a rodent? If you're already pretty small and light? Well maybe you can slowly develop some webbing between your arms and legs, and maybe the more you have, the further you can glide and the better your odds of survival and passing on that trait to your offspring and having *them* survive. Enough generations later you might just get it over with and become a bat. Once you're in range of that evolutionary gravitational well, it's pretty easy to fall into it."

"But I think that's what I'm getting at. The more developed a tetrapod's four limbs, the harder it would be for it to develop a sixth out of nowhere. To put it your way, they started out well outside of the hexapod gravitational well, and only moved further and further away from it."

"Fair enough."

The two resumed soaking up the sights of the night sky. Then, Neil pointed to a small point of light which appeared to be slowly moving against the background, and somewhat low towards the southern horizon. "Look," he said as he pointed. "See that one that's slowly moving? That's the ship. Our satellites wouldn't reflect that much light."

Sadhika put on her PANEs and put in a call up to the ship. "I should share what I've learned with Blair too." When the woman on the ship answered, her image was three dimensional since she was projected onto both interior screens of Sadhika's PANEs.

"Hello Sadhika, enjoying yourself?"

"Oh you have no idea... did you get my initial report?"

"Yes indeed, actually I've been pouring over it. I was particularly interested in your discovery that one of the sets of base pairs are different from those on Earth."

"Yeah, I guess we just struck another blow against the anthropocentric perspective, didn't we?"

"How's that?" Neil asked. Sadhika had relayed Blair's voice to the external speakers on the PANEs so that Neil could hear the conversation.

"Well, astrobiologists have always wondered if there was some mechanism which allowed panspermia, the seeding of life from one planet to the next, and the next and the next. We wondered if life maybe only had one common source and was then seeded from one planet to the next over the eons. If this was the case though, the DNA should have had the same base pairs in use. The fact that life here uses *different* base pairs suggests that life evolved here completely independently of life on Earth."

"I see," Neil considered. "And that means that life is relatively easy to get started without any outside help, which means... that it is likely to be much more common in the cosmos than it would be if either Haven or Earth had seeded the other."

"Or were both seeded by a third source," Blair added. "It also specifically suggests most importantly I think, that cellular life is easier to evolve from scratch than we though. The idea of panspermia was so appealing because once you've got a few cells landing on a planet, the rest is relatively easy. Getting a functioning cell out of random biochemistry is really by far the hard part, and now we can prove it happened twice independently in relatively close cosmic proximity. That's huge! And since animal life is relatively easy once you have cellular life, and intelligent life can only happen once there's animal life..."

"We're really filling in that Drake equation now, aren't we..." Neil observed.

"Well today alone we've certainly really narrowed the error bars, that's for sure," Sadhika agreed.

"I really can't wait to get your samples back to the ship and run full cellular analyses on them," Blair enthusiastically remarked. "I'm intensely curious about the similarities and differences in the cellular physiology."

"Oh me too, believe me!" Sadhika affirmed with equally growing excitement at all the work still to be done.

"Speaking of which," Blair said, "how does the biological environment down there look? Does it seem safe for us to come down?"

"Well, between the shuttle's bio-filters and the air samples Wiremu took, nothing has been recognized as necessarily dangerous to humans. But of course it can only recognize what it knows to look for, so there's no way to eliminate the risk altogether. We'll only know for sure when the first human landing crew actually walks around down here and breathes the air and whatnot."

"Well I'll be among the first crew down Sadhika. I'm betting my life on my belief that the physiology of life down there is just too different for us to be infected or otherwise seriously harmed by anything down there. At least by anything microscopic… I saw the video you sent us of that horned animal you came across in the jungle, talk about the stuff of nightmares…"

"Looked like good eats to me," Neil commented with a grin. Blair responded on Sadhika's screens with a look which was a mixture of confusion and revulsion.

"You must be really looking forward to coming down tomorrow," Sadhika commented, trying to put herself in Blair's position.

"What, are you kidding? I've *literally* been preparing for it my *entire* life."

"Understood." Sadhika knew something of singular existential purpose. "Try to get some rest then, I have a feeling you'll need it."

"Goodnight, Sadhika." Blair said warmly. "You too Neil."

"Goodnight." She took off her PANEs and rested them on her chest. Her mind was swimming with thoughts, her mind constantly switching focus between the day's events and discoveries, questions and thoughts about the nature of her existence, her role in the whole mission, and the part she was meant to play.

"Yup," Neil said, lost in his own thoughts. "Quite a day…"

Chapter 14

"Where's Earth?" Sadhika asked. The question surprised her a little; her curiosity about it seemingly came out of nowhere.

Neil pulled out his pocket scroll and after issuing a few thought commands and observing the results on the screen, he pushed it closed and pointed out to just a few degrees over the eastern horizon. "That star..." he said, "That's Sol. That distant, unassuming star... out there, in the middle of nowhere, amongst so many others."

"It's so... oh I don't know, what's the word I'm looking for Neil? Indistinct?"

"Works as well as any other I suppose. Since we're at it," he pulled out his scroll and briefly consulted it again. He pointed up to a couple degrees off of the sky's zenith. "See that bright blue tinged brownish one that isn't shimmering like the others? That's the binary gas giant in the outer solar system that the ship passed on its way in. Unfortunately none of the others are up right now though. Apparently that one is something like a Jupiter orbiting with something like a Neptune; I really wish I could have seen that... I really hate that they waited so long to wake us up."

"I know what you mean..." Sadhika sympathetically replied.

"Those planets out there though... you know what I've been thinking about a lot since we woke up?"

"What's that?"

"By the time we left Earth, we knew so much about that planet and our Solar System. Humans had spent the better part of half a millennium seriously investigating the formation of the Solar System and the planets, orientating ourselves in space and time, the geological history of the Earth and the evolutionary history of life on

Earth..."

"And?"

"And now we're basically starting over again from the beginning, from question one... sure the large scale and fine grain stuff of the universe at large stays the same, everything we know about stars and galaxies transfers of course, and all the physical laws are the same here, there, and everywhere as far as we know, but... but all the particulars here, it's all different!

"What is the evolutionary tree of life here on Haven? What are the relationships between the myriad of life currently in existence here and in previous epochs? What is the geological history of this and the other planets? Did the planets here initially form as they are in this configuration or did they migrate in and out? Back home we'd already figured out so much of that...

"There's just... so many unknowns Sadhika, so many mysteries, so much to newly discover and learn about. That's what this has all really been about for me. That's why I'm here... A permanent off world foot hold for humanity is just a perk for me. I know it's technically our primary mission, but it's not the real reason *I'm* out here, it's not why I dreamed up this mission in the first place at all. I'm here to explore; to discover, to be a part of the excitement of figuring out all of the answers to all of those questions!"

"I'd like to think the same could be said for all of us..." Sadhika answered thoughtfully. "Well, the original us in any case," she mused.

After a few moments of quiet reflection, the two saw a bright burning streak across the sky. It was clearly orange and red as they watched it from where it appeared low on the horizon to the south, and then burned over the horizon to the south-west. "Meteor showers too," Neil reflected, "we have no idea about any asteroid or comet profiles or regular meteor showers... for all we know at this point we may have arrived just in time to be wiped out by a major impact event," he darkly joked.

"Sadhika, Neil, back to the FDM immediately!!" Wiremu barked in their ears. The two sat up startled and looked at each other with dread. They then both scrambled to their feet and flat out sprinted the short distance back to the First Descent Module and rushed inside.

"-I repeat, Halley, Søren, Ishtar and some others have stolen the other shuttle and descended to an alternate landing site on the opposite side of the continent." It was Asari on the screen, incensed.

"How do they intend to land?" Wiremu asked after nodding to Sadhika and Neil to acknowledge their entrance.

From out of frame, somebody handed Asari an opened scroll which he then quickly reviewed. "How did we not notice that?" he angrily asked with a turn of his head towards whoever had handed him the device. He was clearly sitting at one of the multi-purpose auxiliary terminals on the bridge. It hadn't occurred to him to sit in the captain's chair yet. Halley after all was the captain, and it wasn't his place.

"What is it?" Wiremu asked.

"He sent the other paving drone down to the other side of the continent before you four ever even left," Asari replied in disbelief. "I don't have any idea how they were able to keep something like that hidden from us!"

"What do they think they're doing?" In-Su asked from a top bunk, and likewise out of frame from Asari's perspective.

"They've just completely torpedoed all of our careful planning!" Neil angrily decried from where he was standing behind Wiremu. He'd immediately had a bad feeling about Halley but he'd kept it to himself because it was just an intuition without any evidence.

"What do we do?" the four clearly heard Aset ask Asari from off screen.

"I'll tell you what we do, we launch every single landing drone we have down to where they've made the second runway and take back our fucking property."

"Excuse me!?" Wiremu asked, noticeably alarmed and incredulous. "You absolutely will *not*!"

"You can't do that!" In-Su exclaimed. "We… we have *no idea* what his intentions are, no idea how he'd respond to such an action, everybody is still *way* too exposed at this point to just start winging it here, okay!? We just got here; the mission could still so easily fail at this point!"

"If you just try to brute force storm them like that," Neil warned, "people will get hurt and a lot of people will probably die. Mission property will be destroyed beyond repair and our ability to continue here in *any* way could be *completely* ruined, we need way more information before we take any actions of any kind, let alone such brash and nakedly aggressive ones!"

"But *they started it*!! Like *always*! Dammit *they're* the ones acting *aggressively* here!!" Asari yelled in a roar which bordered on a scream.

"Asari... listen to me, okay?" Sadhika offered in as soothing a voice as she could put on. "This happening at all, *already* compromises the mission. Storming them like that would put us so far out of protocol that the entire mission would *surely* be a failure. Halley has already put the mission clearly at risk; that's on him and we all acknowledge that. But if you do *this*, the mission would *definitely* be a *complete* failure altogether, and *that* would be on *you* instead. Is that what you want?"

"They've landed sir," an unseen voice informed Asari. "Landing parties are armed and standing by at the descent pods."

"Asari, did they taken *any* of the weapons?" In-Su asked as he climbed down to get in view of Asari's video feed. "It sounds like they certainly didn't take everything they could have to have secured an advantage."

Asari gave an angry but inquisitive look to one of his people, and was informed that only four shotguns and one laser rifle were missing from the weapons locker.

"Only five weapons," In-Su repeated," only a small part of our entire inventory. I think that says something about their intentions right there, doesn't it? If they *wanted* conflict, if they were working towards their side ultimately winning completely at your expense, then they would have taken *all* of the weapons, wouldn't they have?

"Right," Sadhika agreed from over Wiremu's right shoulder. "If that was their ultimate intention, then they would've also auto launched all of the descent pods so you couldn't go after them!"

"We've had zero failures so far Asari," Neil explained, "and we stocked everything in duplicate in principle so that there was a spare for everything, but also specifically so that if we did wind up being lucky enough to have zero failures, we could launch a second colony site or eventually even send the New Horizon off again to yet another star. *This can still work,* Asari. It doesn't *have* to get any uglier than it already is. The mission has a greater chance of success with two viable colonies… even if they hate each other."

On the monitor the four sims could see Aset come to Asari's side and hold his hand. "We should talk to them," they heard her say with begrudging acceptance of their point. "We should at least hear them out. I don't like it either but they're right. It would be irresponsible at best, for us to launch an invasion before we are clear about their intentions."

"They still haven't responded to your attempts to communicate?" Sadhika asked.

"No." Asari answered coldly. "They're totally dark."

"Same here…" she said in frustration while trying to reach them through the communications system on her own scroll.

"Well," she said finally and tentatively, "I suggest we simply continue as planned for now."

Wiremu nodded. "We'll see if they make any attempt to contact us," he added, "and then whether they do or not we'll head back to the ship in the morning as planned and prepare for the next phase of the mission. We'll have to make some… adjustments, but we should be able to make it work. Exactly how many of the crew did they take with them?"

"Twenty-four as far as we can tell."

"See Asari? Again, he seems to have only taken what he felt he needed as opposed to everything he could."

"Or maybe he just couldn't round up any more traitors," Asari snarled. "Fine. We'll do it your way. It's certainly not going to be *me* who makes the mission a failure. *He's* the insurgent, not me. So get your beauty sleep simulants… you have a long day ahead of you tomorrow. Goodnight."

"Goodnight Asari," Wiremu answered reflexively as the screen switched off.

"You know…" In-Su offered, "we could go there. Tomorrow morning, or… well, right now if we wanted to. Maybe we could talk to them; maybe we could resolve this right now before it goes any further?"

"I certainly like the idea In-Su," Sadhika said, "but I'd be too worried that they'd be paranoid about exactly the response Asari had in mind. I'm worried that if we were to show up unannounced in *any* capacity right now that they'd just shoot first and ask questions afterwards."

"You're probably right," In-Su admitted with a sigh which revealed a profound sense of defeat. All four of them were quiet for several moments. "How did this… how did this happen? Was it our fault?" he asked.

"Yeah, well… I guess if we want to claim all the good of being our progenitors we have to inherit their mistakes as well." Neil begrudgingly admitted.

"You know, it's like we just transplanted the problems we had on Earth a hundred and sixty years, and… almost nineteen light years away" Sadhika complained. "Each and every one of us," she added, "can in our own way identify with Halley… maybe in his own way he's just doing what we did in leaving Earth to pursue our own path here on Haven. We thought we could just take a particular part of humanity with us and nurture it into something above and beyond… but instead we just set up this disaster of a chaotic cascading return to all the normal petty problems humans have always had… Our progenitors failed to accept and incorporate *all* elements of humanity into the New Horizon mission, and now *we're* paying for it."

"I couldn't have said it better myself," In-Su said.

Chapter 15

Neil stepped out of the FDM and stretched his arms above his head with his hands clasped and his back arched. He stretched as profoundly and as satisfyingly as he ever had in either of his incarnations. It was a beautiful and perfect morning, the kind of morning which made one happy to be alive and led one to appreciate the singular precious moment in time that was this morning. The planet Haven greeted him in kind with the pristine and undisturbed beauty of the planet's alien wildness.

The sky was brilliant blue with hardly any clouds in the sky at all. He could hear what sounded like alien bird calls; he imagined that they served a similar communicative purpose to birds he was familiar with on his home planet, but the actual sound was hauntingly different. It was reminiscent of what one might expect if some sort of reptile were to attempt to imitate a bird call. The sounds were quick and rapid, but had a very deep and resonant sound. While standing outside the FDM and absorbing the scene, Neil saw a few creatures fly over top of the runway they'd built. They were too far away to see in any great detail, but they certainly seemed to move the way he'd come to expect birds to move as they flew, darting and swooping and seeming to play with each other.

He was startled but delighted when one of the birds came by out of nowhere and perched itself on top of the FDM. It appeared to be scrutinizing him as it turned its head to various angles to get different views of him with its side mounted eyes. It was an odd creature, and definitely unlike anything he'd ever seen before. It appeared reptilian but had the basic body design of a bat. Its main body and head were scaled but its wings were smooth skin through which finger bones and arteries could be seen. All in all it looked to him like some kind of miniature dragon. When the creature landed Neil estimated its wingspan to be about two thirds of a meter and now that it was perched its body and jagged horny head only appeared to be about a quarter meter long, with a long skinny tail which was almost as long again. It didn't have a beak which gave Neil pause. He wondered if the iguana like mouth indicated that it was an insect eater, and if maybe it ate those flying red insects they'd seen in the jungle the day before.

The creature engaged in screeching squawks back and forth with several dozen others which flew overhead, at which point it took off to join them. Neil found himself wondering with a shudder if there were other creatures stalking the sky which preyed on the animals he'd just seen. It seemed unimaginable to him that they should have exclusive free reign of the sky, and that no other creatures would ever have evolved to prey on them. He noted that if they were insect hunters it would have helped for them to have forward facing eyes, which he figured made their side mounted configuration an indication that they had to watch out for predators. Also, if they didn't' have any predators he imagined that they would be so numerous that they would blot out the sky. On the other hand, if they had trouble keeping their eggs safe on the ground (assuming they did in fact lay eggs), that alone could keep their numbers in check...

Neil shook his head with a smile. 'There'll be plenty of time to find out...' he told himself. He went on to make his way over to the shuttle which had brought them down to the planet's surface, and which would ascend them back into orbit again later today. It was only a couple dozen meters at most from the FDM itself, and he gratefully patted the faithful vehicle on its hull as he had a twinge of sympathy for it over the inflated fuel tanks now hanging from under the wings. They almost appeared to be bulging with the liquid oxygen and hydrogen fuel it had separated out of the planet's atmosphere. The sacs were made out of an unimaginably strong material and contained the fuel which would get them aloft and overtop of most of the planet's atmosphere. The regular fuel tanks which occupied almost all of the interior of the shuttle which was not the flight deck, housed the bulk of the fuel which would accelerate them sideways into orbit after the hanging auxiliary tanks were sucked back into the wings from the vacuum pressure of being used to depletion.

His first move was supposed to be to prepare some coffee for him and his friends, but when he looked at the electric heating element he was to use, he found himself looking past it towards the jungle just beyond the runway and he grinned. Instead he wandered over to the boundary of the jungle, and venturing just a few meters inward he found and collected some sticks and branches appropriate for building a campfire. "A campfire a hundred and sixty years in the making..." he joked to himself as he gathered sufficient wood for an impressively sized campfire. Once back at the nearby campsite, he arranged the wood into the shape of a fire with the smallest pieces he could find on the bottom for kindling, and the larger pieces on top for once the fire really got going.

The simple act of gathering wood for a fire conjured up a vague sense of memory for him. There was something familiar about the exercise yet no specific memories came to mind, just a sense he supposed that this was something he'd done before. He found himself wondering if this was a feature or a bug of his programming. Was he meant to have these kinds of vague senses of familiarity? Or was there in fact a specific memory which his programming had been cued to recall and then failed to. He of course hoped that the experience was a sign of his programming working exactly as it was intended to, but it was hard to say. He ultimately shrugged it off as an altogether human experience either way. Human memory was certainly imperfect even at the best of times, and for whatever reason his appeared to be as well.

He touched one of the smaller pieces of wood to the top of the heating element he was meant to use, and turned it on to full power until the first licks of flame arose from the piece of wood, at which point he carefully place it into the base of the potential for a larger fire which he'd created. Slowly it caught fire and the flames began to proliferate throughout the whole wooden structure.

Once he had a good fire going, he walked the short distance back to the FDM for some water with which to make his coffee. The module had a more compact version of the atmospheric separators the shuttle employed and overnight it had filled up its twenty litre water tank. Once Neil had extracted the couple litres he required for the moment, the apparatus happily went to work replacing the fluid and topping up the reservoir. He carefully placed the water kettle on an appropriate part of the fire, and prepared three travel coffee mugs with a packet each of dehydrated coffee, and a fourth with tea leaves for In-Su who didn't care for coffee.

It was at this point that Sadhika emerged from the FDM and took what appeared to Neil to be an almost equally satisfying stretch. "It seems like such a waste to sleep... she groggily remarked, "especially since we don't actually need to... seems like such a terrible waste of time."

"As it often seems to humans as well, my dear Sadhika," In-Su remarked as he followed her out of the FDM. "Is that not the point? Likewise..." he added as he rubbed his eyes, "nor do we need to drink or eat, yet nothing in the world at this moment appeals to me quite as much as the tea Neil seems to be so graciously preparing for me."

It was at this point that Sadhika fully clued in to the fact that Neil had constructed a fire. "Oh what a wonderful idea!" she exclaimed as she went over to give him a warm and lingering hug. Neil and Sadhika were very fond of each other. In fact, while Neil had for some time considered In-Su his best and closest male friend, he'd long ago come to think of his friendship with Sadhika as comparable.

Neil got on quite well with Wiremu, but they'd never had as much of a chance to get very close, and they ultimately didn't have much in common besides their mutual passion for the mission. The other three had an intellectual streak which Wiremu did not. Wiremu was the one with a strong and pronounced adventurous streak which was far less pronounced in the other three. None would have founded the mission if a sense of adventure was altogether absent from them though, and likewise an intellectual streak was not altogether missing from Wiremu either. They were a good complimentary team, each with their own strengths and deficits.

"What world specifically were you speaking of In-Su?" Neil asked as Sadhika pulled away from him. "Nothing appeals to you as much as anything in this world, or the last?"

"Either," the man replied with a smile.

"Well, then here you go." Picking up the pitcher by its cool ceramic handle, Neil poured the now boiling water into the four mugs, first handing a coffee to Sadhika, and then the lonely tea to In-Su.

At this point Wiremu finally emerged from the First Descent Module, and Neil happily came over to offer him his morning coffee. Wiremu only grunted in acknowledgement of the kindness at first, but after a few tentative initial sips of the hot liquid and several moments to compose himself, he finally uttered a recognizable "thank you."

They all said the remainder of their hellos and good mornings, and then they all enjoyed their incredibly satisfying drinks in silence for a while as they soaked in the moment and the sounds of morning on this strange new world. It was the first sip of their respective favourite morning rituals which any of them had had in over a hundred and sixty years. Either that or it was their first sips ever; either way the experience was for all four of them delicious, and unbelievably satisfying.

"Will this even work?" Wiremu asked. "I mean… will our physiology respond to caffeine the way a human body would?"

"No… but yes," Sadhika cryptically answered. "I mean not directly… nothing biochemical can affect us directly in a normal biological way since we don't have a… well any kind of biochemical structure at all, so no drugs can directly affect us in the way you mean, no. However, we *were* built to be perfect simulations of human beings, and that includes a subjective experience of the effects of something like caffeine, or any other drug our bodies have been programmed to detect and recognize. Our systems detect the substance, and then our bodies and brains simulate the effect of the detected drug as though we were affected naturally."

"So…" Wiremu asked as he took another sip with an expectant wince.

Sadhika laughed. He understood well enough, he was just ribbing her complete inability to provide a simple straightforward answer to any kind of scientific question. "So, yes, it will work." she answered him plainly. "Sorry."

"Good," he said as he took another sip. "We need like… bacon and eggs or something… and toast."

"Well you should have thought about that before we left Earth," Neil scolded him in jest.

Wiremu nodded in acknowledgement. "Indeed"

"We could cook up the specimen we picked up yesterday..." In-Su suggested. The other three looked at him in surprised confusion for a moment before they started to laugh when they realized he was joking. He was finicky about eating any kind of meat at the best of times, let alone their alien planet mystery meat.

"Maybe once we've examined it back on the ship In-Su," Wiremu laughed as he clapped the smaller man on the back a little harder than he was comfortable with, "maybe once we've examined it..."

Half an hour later, the four were sitting in the flight deck of the shuttle in the same seats they'd descended in. Wiremu and Sadhika were seated in the front swiveling pilot seats going through all of the pre-ascent checklists in conjunction with the New Horizon flight operations team. Aset had had to take over serving as the mother-ship's liaisons with the shuttle and was overseeing the ascent operation herself since Ishtar, the former head of flight operations, had defected along with her husband Halley.

"We're all ready for you up here," Aset reported. She sounded incredibly depressed, and she didn't seem to be putting much effort into concealing it. The four simulants were understanding, but they were also understandably concerned. "Have you been monitoring Halley?" the woman on the ship asked.

"Yes," Wiremu answered. "Satellite imaging shows that they just spent last night sleeping in their shuttle. So far this morning they don't appear to have left their landing strip to do any exploring or anything."

"I'm watching them on one of my screens now," Aset informed them. "It looks like they're moving on to exploring the jungle near their landing site."

"They haven't made any attempts to procure any other modules, have they?" he asked.

"Not that we've noticed, but we've locked all of their Brainchip access codes out of all of our systems so at this point there's not much they could get from us or do to us even if they wanted to."

"Unless they left a mole on the ship to do it for them..." Wiremu immediately regretted saying it and needlessly putting the idea in her head. He realized by her reaction that they hadn't considered such a possibility before he'd mentioned it.

"We hadn't thought of that..." Aset said as she looked off screen, presumably over at Asari.

"I suspect," In-Su interjected, "that if they had any intentions of taking any further actions they would have done so already, they'd have done everything that they intended to do all at once to avoid giving you any chance to respond. I believe they are consciously and deliberately avoiding antagonizing the rest of us as much as possible."

"You may be right." Aset said, but she sounded decidedly unconvinced. "Are you four good to go?"

"Good to go," Wiremu called back.

"Very well... Shuttle One you are cleared for launch. You have the ball."

"Thank you New Horizon, we have the ball."

Very slowly, very small electromagnetic motors turned the shuttle's wheels and drove the ship the few dozen meters it had to go to the very end of the runway, right beside the First Descent Module. It carefully positioned and pointed itself off to the side of the FDM to avoid incinerating it with rocket exhaust when it took off. The shuttle then deployed its auxiliary ascent wings.

The thick stubby wings it began with were in fact three layers of wings folded on top of themselves. During atmospheric entry it was important to have a modest attack profile, but to take off from the ground loaded with as much fuel as it was, and to achieve the high altitudes from which it was meant to rocket hard into orbit, longer more lift generating wings were required. To this end, the outer edge of the descent configuration wing contained a hinge which allowed the auxiliary wing to fold up, over, and out to double the length of the wing and then to unfold up and over yet again, resulting in a total wingspan three times that of the shuttle's original descent configuration.

Once the shuttle had turned around and fully deployed its ascent wings, the three conical main thrusters at the back of the shuttle lit and the shuttle immediately and dramatically began accelerating. Great thrust was required to get it off of the ground, but once the shuttle lifted off of Haven's surface near the end of the runway the throttle was dramatically reduced while the shuttle ascended through the atmosphere as a standard aircraft would.

They spent the first half hour of the flight lazily climbing their way up to about thirty kilometers above the surface, where there became a balancing point between the thinning of the air and the maximum lift profile of the shuttles wings in flight. At this point the thrusters engaged fully and the aircraft became a spaceship as it took off with an incredible acceleration. It wasn't just a question of getting up to orbital height, that was in fact the easy part and they were already nearly there. The really hard part about achieving orbit from a planet's surface, is the energy required to go sideways at a sufficient speed; to fly so fast around the planet that you are perpetually falling over the side and around the planet instead of falling down to the surface. One has to fall sideways so fast that they perpetually miss the ground.

Now in black skies, after twenty minutes or so, the engines abruptly cut out after guzzling a full ninety-seven percent of their remaining fuel. Although they were both travelling incredibly fast, the New Horizon and the shuttle were moving very slowly relative to each other. The shuttle's mothership reduced its speed by just a tiny bit as the shuttle increased its speed by an equivalent amount. The two vessels moved slowly but continually towards each other until they were close enough, at which point the shuttle slowed down just enough for the two crafts to match their speeds exactly.

After retracting its auxiliary ascent wings, the shuttle ever so slowly and carefully approached its mother ship and slid along the New Horizon's long engineering section. It nuzzled up to its docking port and held itself just off of it so that the magnetic seal system could pull the shuttle firmly and decidedly into its properly sealed docking position and lock it down.

Shuttle One was home.

"Docking complete. Shuttle One safely home."

Chapter 16

"I'm not happy." Asari flatly told Wiremu as scientists and technicians went back and forth in front of them.

"No kidding…" the original captain responded ironically. "I'll tell you what Asari, why don't you just think of the other shuttle as being rolled into our expected ten percent failure rate?" He nodded to Blair as she floated past him, towing an armload of equipment behind her in a net as she swam through the micro gravity.

"I'm sorry Asari, one second. Blair what did your analysis of that insect turn up?"

"Well," the woman responded, "it does have a poisonous stinger. It would hurt like hell if it stung one of us but it certainly wouldn't be fatal or anything, not from any biochemical mechanism *I* could discern." She had wisely tied up her long curly black hair since she'd be dealing with micro gravity today and presumably didn't want it floating all around her head. "You prioritized the insect though, so they're only now getting started on the other creature you brought up."

"Good. And the atmosphere samples I brought back good?" The woman pointed to a man named Nekheny as he approached before moving on herself.

"Yessiree, the atmosphere's clean as far as I can tell," the man reported, "I couldn't find any compounds, microbes, or viruses in the samples you brought back that look like they could be hazardous to humans. We're good to go!" He didn't seem to be making any effort to conceal his excitement.

"Thank you," Wiremu acknowledged. The man nodded and continued on his way into the shuttle. Wiremu looked back at Asari to find him positively scowling. "Come on Asari, wouldn't it make you happier to just pretend they're all dead? That they just died on entry? The effect would seem to be pretty much the same; I mean they haven't made any attempts to secure any more mission property. So far their little rebellion has only cost us one shuttle. That, in and of itself is an acceptable loss by the mission protocols, especially since we still have the full complement of landers."

"That's not *good enough*!!" Asari answered quietly but severely. His eyes darted around to see who could have heard his muted outburst. "They, they deserve..."

"Punishment?" In-Su asked, having overheard.

Asari looked at the simulation of a middle aged East Asian man with contempt, but again it was muted. He was clearly making an effort to show deference and subdue the obvious rage roiling under the surface. "...no." He answered simply and unconvincingly.

"They seem to have deliberately landed well away from our chosen colony site *and* they seem to have stolen as little equipment as possible to pull it off," Neil offered. "They could have *completely* fucked us, but they didn't. For now I'm afraid, we need to give them the benefit of the doubt."

"I know it's not what anyone had in mind, but we did plan to eventually set up a second colony site once we were able to," Sadhika added. "This certainly accelerates that."

As Armina passed by with the laser rifle and four shotguns she'd been asked to bring on account of the scary looking jungle beasts the sims had run into, her and Neil exchanged knowing smiles, but this time Sadhika missed it. Returning his attention to the situation at hand, Neil could feel the oppressing tension. To break the awkward impasse, as he floated past them towards the shuttle airlock, he asked one of the crew: "have they finished inspecting the heat shield Nekheny?"

"Yes," he answered, "they just finished. They say it's still flawless and that we'll be able to make several more descents before it'll need to be fully resurfaced, though it may need some spot fixes along the way. Nothing yet from your one trip down though."

"And the fuel?" Wiremu asked while they were on the topic.

"They've finished purging all of the tanks and..." someone passing by handed him an opened scroll and he looked at it for a few moments. His left eye winced a few times as he issued thought commands to navigate through the information on the screen. "We've just finished loading all of our cargo and equipment. We're good to go."

"Thank you" Wiremu answered with a gesture towards the airlock, "go on ahead and we'll join you in a few minutes."

For several moments the four simulants floated alone in taciturnity with the matriarch and patriarch. It was Wiremu who finally broke the deafening silence again.

"Asari… do you understand that I am only refusing an attack because it would only put the mission at further risk than this incident already has? I understand that you feel personally slighted and that you *burn* to respond. Believe me, I really do get that… but in a command position you've got to be able to put the welfare and success of the mission over and above your personal feelings… you've seemed up to that so far and I believe you still are." Only his certainty was a lie; unfortunately he found the patriarch's ability to keep his head only probable. "I'm not going to suggest that we replace you, but I do think I should ask if you'd like to *volunteer* for a… for a temporary vacation from your command responsibilities."

Asari looked up at him with what could only be described as a hurt expression on his face at the suggestion that he might be incapable of carrying out his duties or would in any way shy away from them.

"Don't worry," Sadhika reassured him, "we can't thank you enough for everything you've done in getting us to this point already. He's just offering you an out in case you wanted it but didn't feel like you had a right to ask."

"Thank you… but no." Asari's expression actually seemed to lighten somewhat at their apparent deference and appreciation of the impossibility of his situation. "No, I appreciate the offer, but I am still perfectly capable of performing my duties, so I feel honour-bound to continue with them." He took a deep breath, and let out a long sigh. "Okay… we'll do it your way." He extended his hand and Wiremu shook it. Shaking hands as a greeting had fallen out of fashion well before they even left Earth, but honourable men and women sometimes still employed it to seal an informal but serious agreement.

The four sims pushed and pulled their way past all of their passengers and towards the flight deck of the shuttle, but then looked back through the hatchway. They saw the twenty eager scientists looking back at them. Each and every one of them seemed so magically eager to fulfill the singular purpose of their entire existence.

"Now you all behave or we'll turn this thing right around, you hear me?!" Neil yelled with feigned anger. The crew in the back laughed nervously, but they seemed happy to have their presence more personally acknowledged by one of the famous figures.

With a thought, Wiremu closed the hatch to the rear section and started making his way to his seat. He paused before proceeding though, and returned to the hatch and re-opened it. The other three paused strapping themselves in as they watched him and wondered what he was up to. Although there was seating for forty in the rear compartment, since this was their first landing of human personnel, as a precaution as well as just to make initial exploration more manageable, only a twenty person team had been assembled for this particular phase of the mission.

"I want to acknowledge that you have all had something robbed from you…" he announced in address to all of the humans, "and for that I want to apologize. In the original mission profile… you were all to be the first humans to ever set foot upon Haven. I know that for most of you, the pure thrill of going down to a planet for the first time ever in your lives will be exciting enough, but… still. It's not fair what's happened. I wanted to acknowledge that and… well, apologize for it I guess.

"Even so though, it's a big day isn't it?" he asked them. They all nodded and murmured their excited agreement. "I can't imagine what it must be like for you… to have lived your whole lives on a small ship, and now about to go down to a planet for the very first time… We," he said as he gestured to himself and the other sims, "from our perspective we went to sleep after a life time on and around Earth, and only recently woke up here in orbit around Haven. To us it's just another planet but, but to you well… well, to you it's *the* planet."

"Earth who?" Huli called out loudly from the crowd. The other sims and the rest of the crew broke out laughing, and Wiremu pointed to him with a smile which acknowledged his sentiment and the spirit with which he'd articulated it.

"Quiet right," Wiremu offered, "alright, let's get the hell out of here then," he said as he closed the hatch, returned to his seat, and strapped himself in. After conferring with Aset at mission control on the mothership's bridge, he undocked the shuttle and began his descent sequence.

Before the shuttle initiated its primary deceleration burn to fell itself from the sky, Sadhika had Wiremu wait as she put a communication request through to Halley's Personal Area Network. After a few moments without any response, with some quick thought commands Sadhika forced a line open so that whoever was on the other end would hear what she had to say whether they liked it or not. As she did so, from the first seat to her left Wiremu opened up the satellite imagery of the second site, and brought it up on the heads up display which encompassed the whole interior of the main window out the front of the shuttle. All four sims could see a group of people milling around the shuttle, and the way their behaviour changed to a frenzied attentiveness and moving about once Sadhika began speaking.

"Halley..." she said thoughtfully, "It doesn't have to be this way... you can still come home. We only have the First Descent Module at the other site and yours is as good as ours... we could come down to your site instead right now. We could still work together to build our first colony. We could keep this crew *together* Halley, we could avoid anything else bad happening... we could put this family back together, the way it was always meant to be..." There was no response, and everyone listened very intently to the lack of sound.

"I recognize and... deeply appreciate the care that you've obviously taken to minimize your damage to the mission's ultimate success. A second site makes a lot of sense in terms of overall mission survivability... hell, that possibility is in part why we made everything in duplicate in the *first* place!"

She paused. The futility of her efforts were becoming apparent to her. "Halley we may even be able to negotiate sending you some of the industrial drones... but dammit, you have to *talk* to us! We *have* to be in *contact*! The silence, the mistrust, the, the ambiguity of your intentions, *these* are the things putting the mission at risk now!"

Silence.

"*Dammit* Halley I *order* you to respond right *now!!*" She could be a kind, sweet, and warm woman, but she was also a shark. Her progenitor had been the woman who had singlehandedly built Brahma Biotech, the largest and most successful biotechnology company on Earth at the time of their launch. It was her profits from this original venture which had been the primary financing for the New Horizon mission in the first place.

Silence.

The artificial woman sighed heavily, and with a not insignificant sense of defeat she closed the channel. "Okay Wii... take us down."

Chapter 17

After another blessedly uneventful descent, and a genuine *re*-entry this time, the simulants and their human crew made their way down to the colony site very much as they had the first time, and landed safely on the runway. It was mid-afternoon by this point, and although there were a limited number of sunlight hours left, there was much to do before they could rest for the day.

The four simulants casually made their way out through the door and onto the surface of the planet again. The human crew followed, but much more slowly. Each had a different response, and a different way of greeting the planet for the first time. Some bounded out with great enthusiasm, whereas some others seemed quite reticent if not outright fearful to leave the claustrophobic safety of the shuttle. There were after all, so many things they were being thrown into which they'd never known. Things as basic as the wind, or a horizon, or a space without walls that seemed to keep going forever, these were entirely new experiences for them.

None of them had ever experienced natural and solid gravity before. As much as it was similar to their centrifugally generated artificial gravity on the ship, something nevertheless felt different about it to those who had up until today lived their entire lives in an artificial gravity environment. It might have only been their imaginations, but there seemed to be something noticeably different about the real thing to someone who grew up in one form, and then much later ventured into the other.

Some of the human crew paused at the myriad of fresh scents in the wild air and took a deep breath, while others only timidly and tentatively sniffed at the foreign environment. While some bounded out of the shuttle hatch with unbridled enthusiasm, others stopped at the portal to self-consciously reflect and appreciate the significance of the moment. They seemed to be reflecting on the moment in the context of their lives, their community, and their species, before decidedly stepping out with a sense of import and purpose.

Each initially went off in their own direction to explore different features of the new environment, and the simulants beamed like proud parents watching their children walk for the first time. While there would all too soon be all too much to do, for now they left their crew to their own devices, and allowed them the freedom to explore the space and appreciate the moment in their own ways.

Some of the crew immediately made their way to the jungle wall to investigate the wild environment just a short walk away. Some bent down to feel the solid runway surface beneath them, putting their hand flat on the ground to form a firm physical contact bond with the environment of their new home world. Some just stood around slack jawed, completely dumbfounded by the significance of the moment and the vividness with which the new environment assaulted all of their senses.

About a full ten minutes after the last human exited the shuttle door, Wiremu called all of them to attention. "Okay people, listen up. This is the second reconnaissance phase of the mission. We sims were the primary phase and we cleared the planet for human arrival. It's now *all* of our jobs to as quickly as possible prep the site for mass landing. We have a lot of work to do, and we've gotta get to it. Biological and Environmental teams you're with Sadhika and In-Su. Everything you're interested in is in that jungle there, so knock yourself out. The animal corpse we found is back on the ship being studied in the bio-lab, but I'm sure there's plenty else for you to find in the jungle for further study. For now we're going to avoid killing anything more sophisticated than an insect, but anything of any size which is already dead is fair game for recovery and study. Physical and Engineering teams, you're with me and Neil. Each team take one of the weapons and figure out amongst yourselves who will carry it."

"And don't get lost." Neil added as an important afterthought. "You've all spent your whole lives in a closed environment where it was a physical impossibility to get lost. That is not the case here, remember that. If you have your scrolls with you you shouldn't run into trouble, but it's still important to stick together and not wander off. Hopefully I shouldn't even have to tell you that."

Some smiled at what they thought was a joke while others nodded gravely at advice they were taking very seriously. The group split into two as the Biological and Environmental teams followed Sadhika and In-Su towards the jungle. As they were leaving Sadhika could be heard saying: "Samples people, samples!"

The weather was cool but not uncomfortably so, especially with the general lack of wind. There was an optimism in the air, and it almost seemed to be shared between the planet itself and its new inhabitants.

Wiremu and Neil assembled the Physical and Engineering teams in front of them. "We haven't met most of you-" Wiremu's eyes narrowed as he quickly scanned every face in the crowd. "Correction, we haven't met *any* of you. So... hi everyone, my name's Wiremu and this here is my friend Neil," he said satirically as he put his arm around Neil.

"Hi, Wiremu and Neil." The crowd said in unison, which almost made Wiremu and Neil fall down laughing together.

Composing himself, Wiremu continued: "Okay, you can each introduce yourself to us personally when it's appropriate, but in the meantime... you've all seen the topography and satellite images of the area. A few kilometers in that direction," he pointed, "is the area we've had the paving drone working overnight and this morning. That's where we're going to put the town. Here in this area adjacent to the landing strip," he pointed, "is where we're going to bring down the industry drones. So, Physical team you'll be staying here with Neil to bring down and set up the industry drones, and Engineering team you're coming for a walk with me." All of the human crew had long ago memorized the full mission plan and none were hearing any of this for the first time, but as far as Wiremu was concerned, him issuing the commands himself was as much a part of the mission as anything else was.

The two teams diverged, and Wiremu led the Engineering team down the paved three meter wide road towards the new town site which the paving drone had made on its way there the first time, and upon which it had returned to the landing strip earlier today. Neil and his Physical team, after arriving at the area to be cleared for their industrial zone adjacent to the airstrip, called up to the ship and summoned down the first of the dozen or so industry drones that were to be set up there, although very few were as of yet necessary during this still early phase of the landed mission. Industry was after all an oftly lofty goal when one's immediate concern was survivability itself.

The paving drone was waiting for them, and with a thought Neil switched it to forestry mode and set it to work. When it launched, the machine was about four meters tall and one and a half meters wide, but now that if was fully deployed and at work, it was five meters long and a little over three meters tall. In paving mode, the machine used all of the material it cleared to produce a hard surface for the shuttle to land on, but in this different forestry mode, it ate a five meter strip out of the jungle as it worked in a grid, and left behind it piles of lumber and scrap on a soft ground which could later be used by the colonists for a variety of purposes. Later on the machine could be programmed to log more judiciously and only target specifically appropriate trees, but at the moment it was in clearing mode and was taking down everything in its way as it slowly but methodically cleared the entire multi kilometer area.

While that device created space for other industrial drones to be brought down, Neil ordered one of the industrial atmospheric separators down. This one instead of landing in the industrial clearing, was instead brought down beside the FDM at the end of the runway. The reason for this was simple. In addition to producing tremendous amounts of drinking water per day, it was also capable of creating the liquid oxygen and hydrogen fuel which the shuttle used.

Using this drone to fuel the shuttle, trips could be taken between orbit and the surface much more frequently. This drone itself didn't unfurl; instead out of the same meter and a half by four meter shell, four large bags inflated out of the core, two of which filled with water, and one each of liquid hydrogen and oxygen. Autonomous drills extended out at four equidistant points on its core, and dug into the earth with enough strength to prevent it from ever falling over even when two large bags on one side were full and the other two on the other side were fully depleted.

After Neil was satisfied with the separator drone being properly set up and functioning, the next task was to get the lumber which the forestry drone was creating over to where Wiremu was setting up the new town. He ordered down the next drone to land on the boundary between the landing strip and the industrial area, and its rocket halo soft landed it exactly where he'd indicated. Once safely on solid ground, the lander's outer shell unfurled from the top out, creating a wide basket. In the now exposed core of the large basket lay a large deflated gas bag which slowly but immediately began filling with hydrogen gas supplied by a small atmospheric separator which was incorporated into the drone. Powerful fan units were embedded in the sides of the basket and would swing out to propel the airship once it was fully inflated and airborne, which would only take a few hours. Once fully operational, it would serve as an incredibly valuable airship for ferrying both cargo and people around between the different areas of the colony.

"Alright Aset, send down Hector One please, grid position one."

"Incoming." Aset's face on Wiremu's wrist scroll acknowledged. The wrist scroll was the smallest roll up screen available, and one wore a wrist band with a slot one of the posts slid into, and with the scroll fully deployed the wristband could hold it firm at whatever desired angle it was physically moved to. Every member of the descent crew was sporting the same wrist band with an attached scroll which one hardly noticed when they were retracted.

Wiremu started looking around to the horizon in several directions. "What direction will it be coming from?" he asked. He had expected to have been able to see it by now.

"I'm sorry Wiremu," Aset apologized, "we've had a failure... Hector One didn't survive atmospheric entry... looks like it disintegrated over the horizon from you."

"Damn!!" Wiremu exclaimed. "Well, we expected a failure rate of eight percent... it is after all the *real* reason we doubled up on everything... Oh well, if we only have one failure today I'm glad it's a habitat module, we've got plenty of those... Okay Aset, try the next launch tube, send down Hector Three please, same touchdown position."

The modules were stored in something like missile silos in one section of New Horizon's large habitat ring. They were arranged in a grid, with two stacked on top of each other on both the inner and outer surfaces of the habitat ring. Every primary module was loaded into the front of the launcher, and was the first to come down. To mitigate the possibility of a damaged launch tube causing a failure in two identical modules, backups were always stored behind a different primary module. At Aset's command, the second habitat launched from a fresh tube.

"Incoming."

Wiremu and his crew on the ground first saw it when the parachutes deployed, which were much easier to see than the slender four meter by one meter and a half cylindrical lander. Like the initial First Descent Module, this one's parachutes pulled out of the halo from the top, which initially deployed its rockets some ways up in the sky, and became ever more forceful and aggressive as it neared the ground. The lander retracted its parachutes and touched down softly on the ground before the rocket halo itself finally retracted back into the structure of the lander.

"Hector Three safely down." As Wiremu walked towards it, he issued the initial start-up command by thought, which was relayed through his wrist scroll to the freshly landed device. The outer shell broke apart into four rounded corner sections which extended out to form the corners of the expanding square area within, with thick synthetic material spanning between the corner sections. The interior continued to inflate into an area of five square meters.

It was for all intents and purposes a less sophisticated variation of the First Descent Module. It had less equipment built into it, and was instead maximized for internal living space. They were quite simple in design, and the magic was again in the synthetic material with which it was constructed. The structure was designed to be impenetrable to anything from the angriest bear and the most violent storms. The material was incredibly robust, and at all four hard corners, small drilling rigs drilled down a full meter into the ground, anchoring the module in place. Inflated within along with the overall structure were twelve prepared beds for the crew, and a modest interior climate control system which would keep them warm on cold nights and cool on hot days.

Eventually, these more temporary structures would be replaced with more permanent ones built up layer by layer using industrial building scale three dimensional printers. This phase was several weeks out at least though, since it required a complicated assembly of components brought down in six different landers. It was currently a low priority though since if required these more temporary shelters could comfortably last and house the crew for many months, if not years.

Wiremu watched as the habitat module fully inflated and then anchored itself into the ground. "Okay, good. Send down Hector Four please."

"Incoming."

"So what do you make of it?" Sadhika asked Blair as they poked at another fresh half-eaten carcass of the tree cephalopods in the jungle.

"Well, it's an... octopus," Blair observed. "I mean sort of a, more of a... quatropus I guess," she laughed. I don't see any indications of any vestigial limbs so I don't think it had more to begin with and then later lost them at some point or anything. Also, where octopuses tend to have big knobby heads, this one's has a much lower profile... more of a bump you might say, but it still has a beak underneath the head in the centre of its limbs... You say it was swinging?"

"Oh yeah, hell of a sight too..." Sadhika reflected. "Actually, here:" She pulled her wrist scroll out of its dock and with a few thought commands brought up the video Neil had taken during their encounter. She showed it to the others on the fully unravelled scroll and they all watched as the animals moved through the trees over their heads.

"That's incredible..." Blair commented. "It looks like a video I saw in the archives of monkeys moving en mass through the canopy of the Amazon rainforest."

Sadhika made a sound which she was disappointed to hear come out as a snicker. "I actually saw the real thing..." she mused. "I spent some time in Brazil..." She waited for somebody to remind her that it wasn't actually her who saw any such thing, but nobody did. She wasn't entirely sure what this meant, but it did please her.

Chapter 18

"WOAH! WHOOOAAAAHH!!!"

"IN-SU!!!" Sadhika cried out as he vanished. He appeared to have somehow fallen into the earth without any warning. "Everyone slowly back away from that area!" she barked at the human crew with them as she got down on her stomach and began inching her way towards the spot where In-Su had vanished.

"In-Su?" she called out again. It was more of a question this time.

"I'm here!" he cried out, sounding a little panicked.

"Are you okay?"

"I... I think so. I don't think anything's broken, or well... damaged."

It was at this point that Sadhika reached the hole in the ground through which In-Su had fallen. She could see him lying flat on his face some ten meters down. 'I know we're supposed to be perfect simulations,' she thought to herself, 'but I can't help thinking that that fall would've had to have seriously injured if not killed an actual human...'

"Can you get up?" she asked.

"Is he okay?" Blair called out from the group of humans standing safely away.

"Looks like it," she called out in answer. "He's gonna to try to stand."

"He shouldn't! He could have a spinal..." Blair began to caution, and then remembered. "Never mind!"

Simulant or no, In-Su very gingerly pushed himself up off the floor and onto all fours. He then brought his legs under his torso and stood up fully. He arched his back in a stretch with his arms on his waist and then shuddered a little as he finished.

"What do you see down there?" Sadhika asked. "What did you fall into?"

"I, I don't know I, I can't see anything down here!"

"Scroll," she reminded him.

In-Su pulled his bag off of his back and pulled out the large scroll which he'd brought with him. The wrist scroll had the same function, but could provide far less light. He fully unravelled the large scroll and the material went rigid. With a thought command, both sides of the now stiff material lit up brilliantly with white light. Holding it over his head, it illuminated the space around him.

"What do you see?"

"I see... I see that you're going to want to call the others over for this Sadhika." In-Su said as he looked around in wonder.

"This place is old..." Wiremu commented, "I mean like really, *really* old, like... long before human modernity kind of old..."

They had discovered that what In-Su had fallen down into was a narrow meter wide tube constructed of some kind of bricks which were offset in and out at each brick layer, providing foot and hand hold for them to relatively safely climb themselves up and down as though they were rodents in a vertical hamster cage tube. Some of the bricks slipped out and fell down when they tried to put their weight on them, but remarkably most held their place. They were precisely cut and fitted closely together instead of using mortar between the bricks which by now surely would have crumbled to dust and left none of the bricks in place.

When they got to the bottom, they found a space just under two meters high and several meters wide and long. Even in the relative dark it was unmistakably brick lined like the tube which had brought them down. Shining their lights around, they could see hallways going off in three directions but from where they stood the tunnels remained ominously dark to their lights.

As well preserved as the place appeared to be, it was very obviously quite ancient, and there was a strong sense of danger just being in the room. They all had the strong impression that they shouldn't stay down there any longer than they had to. As remarkably well-constructed as the brick work was, it was in an obvious state of extreme decay and the bricks themselves were cracking and flaking. It appeared though, that the further they looked away from the access shaft they'd come down, the better preserved the construction seemed to be. The elements are the enemy of any structures' longevity, and the further away from the outside world they looked, the less light there was for plants to grow in between the bricks and break them apart, much like how the less water and temperature fluctuation there was, the less heating and cooling of the ambient moisture could warp and damage the bricks.

"What makes you say that?" Neil asked in regard to Wiremu's comment about the age of the place.

"The piles of dust everywhere..." Wiremu answered. "I think they were all objects a long time ago, now they've all just turned to dust... I mean on Earth we get excited about things from a few thousand years ago... and those are mostly just stone or hardened clay... maybe inert metals... stuff like the brick itself here, or the Egyptian pyramids back on Earth." He shone his light up the tube through which they'd come down.

"But see all the piles of dust and unidentifiable bits of decayed stuff in piles of varying sizes against the walls here... for all we know once upon a time those could have been beds, bookshelves... maybe even something like those ancient furniture sized radios made of wood." He almost made himself laugh at the prospect.

"Yeah, or... just dust piled up," In-Su skeptically pointed out.

"Well if they were something like that we'd be able to tell by sifting through the dust," Neil noted, "any technology we'd be able to recognize or understand would leave bits of metal behind, even after this long."

"Quite right," Wiremu affirmed.

"So what do think we can surmise from this discovery?" In-Su asked.

"Well," Wiremu answered, "we don't know who made this place... we don't know the extent of it, and we don't know if they're still around."

"Don't you think those are questions we need to answer now?"

"In time, sure. But for now we have our timetable In-Su. Sure this is a curiosity, but-"

"I'd say it's a hell of a lot more than a curiosity Wii!" Sadhika exclaimed. "Are you totally missing this?"

"What?"

"Intelligence!! It was one thing to find that there was a fully independent DNA system here, but *right now* we're standing *in* the evidence that there is intelligent life of alien origin!"

"Or at least used to be," Wiremu observed with remarkably less enthusiasm, "but I take your point."

"I'm sorry Wii, but this is, this is the single most important discovery since... well since ever! Humanity is not alone in the universe! That is the biggest discovery ever made in the history of humanity! It doesn't matter if they're not *around* anymore! Like the DNA, if it can happen completely independently on two completely separate planets so close together, then that means it can happen *anywhere*! And *easily*!"

"I share your excitement Sadhika, believe me," Neil offered, "but I'm also deeply concerned that this means we've violated a fundamental mission protocol. We were not to colonize a planet with existing intelligent life and you said it yourself, we are standing *in* the evidence of that intelligence right now!"

"Well, frankly I have to agree with Wiremu that they're long gone now. Any sophisticated civilization currently in existence, even if mostly underground, would have revealed itself in our detailed studying of the planet so far, especially since we've had all of our planet facing telescopes in orbit."

"But still..." In-Su said tentatively. "For all the fear that humans have had for so long about aliens from deep space invading Earth... and now to *be* those invading aliens."

"Maybe," Wiremu offered thoughtfully, "it was always just a part of our own nature which we were afraid of, and projected out into the blackness of space. I'm sure some part of us has always understood that the same drive which makes us want to go exploring over the horizon, is the dame drive which can bring doom and misery to whoever already lives over that horizon when someone new shows up..."

"Them..." Neil reflexively corrected without thinking. Nobody objected or agreed. Nobody seemed to acknowledge his comment one way or the other.

Sadhika laughed a little to herself.

"What?" Neil asked.

"Just... *another* biggest human discovery of all time made by a non-human," she said with a smile.

"I wonder... if in a thousand years the human's egos will force them to forget that we were simulants at all," In-Su mused out loud. "Maybe in history we will become human descendants of our progenitors, or maybe our progenitors themselves will be erased from time and will only be remembered as us."

The four ruminated on this for a few moments until, almost on cue, Blair called down to them. "How's it going on there? What do you see? What did you find?"

"Nothing," Wiremu called up to her.

Sadhika assumed a look on her face which was a cross between horror and bewilderment. "Everything!" she called up in correction. "It's a room lined with the same brick work as the tunnel. There's piles of dust against the wall which we think used to be objects which have now long turned to dust. We think the place is beyond ancient, but it clearly indicates the existence of intelligence here in the past at least!"

"Yeah, I figured the same thing just from the brick work we can see up here!" Blair excitedly agreed. "Ancient you say though?"

"Yeah... and there's three tunnels leading out of this room, I don't know if we're going to explore them though, hold on." Sadhika turned to the three male sims. "What do you think?"

"Look guys," Wiremu said, "I definitely agree with you that this is all very interesting and worthy of further investigation. But I' m not as driven by my curiosity as you three all are and frankly that's why I'm here and why I'm your captain. My role is to keep us clear about what our priorities are. Our priority is still, and still has to be, the mission and the establishment of the colony. If everything had gone to plan so far we could be much more loose with the rules about researching this site, but Halley has put pressures on us that we can't ignore. You all know that this could all still go sideways at any moment, and the more progress we make towards setting up our colony site, the less it will matter if things *do* blow up, and the less potential there will be for *complete* mission failure. You get me?"

The other three nodded that they at least understood where he was coming from. Wiremu was right though that he was dealing with three academics who at the moment wanted nothing more than to drop everything else and start studying these ruins, to go down those dark tunnels and see what they could find. Their fundamental curiosity was one of the primary things which had brought them to this point and all the way out here in the first place.

"I suggest," Wiremu stated, knowing full well that these were the three people he didn't have any right to outright order around, "that we keep working at establishing the ability of our crew to survive long term on the surface without any extra help, and being able to bring a lot more people to settle in here. Once we're securely in that phase of the mission I'll be right here with you to explore what's down there," he said, shining his light down one of the mysterious tunnel. "I mean, it's not like I'm not at all curious *myself...*"

The other three nodded their agreement, and then Sadhika called up to Blair: "We're coming up! We'll fully explore down here once our colony is at least minimally established."

"Understood," the woman on the surface replied, sounding quite disappointed.

One by one, Wiremu laced his hands and gave the other three boosts up into the tube by their boots. Once they were all on their way up, he let out a "Hyup!" as he jumped up to grab the lowest rung of bricks, and then pulled himself up into the tube with just the strength of his arms and followed the others up to the surface.

Chapter 19

"Beg your pardon Sadhika, but... but shouldn't we be shifting all of our priorities to investigating those tunnels at this point?" Blair asked. "Isn't the biggest and most ominous unknown now the possibility of intelligent life on this planet?" Sadhika and In-Su had resumed their investigation of the jungle with their teams after Neil and Wiremu had returned to their own work sites.

"The place was old Blair... very old. We think that whatever... or whoever had the ability to make those tunnels is long gone now. If we thought they were still around I'd absolutely agree with you though. Still around or not though don't worry, we still intend to fully investigate but first we need to adequately establish our colony site. As I'm sure you understand I am both pleased *and* dismayed that it is at the top of a very long list of things we need to investigate, a long list of things which demand investigation, but which have to wait until our primary task here is done."

"I understand..." Blair answered thoughtfully. "Still though, I wonder what they were like... and what happened to them."

"Impossible to say at the moment but have you noticed Blair, the total absence of anything like a mammal? So far I've noted various kinds of insects, cephalopods, lizards... but no mammals. Instead some of those cephalopods and lizards seem to have adopted some mammalian qualities, like I have to assume based on the way they were moving warm bloodedness, definitely *some* kind of active metabolism."

"I *had* noticed that... so it's unlikely that whatever intelligent life was here was anything like a mammal, let alone a primate... although, from what I understand people on Earth always thought that cephalopods had the potential to become more intelligent... didn't they always consider octopuses to be quite intelligent?"

"Oh yes, we certainly did... I was thinking the same thing," Sadhika affirmed.

"Of course, it's also entirely possible that we're just on the wrong *continent* to see the kinds of life which *do* resemble mammals on this planet."

"*Or,* the classes of life which we can't even recognize as having *any* similarities at all with *any* kind of life on Earth. To be honest I'm a little surprised that we're finding kinds of life which we can generally recognize at all."

"Well," In-Su piped up, "you *call* them reptiles and cephalopods, but they're not really. Such classifications were even on Earth somewhat arbitrary anyways. We have witnessed animals which converge on a number of similar characteristics as classes of animals we recognize from Earth, but they're not *actually* from the same class or anything."

"You're right of course," Sadhika replied with a smile.

"You know... I still just can't get over how lucky we are," Blair remarked. "I know the mission founders really did their homework before leaving Earth, but there was still a lot of hoping and praying involved."

"Not as much as you'd think," Sadhika answered as the group of twelve made their way through the jungle. "There was a lot we could confirm ahead of time based on the atmosphere's spectrograph... and there was a lot we could pretty safely infer based on it." She paused to consider what the woman had really meant by her comment. "You're quite right though, the planet on a whole really *is* pretty much just as we'd hope it would be."

"It's dangerous to presume too much," In-Su warned. "We've only been here a short time, and there is still much which can yet go wrong." He meant things which were hard to predict with observations so limited in time, like the worst storms, volcanic activity, and earthquakes. They'd have to wait hundreds of years to see what weather events happened only once a century, and thousands of years to see what geological events happened only once a millennium. He reflected to himself that at the moment they should really be more immediately concerned with the group which had broken away from the crew. At the moment this undeniably remained their greatest threat.

The man with one of their two shotguns, who was at the front of their group as they moved through the jungle, shushed everyone and motioned for them all to get on the ground as he himself laid down with his weapon in front of him. The others followed his lead and laid down themselves. After a few moments of silence, everyone started wondering if he'd errantly imagined some danger.

Then, they first heard the sounds. To the human ear they sounded like squishing and sloshing sounds, but In-Su thought that maybe he could detect a certain patternicity to it. Then the three figures came into view and the crew became able to put image to the sounds they'd been hearing. So far undetected, the group watched as the animals moved past them at an angle, first they got closer at they moved, and then as the humans and their simulant leaders watched, they passed by and began getting further away while continuing to make their odd but distinctive sounds.

The creatures were a little over one meter tall, and supported themselves on three limbs which looked like the blunt cylindrical legs of an elephant. There didn't appear to be any joints in their legs, but they appeared to go from being rigid when weight was put upon them, to somewhat loose and limp when swinging through to their next step.

The creature likewise had three arms, each rooted in-between two of the legs so that there were six equidistant projections from the dome topped round cylindrical main body of the creature. The legs came down from the core of its body, while the arms projected down to the side from higher up on the outside of the body. All of this was topped by large black eyes at the end of short antenna like structures projecting out of the top of their bodies, which moved the eyes around to allow the creature to survey its environment. Overall it looked a little like a giant squid which had stood up on three shortened tentacles, and brought three other tentacles up to operate more like arms.

When they were at their closest, Sadhika could see that at the end of their arm tentacles, the appendage was split into four smaller tentacles which appeared to have as free a range of motion as the arms, both of which appeared capable of fully omnidirectional motion like an elephant's trunk. She remarked to herself that some-thing like that would be at least as effective for using tools as a human hand, if not even better or more resilient.

The group watched as the animals moved off and eventually went out of sight and presumably earshot as well.

"Wow..." Blair said quietly.

As they all slowly got up, ever surer that the creatures had moved on, they were caught by surprise. A different, much larger, and much deadlier creature surprised them all by emerging from an obscured ridge behind the group, and aggressively charging at them. The ground could be felt to shake with the weight and aggression of the attack. It was the same kind of horned panda dinosaur the simulants had encountered the day before. Its coloration had helped it camouflage into the foliage of the jungle.

It only took a couple seconds to reach them, which was far faster than anyone had any chance to react. It charged and gored Blair in the back and through her chest, lifting her up several meters into the air. Her limp body briefly paused in midair, and then fell back down to the ground where she was viciously pounced upon by the beast who held her down with its front feet and began tearing at her flesh with its teeth and biting out whole mouthfuls of flesh and bone. It availed itself of Blair's corpse seemingly without any interest in nor fear of the rest of the group at all. Within seconds the man and woman with the shotguns had fired and killed the animal, but Blair was already long dead.

Shaken and in shock, In-Su and Sadhika's group somberly carried Blair's body out of the jungle and back into the clearing where the shuttle and FDM were situated on the shuttle's runway. Everybody else's objectives of the moment were paused due to the tragedy, and all were reassembling in the staging area. Even these industry drones at the other end of the runway had been switched to standby to silence them. On his way back to the landing strip area from the clearing which would become the new town, Wiremu and his team had retrieved the corpse of the beast so it could be analyzed in detail on the ship along with the quatropus they'd already brought up.

There had been a variety of reactions to her death, and the kind of death she had suffered. Some were devastated, others seemed indifferent, but most were simply still in shock and had yet to really process the reality of what had just happened.

"Expected losses... *acceptable* losses." Wiremu whispered grimly to Neil out of earshot of anyone else. In-Su and Sadhika were closer in with the rest, and he seemed to be saying it to reassure himself as much as anybody else. "No different from the habitat module I lost earlier today... The problem though, is that they all know that as well as *we* do, but we all still have to stop everything and wait for them to-"

"They knew her..." Neil offered softly. "To them she was family... their sister."

"Yeah," Wiremu sighed as he arched his back and stretched, "I know..." The simulation of a grizzled old half Maori sighed deeply and allowed himself a moment to acknowledge the gravity of the tragedy. "She seemed like a lovely person and I'm sure if I'd have known her better I'd be a lot more beaten up about it."

"What's this?" Neil asked as he and Wiremu saw Sadhika and In-Su walking over to them with the rest of the crew.

Armina Shostak was at the front of the group with the other two sims and she said: "We've all been training for this mission since we were born. We've always known there was a good chance that we would lose people... we all know that there's a good chance she won't be the last... We know this, and we know that the mission goes on; we all know that that's what she'd want. We will all grieve in our own way, and in our own time."

Wiremu stepped forward and put his right hand on the woman's shoulders and rested it there while he placed his left hand on her cheek. He was moved; he hadn't expected that reaction from them. He was proud.

Although he was too proud a man to actually allow himself to cry in front of the crowd, it took considerable effort for him to control himself. Despite his best efforts, a gloss nevertheless came over his eyes as he said softly but firmly: "I'm proud of all of you... and I will help you bury her when the time comes."

Chapter 20

"Aset, given what happened to Blair, I want everybody on the planet to be armed at all times. We don't have enough shotguns and laser rifles in the armory for everybody, but they're too unwieldy for just carrying around anyways. Get a team together to manufacture us some small arms. You should be able to make all of the components with the ship's printers and material reserves. When they're ready load them and all of the armory's larger weapons into one of the personnel landers and send them down to us."

"You really want to put *all* of our remaining weapons into one flaming basket?" she asked. Wiremu paused and considered this. She was right; it was against a general principle of the mission.

"No," he answered, "you're right. Just see to it that twenty handguns are manufactured and when they're ready send them down to us with as many extra people as you're able to fit into the capsule. Other than the danger posed by the... animal life, we've demonstrated that it's safe otherwise to start bringing more people down anyways. You can leave the remaining shotguns and laser rifles on the ship for now. Maybe we'll send them down with other crew when they eventually descend.

"Understood."

"And Aset, go ahead with bringing down the other four habitat modules we're gonna need tonight. Do it one at a time and in the order and placement I indicated to you earlier. I don't have time right now to personally go back and oversee it, but they seem to be working properly once they actually make it through the atmosphere."

"Understood," she answered professionally, but despondently.

"Were you, were you close to her?" he asked, realizing now what must be newly bothering her.

Aset looked up with an expression which was somewhere between confusion and pain. "I… I grew up with her."

"Right… I'm sorry." Wiremu thought the channel closed and shut his wrist scroll. He stood alone for a few moments, shaking his head to himself. There was an odd comfort he thought, that at least now the things which they had planned on possibly going wrong were the things which were actually going wrong. Crew deaths and burn ups on entry, these were unfortunate but at least they were contingencies which were expected and accounted for, but a rebel faction and dissenting colony site… well, there were no contingency plans for that and it still weighed heavily on him. He composed himself as best as he could, and then walked back out from behind the shuttle and rejoined the group, where there appeared to be some kind of argument going on.

"Are you aware of this man's qualifications?" Neil was asking a brown skinned man named Nekheny, one of the crew who had come down with them.

"I am aware of Kim In-Su's qualifications, yes!" Nekheny retorted with an intense contempt in his dark eyes.

"Don't give me that," Neil barked, "this man *is* Kim In-Su and *then* some, and *given* that, are you *aware* of In-Su's qualifications, right!?"

"Yes," the man said through gritted teeth.

"Grand, and is there anyone else in this crew with comparable linguistic capabilities?" Neil asked.

"No."

"Exactly!"

"What are we talking about?" Wiremu asked.

"In-Su thinks that the animals they saw in the jungle before… before Blair, were speaking a language."

"Really…" Wiremu said, wondering on the prospect.

"But it's not true." Nekheny decidedly declared. "It can't be!" Neil glared at him.

"Why not?" Wiremu asked.

"Because they're just alien *animals*!! And even if it *were* true, how could a damned *simulant*, let alone a human *being*, be able to decide that based on just listing to the noises they were making for a few seconds at *most*!?"

For the moment ignoring the aspersions cast on them as simulant, Wiremu turned to In-Su and asked: "In-Su?"

"I'm not saying... that it was a full language... and I'm certainly not saying I could even begin to understand any of it, but I know language. And you know, I haven't just studied human languages, I-"

"In-Su studied." Nekheny tried to correct him.

"Shut up." Wiremu flatly commanded him. "That's enough out of you; you've made your point. Go on In-Su."

"As I was saying, I haven't just studied many human languages; my interests have led me to study more primitive animal communications as well... I wanted to understand the difference, and... try to understand what makes human language so special and how it could have emerged out of more simple direct communication. I know what I'm talking about."

"We know," Neil reassured him. "Go on... tell Wiremu what you told me."

"Of course I'm only guessing based on that knowledge and experience, but from what I heard, I don't think I heard a fully developed language or anything, but there was definitely a distinct... patternicity to it. It sounded to me like something *far* more sophisticated than what you'd expect from say primates or dolphins, while still being much less sophisticated than humans. Maybe, *maybe* something on the level of just simple nouns and verbs, but definitely no kind of grammar to speak of. It really didn't sound sophisticated or complex enough for that."

"Well you were wearing your PANE during the encounter weren't you?" Neil asked him. "You could review the recording's audio."

"Yes, you're right, of course," In-Su answered. "I will; I think that would be very helpful."

"Alright everyone, as you were," Wiremu ordered. "We'll take a dinner break, and then we've got to get some more work done before we can call it a night. By now the habs should be down and deployed at the town site."

Sadhika had come to be standing in the back of the crowd by now, and Wiremu motioned for her to come over. He gathered up his team and spoke to them privately.

"Now..." he said with a somewhat pained expression, "obviously I'm not the scientist here, but based on how Sadhika described those... squiddy things, and what In-Su is saying about them now, I think it's a safe assumption that there's some connection between those squiddies and the underground cavern we found." The other three solemnly nodded.

"How certain are you that you couldn't detect a sophisticated language In-Su?"

"Quite, but I could be wildly wrong of course, it's totally alien life."

"I ask, because I have to imagine that any species capable of working communally to create bricks, to cut them exactly, to excavate..."

"I see where you're going," In-Su offered.

"And yet," Sadhika noted, "things like termites and bees can create some pretty amazing structures for what they are."

"Sure, but... that was no termite mound Sadhika," Neil stated. "I mean, insects at their best tend to be able to do remarkable things with a single building material like wax or mud, you get me? We're talking chemistry here, tool use, far more sophisticated stuff."

"If we found evidence of technology, any kind of electronics..." Wiremu mused, "that would clinch it."

"But what about how old it seemed down there?" In-Su asked.

"I was thinking the same thing..." Neil agreed. "If they were intelligent and sophisticated you'd think that they'd have built something more obvious more recently, that they'd have advanced *beyond* that in the intervening thousands of years..."

"Too many mysteries... not enough answers," Wiremu said.

"Wiremu?" Sadhika asked. "I think we may need to adjust our priorities. I think we have to investigate this now. We need a lot more information here, about the squiddies, about how sophisticated they are, about what else is waiting to be found underground in those tunnels... we may have to find a new colony site."

"I'm inclined to agree, Sadhika. I'm worried now about the possibility that we really have violated a principle mission parameter. There may very well be life we recognize as intelligent here." The other three solemnly nodded their agreement.

"Let's at least hope for now," Neil offered, "that unlike that damned panda dinosaur thing, the squiddies are far more scared of *us* than we are scared of or curious about *them*."

"When did we start calling them squiddies?" In-Su asked. "Is that what we're calling them then?"

"Has a certain ring to it," Neil said with a strained smile.

"In any case," Wiremu said, trying to keep them on topic, "there's really nothing we can do *tonight*. We need to get the town camp set up so that the crew has somewhere to sleep safely tonight. Let's just get set up and call it a night, and then in the morning we'll convene an investigation team. I can oversee a reduced but combined engineering and physical team. In-Su with your horticultural background you should be able to oversee a reduced biological and atmospheric team while Neil and Sadhika can gather up the rest of the people we have to investigate the underground, the squiddies, and whether or not there's any connection there."

"Plus," Neil reminded them. There's no reason why tomorrow we can't start the next mission phase and bring down more people to help."

"While that is true," Wiremu observed, "The situation now being what it is, I don't want to bring down any more people until we know more about the mysteries we're going to investigate tomorrow. I don't want to put any more people at risk until we have a better idea of what we're dealing with and whether or not we have to shift to an alternate site. I'll have a few people coming down with the weapons but that's it."

The three looked up as they saw the last new habitat module sail overhead and deploy its parachutes on its way to the new town. "You're right of course," Neil agreed, "we should wait until we know more before bringing more people down."

"What do we do with Blair?" In-Su asked.

"Cold storage," Sadhika said thoughtfully as she looked down at the ground. "We'll have to bury her later, so... in with the animal corpses for now, I'm afraid."

'Like so much meat,' In-Su silently lamented to himself. 'Now she has far more in common with her lifeless killer than she does with we machines.'

Chapter 21

Much later that night Sadhika was fast asleep. As she lay in one of the four beds which the simulants' private habitat module was equipped with, her wrist scroll began vibrating from under her pillow. Keeping it there was an old habit she'd picked up from back in the days when she ran a multi-billion dollar transnational corporation. She hated the idea of ever being out of contact; she hated the idea of ever being unreachable if she was ever needed for any kind of an emergency. Reflexively she woke and took the device out from under her pillow. Pulling the scroll apart to see who was trying to reach her, she saw that it was a private communication request from Halley. She was at once surprised, excited, and concerned, so she held the glowing screen to her chest as she left the hab in order to be able to respond without waking up the other Sims.

Once outside and walking away from the habitat module, she thought an acceptance of the comm request towards the device and Halley's face appeared. "Halley, what-"

"Sadhika, listen." He stopped her. "I have your shuttle."

"What?" she asked, incredulous. "That's ridicul-" this time she stopped herself. There's no way he would contact her out of the blue just to make up a story and lie to her about something like that. "How?" she asked instead.

"I... I don't want to talk over the comm line, but... I have an offer for you. If you'll meet me at your airstrip, I'll pick you up in the shuttle and take you back to our camp. When we're done talking, you have my word that you'll be allowed to safely return back to your own settlement, and with the shuttle back in your possession."

"What's going on Halley?" she asked with growing concern. She had a thousand questions, and there were a thousand ways that this situation could have arisen, and while most of them were bad some were positively catastrophic. She didn't doubt the sincerity of his offer on its face though, again if he already had the shuttle there seemed little to gain from capturing her as well. She was in fact encouraged that he seemed rather stressed about finding himself in possession of both shuttles.

"Death…" Halley answered somberly. "And there will be many *more* deaths if we don't meet to resolve the situation before it escalates."

Reason enough, Sadhika figured. Whatever he was talking about it sure sounded ominous. "Okay," she agreed.

"Meet me at the airstrip in forty-five minutes."

"Understood. I'll see you there." The line went dead and the small screen on the scroll went dark.

'That should be enough time,' she thought to herself. She'd have to get moving pretty quickly but it was a reasonable amount of time, especially since the paving drone had already created a good reliable road between their infant town and the landing strip.

Sadhika walked back over to the simulants' hab and opened her personal exterior storage locker. She took her coat and her PANEs, and then quietly opened the hab's door and silently removed the shotgun from beside Wiremu's bed. She then exited again and quietly closed the door behind her. As she walked off, she thought dictated a text message for the other sims when they woke up, explaining where she'd gone and why. The simulation of a middle aged Indian woman then disappeared alone into the alien darkness on the road to the airstrip.

Wearing her PANE, the darkness wasn't a problem. The cameras in the glasses were equipped with low light and infra-red cameras, which were then projected onto the interior of the lenses. This allowed her quite fair visibility, thought it was in red and black and absent of any colour vision. Using red light instead of white in the display reasonably preserved the user's dark adapted vision so that if they had to take the PANEs off for some reason, their eyes wouldn't take twenty or so minutes to newly adapt to the darkness about them, but would instead already be so adapted. Holding the shotgun out in front of her, she scanned from side to side as she carefully made her way down the road. Although the path she was walking was evenly paved, it was a new and unsecured road which meant that there could be any kind of obstruction newly lying in her path, as well as anything waiting to attack her from the jungle wall only a couple meters away on either side.

As she made her way towards the landing strip, she periodically heard a blood curdling shriek. It came out in a long call which was then followed by two shorter bursts. Sadhika comforted herself with the thought that as frightening as it sounded, it probably came from a creature which looked far less scary than it sounded. Her ever elaborating mind then considered that even if it didn't look particularly scary to her that certainly would not exclude it from being extremely dangerous. On Earth some of the most vicious or toxic creatures could look tragically and deceptively benign to human eyes or even worse, cute.

The scary intermittent sound though, was made all the more eerie and disturbing by the fact that it was the only sound she could ever hear. It was punctuation to the oppressing absolute silence of the night which she found intensely curious given how the daytime sounds of the jungle were an endless cacophony of strange alien animal noises. She knew that there must be a very good reason for everything to get so quiet at night, but for the life of her she couldn't imagine what that reason might be. Her inability to conjure even a single plausible ex-planation was what scared her the most about the phenomenon.

She tripped over something and almost fell, but she caught herself. When she looked behind her there was no evidence of what she may have tripped over and she found this somewhat unsettling. Either she had tripped over nothing, or she had tripped over something which had then scampered off. Both possibilities were equally unsettling for her, and either way she resolved herself to stepping more carefully. She was making decent enough time after all, and it was no longer necessary to be in such a hurry.

As she got moving again she figured that she was only fifteen or so minutes away from the landing strip where she'd agreed to meet Halley. At this point she received another communication request from him, and was again notified of it by the feeling of her small scroll vibrating in her pocket. Instead of taking the device out and opening it, she instead issued a thought command which put Halley's image up on the top left quadrant of both of her PANE lenses, and enabled the microphone and speaker system in her EAR.

"I've landed," he informed her. "Are you near?"

"I'm about twenty minutes away," she answered. "So are you going to tell me how you came to be in possession of both shuttles?"

"I'd... I'd still rather not talk about it over a comm line."

"Fine." Sadhika was irritated, but it was a reasonable precaution since their communications system wasn't especially secure. It wasn't designed to be; it was never foreseen that it would ever need to be. It was *hoped,* that it would never need to be. "Like I said I'm almost there. I'll see you soon."

When Halley could begin to make out the figure of Sadhika emerging from the darkness out the shuttle's front window, he went to the side door and opened it. He stood in the doorway with his arms folded and leaned up against the doorway. "Fancy meeting you here," he said, and immediately regretted it. The statement came off as glib and playful, which was well outside the bounds of the gravity of the situation he was about to drop on her.

"What to happen?" she asked very seriously. "Who died?"

"It wasn't my doing..." he started to plead. "I never wanted any of this to happen." Sadhika only widened her eyes at him expectantly.

"Well I guess I should start from the beginning... We were woken in the middle of the night to a shotgun blast near our camp in the jungle. We could tell that it was coming from somewhere between our airstrip and our settlement, which as I'm sure you know are much closer together than yours are."

"Okay," Sadhika prodded as she followed him into the shuttle's flight deck. "Go on..."

"So, we... went to investigate. When we arrived a minute or two later, we saw Nekheny firing a shotgun at one of the indigenous... wait, have you even met them yet?"

"Giant... jungle squid things?" she asked, to which Halley nodded. "Yeah, we've been calling them squiddies. In-Su and my teams briefly encountered a pair after we discovered what we later figured to be ruins somehow associated with them. In-Su swore up and down that he detected some kind of limited complexity in the sounds he heard them making."

"Really..." he seemed particularly curious about that.

"That's right, and if you hadn't entirely cut off communications we could have told you about them, we could have shared information and learned about everything much quicker," she scolded him with an obvious anger which she hardly even bothered trying to keep in check. "Then what happened?" she asked as she entered the shuttle and the two stood talking to each other.

"What kind of ruins did you find?"

"Does it really matter at this point?" she asked in obvious impatience. She was here to find out what happened with the shuttle and apparently Nekheny, whom she really didn't know much about.

"I'm sorry, but yes it does if you'll indulge me," Halley cryptically responded.

"Well it was tight unmortared brick work, some kind of vertical tunnel In-Su fell into and when we went down to investigate, we found a room several meters wide and long of similar construction and a few tunnels leading away from the room. We were planning on investigating the tunnels further in the morning."

"Fascinating..."

"What?"

"We had a similar experience," Halley answered. "One of my own people fell into a similar tube and almost broke her neck but was able to stop her fall some ways down the shaft. We found a similar room initially, but we *did* investigate right then and there."

"...and?" Sadhika found that she couldn't help herself. Despite whatever else may be going on, she was dying to know what they found, and what she and her people would have found if *they* had instead chosen to investigate right away.

"They're *sentient* Sadhika! In-Su was right, they're sentient!" Halley excitedly exclaimed. "At least... at least they certainly *used* to be. I don't know what happened, but we found ruins that we think were definitely built by them, but a long, *long* time ago."

"How do you know that for sure?" Sadhika asked. Her people had already suspected as much, but she was excited at the prospect of there being positive evidence for it. Being a trained scientist she was appropriately skeptical; such an extraordinary claim especially, required equally extraordinary evidence.

"Because in an adjacent room we found writing scratched into the brick walls, and some crude drawings which included depictions of the... I'm sorry, what did you call them? Squiddies?"

"Really!? That's amazing!!" Sadhika exclaimed. "And yet... well really a little strange. I mean that brick work suggests far more sophistication than mere scratches on a wall, although not if it's actually coherent written language..."

"It actually gets even stranger, and... well frankly, more ominous. We sifted through some of the piles of dust we found, and we identified metal and glass bits, like... like *electronic* bits, Sadhika. It didn't seem like particularly sophisticated electronic technology, but-"

"It doesn't matter," she said with a clear understanding. "Any understanding and technological utilization of electromagnetism is an undeniable dead ringer for industrial level intelligence..."

"You seem saddened by that," Halley observed. "I would've thought you'd be more excited."

"Well," she said with a heavy heart, "the scientist in me is ecstatic of course... but as a mission founder I'm deeply disturbed. This is something we specifically wanted to avoid. Signs of industry were supposed to strike a planet from our candidate list. Of course... more importantly at the time, such signs of industry on another planet might have been the most important scientific discovery of all time and a much bigger deal than the mission itself altogether, but... still. It *also* would have excluded this planet as a candidate for the mission."

"Which raises the question though, why *didn't* you see it? I mean, whatever they may have been and been capable of in the past, they are clearly no longer that sophisticated. Today the atmosphere would show no more indications of industry than it would have on the day you left."

"Right... Wiremu figured that the debris we found in the underground room had to be tens of thousands of years old at least..."

"We figured about the same thing."

"So what happened to them? What could possibly cause a species to regress like that?"

"That's where we draw a blank," Halley admitted. "Anyways earlier today we ran into a couple of them in the jungle and had a brief exchange with them before they ran off. Of course we couldn't understand each other in any way shape or form, and we couldn't even be sure that the sounds they were making were any kind of language the way In-Su seems to have been able to, but it *seemed* like they were trying to communicate… we certainly got that impression."

"What happened with Nekheny?" Sadhika asked, only now being able to rip herself away from the fascinating conversation about the squiddies.

"Well, that's just it…" Halley said as he gestured an invitation with his hand for Sadhika to take the co-pilot seat. She obliged and he followed her to the front to take the captain's seat beside her. "When we arrived… well, he'd run into a group of three squiddies. The first was already down and he was firing on the second as we arrived. We… then saw him turning his weapon on the third, and…" he seemed reluctant to finish the sentence.

"And?" Sadhika prodded, almost afraid because she was already pretty sure of the answer.

"And I shot him. I shot him dead."

"Oh no…" Sadhika was mortified.

"He… had already killed two," Halley explained. "I was thinking about the family we met earlier… at least what we *thought* was a family… I think I was imagining that he was about to kill a younger one after killing its parents…

"Halley…"

"I know Sadhika, I know… We investigated his PAN and found instructions given to him by his parents to spy on us. After that it didn't take long to realize that we had both shuttles and… where we would find the second one."

"Wait, what? His parents?"

"Of fuck… you didn't know?"

"Know what?"

Halley sighed heavily. "Nekheny is… Aset and Asari's son."

Sadhika's jaw dropped and her eyes opened wide.

"Now Sadhika, you've *gotta* believe me. I couldn't see who it was specifically when I shot. I had no idea who it was, I just… reacted instinctively to protect the... the squiddies."

"Halley..."

"I know. I mean, I don't know if I'd have acted any differently in the moment if I'd have known who it was ahead of time, but... it's important to me that you know that I didn't know, and that there's no way that I shot *because* of who he was... if anything it would have made me hesitate. Believe me, I *know* how on a razor's edge I am already."

"And that's when you contacted me?" she asked.

"That's right," he answered as he informed the shuttle by thought command that he wished to take off and what his intended destination was. Like road pods back on Earth, automatic piloting programs had proven themselves time and time again to be superior to and more reliable than human pilots, and with the exception of Wiremu, most everyone else just left the actual flying to the shuttle's onboard systems.

In earlier days autopilot systems had still made humans uncomfortable with the idea of relying on the technology completely. By the time the New Horizon had left the Earth though, people in general trusted autopilot systems so completely, that they had instead become reluctant to trust human pilots. More common now was their frustration with those who still wished to pilot land, sea, air, and space vehicles personally, since they were the only ones who ever had any incidents with piloting error anymore.

After receiving and processing Halley's commands, the shuttle swung around and aimed itself back down range of the runway. After deploying its auxiliary atmospheric wings, the shuttle's liquid rocket engines lit and fully engaged, and it was quickly in the air and climbing on a direct parabolic trajectory a third of the way around the planet to Halley's colony site. "I'm not afraid to say Sadhika... that I don't know what to do. I planned our defection very carefully, I imagined every scenario I could and worked out every detail I could imagine. I... I didn't plan for this and I don't know what to do. I'm scared."

Sadhika laughed out loud, and much to Halley's surprise. "What?" he asked.

"Really?" she asked. "You really don't get what's so funny about that?" He shook his head. "How you feel right now, is *exactly* the position you put *us* in when you decided you were gonna to fuck *us* over. It serves you right… at least now you know what you did to us, and I hope you appreciate that *everything* that comes afterwards now is *your* fault." He declined to respond to that assertion directly.

"Regardless… I didn't want this Sadhika. I did everything I could to avoid my actions leading to an escalation or any kind of open conflict, but when Aset and Asari find out about this… I'm pretty sure I'm going to need your help if there's any hope of averting a cata-strophe. They'll… they'll never understand. You need to *make* them understand, you need to tell them the story that I just told you, for there to be any hope at all."

"I can't say I entirely disagree. Speaking of which, why don't they know already? Wouldn't they have been monitoring Nekheny's progress? Can't they tell that he's dead by his beacon having gone dark?"

"Well," Halley answered a little sheepishly, "I immediately set up a false broadcast of his beacon to prevent them from being able to know that until I figured out what to do…"

"Of course you did," Sadhika replied with a total absence of surprise.

"As for why they haven't been watching with the satellites or wondering why the shuttle has come to you and is now heading back… well, either they're sleeping since it's the middle of the night and they were going to check on his progress in the morning, or they are in comm blackout so as not to put him at risk by tipping anyone off that they sent him out. As for satellite imaging, cover is intermittent at best as you know. They may be up there dying to know what's going on but afraid to say or do anything, or they may still be completely oblivious. It's hard to know."

"Halley…" she sighed, mentally exhausted, "what the hell were you thinking? Why do any of this at all? Why break up and endanger the mission in the first place? How could you possibly think it was really worth all the risks?"

"Well," he said with self-conscious reflection, "do you want the real reason or my principled justification?" he asked.

"Both," she answered, not amused. "Start with the real reason."

"I simply couldn't bear to collaborate with Aset and Asari anymore… I wanted the chance to really *lead,* to create something different and to… to create a different kind of colony from the one you planned."

"Different how?" Sadhika asked.

Halley sighed heavily. "I've studied you a great deal, all of the progenitors of you sims. You thought of so much… and yet there was so much you missed. That problem has been magnified over the course of the whole mission and was part of why the Midway schism happened at all in the first place."

"What?" Sadhika asked pointedly, now frustrated at his evading the real question. She was also a little insulted at his impugning of how they had prepared and planned for the mission.

"You thought of everything, absolutely everything… except the human part. "You failed to adequately *psychologically* vet the people who launched, you were so concerned with their professional qualifications that you… that you didn't give enough thought to the fact that you were creating a society, not a crew but a *society*!"

Sadhika didn't answer; instead she just listened.

"I don't… I don't *blame* you, or any of the other mission founders. It's truly miraculous what they *did* achieve in getting us here at all, in *any* condition. But I do believe that that original oversight is the root of all of the problems which came after, even my own original progenitor I have to admit is somebody who never should have made it onboard in the first place. Every-thing that's happened since is just… ripples from that original error."

"But everything *you've* done since our arrival here has only added *further* ripples, only *aggravated* the problems you're describing, can't you *see* that?" Sadhika chastised him.

"Of course I can… but I think you underestimate just how politically factionalized the ship already was before you woke up. There is a profound ideological divide which most of the crew falls decidedly on one side or the other of. "*They* consider my very *existence* an affront to them. *I* consider them being married as patriarch and matriarch an affront to the mission and I renounce their open discrimination of me. *They*, think the group comes first, while *we* think the individual does. *They* want to adhere to mission protocols as strictly and dogmatically as humanly possible, while *we* are comfortable improvising, and considering the original intent with which the protocols were written in order to act accordingly.

"I founded the second colony to provide a relief valve, so that we could live apart in peace, while we tackle our mutual larger problem of human colonization of Haven. I thought that space between us could cool tensions and eventually allow an equal and balanced dialogue. Well, that's my 'principled justification,' anyways. I never wanted it to turn into any kind of war though… I specifically did everything I could to avoid it coming to that. I was hoping to just get away with taking a shuttle and leaving the rest to you and them, I knew we were capable of figuring everything else out for ourselves. In part we wanted to build and discover a more natural life which was relatively free from the technology we've been bathed in our whole lives. We also hoped that based on our taking only a minimal amount of equip-ment, that you'd be able to convince Aset and Asari to let us go."

"We *had* Halley," Sadhika affirmed, "but that was before you gunned down their son."

Chapter 22

Not long after they landed, Sadhika's scroll began vibrating and chiming. Unless she specifically turned the feature off, urgent communication requests could override her having set it to vibrate only. Looking at the screen she saw that it was a comm request from Wiremu, and she thought to herself that it made sense he'd feel his communication attempt urgent at the very least at this point. With a thought she answered the call and Wiremu's face appeared on the small screen.

"Sadhika, what the hell?" Wiremu asked, somewhere between anger and concern. "Your tracker shows you all the way over at Halley's camp, and with *our shuttle*! What the hell are you *doing* over there?" He didn't seem to know what to think, but he definitely seemed worried.

Secure channel or not, Sadhika had to tell him the whole story. She told him about being woken up in the middle of the night and about discovering that Halley had their shuttle, including how it had come to be in his possession. Wiremu's fog of confusion and concern burned away to outright anger.

"Are you telling me, that Nekheny was Aset and Asari's son, and that he *stole* our shuttle to go *spy on them* in the *middle of the night*!?"

"It would appear so, yes." Sadhika somberly answered.

"God… *damn* it!" Wiremu exclaimed. "They must have ordered him to do it, too!"

"Yes," Sadhika confirmed, "they found those orders on his PAN when they searched him afterwards.

"And now he's dead… and worse still personally killed by Halley. This is a serious problem…" Wiremu stated grimly. "We were already sitting on a bomb just waiting to go off… I don't see any way we can avoid this place from totally blowing up now. Asari was barely containable as it was, this is… catastrophic."

"So what do we do?" she asked him quite plainly.

"Hold on," Wiremu told her as he opened channels with Neil and In-Su, and all three appeared on the screen of her wrist pad. "They've been listening in on your story," he explained.

"Oh, and In-Su," Sadhika remarked, "I know we have more important things to worry about right now, but you should know that you were right about the indigenous. There's actually a bit more to the story here, but I hadn't mentioned it yet because it wasn't relevant to our new and more immediate problems. The reason that Halley was so keen to protect the squiddies Nekheny was attacking was because he'd *also* discovered evidence of their intelligence."

"What kind of evidence?" In-Su asked, intrigued.

"Well, they apparently had a similar experience to ours. One of them fell into a tube like the one you did which led them to a room which he described quite identically as being like the one we found. Unlike us though, they took it upon themselves to investigate right away, and they found other rooms with what they believed to be writings and drawings carved into the brick walls like… like prehistoric cave drawing on Earth but with what they believed to be some kind of writing."

"Really…" In-Su uttered in wonderment. He was lost in thought about what it all meant.

"And Neil, you'll be interested to know that they did indeed find metal and glass components which led them to think it was evidence of some kind of rudimentary electronics technology but like Wiremu suggested, they also figured it to be tens of thousands of years old at least."

"That is… at once fantastic, and mortifying…" Neil managed to say.

"I know," Sadhika affirmed. "But whatever capabilities they once had in that respect, they've long since lost them. So… there's no way we could have known about them before coming here, but either way it doesn't look like the *spirit* of our mission protocols have *really* been violated. The *big* mystery though, the one I can't stop thinking about even when I really should be thinking about more pressing things…

is what made them regress like that? I wonder on both a pure curiosity level, but... as well I find myself concerned that whatever happened to them might pose a threat to us as well."

"Right, right..." Neil agreed, now as lost in thought as In-Su. "It is also interesting, and telling, that they built so similar structures so far away from each other and on a different continent altogether. It means that their civilization... or whatever, was remarkably widespread and apparently connected."

"Speaking of the more pressing things at hand," Wiremu stated in an attempt to recapture their attention to the immediate threat, "we have a big fucking problem." He was irritated with what appeared to him to be their superfluous interests in rather trivial concerns at this point, given the serious threats to the mission which currently faced them. "I'm sure this is all very interesting, and if we weren't under immediate threat I'm sure I'd be almost as taken with it all as you three clearly are, but we have more immediate concerns?" The other three nodded their acknowledgement.

"You know..." Sadhika thoughtfully added, "I didn't consciously excluded the information at the time, but I never told Halley that Nekheny had only hours earlier been arguing with Neil and In-Su that there was no way they could possibly be sentient or intelligent."

She looked back over at a crowd that seemed to be forming at the far end of the airstrip. "Now that I think about it I'm worried that telling him so now will only help him to feel justified in his actions and his fabricated sense of moral superiority around what happened."

"That's probably wise," Wiremu reassured her.

"Sadhika!" Halley called out to her from across the airstrip.

"Oh, gotta go," she said to her colleagues.

"Please put your PANE on and feed us the live stream," Wiremu politely ordered.

"Oh, okay sure, good idea," she said as she put the glasses on and thought activated the live feed over the comm channel before hustling over to Halley.

As she approached, she saw that Halley and his people were having another encounter with the squid-dies, now thought to perhaps be the planet's indigenous intelligent life. She wondered if they were coming to investigate the deaths of their fellow beings. Halley had told Sadhika that after he'd saved the third squiddy which Nekheny was about to kill, it immediately disappeared back into the jungle.

She wondered if the one which had survived the encounter had somehow managed to convey to the others what had happened and gotten some friends to return with it. She suspected that there was no way for Halley and his people to be able to tell if any of the animals who were showing up now were the same one which had originally escaped. There didn't seem to be any distinguishing features which would differentiate one from the other, at least not to human eyes. They weren't all exactly the same size and shape, but that was about all the difference she could make out.

Halley appeared to be trying to communicate with the creatures, and despite herself Sadhika was amused with the futility of his efforts which she could immediately recognize. He was trying to talk to it in slow and simple English as though it were just a slow and simple English speaking human. The hand gestures he was trying to use were things which Sadhika could immediately and clearly recognize as human cultural artifacts which had no reason to translate in any way to an alien species on an alien planet. Yet there he was making the attempt, and it amused her. He held his hand to his chest and said his name slowly and clearly, and then tried pointing to other things and saying their English names while trying to encourage the creature to reveal its own words for the same objects.

The creatures only appeared confused. Sadhika was amused because she understood that there was no reason why they should even be expected to understand the concept of pointing itself. She arrived and made her way to the front of the crowd which was watching Halley's inept attempts, and allowed her friends watch-ing from the primary colony site to survey the scene along with her.

"Fascinating," In-Su observed in her ear. "How I wish I was there to try… I dare say Halley is making a fool of himself."

Nekheny' body was still lying beside the bodies of the two dead squiddies but under a blanket, and Sadhika wondered if they somehow understood that Halley had helped them by preventing him from killing the third. She figured that that alone would be a pretty solid indication of some kind of sophisticated intelligence. It would be, she thought, a pretty difficult cognitive task to not simply see all the newcomers as equal, and jointly responsible for all of the activities engaged in by any of them. At this point, from their perspective, what reason could there possibly be to see them as being in two different and independently operating groups?

Sadhika moved forward and stood beside Halley to get closer to the creature. She held her hand out to it, and with its large black eyes the creature looked at her and rippled its arm tentacles up and down a bit. It produced a noise which sounded something like a falsetto gargle. The texture of its skin appeared smooth but firm, like a dolphin or orca back home. Its three thick cylinder shaped legs appeared to be quivering ever so slightly under the strain of remaining turgid and supporting the creature's weight. If they were in fact anything at all like the cephalopods she was familiar with back on Earth, then they were surely invertebrates and devoid of any kind of comprehensive skeletal structure. Humans could stand and walk with relatively little energy spent because they suspended their weight on bones with ligaments. Much of the effort which went into a human being standing upright merely consisted of small muscular corrections to keep their weight properly balanced and suspended on their solid internal structure. Sadhika got the impression that this creature lacked a similar system and was condemned to spend much more of their energy merely keeping themselves upright as a result.

She put her hand out a bit more and tried to appear as friendly and non-threatening as possible. On the inside she took a moment to laugh at herself though, for being equally as ridiculous and hopeful as Halley seemed to be in his own attempts to communicate. She silently but with good humour chastised her hypocrisy in seeming to do exactly what she had just mocked him for trying. Then to her shock and delight, the creature tentatively reached out one of its three arm tentacles and touched her hand. It then opened up its four small finger tentacles at the end of its arm, and grasped her hand while its antenna mounted eyes looked into hers.

"Outstanding..." In-Su uttered in her ear. "Please Sadhika... *please* come get me."

"Not a chance," Sadhika said with a gentle mirthful laugh. "I'm not going *anywhere,*" she explained while still holding the creature's hands and returning its curious gaze. "I *will* however, send the shuttle back to you on autopilot."

Chapter 23

In-Su and Neil stepped out of the simulant's habitat module and into the early morning light. The sun was just promising to rise over the horizon above the jungle, and the soft gold, yellow, and red light was slowly but persistently getting lighter by the minute. They found something ugly about the beauty of the pre-dawn environment. It seemed to be lying to them. This new world seemed so peaceful and so beautiful, as though it didn't know what danger was afoot, and what malice hung in the air. The bomb was set; the fuse was primed and lit. What was the worst though, was that none of the sims could see any way out of it, none had any good ideas about how to extinguish the fuse altogether and prevent the bomb from detonating in the first place.

Ostensibly Neil and In-Su had come out to head towards the airstrip and secure the unpiloted shuttle when it arrived, but at the moment they both felt like they just needed some air, as though getting out of the hab could get them away from the danger that now hung over all of them. Neither one spoke; they were both thinking about what was happening, and how they could potentially avert the coming disaster. Unfortunately no good ideas came to mind for either of them though. They both knew that two forces determined to fight each other eventually usually found a way to.

"Heavy…" Neil said softly to In-Su, as they mulled around outside the habitat module, looking down with their hand in their pockets and kicking the dust on the ground.

"That is certainly one word for it," the linguist offered in agreement.

"This could be the end, In-Su. Can't you feel it? There's enough going on here, enough volatility in the air already, so much in play, so many forces coming to a head which were building for decades before we even woke up and got here... It's like, it's like we're stuck in somebody else's conflict. It's like we just woke up in the middle of it, and just as we start to get our heads around it and start making progress in our own mission, bam!" He snapped his fingers to accentuate the word, "the whole mission could explode because of a conflict decades in the making... All of our hard work, all of that careful and detailed planning..."

"I know..." In-Su somberly agreed.

"I didn't think we missed anything, I *still* can't really see what they think we missed! I think they're just trying to blame their petty and myopic blood feud on us to take the blame off of themselves. I mean if they're right, how could we possibly have gotten so much wrong when we spent so much time planning every detail to such a fine degree, and trying to account for every possible eventuality? What could we really have possibly missed In-Su?"

"We missed the human part of the equation Neil..." In-Su somberly answered upon careful reflection. "We were too fixated on all of the technical aspects of the mission, on all of the engineering problems. We worried exclusively about taking as much technology, information, and culture with us as we possibly could, and as we needed to don't get me wrong, but... but we never really thought about the fact that there would be real people living *on* our blueprints, and *in* our dreams... complicated people, sensitive people... *damaged* people. We instrumentalized living, breathing... *vital* people, Neil. They were people who had to live their entire lives under conditions which we chose for them without adequately thinking about how they could aversely react to that lot in life, and without leaving them behind any of the tools they required to adequately confront what was done to them or what to do when things *didn't* go exactly according to plan. I'm ashamed to say I'm guilty of it myself... I was so preoccupied with the education system and with preserving and bringing with us as much human culture as possible, that I was too fixated on future crew as people without adequately considering them... as *persons*."

Neil just sighed heavily. "You're right of course... In retrospect, what a nightmare it must have been for them. I mean I really can't imagine *myself* being one of the, what did they call it? Children of the void? It's certainly apt... I don't know why I couldn't look forward to see that problem for myself... I mean now that I really think about it, I shudder to think of how *I* would have reacted to being born into that situation... why couldn't I see that before? Why couldn't the original Neil and In-Su see that before we launched this... this mother of all Hail Mary passes? Now that I really think about it, being born into the void and being condemned to die in it with no hope of any other fate being available to me... that's like, the worst thing I can possibly imagine!"

"Maybe we are superior to our progenitors," In-Su uncharacteristically suggested. "Or maybe it's just being here, actually *seeing* the consequences of our oversights and having personal experiences with the people who are ostensibly our victims, perhaps this has sensitized us to the gravity of what we've done."

"Or worse," Neil gravely uttered, to which In-Su looked at him inquisitively.

"Maybe we *did* think about it," Neil continued. "Maybe we understood all too well that there was no fix to the problem, so instead we just worried about the things we *could* control and plan for."

"Hmmm..." In-Su uttered in agreement while nodding his head. He had to admit that as unsettling as the prospect was, it was indeed a possibility. "I have an even scarier proposition for you," the sim further offered. "What if they *did* know, *exactly* what they were doing, but *deliberately* left that awareness out of our programming so that we wouldn't feel any responsibility for it when we woke up? What if there were a lot of things which were consciously and deliberately left out of our programming for a myriad of intended effects of the omissions?"

Neil shuddered at the prospect. Merely the attempt to faithfully recreate his progenitor itself would have been hard enough without any of that kind of manipulation. But In-Su was right, if they wanted to, they could have subtracted or for that matter added any knowledge or quality at all to their simulations, and for whatever reasons suited them whether justified or whimsical.

How was Neil *really* to know just how faithful a simulation he was of his progenitor. Whether or not there was any kind of formal conspiracy as In-Su suggested, the original Neil Sagan could have either consciously or unconsciously misled the simulation team about his memories and innermost thoughts and feelings. For all he knew now, he could be some kind of idealized fiction of the original Neil Sagan. For as well as he *did* know himself in his existential condition, he'd have to admit it was something he couldn't altogether put past himself doing.

It made him wonder about the human condition too. He didn't imagine that this particular dilemma was all that different from the one real organic humans faced in their own lives. How were any of them to confidently know the truth about the world and themselves? How were they to tell the difference between the things they'd actually learned for themselves and the things they'd just been programmed to believe by parents and teachers and the media? How were they to know when their mind was faithfully representing the world to them or when their subconscious was altering how they perceived it with no rational regard for whether it helped or hindered them in the living of their lives?

The two simulated men watched as the shuttle silently glided over their heads in the rapidly brightening sky. They watched as it once again receded over the horizon, which was quite high from their perspective since it was well obscured by the jungle's high canopy.

"We'd better get moving," Neil said, trying to shake his disturbing musings from his mind. "It's still a bit of walk to get to the airstrip."

"There's something that's been bothering me Neil," In-Su said. "Won't Aset and Asari be able to tell that their son is dead? I mean they wouldn't be able to tell that it was Halley pulling the trigger unless there happened to be a satellite overhead at just that moment, but won't they be monitoring his Brainchip and won't it register and reveal to them that he died?"

"Well, yes and no," Neil explained. "They'll certainly have lost contact, but as far as they know it could just mean that his scroll was destroyed. The Brainchips themselves don't have the range to be directly accessed from orbit; they just have enough range to access things like the scrolls within a few meters around them."

"He's *dead*!??" Huli shrieked in shocked agony. "He *killed* him??" He was standing in the doorway of one of the habitats that Neil and

In-Su had previously had their backs to.

"Huli..." Neil pleaded in mortified panic. "Ho- hold on now, just... just calm down for a minute." Neil said with his hand outstretched as if the saying 'stop' with a hand gesture might accentuate his plea.

"Oh no-" he cried as he closed and sealed the door to the habitat behind him.

"WII!!!" Neil yelled as he and In-Su ran over to the hab Huli had locked himself into.

In-Su pleaded from outside. "Wait, please! Don't tell them, you can't tell them yet, not without context, not without an *explanation*!!"

"To *hell with you!* You're not even *people!!* And you would keep something like this from the *real* mission crew!? How *dare* you!!" Huli yelled feverishly from inside the structure.

As Wiremu emerged from the simulant's hab and began running towards them, Neil and In-Su could hear from inside Huli's hab that he was on the comm with Aset and Asari, telling them that their son was dead and that Halley had killed them. From what they could make out Huli was a close friend of Nekheny and was likewise quite close to his parents, especially with being a department head. The two sims continued to plead with him through the wall but they had ceased to be listened to.

As Wiremu arrived and stood alongside Neil and In-Su, all three of their wrist scrolls began chiming in unison with an incoming comm request. It was Asari, and all three exchanged worried looks with each other as the chirping scrolls seemed to ring out deafeningly in the silence of the otherwise tranquil and peaceful morning.

"I think we have to answer," Neil flatly stated with a note of defeat.

"Of *course* we have to answer..." Wiremu snapped, momentarily and errantly lashing out at Neil in frustration. He immediately felt bad about it but instead of apologizing, he opened his scroll.

"How... *dare* you." Asari's face demanded from the small screen. Despite the small display size, there was no mistaking his state. His eyes seemed on the verge of burning through the screen, and his voice was slow and even, despite the way he was visibly shaking.

"Now Aset you've gotta listen to me-"

"No you listen to ME!!!" Aset screamed, incensed. "He was my

son!" he uttered through tears of rage.

Wiremu, did not like his tone. He didn't care who he was, he didn't care what had happened. He was Wiremu *fucking* Tynes. *He* was a principal mission founder. He and his friends, were the living embodiments of the mission itself and he was not about to just stand there and allow himself to be accused of betraying his own mission. He *was* the mission!

"How dare *we*? Just who the *fuck* do you think you *are*?? What the *hell* was he doing spying on the other camp in the *first* place!? This is as much *your* fault, as it is *Halley's*! *All* of this, *every* part of this *clusterfuck* is as much *your* fault as it is *his*!! Yes the clones should never have been made in the first place but as far as I can tell since they *were*, they only ever sought to be accepted so they could peacefully contribute to the mission! It's *you* and *your* kind who have always refused those offers of peace and *kept* the conflict going, it's always been *you* who have escalated things and then *refused* to back *down*!"

"You're defending him? You are defending all of them?" His voice was suddenly cold and distant as though he were now completely removed. He seemed a man who had just had his carefully constructed world view overturned, and was now recalibrating to see where all the pieces fit. He looked down as his eyes darted back and forth. Then, he looked back straight ahead at Wiremu and ominously stated in a cold and eerily even voice: "You're a traitor." He knew exactly what he was saying, and what saying it meant. "You must be defective. You are clearly no longer capable of leading this mission. You don't *deserve* to lead this mission anymore."

Wiremu, quite simply, appeared as though he was about to explode. He softened just slightly though, and just barely enough, when In-Su delicately placed his hand on his shoulder. He gently ran his hand down Wiremu's arm, and softly but deliberately removed his wrist scroll. He walked away, cradling the device in his hands as though it was an explosive which might go off in his face if he jarred it too much. Without a word he left the other two simulants and the small crowd of humans who had gathered around to see what all the commotion was about. In-Su traversed the short distance to the edge of the jungle and entered just enough to be out of earshot of the crowd he had just left.

"Asari," he said softly, "this is an incredibly severe moment. I have… infinite sympathy for your loss. It is… one more senseless and unnecessary tragedy on a list of senseless unnecessary tragedies which is already far too long. I can't even… *imagine* how much you're hurting right now." In-Su certainly could imagine, but he was a sensitive enough person to know that no person in the throes of such suffering ever thinks that anybody could ever possibly understand what it was like to be suffering as they were suffering. The simulation of an aged Korean man was already beginning to cry himself in simple empathy as he was very much sympathizing with how Asari must be feeling in this moment. "But I know for a fact, that Halley and his team did not want any of this either. Of course they were wrong to launch a parallel landing, but it's already done, and they did everything they could to minimize the risk to the rest of us.

"I know it doesn't lessen your loss in any way Asari, but Halley did not act maliciously. He had discovered that there is an indigenous life form here for which we have found evidence of their intelligence. Your son… panicked; he had already killed two and was turning his weapon on a third when Halley fired upon him to defend the indigenous. He *did not know* that it was Nekheny he was shooting at. Asari, for all he knew when he shot it could have been one of his own people who he was firing at."

Asari said nothing; he was still looking through the small screen with intense eyes which were at once distant and burning with rage. Something in his face made In-Su believe that maybe, just maybe he was in some small way getting through to him.

"I know what you want to do Asari… I can see it in your eyes, believe me. But I'm telling you that if you choose *this* path, if *you* make *that* choice… many *more* will die. *Other* people's sons, other people's daughters, many more people you personally care *deeply* about will be hurt and die, and you'll be putting *their* loved ones, *their* parents, siblings, and friends, all through *exactly* the same misery that you're feeling *right now*. Even worse, it'll mean the end of the mission itself, and you know as well as anyone that mission *failure*… means death for *everyone* in time." In-Su swallowed hard.

"Please…" he begged, "*please* don't do this."

Without a word, Asari cut the comm line and the scroll's screen went blank. The great communicator, had failed to get through to him.

Chapter 24

"Front and center, every one of you!" Wiremu bellowed at the rest of the habitat modules. He yelled loudly enough to be sure everyone could hear, and angrily enough to make sure that everyone immediately complied. His military training was asserting itself in the extreme situation. All of the other landed crew members groggily stumbled out of their new homes and gathered in front of the simulants; it was after all still pretty early in the morning. "You too Huli. Don't be afraid; you've already *served* your purpose," he said with a sneer.

Cautiously, Huli emerged with the others from his habitat module and joined the group which was already forming in front of Wiremu, In-Su, and Neil. His initial indignance seemed to have faded away now. He still sported a miserable scowl, but he seemed to have also taken on something of an air of sheepishness. Perhaps now that his assertiveness had indeed served its purpose, he was fully aware that for better or worse he was now stuck down here with these simulants whom he had just so angered.

The crew had formed a proper line facing the simulants and Wiremu walked up and down the line slowly, looking into each of their eyes in turn, one after another. He walked the line using a big branch he'd found in the jungle and had been using as a walking stick, and although he hadn't really had it in mind when he'd picked it up, he now appreciated its equal appropriateness as a beating stick. He remembered an old expression he'd once heard, something about speaking softly but carrying a big stick. Well, In-Su was the soft talker, and he'd failed. *He*, was the big stick. That was *his* job; that's why *he* was here.

Wiremu still didn't know the names of most of the men and women in front of him. He recognized Huli of course, and Armina as well, but the rest were still unknown to him. He was trying to size up their souls, trying to intuit where their loyalties would lie when it really came down to it. Were they more angry or scared? He figured if he could intuit that, it would tell him all he needed to know. Fear was good; fear meant they were still on the mission's side and still afraid of failure. Fear meant there was still something they were afraid of losing.

Anger meant the opposite, anger meant irrationality. Wiremu knew anger all too well; it had long travelled with him like a shadow. Between his military training and experience, as well as simply the passage of time, he'd learned how to harness and control it by now; rarely did it ever control *him* anymore. But these people were young and untrained, anger could still control them, still make them want to burn everything to the ground rather than see their enemies prevail. Scorched Earth angry, that's what they'd called it back home. He didn't know what they'd call it here, but he could certainly see it in a few of their eyes.

"This mission..." he said as he paced slowly in front of the line after his close inspection of those in it, "has now officially split. As a result, I now need to know with absolute clarity who is on who's side. Given what's happened, we can now expect Asari and Aset to launch some kind of assault on Halley's colony site and in order to prepare for it, in order to do what we can to neutralize this threat to the mission and to limit the resulting damage, I need to know now who is on my side; I need to know who among you is still on the *mission's* side.

"Now I will make myself absolutely clear. None, I repeat *none* of you, will be punished in *any* way if you side with Asari and Aset, and refuse to help us. I know very well that life on a deep space ship can socially be very complicated. I know that you've all literally had a whole lifetime to develop complex social webs and personal bonds I can't even imagine and frankly don't really care about right now.

"But I promise you this... this I promise you, and you'd better believe me. If you side with us now, only to betray us later, I *will* execute you *myself* for treason."

Neil and In-Su looked at each other very uncomfortably, and then turned back to look at Wiremu with grave concern. Such a thing was inconceivably beyond the scope of any of the mission protocols, but they daren't question him right now, certainly not so publicly in front of all of the humans. He sounded cold as he made the pronouncement, and they could at least be certain that none of the human crew doubted his sincerity.

"So here it is people, and I'll only ask once. Who is not with us? Who among you cannot commit to obeying our orders without question in service of bringing an end to this crisis with minimal loss of life and destruction of materiel? Let's have it." Five people timidly raised their hands, including Huli. Wiremu was relieved that among them were the four whose eyes he'd found the most trouble in.

"That includes," In-Su added, stepping forward and putting a hand on Wiremu's shoulder, "those of you who don't want to take *any* side in what's about to happen, who refuse to fight, or just don't think you're *up* for a fight." Seven more sheepish hands went up.

"Fine." Wiremu barked. "Split yourself into two habs and find a way to mark them as neutral." The twelve who had raised their hands silently obeyed and made their way back to the habs.

Neil and In-Su pulled Wiremu aside as the rest of the humans mulled about and talked among themselves about the situation. Many of them had just been woken up and still hadn't heard exactly what was going on. "Wiremu," Neil said, "were you serious?"

"About what?"

"About what?" Neil asked back incredulously. "About threatening field executions?"

Wiremu sighed heavily as he looked back at those who claimed to be with them. "Let me put it this way... I really hope we don't have to find out."

Neil and In-Su looked very apprehensive. "Look guys, I'm sure it won't come to that. In any case, Neil I need you to pick a team of three and head over to the airstrip. I need you to link up the industrial atmospheric separator drone and super-fill the shuttle's cryogenic fuel tanks. We need to be capable of orbital insertion as soon as possible."

"Understood," Neil gravely responded. As uncomfortable as he may be, this was indeed exactly the kind of situation Wiremu was here for, exactly the kind of situation for which mission protocols stipulated that Wiremu was in clear command. Neil went over to the crowd of humans, selected Armina Shostak and two others, and together they headed down the road towards to the landing strip.

"As for the rest of you," Wiremu said in address to the rest of their loyal crew as he and In-Su approached them again, "I'm afraid at the moment there's nothing left to do but wait." He looked up into the clear blue of the morning sky as his thoughts elevated to their mother ship in orbit. "They won't be coming *here* anyways…" he said in a lower voice which has as much just to himself as for anyone else to hear.

"Waiting," one of the people in the crowd who hadn't introduced himself yet said with a heavy hearted sigh, "is something we're all too familiar with Wiremu."

"Right," the simulant acknowledged in a low voice, and almost apologetically. "In-Su, come with me please." He led the other simulant back to their personal habitat module, held the door open for him, and then entered behind him. "Time to call Sadhika," he said, and In-Su nodded.

In-Su was somewhat shell-shocked by the whole situation. As familiar as Wiremu was with conflict and aggression, it was equally as alien to In-Su. He was an academic through and through, and he'd never even seen a fight in person let alone been in one. The nastiest conflict he'd ever personally been in was a heated formal debate about who the best nineteenth century Russian novelist was. He felt so far in over his head at this point that he didn't even feel like he could see light at the surface anymore. What's worse, he'd taken his failure to get through to Asari very personally. It was exactly the kind of thing he was here for, and he knew full well that if he'd succeeded, nothing which now came after would have ever occurred or been necessary.

Wiremu thought up a comm request to Sadhika, and within a few moments her face appeared on a screen in the wall of the hab. Wiremu took a moment to be grateful that Asari hadn't locked out their access to the satellites and comm system. Being on the ship he certainly had the power, and Wiremu certainly would have in his situation. He stole a moment to wonder if he had chosen not to or if it was just an oversight due to his lack of tactical training, or if his anger was clouding his judgement. He figured the latter to be much more likely.

"What's up?" Sadhika asked from the screen.

"Asari knows," In-Su informed her in a soft voice.

"Asari's *pissed*!" Wiremu clarified with an odd and slightly frustrated look up at In-Su who was standing be-hind him. "Huli overheard Neil and In-Su discussing the situation," Wiremu elaborated, "and he learned from them that Nekheny was dead and that Halley pulled the trigger. He immediately locked himself in a hab and told Asari, who then contacted us in a fit of rage"

"I see." Sadhika responded. "I saw his comm request to all four of us but I thought it best to let one of *you* answer it since you were all together."

"Maybe you *should* have answered it..." Wiremu suggested. "*I* certainly didn't help. I threatened him..."

"Oh Wii..." the simulant woman responded while gently shaking her head.

"I... I tried to reason with him afterwards, but... but I failed to get through to him," In-Su said sadly, still very disappointed with himself.

"In-Su... this isn't even about us," Sadhika reassured him. It's not your fault you couldn't get through to him... I'm sure if *anybody* could have gotten through to him it would have been you. No, I'm afraid we're caught in the middle of something here that's been brewing for well over a century."

"Yeah," In-Su agreed, but then he added: "in a pot *we* put on the stove..."

Nobody said anything in response to his sentiment. They all knew it was true and none of them had anything particularly helpful to add. Eventually Wiremu broke the silence and continued his report to Sadhika.

"Anyways, I sent Neil to go link up the shuttle to the atmospheric separator drone so it's ready for orbital insertion as soon as possible. I'm convinced that Asari and Aset are going to launch some kind of assault on your position with the landers. I intend to go up to the ship as soon as possible to stop him... any way I can. I doubt we'll make it up there before he launches though, so... you need to be ready."

"What makes you so sure that that's what he'll do?" Sadhika

asked.

Wiremu shrugged despondently. "It's what I'd do..." Again the other two didn't have anything helpful to add.

"So... what do *I* do?" Sadhika asked. She was after all the one in the line of fire now.

Wiremu let out a heavy sigh and rubbed his eyes. "Well, you could fight..." Wiremu answered, to which In-Su audibly cringed. "You've got a weapon, and you're certainly capable of helping Halley and his people defend their position when Asari's forces come, but if you stay with them they'll be gunning for you as much as anyone else over there.

"Or... you could run away. You could disappear into the jungle and take your chances there while you wait it out. I'm not going to order you either way Sadhika, you know as well as I do that we shouldn't be helping *either* side. If you stay you certainly might be able to be some kind of neutralizing force at some critical moment, but... in all reality you're far more likely to just get yourself killed if you stick around. On the other hand we know all too well that the jungle itself is far from being a safe haven either, but... at least there you won't have to get involved or take a side, so.... it's up to you. You're the one who's out there after all..."

Chapter 25

"Catch all that?" Sadhika asked without looking over at Halley. With her permission he had been listening in on their conversation, but out of view of Wiremu and In-Su. They were both sitting in the forward seats of the flight deck in Halley's stolen shuttle.

"Yup." he replied distantly. "I tried so hard… for it to *not* come to this. I was a fool. I should have just killed them and stolen everything I could… I never should've even left them the *option* of coming after me."

"Are you fucking *kidding me*!??" she roared as she stood up and wheeled around to stand over him. She paused, thought about it, and then decked him in the face as hard as she could right where he sat in the captain's chair. She felt eminently justified about it given everything that had happened, not to mention his current attitude. She unloaded with everything she had and knocked him back off of the chair and onto the ground. She shoved him out of the shuttle and onto the ground below, booting his ass on the way out. It felt *so* satisfying; she *so* felt like he'd had it coming for a long time now.

"What the fuck is the *matter* with you??" she said as she chased after him, continuing to kick him along the ground as he tried to scurry away. She wasn't kicking him as hard as she could or as hard as she'd punched him in the shuttle; it was more like she was kicking at him to further accentuate her words and to clearly drive her points home. "Who the *fuck*, do you think you *are*?? Are you *completely* fucking cracked?? Can't you see that *all* of this is *your fault*!? *You* started *all of this*!!" she screamed at him.

At this point most of Halley's people had gathered around to help him. Søren and Ishtar grabbed ahold of Sadhika and held her back.

She feigned to struggle to get away at first, and then stopped trying to advance on Halley and instead forcefully freed herself of their hands, which they allowed once she'd signalled that she was truly finished with her assault. Halley stood up, and then wiped some blood off of his face with the back of his hand and looked at it. He then glared at Sadhika as the blood continued to accumulate on his face out of his mouth and nose.

"Yes your kind was treated unfairly Halley, and yes if you'd stayed there would have continued to be a lot of tension, but it *never* would have come to *this* if you hadn't *wanted* to strike off on your own, if you didn't have something to *prove*. *You* could have *chosen* to make it *work* Halley... but instead you ran away. Instead you instigated open conflict; you took your grievance and incited a level of hostility which things never had to get to! Don't you get it? Their mistreatment of you is *their* fault, but your response, this situation that we're *all* in now is *your* fault, *regardless* of what *they* did in the *past*!"

"How is what I did any different from what you did when you left Earth?" Halley coldly asked. "I left the main group to go off and create my own smaller colony, knowing full well that there were inherent risks. *How* is that any *different*?"

Sadhika looked at him with an expression which was a mixture of hurt, confusion, and rage. She made a rush towards him again like she really wanted to kill him this time, but Søren and Ishtar held her back again. "How *dare* you," she roared with daggers in her eyes. "For *starters*, nobody had to *die* for *us* to launch. *We* never stole resources and put everyone *else's* survivability at risk! *We* had the *consent* of our parent population; *our* mission was *celebrated* the world *over*!! *We* were a god damned high water mark of *humanity itself*!!" she screamed. "How *dare* you make *any* comparisons be-tween what *we* did and what *you've* done, how *dare* you try to attach your petty personal griping to the noble *dream* that was the New Horizon *mission*!?"

"Let her go." Halley's friends obeyed and let her go again. "Sadhika... we were both running away from *something*. I know full well what the mission was *really* all about... you were running away from the emptiness of your lives, running away from the boredom of paradise, running away from an empty life left meaningless without struggle and challenge. You created the mission just to alleviate your own petty existential boredom, and without a thought you condemned *us* to the void in the process."

"No. No, you're *wrong* Halley... Maybe some of the crew were running away from any number of issues they may have had back on Earth, maybe Markus was running away from something Halley, but not us... and yes, it *definitely* turns out that we should have done a *much* better job of selecting the right crew to launch with... but *we* weren't running away. We mission principles were *not* running away Halley; we were vibrant, creative, and curious people. I've never been bored a day in my life Halley, and neither have Wiremu, Neil, or In-Su. There was always more to do, always more to learn, to discover... to experience! We built this mission to create *more* opportunities for people to learn and to discover, not to just... not to just distract ourselves from boredom! What a sad and narrow view you have of something *so* glorious...

"Dammit Halley, that's *never* what this mission was all about, that was never what motivated us to put it together in the first place at all! It was an eminently peaceful mission, we were a beloved *part* of the world we came from, an outstretching hand of Earth culture and civilization itself! We stood on the *shoulders* of all of the giants who came before us and we reached out as far as we could on their behalf, and for *everyone* in our past who dreamed equally grand dreams but never had the means or technology to make it a reality! And now it's all coming apart, that glorious dream is *evaporating*... and all because of *you*, because of *your* childish and myopic pettiness. You can't see beyond what you are because you can't even see past the bridge of your own fucking nose. You're a selfish coward."

This time it was Halley who rushed forward towards Sadhika like he wanted to kill her for what she'd said. She happily raised her fists again in kind, ready to beat the shit out of him all over again, but this time it was Halley who Søren and Ishtar held back for his own good.

"*Fuck you*!" Halley screamed as his friends held him back.

"Oh, *very* mature," Sadhika retorted, taunting him with an overdramatic eye roll as she planted her fists on her hips. "And that goes for *all* of you too," she said, surveying the crowd. "You're *all* children; you're *all* spoiled little brats and selfish cowards. It's *easy* to run away Halley," she continued, turning back to him now, as his friends released him on his promise that he'd be cool. "It's *easy* to justify doing whatever you already wanted to do in the first place, it's so *easy* to go it alone, and then blame somebody else for what you 'have' to do," she accentuated the word gesturally with air quotes. "It's so *easy* to provoke someone you want to kill anyways and then claim self-defence when you 'have' to kill them." Again she used air quotes to accentuate the word. "But you know what's *not* easy Halley? You know what's *really* fucking hard?"

She paused for dramatic effect, just long enough to sense them all leaning forward ever so slightly to hear what her answer was. "*Peace,* Halley. Peace, is *very* hard. Peace takes a lot of *work,* peace means talk with people you *hate;* it means compromising with people you completely and fundamentally disagree with. Peace, is so much *harder,* than *war.* Peace, means the courage to *take* abuse without retaliation to gain the moral high ground over your aggressor and to avoid betraying what you believe in. Your *father* understood that..."

Halley looked up at her, surprised. "Didn't he?" she asked, but he didn't answer. Instead he looked away.

"You know what makes war and conflict so damned wasteful Halley?" she asked in a soft voice. "The fact that it can never last forever. Eventually there's nothing left to fight with and peace inevitably breaks out again, and usually without anything ever really being resolved by the fighting. War is just a break from peace, and can only ever end again with a return to peace, which makes every moment of war in between nothing but a terrible senseless waste.

"And you know what Halley? Peace isn't just hard, it's also the *only* way to actually *change* anything. The courage to take abuse in order to gain and keep the moral high ground over your enemies is the *only* way to ever really change *anything.* Violence only reinforces hate on both sides, only *shame* can really create changes in the behaviour and attitudes of your oppressors.

"Only peaceful cooperation or competition can ever really build anything of *true* value. Hate and division... can only ever destroy; it can only ever destroy something like the dream that was the New Horizon's mission. You think Wii, Neil, In-Su and I agree about everything? Hell no! We're *very* different people and we had *very* different ideas about *critical* aspects of this mission! Wii, ironically enough, *hated* simulants and was mortified not only over having them on the ship at all, but *especially* over having one created of himself, but you see we all *compromised.* We all got things we wanted and we all had to live with things we didn't. And you know what that got us?" Again she hesitated for dramatic effect, to allow a moment for everyone to ponder what her answer might be.

"Here." she stated simply. Her point seemed to land as poignantly as she'd hoped it would. *"Here."* she said again more softly and more sincerely. Everyone in the small crowd suddenly looked somehow uncomfortable, as though something they hadn't wanted to see about themselves and what they'd done had suddenly been revealed to them against their will and exposed for everyone to see. She'd succeeded in shaming all of them, all but one. Halley just blinked.

"We have to get ready." he stated indifferently as he turned and headed for their much shorter road leading to their colony site. Before he could get very far though, an alarm started sounding off from his wrist scroll. He flicked it open and saw that it was the warning alarm he'd programmed to alert him via the mission network if there were any launches from the New Horizon. He turned around and looked at the crowd he'd started away from, and then more deliberately at the simulated woman who'd attacked him. "None of that matters anymore Sadhika," he said. "They're coming." There was still much anger in his eyes, but it was now shaded with a not insignificant amount of fear as well. "They just launched the landers… every single one of them.

"Alright everyone, listen up." It was a few minutes later and Halley was laying out their defensive plan after consulting with Søren and Ishtar. "As you know, we only have four shotguns and one laser rifle." As he addressed the group, they were all using their standard issue hunting knives to whittle spears out of appropriate sticks they'd found in the jungle.

"You two," he said as he pointed to two of his people for whom Sadhika had never learned names, "you see that ridge over there just beyond the tree line?" he asked while pointing out the area he had in mind just adjacent to the airstrip, "I want you there with the laser rifle when they arrive, but for now just find a place nearby to wait. They'll be able to spot our positions with the satellites, so wait until the last moment to take up your final position so they can't know exactly where you are when they actually get here. Use the rifle's multi-spectral scope to cover us as best you can from the elevated position." The two he'd been speaking to nodded their understanding.

"Now," Halley continued, "We have every reason to expect that they might be brash enough to land right here on the airstrip directly, but we can't be sure. They also might be foolish enough to attempt to come down right through the jungle canopy some ways away and try sneaking up on us. Either way we can be sure that they know we know they're coming. They'll all be armed, and with ten landers completely filled if they all survive the descent... they'll outnumber us more than four to one.

"Nyala, I want you to take a shotgun and take up a position inside the shuttle that'll allow you shoot anyone who tries to come through the door, and then leave the hatch open. The shuttle's hull will prevent the satellites from seeing that you're in there.

"As for the rest of you, set your PANs to notify you after each pass of a satellite. Once we know they're nearby, reposition yourself after every pass so they can't know exactly where any of you are when they actually attack. Take up random positions about the perimeter of the airstrip where you can ambush them with your spears as they enter or exit the clearing, and try to get your hands on *their* weapons to use instead since we only have enough shotguns to hand out to a few of you.

"People... I'm afraid this is all we got. I put us at this disadvantage deliberately; I was hoping that it would avoid anything like this from ever happening at all, but... well here we are. Are there any questions?" Nobody spoke up. "Does anyone have any suggestions?" he then asked.

"Yeah," Sadhika answered. She was standing at the back of the crowd with her arms folded and with a sour expression on her face. "Surrender." she emphatically suggested. "Completely," she further elaborated. "Call Asari and tell him that he wins, that they can have the shuttle back and that you'll personally take responsibility for everything that's happened here. You could do that and avoid *everything* that's about to happen. You could save the lives of all of these people here who are about to *die*."

Halley looked at her with a strange expression on his face. He cocked his head to the side slightly as he blinked at her. He didn't understand.

Chapter 26

"There they go..." Neil said as he watched the landers leave from the ship on the shuttle's heads up display. The three simulants were in the shuttle, with Wiremu and Neil in the front seats, and In-Su between them looking over their shoulders as he leaned against the backs of their chairs. They could all see the same thing, so Neil was more idly commenting than actually informing anyone of anything. There wasn't much any of them could think to say at a time like this, so they just watched.

Neil had successfully linked up the industrial atmospheric separator to the shuttle, and its cryogenic oxygen and hydrogen tanks were now almost full. It was still a slow process, but now they expected to be fully fueled and ready to ascend to orbit within the hour. It was impossible to try to launch any earlier, since even with all of the auxiliary fuel tanks bulging full there was only just barely enough fuel to actually achieve orbital velocity; there wasn't much margin for error.

The three morosely watched the image being projected onto the flight deck window as all ten lander drones were ejected from the New Horizons' launch tubes in regular succession, one after another. Whether deliberately or by oversight, Asari and Aset had still neglected to block their actions from being monitored over the network which linked together all of the mission's shuttles, landers and scrolls via the ship.

From his seat to the right of Wiremu, Neil with a thought took control of one of the New Horizon's four mounted telescopes and directed it towards the landers as they entered the atmosphere. After he put the feed up on the HUD, the three watched as one by one the landers gradually became engulfed in energetic plasma as they were slowed down from their orbital velocity by their frictional interaction with the planets' atmosphere. Finally, the last one streaked over the planet's horizon and out of sight of the ship's telescope. The landers were similarly cylindrical in shape like all of the other drone landers, but they didn't unfurl to a larger shape and were simply hollow inside with two levels. Five people could be uncomfortably shoe-horned into each level creating an emergency descent vehicle for ten people.

They were hoped to never need to be used, and were expressly for emergency departure from the ship in the case of some kind of disaster. Mission protocol called for everyone to be ferried down in the shuttles, especially since they could take far more people down with them on every descent trip than they could ever take back on an ascent to orbit. The landers only existed in case there was some kind of catastrophe, like if the New Horizon itself was doomed or both shuttles were somehow destroyed or otherwise rendered incapable of ferrying passengers down to the planet, whether en-route or after their arrival.

"Wii?" In-Su asked, "I don't um... I don't know what to hope for here. I don't know... who I want to win, or... or if I really want anyone to win. Part of me doesn't want *either* side to be... to be *rewarded* for what they're doing." Kim In-Su had always been an eminently peaceful man. He'd never been an explicitly avowed pacifist, but in his life he'd never encountered a situation where violence had been the only, smartest, or best option. He understood on an intellectual level that in some extreme situations and circumstances violence can be left to one as their last recourse, but such cases and examples had always been so academic to him. A line from Isaac Asimov's 'Foundation' book series had always stuck with him, that 'violence is the last refuge of the incompetent.' The sentiment had never failed him to date, in fact it had never revealed itself to him as being anything other than perfectly accurate.

"I know In-Su... I know." Wiremu replied as he brought up a stylized terrain map on the interior of the shuttle's window, and then waited for icons representing the landers to reappear once they passed through the dangerous burn phase of their descent. He knew that it was long odds that every one of them would survive the inferno.

"I have far too much experience with just this problem from my Peacekeeper days... You go into a conflict zone, and all you see are bad guys... both sides are usually clearly in the wrong somehow. Don't misunderstand me, sometimes there really is a clear ag-gressor and a clear victim, but too often... too often it's just a bloody mess, just like this... Too often it's a situation where the question of who's guilty and who's innocent... become a nonsense question a long time ago. Far back in time, further back than anyone can usually remember, one side had to be the first to wrong the other sure, but... but by the time we showed up there were always enough atrocities committed on both sides to make it not really seem to matter anymore." He sighed heavily, now lost in very painful memories, and in deep dread that this situation was as intractable as some of the ones he could all too clearly remember.

"What I can tell you though In-Su, is that nothing productive can ever happen until the destruction finally stops, until one or both sides finally decide to pull back from the brink and realize that they have nothing to gain from keeping the cycle of violence going anymore... that was after all the whole idea behind peacekeeping missions in the first place. Sometimes you've got to kill a few more people who refuse to get the message, but the whole point is to grind the killing to a halt overall and prevent either side from being able to gain anything by committing any further violence. Once it's started... it quickly doesn't really matter who started it in the first place or who is right or wrong anymore. Once the violence starts, nothing matters but ending it. Only when the fighting stops can thinking and talking re-sume... My advice In-Su, is to not even try to find a side to root for, just hope for as few deaths as possible before the killing finally stops."

"They're coming out of the clouds now," Neil observed. Together the three counted the landers as their respective infernos dissipated and the signals of their transponders could reach the satellite network again. One by one they counted as their icons showed up on the map of the planet's surface. One, two, three, four, five, six, seven, eight... and that was it. They waited and waited in agonized anticipation, but the last two landers never reappeared on their screens.

"Oh no..." In-Su uttered with tears in his eyes.

"Twenty people…" Neil uttered in shock.

Wiremu only winced, and calculated in his head that overall, their expected lander failure rate was now at par. "Touchdown in thirty minutes." he grimly observed.

Although somewhat intermittent, between the ship's telescopes and satellites, they often had real time video of the landers as they tracked them down to the surface. When video was unavailable, the image on the HUD switched back to the stylized map with their transponders locating them on it. Although direct video was intermittent, the system was designed to be able to provide an exact location for every piece of mission equipment at all times.

The three watched in horror as the landers attempted to come down through the canopy of the jungle several kilometers away from Halley's landing strip. Between the intermittent video feed and the locating transponders, they were able to tell that three of the landers didn't make it through the canopy and instead became lodged within it, and just being stuck that high up was going to be dangerous enough to the crew inside. There was a good chance that the thick tree tops would block the hatches on the landers from fully opening, and there was no easy way for anyone to climb down from that height since the bottom four meters of the trees' tall trunks were quite bare of any branches to climb down on.

At one point while an overhead satellite provided direct imagery, the three simulated men had to watch aghast as two of the three stranded landers burst into flames. The rocket halos which were built to set them down gently on the surface in a clearing, instead ignited the drier parts of the canopy around the lander. They could see a few people emerge from the flaming capsules, but as they exited they were all engulphed in flames themselves, and they either quickly became motionless in the burning canopy, or they fell out of sight. Those that disappeared presumably fell all the way through the tops of the trees and down to the ground far below after hitting other branches and trees on the way. The only luck they could be said to have, was that the jungle was lush and damp enough that the fires didn't grow into a much larger wildfire. They continued to burn in the area around the landers, but the fires blessedly did not spread. The three simulants were silent as they considered the fate of the men and women trapped in those landers, squeezed tightly into small metal boxes, and then roasted alive for so ignominious a cause.

Chapter 27

Sadhika waited restlessly for the madness to descend upon her. She had been in intense situations before, real pressure cookers in fact, but never before in her memory had her life been so directly and overtly under threat. It was an awful kind of restlessness; the kind one only feels when one's life is on the line with no meaningful control over how it's all going to turn out. Put more simply she was scared; she was in mortal fear for her life.

She had been monitoring the descent of the landers on her wrist scroll and had been forced to witness all of the same horrors as her fellow simulants. She was still rather in shock at the idea that dozens of people had just died, dozens of *her* people. Nothing in the memories lent to her by her progenitor had in any way prepared her for such a thing. Commercial and professional stress she was supremely familiar with, and was cool as a cucumber under that kind of pressure, but she just didn't have the kind of job... the kind of life which meant that anybody under her supervision or direction had ever died on the job. Part of her knew with great certainty that it would all hit her like a brick later on, but at the moment she was only numb to what had just happened.

On some level she also knew far too well that they would not be the only people to die today. A massacre was brewing, and she lamented a thought which she had, that maybe those who burned up on entry were the only lucky ones today. At least they didn't have to suffer being burned alive, or being shot by their brothers and sisters, or being stuck forever on the ship above or dying of starvation or exposure below after the mission was a complete failure.

At first she'd thought it would be a good idea to stay with Halley and take up a defensive position with his people. She didn't have any intention of actually fighting, but she'd hoped that being there she might be able to talk some sense into him or his people. Before long though, she realized it was utterly futile. She understood that all of them had stopped listening to her a long time ago. Upon that realization, she'd abandoned them and headed out into the jungle as Wiremu had suggested as an alternative. She knew it wasn't much safer out there but it was somewhat safer, and in her heart she found that she'd far prefer to be mauled to death by some kind of mutant panda dinosaur than have to suffer being killed by (or worse having to kill) one of her own people. She loaded what gear she'd brought with her into her backpack, picked up her shotgun, and walked off on her own into the jungle.

Many had protested her taking the weapon with her, including Halley himself at first. Being so minimally armed, just that one shotgun would have made a huge difference to their overall defensive capabilities. Sadhika made it clear though, that leaving them her shotgun was totally unacceptable, because her intentions were to remain absolutely neutral. To leave them her personal weapon would be tantamount to supporting their side, and she solemnly swore that if they took it from her by force she would in response commit total and unwavering support to the forces which were coming against them. Although she chose not to mention it because she didn't think it would penetrate much with them in their situation, she was worried about her safety out in the jungle, and she knew that her odds of surviving *that* danger went up significantly if she were armed.

The truth in Sadhika's heart, was that it was an idle threat to suggest that she would ever join the other side against them. She absolutely just didn't have it in her to raise a weapon against any member of her crew, and she *did* still think of them collectively as *her* crew, even *if* they were factionalized and about to start killing each other. They were all her crew, all her people… all her children in a way, and that's what hurt her the most, the idea of people she cared so much about killing each other, and her being totally unable to do anything to stop it. Beyond needing the shotgun for her own protection in the jungle, she didn't want to leave it behind, because she knew that it would be used to kill members of her crew. She found that unacceptable. She brought the weapon in; and she felt it was her duty to make sure that she brought it out with her again.

After leaving Halley's camp, she found herself very much alone out in the jungle. By now it was early nighttime again, and it was as eerily and disturbingly silent as it had been before, except again for the mysterious shrieking of one particular species. She realized that the night must have been what Asari was waiting for and what took him so long to launch his incursion. They must have been waiting for the dark-ness. Fortunately for Sadhika though, with her PANEs on she could clearly see in the dark just as well as if it were brightly daytime, with the exception of her vision being reduced to black and white or in this case, black and red. The cameras in her PANEs picked up low light and infra-red signatures to compile as faithful as possible a representation of what was out in front of her, even in pitch black.

The nights were dark on Haven... as dark as nights ever got on Earth, but every night. There were no artificial lights to create light pollution, and there was no large luminous moon. There were only the stars and the grand expanse of the Milky Way. It was usually dark, but on this night off in the distance Sadhika could see a dim dancing glow which she intuited must be the fires from the landers trapped in the jungle canopy some distance off. Not too long after noticing the fires, she began to see the faint signatures of the surviving crew approaching her position. It was either dumb luck, a terrible careless mistake, or a subconsciously deliberate choice, but for whatever reason she had managed to walk away from Halley's camp in the direction of the area where the landers had come down.

When she realized they were coming her way, she immediately started moving straight to her left to avoid running into them as they advanced towards the landing strip. Once at what she considered to be a respectable distance, she issued a thought command at her scroll to begin broadcasting an identification signal which would show up in their PANE displays. It identified her as Sadhika, and as a neutral non-combatant. It was her hope that by announcing her presence from a respectable distance they would choose to ignore her, or at the very least not shoot her if they did happened to see her and suspect that she might be one of Halley's people waiting to ambush them. After all they knew she'd been at Halley's camp, and she hoped that they could intuit exactly what'd happened, that she'd gone out into the jungle because she didn't want any part of the conflict.

After she began broadcasting the signal, she watched as they seemed to pause to discuss something, and then resume their advance on Halley's airstrip. She hoped that her plan had worked and that they'd identified her, decided that they didn't need to worry about her and moved on. Her own personal identification protocol was heavily encrypted, and they must have known how unlikely it was that anybody else could be out there pretending to be her for whatever reason.

She was relieved when they seemed to ignore her and continue on their way towards the airstrip. When they advanced to about the point at which she'd originally detected them in the first place and turned to her left to avoid them, she saw a sudden and panicked eruption of chaotic flailing and thrashing. She zoomed in with her PANEs and to her horror was able to see what was going on. Three of the horned panda dinosaur things had attacked the humans. One large beast was accompanied by two smaller ones, which she figured to be children of the larger one.

Sadhika watched with dread as she saw the first person get gored by the larger of the three beasts. When she saw the first of the landing party shot down by another human trying to hit the animal and missing, she stopped thinking and took off in a flat out run towards them. She watched as a second person, and then a third was gored by the two apparently equally vicious smaller ones, and then as two more were trampled by what she took to be their parent.

If she'd had time to think and back rationalize her actions after the fact, she'd say that it wasn't a violation of her neutrality to help them because they were facing a planet related threat which wasn't part of the crew's conflict. In truth though, she was absolutely intervening in the conflict but just in an unexpected way, and deep down she probably knew it on some level. The animals here were just an inherent hazard of the terrain this battle was to take place on, and the more of the landing party which were taken out by the jungle before even getting to Halley, the greater his chances of ultimately triumphing. Sadhika's ultimate truth though, was that she just wasn't the kind of person who had it in her to watch people in trouble without trying to help if she had the power to. She was a helper, a builder, an engineer… a doer. That's why it was so hard for her to accept that she couldn't help either side of the conflict in the first place.

There was wild and undisciplined firing of lasers and shotguns all over the area, and the closer she got the lower she had to keep her head until eventually as she arrived she found that she had to lie right down on her stomach to avoid being hit by any stray buckshot or weaponized coherent light beams. Tossing her backpack aside and flipping over on her back, she quickly emptied her shotgun of the buckshot rounds it was currently loaded with and slipped them into the left outer thigh pocket of her coveralls. She then took out the solid slug rounds she had in her right thigh pocket and loaded them one by one into the weapon until it was full. Turning back over on her belly, she waited patiently and as calmly as possible (which was apparently far calmer than any of the landing party), until she had a clear shot at one of the beasts with reasonable assurance of not hitting any of the colonists. When she felt like she had the shot, she fired.

She was deadly accurate, hitting the animal exactly where she'd intended to on its side, above and behind its front shoulder where she figured its heart should be if its physiology was in any way analogous to similar animals back on Earth. Whatever she did hit within the animal, it immediately fell hard to the ground with a heavy thud. Its limbs flailed some in pain and panic, but less and less as it died, until it stopped moving altogether. The two smaller animals, presumably scared off or confused by the sudden loss of their parent providing direction and security, promptly ran off. One appeared to be slightly wounded and limping a little from a previous grazing shot, but the two nevertheless made off with reasonably good speed.

Sadhika stood up, perhaps a little too soon and too quickly given the circumstances, and all fifty remaining colonists turned their guns on her. She put both her hands up and held her gun high above her head in conciliation, and began walking backwards without saying a word. None of the humans said anything either; they'd all seen that it had been her who had just saved them by killing one of their attackers. Given that, none wanted to stop her by force, nor were any of them particularly inclined to have a chat with her at this point either. They kept their aim on her as they watched her retreat back into the thick darkness of the jungle, and then when she had retreated enough for their comfort, they regrouped and continued on towards their enemy's airstrip.

When they had advanced enough, Sadhika moved in behind their position to follow them to the airstrip. She still had no intention of involving herself, but she was now determined to at least bear witness to the encounter. She thought, still *hoped*, that at some critical moment she might be able to intervene to stop the madness, to maybe clue them in that one side had already clearly won or that they'd both already lost and that nobody else had to die today. She thought that maybe just by being around there was a chance that she might somehow be able to save a life or two.

She heard the first gunshot, and then a violent eruption of gunfire ensued. The laser rifles made little sound and none whatsoever from a significant distance, but the sound of conventional weapons fire was unmistakable and the sound chilled her to the core. People were dying, *more* people were dying, *her* people...

In addition to the heavy booming of the shotgun blasts, she could also hear what sounded more like harsh popping sounds, which she immediately identified as the handguns being fired. It was then that she realized that they'd brought with them all of the small arms Wiremu had ordered them to print for the landed crew to protect themselves against the panda dinosaur things. It made complete sense at the time, but now she found herself decidedly wishing he'd never given such an order. They'd never have had enough time to fabricate them for this incursion if they hadn't already started making them for more legitimate purposes.

Suddenly she became aware of a rustling behind her. Despite her listening intently to the battle taking place not far away, the sound was close and ominous enough for her attention to be immediately and completely drawn to it. The sound became steadily clearer and louder, and startled Sadhika into turning around to see what was coming her way. To her shock and horror it was a mass of squiddies. There seemed to be a hundred of them at least, and that was only what she could see from where she was crouched down; there could have been many many more. She was afraid for them, they seemed to be walking right into a combat zone and into a slaughter, and what's worse their presence would only add to the confused fog of war which already existed at the airstrip. Little did she know, she should have been more scared *of* the squiddies, than *for* them.

Confused and afflicted with a simulation of rampantly surging adrenaline, Sadhika hunkered to the ground and laid herself down in a nook between a fallen tree and the ground to shelter herself as they passed by, at least she was *hoping* that they'd just pass her by. She had no idea what could possibly be prompting them to this strange behaviour, but she felt lucky when they didn't seem to notice her at all and just passed her by. It took several minutes for the entire herd to pass over her, and they seemed to be moving at a pretty good speed too. She figured that she'd been right, there seemed to be at least a hundred of the creatures passing by her as she hid. Once they had passed her though, she was consumed with dread as all doubt was removed from her mind that they were heading directly towards the airstrip and the battle, for some reason she couldn't even begin to understand or explain.

Not long after they'd passed her by she heard a distinct change in the sounds coming from the battle at the airstrip. The faint vestiges of shouting she'd heard had until this point been simply anger, clearly emblematic of the kind of rage one would expect from those in the throes of a violent bitter struggle. She heard a sharp decline in the number of shots being fired which was then punctuated by shouts which sounded more like those of confusion and panic than what she had been hearing before.

She then heard a sharp uptake in the gunfire, which then began trailing off again until it eventually died off altogether. Several times when she thought she'd heard the last shot fired, she'd find that she was wrong and another would ring out in the night as she listened intently, wondering if this time it would indeed be the last. Now all her ears could detect in the silence of the night was a slight ringing simulation of what humans heard when the loudest sounds in their environment were blood passing through their inner ear and the residual vibrations of hairs in their cochlea. There was an eerie stillness in the air; it was as though the horrific battle had never taken place at all. She was about to begin advancing on the airstrip to investigate what had happened, but as she began to move she was prompted to resume hiding when she saw the squiddies coming back towards her.

As they passed, she realized that it was unlikely that she had just happened to be in the way of one group's approach to the airstrip, and she came to suspect that many more such groups might have approached the area at the same time but from a variety of directions. If that was the case, there could have been thousands of the creatures on the scene, and she still had no reasonable hypotheses whatsoever about what might have drawn them to the battle in the first place. Unless...

It took several minutes again for the creatures to pass her by, but this time when they'd passed, she didn't waste any time once she felt safe. She made her way as safely as she could through the jungle and towards the now ominously silent airstrip. When she was just about at the clearing, she tripped over something and nearly fell to the ground. It was a body. When she looked down she could see in clear red and black relief that there were in fact more than half a dozen bodies stretched out in front of her, both human and squiddy. They were all silent, all motionless. She did her best to respectfully step around them.

Once she was out in the open the sight was devastating and it hit her like somebody had kicked her in the gut. Bodies... bodies everywhere... she was sure that there must be even more which she couldn't see around the inner perimeter of the jungle, but with the aid of her PANEs, she could see the ones out in the open as clearly as if it were daytime.

Out of nowhere she was frightfully startled by the roar of the shuttle's engines powering up. Her understanding of what the sound meant filled her with dread as she immediately turned and ran towards it. As she arrived all of the craft's running lights came on, and as she ran around to the front of it she was momentarily blinded by the vessels brilliant headlights.

Ripping her PANEs off and blinking away the sharp pain of such a dramatic and sudden illumination, through her squinting she could just barely resolve Halley sitting in the pilot's seat looking haggard and intense. She could also see one of his people whose name she didn't know in the co-pilot's seat but she hardly noticed this other person. It was Halley she was focused on like a laser beam. Defiantly she put her hands on the front of the shuttle as though she could stop it from moving with her own meager strength. She looked Halley directly in his eyes and slowly shook her head at him. Without words she was ordering, asking, pleading, *begging*... whatever might possibly make him stop.

"Don't..." she whispered, knowing that there was no way he could hear, but also knowing that he must be able to read it in her eyes. "Don't *do* this Halley!!" she roared as loudly and angrily as she could, while banging her fists hard on the front of the shuttle several times with desperately violent intensity.

But Halley just blinked at her. For a slight moment he seemed to find her behaviour curious, but he soon snapped out of it. His eyes narrowed down with an ominous intensity that chilled her right through to her artificial bones. She could see that he was in the most devastatingly dangerous state a human beings could ever find themselves in, at the intersection of hate and rage.

Chapter 28

"Oh no… the other shuttle's taking off," Neil reported in deep dismay. In response Wiremu issued a thought command to put a communication request through to Sadhika.

"Oh shit," In-Su uttered after another satellite passed overhead of the battlefield and revealed in disturbing detail the outcome of the fighting. It was still dark, but they could all see the devastation for themselves. Between radar, locator beacons, and the infra-red signatures of the still relatively warm bodies, a clear if unsettling picture of what had happened was easy to see. The airstrip was littered with dozens of bodies. The only place where bodies couldn't be seen was the narrow strip down the middle which Halley had cleared so that he could take off in the shuttle. Neil and Wiremu were too stressed and distracted to notice at the time, but it was the first time either of them had ever heard In-Su curse. Ordinarily he looked down on profanity as a failure of vocabulational imagination. These however, were not ordinary circumstances.

"Oh shit indeed…" Wiremu added more coldly as the first light of dawn broke over them and out the front window. For now it remained pitch black over at the site they were monitoring and where the battle had taken place. "Come on Sadhika…" he uttered with increasing fear for her. "Come on, answer… Don't you *dare* be dead." He added in an angry whisper.

Wiremu brought up her locator beacon, and the display they were watching zeroed in on her location and zoomed in with a blinking crosshair. They were all panicked momentarily when they saw her lying motion-less on her back, but breathed a sigh of relief when she reached over to flick open her wrist scroll. Wiremu wondered why she had waited so long to answer.

"I'm here." she answered despondently with a ghostly vacancy in her voice. Her face appeared on the left front window of the shuttle's flight deck while the right window continued to display a semi-transparent overview of the battle field and her location within it, compiled from different information streams.

"Wii... Halley." she said distantly. "You have to go after Halley. Now." She was lying on her back in the exact spot which the shuttle had been parked until Hal-ley had taken off in it. She seemed profoundly dazed, to the others she gave the appearance of being completely emotionally drained.

"The other shuttle?" Neil asked. They all knew what it meant if he was returning to the mothership at this point.

"The other shuttle." Sadhika miserably affirmed.

"We'll come get you first," In-Su suggested, though in his mind it was much stronger than a suggestion. He was deeply concerned for her; he'd never seen her act or sound this way before.

"No time." she replied, softly rotating her head back and forth.

"She's right," Neil confirmed. "It would take us hours to fully refuel again for an orbital insertion after picking her up, especially without a super charger."

Wiremu turned to address In-Su in the back seat. "I'm sorry In-Su, but she'll be fine. She'll certainly be safer than us!" he added with a bit of a harrumph. He then noticed the empty seat across from In-Su and then looked up into the sky through the ceiling window. He undid his seat restraints, stood up, and then opened the door behind the empty seat opposing In-Su and exited the craft.

Wiremu put two fingers to his mouth and whistled loudly. "I'd like to speak to everyone here who is neutral, *now* please." he said loudly and authoritatively. Ten or so people were working on and around the airstrip and new industrial area. They had all spent their entire lives waiting for this moment. For a long time they'd been preparing and practicing all of the things they would need to do upon their distant and eventual arrival. Now in this crisis, with nothing they could do to avert or alleviate the situation, many had simply reverted to the tasks and duties they would have otherwise been responsible for had none of this ever happened. They didn't know what else to do, and it provided a certain comfort for them. It was a physical manifestation of their hope that everything which had happened to get them here had somehow not been in vain.

They acted this way in part as a result of simply not knowing what else to do, but it was also a hopeful gesture, continuing to work on the mission was itself an implicit hopefulness that things would work out, that the crisis could be averted and the mission at some point resumed. These were crew members who had no strong allegiances to either warring faction at this point, people for whom their allegiance remained to the mission first and foremost. As requested, all of the crew members who had previously affirmed their neutrality gathered in front of Wiremu again in the early morning light.

"The battle was a senseless bloody slaughter," Wiremu grimly told them. "Everyone is dead, almost half of the ship's entire crew, including *most* of the adults of breeding age. You fourteen are in fact, basically most of the breeding adults left." It only occurred to him a moment before he said it, and he looked at these people a little differently now as a result. Neutral, loyal, already on the planet and reproductively capable, he now saw them as the most important humans alive in the universe. In a worst case scenario now, it could very well all come down to just them alone in the alien wilderness with only what hardware had already been deployed for them.

"The worst part though people, is that it's not over yet. Halley and possibly a few others have taken the other shuttle back to the ship. Their intentions are... impossible to know for sure at this point, but given what's happened and his unwillingness to communicate with us... we think it's fair to assume his intentions to be hostile. We have the other shuttle, it's ready to ascend... and we intend to stop him. We intend to put a stop to this madness *today*, one way or another. At least... we're gonna try. We don't have time to go get Sadhika first, so... we have an extra seat on our shuttle. I'm looking for a volunteer. You all know my background... this is a peacekeeper mission, not an assault. It will be dangerous and there's a good chance of you getting killed; our objective is not to help either side win, but to save the mission itself. Our goal is explicitly, and simply, to end the conflict however we have to, with as little further loss of life as possible."

Before anyone else could raise their hands to volunteer, Armina

Shostak stepped forward. "I can't allow anyone else to volunteer Wiremu, as the keeper of combat this is *my* duty, and my duty alone. I've *literally* been training my *entire* life for this. This is *my* life task, finally, and I am happy to serve."

Wiremu smiled at her. She had just demonstrated herself to be his kind of woman. "Very good. As for the rest of you... as you were."

The simulant put his arm around Armina's shoulder as she passed him on her way to joining him and the others in the shuttle. "Thank you," he said. "Let's go."

The two were greeted by In-Su and Neil who had watched the entire exchange from the shuttle's hatch. "Welcome aboard," Neil offered to Armina, who only smiled back at him.

"What's the weapon situation?" she asked as Wiremu headed for the captain's seat.

"One for each of us," Wiremu answered her, "three shotguns, a laser rifle, and my own personal side arm."

"Well at least there's that..." she replied.

"Why don't you take the co-pilot seat Armina," Neil offered. "I think I want to sit back here with In-Su."

"Sure," she answered, and then slid into the seat beside Wiremu, who smiled at her in acknowledgement. Neil likewise took his seat across from In-Su in the back and strapped himself in.

Wiremu rushed through the pre-flight checklist. His complete and absolute professionalism forbid anything less, even in this situation.

Hanging under the wings were four inflatable bags which were torpedo shaped, with a cylindrical body and a rounded cone on either end. Of the two large bags under each wing, which very nearly touched the ground when completely full, one held liquid hydrogen and the other liquid oxygen, the same rocket fuel which had been launching humans into orbit from a planet's surface for over three and a half centuries.

As the fuel in the sealed system was used, vacuum pressure retracted the bags back into the wings, and they were fully retracted after the vessel left the atmosphere, but long before orbital velocity was achieved. It was an extraordinary amount of fuel which was required, but it was a truly extraordinary speed which was required to allow them to fall so fast sideways that they perpetually missed the ground in order to achieve orbit. For shorter point to point flights across the planet's surface though, the auxiliary fuel tanks weren't required and thus weren't deployed, since such ballistic flights required far less speed and energy. However, if for whatever reason on a point to point trip one wished to carry more crew than could fit into the flight deck, the main internal fuel tank could be purged to carry crew (as in a descent from orbit), and in such a configuration the auxiliary fuel bags could serve as the primary fuel tanks.

"Launch." Wiremu stated unceremoniously as he hammered the throttle immediately after finishing his abbreviated checklist. They rocketed down the airstrip and lifted off with only modest room to spare, and only a few meters clear of the canopy as they passed over top of its edge. The shuttle's engines powered back to slowly gain altitude in as energetically conservative a manner as possible. In this phase of their ascent it would take twenty minutes or so to achieve the required altitude for an orbital insertion burn.

Chapter 29

"I've been doing some calculations in my head In-Su..." Neil remarked to his old friend.

"Oh?" the simulated man asked as they waited for the shuttle to gain sufficient altitude for their orbital insertion burn.

"Yeah..." he acknowledged with a sense of grief. "Well, you know how the fundamental premise of the mission was always based on the idea that with total success, we should be able to institute a human population with approximately the same level of technological sophistication as the civilization we left from, as in Human Earth circa 2164."

"Yes..."

"Well, that was based on the assumption of *everything* going *perfectly*, on all of our equipment being *perfectly* deployed within expected failure rates, on finding a *perfect* colony site with *perfect* conditions, on our whole knowledge base being *perfectly* preserved and under-stood, et cetera, et cetera, et cetera."

"Right..."

"Well, what I'm thinking about now, is that... well see, the more advanced a civilization, the more people are required to sustain it, and to... you know, keep everything running. I mean, you just can't expect a hunter gatherer tribe of just a hundred and fifty people to develop a space program! You need a colossal distribution of labour, you need a bunch of people doing rocketry, a bunch of people doing material science and chemistry, a bunch of people studying human physic-ology... and a ton of people doing a thousand other things. You need a veritable army of people mass producing all of the things that support the people doing *those* things, *and* the people who do the fine crafting of all of the components that can't be mass produced!"

"What are you getting at?" In-Su asked.

"Well we brought two of everything because... well, for example if one of the shuttles blows up, we can't just make another. It took the whole civilization of Earth to develop the knowledge and know-how required to build something this complicated... and every single sophisticated element it employs."

In-Su continued to look at him expectantly.

"Sorry In-Su, I... I don't think I really have a particular *point* here, I'm just... I guess I'm just thinking out loud."

"Well no, I... I think I know where you're going," In-Su reassured him. "I mean if everything had gone great otherwise, but the whole three hundred person crew had been magically dropped on the planet with no techno-logy whatsoever, we'd have been lucky to establish a Victorian era level of technology from scratch completely on our own. Even if we were able to drop a library drone with every bit of information we could possibly need it could only help so much. And then with only a couple of dozen people left on the planet without any technology at *all*, they'd probably be reduced even further to something more like a *medieval* level to techno-logical sophistication if they were *lucky*. It just comes down to a question of there being enough people to do enough different and varied jobs to produce a sufficient level of complexity."

"Exactly. So our long term goal for this mission was to land, and for the humans to reproduce quickly enough to generate a large enough population to sustain a 2164 era level of technology, and be able to make new versions of everything before all of the original equipment we brought with us started breaking down. The hope was that we'd have a broad enough population base to be able to reconstruct our technology for *ourselves, before* it all started breaking down. We hoped, again just for example, that we'd be able to construct a brand new shuttle for *ourselves, before* the ones we brought with us were degraded beyond repair.

"So I guess what's bothering me... is that it's only now finally dawning on me that that scenario is *completely* out the window at this point. It's now all too safe to say that it's completely impossible for the mission to make it through that population and complexity bottleneck, and for the humans here to be able to sustain the technological sophistication we arrived with. I've just been wondering… I've been wondering what exactly that ultimately means."

"Well let's see…" In-Su suggested. "A couple dozen people without any technology could sustain a medieval level of sophistication, while the full intended crew compliment of three hundred was supposed to be able to sustain 2164 era level of technology…"

"Right, so like I said, I've been doing a little math in my head, and we're basically talking about a seven hundred year spread give or take, and divided by three hundred people… that gives us two and a third. So with those calculations, every single person we lose, effectively reduces the level of technological sophistication we'll ultimately bottom out at when everything is said and done… by twenty-eight months."

"How does that help us?" Armina asked from the co-pilot's seat after swiveling around to face them.

"I… I guess it doesn't." Neil admitted.

"Now you know what *I* have to put up with," Wiremu remarked to Armina. "He just finds it interesting to figure out stuff like that at inappropriate times."

Ignoring Wiremu's comment, Neil then offered to the woman: "At this point Armina, if we're *lucky*… in hundreds of years, your descendants will look at this shuttle and your scroll as mysterious and powerful artifacts which their people *used* to know how to make but no longer understand, like the pyramids to later Egyptians, and the Roman roads and aqueducts to later Europeans…"

"Maybe," she suggested before hopefully adding, "maybe knowing that will only serve to *motivate* them to recapture their former glory, maybe knowing that they came here from somewhere else will serve to motivate them to find their way back to wherever they originally came from."

"Or they could choose to completely forget that they ever came from somewhere else in the first place," In-Su soberly added. "Modern human originally evolved in East Africa, but wherever in the world they eventually found themselves, they always wound up believing that that's where they'd always been since the beginning of time…"

"It could make a big difference for them if the New Horizon stayed up in the sky though…" Neil imagined. "It could serve as a reminder of very important things; it could keep alive a certain urgency to figure out how to find their way back to it... Without a significant moon it would be the brightest object in the night sky and would move unusually fast across it... it'd be hard for them to ignore. Could you imagine if some people were permanently marooned on the ship? Eventually the two populations would lose the ability to communicate with each other, and there'd be two completely independently developing human populations only a few hundred kilometers away..."

"Alright, that's enough," Wiremu chirped in frustration. "Can we please focus on the existential threat *currently* facing us?"

"Yes of course Wii, I'm sorry," Neil offered. "You know how I am; when I'm nervous... the mind wanders."

"Yeah I know, and it's alright. But now it's time to focus. We're ready for our insertion burn."

The shuttle engaged its rocket engines to full thrust, and the four people inside were pressed into their seats. The strength of the acceleration triggered a swivel mechanism in the rear seats, and Neil and In-Su were swung around to face forward so that they were pushed back into their seats instead of being pushed sideways out of them. The forward facing position made it easier for their bodies to evenly distribute the heavy force load, though it was a greater concern when there were human bodies in the seats.

The shuttle powered out of the atmosphere which made their conventional flight surfaces usable, and dumped an inferno of fuel out behind them to achieve the ludicrous relative speeds required to sustain orbit against the planet's gravity. The shuttle was vibrating as violently as it always did during this phase of the ascent, but it seemed more ominous this time than it had before. So much had gone wrong already, that it wouldn't have surprised anyone onboard if this time the shuttle simply blew as an exclamation point to the events of the last couple days. The darker thought which lurked deeper in their minds though, was that at this point so quick and unceremonious a fate would be far too easy, and that thus far they had not proven themselves to be that lucky.

"I've been trying to contact Aset... well actually I've been trying to contact *anyone* on the ship..." Wiremu had to speak quite loudly for the others to hear him over the continual roar of the ships rocket engines and the resultant vibration of the entire craft. "But there hasn't been any response."

"I'm not surprised," Neil answered. "I wouldn't want to talk to us either if I was them... They must know everything we know... They must have seen the after-math of the battle as clearly as we did and seen for themselves the other shuttle launching."

"You know..." Armina tentatively suggested, "if we do get there, and for whatever reason Halley is still on approach... this shuttle's laser cannon *is* powerful enough to take them out."

For several moments all that could be heard was the roar of the engines and the vibration of the shuttle as the three male simulants considered what she'd said.

"They could also start shooting back at us if we don't completely take them out with the first shot..." Wiremu considered out loud, "or if we make them too nervous that we're going to," he added. "They could even start firing on New Horizon. That is a completely unacceptable risk. I'd rather dock and take our chances with a close quarters firefight on the ship than risk an all-out dogfight around the New Horizon. As Neil described all too clearly only a few minutes ago, the shuttles are just too valuable at this point without the landers and we absolutely *cannot* risk losing them."

"At, at least facing them in person we can try to talk to them," In-Su offered, for a moment surprised at how much he had to speak up to be heard over the noise. "Even if they won't listen..."

"We're personally at far greater risk if we board the ship," Wiremu agreed, "but... it's far less risky for the mission overall, there's far less chance for total catastrophe if we dock and try to pacify them onboard, whether we can talk them down, or have to *take* them down."

"I agree." Neil stated.

"For what it's worth I agree as well," Armina added.

In-Su added nothing.

"You know it's funny," Wiremu added, "you two and Sadhika," he laughed, "thought arming the shuttles was a terrible idea but I insisted we did. Now here *I* am, the one who insisted we *have* the cannons, saying it's too risky to *use* them."

Neil and Armina could see the humour in it, but In-Su didn't find it funny at all.

Chapter 30

The roar of the shuttle's powerful rocket engines died off as abruptly as they always did, and its passengers once again experienced the weightless feeling of bumping back and forth between seat and restraints. There was always, even in so extreme a situation as this, such a peaceful and transcendent feeling of release upon arrival in orbit. After the energetic violence which inserted one into it, the contrasting relative absence of stimuli; the silence, the loss of weight, and the blackness out the window above the planet was always striking. This sensation was simultaneously overwhelming when paired with the view of the sprawling expanse of the planet beneath them, forever forbidding the shuttles inhabitants from shaking the overwhelming sense of scale wrought on their senses; their absolute smallness and insignificance in the grandest of contexts.

"We're in the right orbital trajectory, but we need to catch up with them," Wiremu told the others. He lit the much smaller and weaker orbital jets which were nestled between the three more massive and intimidating insertion boosters. Even with these smaller thrusters he only needed a twenty second burn to sufficiently accelerate his relative speed to inevitably catch up with the mother ship which was currently over the horizon. The shuttle then continued on with its increased velocity, steadily closing the distance to the ship as displayed on the flight deck's HUD.

The shuttle had thrusters which could adjust its three dimensional orientation in space, but to significantly increase or decrease their orbital velocity, such as was necessary to catch up with the New Horizon, these smaller rocket jets were required. These same rockets were the ones which were just powerful enough to sufficiently slow the shuttle's orbital velocity for it to fall back down into the atmosphere instead of continuing to sail over top of it.

As they gradually caught up with the ship, when it came over the horizon it was still too far away to be able to see with the naked eye. Their displays were able to indicate the exact moment for them, but Neil still pointed the New Horizon out with his finger when he was able to see it for himself, and he was only able to spot it as early as he was because of their instruments telling him exactly where to look. The landscape before them was so vast, and the ship he was looking for so relatively small, that it would have otherwise taken much longer for him to be able to successfully point out the ship without risking only imagining having seen it.

"Look," Wiremu said as he pulled up the other shuttle's location on the display. "The other shuttle's already docked."

It was still too far away for them to be able to make out the much smaller shuttle pressed against the mother ship, but the crosshairs on their screen betrayed its presence nonetheless.

Neil opened a general communication request to the ship. "Aset? Asari? Please respond..." Silence. "This is Shuttle One, calling anyone on the New Horizon, please respond."

He opened a general hail and tried again. "This is Neil Sagan aboard Shuttle One in orbit and on approach. I am trying to reach anyone who can answer; I repeat anyone onboard the New Horizon, please respond." There was only silence in response.

"Nothing." Neil stated as he thought the channel closed, more to himself in frustration than to any of the others present, all of whom could hear the absence of response as well as he could. There was no response, but as they moved closer they could begin to resolve Shuttle Two with their own eyes; it was docked at its port in the central engineering section.

"There should be over a hundred and fifty people left on the ship..." Armina offered. "It should mostly be the young and the old left at this point, and most of them *must* be non-aligned in all of this and just... hiding out. I'm sure they would have responded if they'd heard the hail."

"Unless..." In-Su began, but he couldn't finish his thought. All four in their mind filled in the blank with horrible scenarios in which there was nobody *left* to respond.

"They must have blocked the ship to ship comm channels..." Wiremu speculated.

Neil turned to Wiremu. "Well boss, what's the play?" Wiremu reached back, grabbed his headrest, and pulled as he stretched out his legs and feet. He was thinking.

Much to their surprise, before he could come up with an answer, the comm line opened and they heard Aset's panicked voice. It was *just* her voice; she was not transmitting any video. Even if Asari had locked out ship to ship communications, as matriarch Aset's command codes would have been able to override the lockout for her own use.

"Neil? We need your help," she stated, sounding panicked. She was whispering, and she appeared to be just outside the heavy door to the bridge.

"What's going on?" he asked.

"It's... it's bad. Halley is cutting through the airlock; I don't even know how he's doing it! But, but... we hardly have any weapons left, most of the people left on the ship now are *children*!! We sent every able bodied adult down to take the second site, we... we don't have *anything left*!" She was panicking, almost hysterical.

"Aset why won't Asari answer us?" In-Su asked. "Why are *you* talking to us in secret?"

"He... he doesn't trust you. He thinks you must have helped Halley to win the battle, he's worried that you're just here now to help him retake the ship, he's... he's not himself."

"I should hope *not*!!" Wiremu exclaimed with a rising indignant anger. Armina put her hand on his knee as if to soothe him a little and remind him that getting angry wouldn't help the situation. This tender gesture from Armina surprised Wiremu a little, but he was too distracted to give it much thought at the moment.

"I'm... I'm scared," she said. "I don't... I don't know what to do."

"Unlock the other airlock, Aset." Armina softly and compassionately implored her. "These men are here to help you."

"You'll... you'll help us?" she asked, in some nexus between surprise, hopefulness, and fear.

"Absolutely not." Wiremu answered almost reflexively, and in contradiction to what Armina had said. The other three in the shuttle looked at him in bewilderment. "No Aset. We will not help you defeat Halley. We are *not* going to pick sides here. We have not, and we *will* not. But I promise you that if you let us onboard, if you unlock the airlock for us, we *will* do whatever we can to protect and secure the mission. The *mission,* Aset. Don't you remember?"

"Yes." She replied. As a child, she had believed in the mission blindly and in a way, she still did. She'd been taught since before she could remember that it was the meaning of life itself, that it was more important than any of their individual lives. It was the reason why they lived and died; it was the singular purpose of their existence. With everything that had happened since, her faith had somehow become confused and corrupted. She'd allowed herself to be misled into believing that everything her and Asari had done had been in service of the sacred mission, but the death of her only child, and now Wiremu's harshness, had just shaken her to a horrid realization.

She could see now in agonizingly clear detail how she had betrayed the mission and violated its very spirit. She thought that her and her people were the last true and virtuous defenders of the faith, but now she could see that her side's actions were as much a betrayal of the sacred mission as her enemy's were. A part of her could now remember that something far more important than the immediate conflict was at stake. The monumental efforts of hundreds of lives, and a dream hundreds of years in the making, was all about to be unceremoniously thwarted and cast aside. Wiremu and his people were the embodiment of everything of value which she could remember. She now understood why there were simulants included in the mission, why they existed at all; they were here to remind them of who they were if they lost their way; they were prophets sent to them by their sacred founders.

"That means," Wiremu continued, seemingly able to see in her eyes the profound revelations taking place, "that once onboard our goal will be to end this conflict with as few lives lost, and as little damage to mission property as possible. That is all I can offer you; it's all I would ever promise."

Aset started to cry. She knew what she had to do, but it required her to betray her husband and patriarch. As much as she understood that it was ultimately worse to be betraying the mission, it was still hard for her. It was taking time for her revelation and newfound under-standing to cascade its way through her psyche and recalibrate all of her decision making algorithms. The hardest part for her, was the realization of her personal blame in everything which had happened. She'd stood in solidarity with her husband for all of the terrible decisions which had brought them to this moment. She'd stood beside him even when she was uncertain, even when she thought he was taking things too far.

"Asari…" In-Su implored her, "consider the alternative. Of the options currently available to you, which will you least regret tomorrow… and for the rest of your life?"

A deep part of her was now agonized to understand that now, after a lifetime of hate, her side was just as responsible for everything that had happened as Halley's side was. What now left her truly chilled though, was her fear that her husband was at this point too far beyond reach. She knew that he was too far gone in his anger and self-righteousness to ever be able to come back from the brink the ways she was; she knew he could not be reached the way she had been. Aset had wanted to find her way back, but she knew that Asari had no such desires. He was at war. The why didn't matter anymore; all that mattered to him now was winning, vanquishing his enemies and defeating those who had ever dared to defy him. She had seen it in his eyes, and it was the fear he instilled in her as a result which prompted her to sneak away and contact the sims in the first place. She was now also terrified of how he'd respond when he found out what she'd done.

"I don't want to risk trying to do it remotely…" she stated despondently, "I'll meet you at the airlock." Her voice was shaking. "What's your ETA?"

Wiremu looked down at his instruments display. "Approximately six minutes."

"I… I think I can make it by then… and before Halley gets through."

"Aset you're doing the right thing," Neil tried to reassure her, "I promise."

"I know." She didn't seem particularly comforted to know it though. "I'm gonna hold you to that six minutes Wii."

"Asari, I swear I do not have it *in* me to let you down. I *will* see you in six minutes."

Now close enough, Wiremu flipped the shuttle up end over end so that they were now upside down relative to the position they had previously been in, with the planet up above their heads and the New Horizon somewhere behind them. He thought activated the twenty second burn which would cancel the speed he'd added to their orbit to catch up with the mother ship in the first place. Once the short burn was complete, their speed relative to the ship was zero and they orbited perfectly in parallel with the larger craft.

When he once again flipped the shuttle up and over, they again found themselves facing the ship but this time holding a steady relative position a little over a kilometer behind it on the port side. Using the far less powerful compressed air thrusters, Wiremu slowly closed the gap. He then cancelled this more minute forward motion again with the forward facing thrusters in the shuttle's nose.

As nimbly as any master who had performed such an operation so many times they could practically do it in their sleep, Wiremu slid the shuttle into position in the long crevice between two of the four long narrow engineering section cylinders until it was holding position just off of the airlock. With a few final bursts of air, the daughter craft gently rested against the airlock, and strong magnetic seals held it in place while manual hooks and cranks mechanically anchored the two vehicles into one jointly orbiting assembly. The whole operation could have been performed on autopilot alone, but it could be argued that Wiremu's abilities, as a sim based on a veteran pilot and subtly augmented with an autopilot's capacities, made his abilities superior to any autopilot known to exist.

Whether or not this meant that he himself was the most sophisticated autopilot in the known universe, was a question that neither he nor the human being he was a simulation of, had or ever would have had the slightest bit of interest in considering. They just weren't that kind of man.

Chapter 31

Sadhika lay flat on her back looking up into the early morning sky, and pondering her many failures in life. Not even the other sims who were her closest friends in the universe, or anyone close to the original Sadhika back on Earth, really had any idea whatsoever just how hard she could really be on herself. She readily acknowledged that her harshness with herself was part of what had made her so successful back on Earth, but it also had a bad way of incapacitating her in moments of truly profound failure, moments like this.

It was quite remarkable she reflected, that she had been simulated so completely. To fully simulate and capture the true essence of a person, the best simulators back on Earth exhaustively investigated three primary axes of personality. They studied the person the subjects thought themselves to be, the person those who knew them best knew them to be, *and* the person who their behaviour revealed them to *actually* be.

This last axis was best revealed by detailed mapping and study of their brain activity patterns in conjunction with their virtual identity which included the things they searched and the media they consumed. By painstakingly analyzing their Brainchip and PAN records, the researchers could ascertain who somebody was in the privacy of their own mind and when nobody was watching in a way that self-reporting could never capture. People after all, habitually and routinely lie to themselves as much as they do to *others* about the kind of person they are.

If one were to simulate a person based on any one of these axes in isolation, the simulation would inevitably be a failure, or at best incomplete. Oh it would certainly mechanically function as it was built to, and in all the most superficial ways it could fool many people, but it would not *truly* be the person it was meant to replicate in any real sense. It could never fool those with any more than a passing familiarity with the original person, and stood up to very little close scrutiny. Persons after all, are not any of these axes of identity alone. People are not just the person others think them to be or who they perceive themselves to be any more than they are just the person who their intimate behaviour reveals them to be. People are all of these; people are none of these.

People keep secrets, wittingly or not, from those whom they are closest too. Weaknesses, vulnerabilities, and darknesses which they never want anyone else in the world to know; this is what one's virtual identity and presence reveals them to be. Assessing other's views of who a person is reveals how they behave in the world, but this is usually remarkably different still from how that same person perceives their own behaviour. Those who observe us closely usually have a different explanation for our behaviour and way of being than the ways in which we would explain away our own behaviour. Both explanations in isolation are always incomplete at best, but when taken as complementary they can reveal surprisingly accurate assessments of what the true essence of a person really is on a more fundamental level.

Sadhika was despondent; utterly paralyzed by her sense that she was responsible for all of this, if not directly then certainly indirectly. She kept thinking about how she created the conditions for this to happen, she had *personally* failed to project the problems that had arisen en route and to accommodate for them. The way she saw it, she couldn't even offload much of the responsibility onto the other sims. Sure the original idea for the mission in the first place had been Neil's, but she'd been the money behind it, she was the real facilitator. Granted she certainly couldn't have pulled off the mission just by herself, after all it took far more than money alone.

She wasn't even sure if she'd have been particularly inclined to *try* to put the mission together if she hadn't met the others though, and been infected by their passion. It was all four of them who had come together to do something which none of them could have ever done on their own, something they all had considered truly extraordinary. That's why she'd gotten involved in the first place... for the extraordinary. She'd already accomplished so much in life; she was starved for exciting new challenges. The New Horizon mission seemed to her the potential for an ultimate crowning achievement on top of her already legendary career. Once upon a time she'd been very proud to know that the mission never could have happened if it weren't for her contributions. Now she was left to surmise that at this point it might have been for the best if it hadn't happened at all, given how it all seemed to be turning out now.

Which all left her here, a bitter failure lying profoundly depressed on the surface of an alien planet, possibly condemned to be alone on it forever, or until her machinery finally broke down, whichever came first. If both shuttles were damaged in the conflict currently taking place in orbit, with all the landers already down, there would be no way for anyone else to ever come down to join her or for her to ever return to the ship. That was only a problem though, given the assumption of anyone left alive onboard for her to commiserate with over the grim reality of their situation when it was all said and done. For the moment she'd forgotten about the people left at the primary site half a world away, and even if she'd remembered, left alone to fend for themselves on an alien planet after living their whole lives on a ship, she wouldn't have given them much chance of surviving anyways.

Failure. All this bitter sound and fury... for nothing. Even if the other sims succeeded in retaking control of the ship and the mission... she was left to wonder at what cost. They'd already lost too much, too many had already died and too much of the mission had already gone off plan. Too much equipment was likely in the middle of being destroyed at this very moment. With regards to the last wish left to her by her progenitor, to be extraordinary and to outshine her star… she had to conclude that she'd failed. Even if the others were successful at this point... too much was already lost for the mission to ever be properly put back on track.

She heard a moan, and her attention and focus snap-ped back to reality. Was that faint hope she heard calling out to her? She bolted up into a sitting position, supporting her torso with her hands on the ground behind her. Where had it come from? Somewhere to her right she thought… but nothing was moving. She heard another stirring, but this time to her left. Sitting up and focusing, she was immediately able to localize the rustling of a body just a few meters to her left. It was Søren.

She leapt to her feet and rushed over to his body and knelt down beside it. She could tell he was breathing, and now quite obviously so. "I thought you were dead!" she exclaimed. He was still unconscious and incapable of responding, but she was incredibly relieved to have someone to speak to regardless of whether or not he was conscious enough to hear and understand her. "Why aren't you dead..." she asked him, though obviously more to herself than of the unconscious man.

She got up to check on the other bodies around her. Many were still all too clearly as dead as dead could be, and some too obviously so with very gruesome physical injuries, but some of them were alive. As far as she could tell none of the squiddies were showing any signs of life, but some of the humans were *alive*!!

She ran over to the makeshift shelter the rebel group had created after their landing; it was off to the side of the clearing they'd made for the landing strip. After frantically rifling through the haphazardly piled heap of supplies they'd brought with them, she found their medical kit and took it with her back to Søren. Among many other things Sadhika was a trained paramedic, and like Wiremu with his piloting, her simulated actual training and know-how were subtly augmented by software from the android doctors on Earth and the coffin shaped automated medical units on the ship.

In these devices one would lay down to be scanned and after being assessed, treated with anything from topical application of an ointment to open heart or brain surgery if deemed necessary. Medical technology had progressed to the point where it was quite unusual indeed for so dramatic and invasive measures to be required though. Medical intervention was always much less invasive the earlier any problems were detected, and complete understanding of human biochemical physic-ology meant that the body could usually be compelled to perform for itself most of the corrective measures which used to require dangerously invasive procedures. Several of these drone medical chambers were permanently installed on the ship, as well as two single unit drone landers, which were presumably still waiting patiently in their launch tubes up on the New Horizon.

Although she'd never really thought about it, if called upon in a moment of need, she would discover that not only was she a perfectly qualified paramedic, but a fully qualified surgeon and general practitioner as well. Once back on the ground beside Søren, she opened the medical kit and popped a vial of liquid mild stimulant into an adjustable transdermal.

After adjusting the dose, she firmly held the device's round applicator ring to the skin of his neck, and pressed the button. A small amount of the standard dilating vapour filled the sealed void between his skin and the main bulk of the device. This vapor greatly increased the permeability of his skin, and after a moment the calibrated amount of stimulant was released into the void and with some gently applied positive pressure, was all absorbed through his skin and into his bloodstream. It was quickly taken up by the main vein and artery in his neck which took the chemical up into his brain, down to his heart, and through the rest of his body.

After only a few seconds, his eyes shot wide open and began frantically darting about before calming down, composing themselves, and then quickly surveying their entire field of view before settling on Sadhika's face. She'd given him a modest dose of a mild stimulant, one known to be difficult to have any significant complications with. The dose she'd given him was essentially the equivalent of him drinking an entire pot of coffee all at once. She was glad to see that it worked, and that so far there didn't appear to be any ill effects as a result of giving it to him.

Søren sat up alertly much as Sadhika herself had when she'd heard him stirring, and set himself to work trying to newly orient himself in space and time after being unconscious. She watched as his brain cued up all of the information he needed to understand his situation, how he'd arrived where he was, and what it meant for him to be there. "What happened?" he asked.

"You tell me," Sadhika replied. "By the time I made it here, you were all... well I *thought* you were all dead." She looked around and then added, "most of you still are."

"I wasn't shot..." he said as he started feeling all over his body for possible points of injury.

"No," she agreed, "but when I checked on you earlier I couldn't detect a pulse, and… and you didn't seem to be breathing either. I was sure that you were dead. I thought you all were," she repeated as she looked around and was pleased to see several more bodies stirring to life.

"The squiddies..." Søren said, still groggy.

"I know. They almost ran me over on their way to the battle."

"The last thing I remember... is several of them coming right at me. They'd leapt on top of me before I could shoot them... I don't remember anything after they hit me. Sadhika, we were losing... we were about to be totally overrun, but then this whole area became flooded with those squiddies... Now I remember, I saw them leaping and dog piling onto others too before they got to me."

"You're saying you lost consciousness as soon as they touched you? You don't remember any bites or stings or anything?"

"That's how I remember it, yeah."

Sadhika pondered the possibilities for a few moments. "Maybe they secreted something through their skin... some kind of toxin they can selectively cover their skin with as a defence, or in this case... offence. It would make sense for them to have some kind of defence like that; it would serve them well against those panda dinosaur things... which we really need a name for by this point now that I think about it."

"Well... it sounds strange, but yeah, that would explain what I saw and... what I experienced."

"Maybe it's *supposed* to be lethal but is only *nearly* so for you humans. Maybe it really did nearly kill you. Like I said, you sure *seemed* dead when I examined you."

"I feel like I *was* dead..."

"Right after I heard the guns stop, they left the scene right away again and I had to hide to avoid them a second time... I wonder what provoked them..." she wondered out loud. "Maybe it was something about the sound of the weapons fire itself... maybe they already associate it with their fellow creatures getting killed. It could be a lot of things," she remarked. Clear across the airstrip, she was comforted to see another person cautiously and gradually get up onto their feet and look around. "Now that I think about it... the nights are eerily quiet here. Maybe that's why... Maybe for whatever reason the squiddies attack anything making a lot of noise."

"Well if you're right," Søren said, now looking around for himself as well and seeing the others stirring, "it certainly wouldn't be the strangest thing about this planet so far."

Chapter 32

Wiremu cautiously tried to open the airlock door. "She did it," he reported after discovering it to be unlocked. He then slowly proceeded through.

"You smell that?" Neil asked from behind him as the air of the shuttle and the ship began intermingling.

"Yeah... hard not to." Wiremu replied as he pulled and pushed himself through the circular portal. Once through he held a railing with his right hand and wedged his right foot between another railing and the wall. In the absence of gravity this allowed him a stable enough position to help the others through, or if necessary to shoot his weapon. He helped Neil through the airlock who then took up an equivalent position himself on the other side of the door. The grip points they were using were located all around the circular tube like structure they were in since in this part of the ship there had never been, and would never be, any kind of gravity at all whether genuine or simulated.

"Smells like burning," In-Su remarked as he emerged from the shuttle a little too eagerly and nearly floated past the other two sims. Before he could though, they both grabbed him and arrested his forward motion.

"Gunpowder and burned insulation off of the wires in the walls..." Armina offered in explanation as she exited from the shuttle behind them. "There's been a firefight here."

"So... do we uh... need to worry about being um... you know, engulphed in flames or anything?" In-Su asked, trying to sound nonchalant. He was self-conscious over how the other three around him seemed to be remarkably calm and restrained in the extreme and dangerous situation. As soon as he finished speaking he realized that he'd significantly overcompensated and felt rather like an ass for it.

"No, no fire risk In-Su, not in this part of the ship anyways," Neil answered. "Fire can't really persist in micrograv. In a gravity environment the hot air of a fire rises and pulls in fresh cool air at its base which further fuels it. In the absence of gravity, fire just burns in a ball until it's finished consuming whatever fuel it had around to begin with. After that there's no convection to keep it oxygenated so it's impossible for it to sustain itself or to grow larger."

"Shh." Wiremu ordered and the other three quieted down to listen along with him. They were at the end of a narrower six meter tube which intersected the much longer and wider access tube laying along most of the engineering section, and providing access to the fuel and cargo pods, as well as the shuttle ports.

Most of the habitat ring where people lived was quite beautified with every effort taken to make it as pleasant and liveable as possible. In somewhat stark contrast however, the zero gravity engineering section was entirely Spartan and had a certain brutal architecture to it, with bare metal grates, dull silver foot and hand holds, and only the most basic and functional lighting. On the opposite side of the tube they were currently in, which led from this main corridor to the shuttle's docking port, was an identical mirrored airlock for the other shuttle which they could clearly see from where they were floating.

"Stay behind me, and stay quiet," Wiremu ordered. "Armina you take the rear. We're going to go investigate the other airlock and assess the other shuttle. If it's still operational we need to send it down to Sadhika while we still can, just… just in case." He thought about it, and then surmised that it really wasn't necessary to finish his thought. They all knew what possible outcomes he was referring to. Holding up his shotgun in front of him with his right hand, Wiremu progressed forward with his left hand and both feet, moving from one gripping point to the next. He reached the intersection with the main engineering access tube, and cautiously peered up towards the nearer forward end where the fusion core and recreational zero gravity bubble was located, and then back down the long corridor to the far rear of the ship where there was engineering access to the ion engines.

"Smoke." he said. "More smoke." Over the length of the corridor he could see a haze which he couldn't see before with a restricted field of view. It was thick enough that he couldn't quite make out the far end of the corridor. One by one they crossed the intersection, first Wiremu, then Neil behind him, In-Su, and then finally Armina.

They could all feel an oppression of danger. The last time they'd spoken to Aset, she'd reported that Halley was still trying to cut his way through the airlock. He'd clearly already made it through, but it could have been the very minute before they opened their own airlock, or he could be long gone up to the habitat ring. If he was still around, they had no way to know how he would react to seeing them there. They had no way to know what state he'd be in; he might just ignore them, or he might be so far gone that he'd shoot at them as soon as he saw them. There was just no way to know.

As they got closer to the other airlock, it became increasingly apparent that it was badly damaged. There was a crescent cut out of the side of the airlock door that intersected the mechanism which locked it closed. This meant that it was impossible to lock and seal the airlock door in order to launch the shuttle.

"Well I guess that would in part explain the smoke..." Neil observed as he touched the damaged airlock.

"Yeah..." Wiremu added, "it also means that we can't launch the shuttle down to Sadhika. There's no way to seal this airlock after it disengages. The shuttle itself is the only think keeping an atmospheric seal. If it were to disengage this whole section would vent out into space."

"Well then let's hope nobody remotely issues that command." In-Su plainly remarked.

"We should evacuate this area immediately if that's a risk," Armina advised.

"I've got a better idea," Neil offered, "though I wish Sadhika were here to help. There's got to be a way to manually destroy or otherwise physically disable the mechanisms that would disengage the shuttle. I mean it's securely winched down, it would require a mechanical process to release the tension..." He waved open his wrist scroll and looked intently at it for a few moments as he investigated how to do such a thing. "Mmkay... it doesn't look like it should be too hard."

Neil removed a wall panel beside the airlock and looked back and forth between what he saw in the wall and the schematic on his scroll.

"It would be best I think," In-Su offered, "not to make a mistake Neil. Could you not easily vent *us* into space if you're wrong?"

Neil looked back at In-Su in somewhat playful disbelief. "Thanks for the vote of confidence." He looked over at Wiremu with a look which asked if he should proceed or not.

"If you're confident," Wiremu answered, "it's the prudent thing to do."

Neil nodded and returned his attention to the wall. He traced a particular wire with his fingers until it reached the mechanism which if commanded would release the winch that mechanically maintained the seal between the shuttle and the ship. Checking one last time on his scroll that he was not about to inadvertently release the seal, he then ripped the wire out which supplied power to the unit. All four looked around, casually waiting to see if they were going to die or not. It turned out not.

"Okay then," Neil said. "Anyone including us could easily repair that if they came back here to do it, but at least now nobody with an idle thought can vent this whole section and us along with it... not to mention an even larger section of the ship if we don't seal bulkheads behind us as we make our way up to the habitat ring."

"Why didn't Asari do just that to stop Halley from making it any further?" In-Su asked.

"Local commands take precedence in the system; it's a safety feature." Neil answered. "As long as Halley was physically here he could prevent him from doing so. After he was already gone though... I guess there wasn't any point. Maybe he even realized that doing so after Halley had already gotten through would mean losing the entire engineering section."

"Right. Ok, now what..." Wiremu asked himself as he flicked open his wrist scroll. In response to his thoughts, after opening the screen, it displayed a wire mesh diagram of the entire ship, which was then populated by little red dots indicating individual people still left on the ship and what their location was. The ship could make inferences about the locations of children still too young to have received a Brainchip based on their manual use of the same technologies, but anyone with a Brainchip could be directly tracked in this way. The display revealed a significant grouping of the dots in the dining hall, three seemingly on approach to the bridge, and four already there.

"Look," In-Su said, pointing at the screen over his shoulder, "all of those people in the dining hall, that must be where they've had the young and the old hide out." In-Su took on a deeply disheartened air when he added, "now they're the vast majority of all of the people who are left..."

"It looks like Asari is still on the bridge," Wiremu observed. "He must be bunkered there as his last line of defence. It's the smart thing to do in his position; after all I did build that bridge like a bunker..."

"He's just left the children undefended?" In-Su asked, seemingly quite bothered by the idea.

"Yes," Armina affirmed, "well, they've got the older crew there looking out for them too. Either way though I find it hard to believe that either Halley or Asari would do anything to hurt them... that is if they've even given it any thought at all. The people in the dining hall aren't anybody's enemy. Besides, I'm sure both sides figure that if they succeed in defeating the other, everyone left will de facto become *their* people."

"Armina I find it difficult to believe that all of the elderly were neutral in everything that's gone on." Neil commented.

"You'd be surprised..." she answered. "They all watched Asari, Aset, and Halley grow up together and were mostly quite disturbed by all of the bad blood between them."

"Ok, well that's good to know," Neil remarked. "It's actually a little reassuring at this point."

"Isn't it a good thing that Asari has locked himself in the bridge though?" In-Su asked. "I mean, it's ultimately a rather temporary solution isn't it? There no quick or easy way onto the bridge once it's sealed, correct? Like you said, that's kind of the whole point."

"Yes yes..." Wiremu commented, obviously distracted. "What's bothering me now though is that I can't see Aset on here..." He knew as well as the others did that since the Brainchips were directly powered by electrical activity in the brain, they ceased transmitting quite abruptly upon death, and there was no easy way for one to prevent them from transmitting their location on the ship.

"We should make our way up to the habitat ring," Neil suggested.

"We should check on the children and elderly, don't you think?" he asked Wiremu, choosing not to contemplate what might have happened to Aset.

"Yeah," Wiremu confirmed. "Yeah, we definitely need to get moving." The four made their way back to the engineering corridor and forward into the smoky haze towards the front end of the ship where the rotational collar was located. It was just ahead of the fusion core and the zero gravity bubble, and was the structure about which the entire habitat ring rotated. In this cylindrical area where the two main sections of the ship met, four tubes which were perfectly equidistant from each other (which the crew more commonly referred to as the struts); each extended all the way up to the habitat ring from the engineering section. The tubes were just the insides of very strong structural supports which firmly grasped the rotating habitat ring while it was rotated about the non-rotating engineering section of the ship.

Wiremu arrived in the space where the four access tunnels were slowly rotating around him, and Neil asked "Which tube Wii?" The tubes spun slowly here at the source, but at their furthest projection all the way up at the habitat ring they spun fast enough to simulate the same gravity as on the planet's surface.

"Number three. It'll take us closest to the dining hall."

One by one they entered Tube Three, and began making their way down it. Quickly into the trip the simulated sensation of gravity became progressively perceptible and it became increasingly necessary to hold onto the ladder to avoid falling all the way down the tube, as opposed to using its rungs merely to propel oneself along. Wiremu was at the front of them, and when he looked down he was the first to spot the figure which lay motionless at the far end of the tube, and on the floor of the top level of the habitat ring.

"Oh no..." he uttered as he stopped methodically climbing down the ladder and more liberally slid down with his hand and feet only braking his descent against the posts of the ladder. It was Aset who lay there, ominously devoid of any signs of life.

Chapter 33

"This is a problem." Neil stated coldly. He was somewhat numbed by seeing the poor woman lying there. All of the terrible mourning he had been so far putting off was finally starting to catch up with him whether he liked it or not. He was at the point of having to coldly shut down all of his emotions altogether in order to avoid being completely overwhelmed and utterly compromised.

"You think?" Wiremu snapped with anger and frustrated irritation. The stress was catching up with him too, but he'd learned in his years of experience that it could help to periodically release some negative energy like a safety blow off valve so that it didn't over pressurize within him.

In-Su knelt down and tenderly inspected her body. "I don't see any wounds from... from any kind of weapon," he observed as he closed her still open eyes. "It looks like she broke her neck after falling down the interior of the strut." Her head was indeed turned at an angle which didn't seem possible for someone who might still be alive. "Her leg too..." he soberly added. Like her neck, her upper right leg appeared to have a bend where no joint was ever meant to be.

"Either way..." Neil leadingly offered to Wiremu who sighed heavily in response.

"Either way... this will only make getting through to Asari that much more impossible when the time comes." The simulant leader concluded. "I don't know what happened... we made it in the six minutes I promised."

"Halley must have made it through the door before she could make it back up to the habitat ring after releasing our airlock,"

Armina suggested. "She may have been so panicked trying to get away from him that she just rushed and lost her hold on the ladder, and..." she looked up the long tube, "fell the rest of the way down."

"Without her we never would have made it onboard," Neil acknowledged. "She's dead because she decided to help us."

"She knew what she was doing," Armina stated with respect. "I could see it in her eyes; she remembered. She was paying her life debt to the mission. She was... redeeming herself."

Wiremu took another look up the tube, trying to put together the information they had. "So... Halley comes down this tube behind her, ignores her body, and then..." he pointed back and forth between the two directions available to them along the floor's main central hallway. "And then what?" If the group was to travel in either direction available to them long enough, they would eventually circle all the way around the entire habitat ring and return back here to the same place.

Armina knelt down with In-Su beside Aset's body, and tenderly put her left hand on her cheek. She then with her right hand removed Aset's printed handgun from its holster which was strapped to her grey jump-suit. While continuing to look down at the dead woman she'd know very well, she said to the others: "I don't think we should waste the time it would take to check on the people in the dining hall. It should suffice to merely contact them over the comm line and make sure they're okay. We can just tell them to stay put there until they hear from us again."

"I agree," Wiremu said. "If I was right that it was only the ship to ship comms that were blocked we should be able to reach them now."

"See if Kim Bao is there," Armina further suggested as she stood up with the sims. "I guarantee you she's neutral, and she's respected enough that everyone there should listen to her and whatever instructions we relay through her."

"Yes, of course, my great granddaughter," In-Su recalled, to which the other sims looked at him with what could only be described as bemusement. "I met her in the arboretum soon after we woke up," he explained.

Wiremu made a hand gesture towards In-Su which said: 'well get on with it then...'

In-Su pulled his wrist scroll out of a pocket and as he pulled it open he put through a communication request to the great grand-daughter of the man of whom he was a simulation. Before long the old woman's face appeared on the screen. She seemed concerned, but she didn't appear to be anything which could be described as panicked or terrified.

"In-Su!" she exclaimed. "What's going on? Asari ordered us all into the dining hall without any explanation whatsoever and just told us to wait! All he told us was that somebody was on their way to attack us. It seemed preposterous, but he refused to answer any of our questions."

"It's Halley... he's on the ship, and... and well, he's gunning for Asari. It's a mess Bao, Halley carelessly killed Nekheny, who'd been sent to spy on him, and then Asari sent a strike force down to attack Halley and his people in response... according to Sadhika they're all dead now except for Halley and the two people he brought back with him. All of you in that room are most of the crew we have left, and... and everyone else who's left are all still trying to kill each other."

Bao didn't say anything at all; she was stunned. She clearly was totally unaware of any of this. "What... what... what now?" she finally managed to ask. "How can we help?" In-Su had a sense that she immediately understood the broader consequences of so much having gone wrong already. She seemed to understand that the mission in some fundamental sense had already failed.

"Nothing. We were going to come check on you to make sure you're all okay and fill you in on what's going on, but now we'd rather not waste the time if we don't have to. Things have gone from awful to worse so now we're just checking in with you over the comms to save time before we press on."

"Nobody's hurt or anything if that's what you mean..." Bao offered. We've just been very... confused, and scared."

"Good," Wiremu said. "Tell her to keep everybody together there and wait to hear from us that it's all over."

"You catch that?" In-Su asked, presuming she could hear Wiremu's voice.

She nodded. Somebody off screen said something, and Bao looked over at them and nodded. She turned back to the screen and said: "In-Su there are several people here who really want to help. There's *got* to be more we can do than just wait here and hope!"

"We appreciate that, but..." In-Su looked over at Wiremu, who only shook his head at him. "We've got it covered Bao. This... this isn't the kind of fight we can win by just involving more people, I'm afraid."

"If we fail..." Neil stated with a haunting note in his voice. He seemed quite distant as he said the words. "If everything keeps going wrong... the two shuttles are still down there. They could fit more than half of the people left into the shuttles... it won't be safe on the ship here anymore..." It was a grim prospect he was considering and his face showed it.

"Bao, listen. If it becomes necessary, fit as many people as you can into the two shuttles, and go down to meet Sadhika on the surface; the shuttle autopilots can bring you down on their own. You should immediately start fueling the shuttles for an autopilot return to pick up the rest just in case it was still possible when they're fueled. Being marooned on the planet like that may be a grim prospect but, well... there's no other alternative if things really do get that bad. You also need to know that you'd have to launch Shuttle One first since Shuttle Two's airlock is damaged and when it launches it'll vent the whole section. You'll also need to repair the release mechanism for Shuttle Two but it won't be difficult if you look up how to go about it on a scroll."

"Tell them to launch every last drone lander before they leave, too... they'll need them if it comes to that." Neil added with the same vacant look in his eyes. He was lost in thought considering how as bad as things would be for everyone even if they succeeded in pacifying Asari and Halley, it would still be so much worse for the children and elderly left alone if they failed.

"Neil also says that if it comes down to that you need to make sure you launch every drone lander you can before you leave. They won't be any good to anyone if they're left in their launch tubes."

"I understand... You're sure we can't help?" Bao asked, almost in a whisper.

"You are helping Bao... You have to lead them if we fail. Understand?" The old woman nodded her acknowledgement.

"Good luck," In-Su offered.

"To all of us..." Bao replied with a heavy heart before closing the channel.

"Well... there's only one place Halley is going," Armina said, stating the obvious. "Only one place *we* need to go."

"The bridge," Wiremu replied.

"The bridge," she confirmed. "I think Halley's lost it... I think he only has one thing left on his mind now that everyone he cared about is dead. All his hopes and plans are ruined now, he can only *have* one remaining sense of purpose now; the same goes for Asari too, *especially* when he finds out what's happened to Aset. There's only one thing left blindly driving either of them forward now."

"Revenge." Wiremu said.

"Revenge." Armina affirmed with a slow nod of her head.

Chapter 34

By the time the sims and Armina arrived at the scene, there was already an all-out firefight taking place. There seemed to be constant discharges of all three kinds of weapons in use, shotguns, laser rifles, and handguns. Between gun powder residue and damaged electrical systems smouldering, there was a pronounced smoky haze in the air similar to that observed down in the engineering section, but far thicker. There was shouting and yelling, but it was too chaotically sporadic for them to clearly make out what anyone was actually saying.

At the end of the corridor leading out of the bridge, the hallway split into two opposing directions. Halley and the two survivors he'd brought up with him were shooting from around one far corner past the split, and Wiremu and his people were approaching from the other direction. As they rounded the last corner they saw Halley directly ahead of them and immediately retreated back around the corner from which they'd emerged. Wiremu opened his scroll and then informed the others: "The mechanism which opens and closes the bridge door has been destroyed. It's stuck open and can't be closed now… they're just shooting at each other across the hallway and from behind corners."

"I wonder how Halley got Asari to open the door in the first place," Armina asked. "None of the people I saw there with Halley are technical experts. From what I understand even if they were, the bridge door is designed to be essentially unhackable isn't it?" she asked.

"Absolutely," Wiremu confirmed.

"Given the state he's in," In-Su suggested, "I doubt it would've taken much. They both wanted the fight didn't they? I imagine Halley just taunted him to confront him face to face, and if that didn't work by itself... he'd probably only need to tell him about Aset."

"I could see it," Neil replied in dismay, "taunting him about being responsible for the death of his son *and* his wife?"

"Yeah I think that would do it..." Armina nodded in dark agreement.

"And then once they'd opened the doors Halley only needed to shoot out the mechanisms in the wall to prevent them from ever closing again," Wiremu concluded.

"So?" Neil asked Wiremu, "how you wanna play this?"

For a moment Wiremu considered his options. There were no good ones. "You and Armina backtrack and go flank Halley's position up the other hallway. Get a clear line of sight and then just wait for my signal. When I give it, you distract them whether it takes just yelling at them or if you actually need to fire some warning shots around them. Don't shoot to kill unless it becomes absolutely necessary. You know as well as anyone how invaluable to the mission every single human life is at this point... even *their* lives."

"Of course," Neil acknowledged.

They were all distracted by some piece of equipment exploding out of one of the walls in response to being shot at too many times. The four all felt lucky that as a last resort bunker the bridge was buried in the centre of the habitat ring and was surrounded by multiple sections on all sides between this location and the outer sections which were adjacent to open space. Fortunately there was very little chance that any of their weapons could penetrate all the way through to the outer walls and expose the section they were in to space. The two sides enthusiastically shooting at each other sure seemed intent on putting this engineering principle to the test though.

"Make no mistake that *our* lives are more important than *theirs* though," Wiremu clarified. "There is to be no sacrificing ourselves for the likes of these bastards."

"Naturally," Neil again acknowledged, but this time with a wink of morbidly playful understanding between the two simulants.

"At my signal, play your hand and distract them. At that point In-Su and I will sneak past them and push our way through to the bridge door and get a clear shot on Asari and *his* people."

The simulated man sighed in dismay. "Sure wish I had a few flash bangs with me though…" he muttered to himself. "Would sure make getting through a hell of a lot easier…"

"Not that kind of mission," Neil likewise sighed. "Of course if we'd have somehow known ahead of time, then between the printers and the chemical reserves we certainly could have made one. There's a *lot* we could have done ahead of time if we'd have known to…"

"I always knew this day would come…" Armina said with a smirk as she produced from her pocket a device which looked suspiciously like a flash bang grenade. "Meet 'Doug.' I made it around the time we entered the system when I first started sensing that the whole mission might go completely sideways on us. There were rumors going around that Halley might be up to something, and I had in retrospect now some very prudent paranoia. I suspected Doug here might come in handy someday."

Wiremu patted her on the head with great approval as Halley and Asari's people continued to shout and fire at each other. "Nice," he said. "You're now officially my favourite human," he said with an approving smile.

"So *we* distract Halley and company while *you* sneak onto the bridge with Doug's help," Neil recounted, "and then what?" he asked.

Wiremu looked around the corner and thoughtfully threw the grenade up and down in his hand. "We talk them down," he plainly stated.

"Really? *That's* the plan? We talk them down?" Neil asked incredulously.

"Yes."

"Uhh… *really*?" It was unusual for Neil to so blatantly challenge Wiremu.

"You have a better idea?" Wiremu asked, getting defensive as he turned around to face his fellow simulant more directly.

Neil sighed in frustration and rubbed his eyes. "No. Certainly not a less lethal one anyways…" he added with an exhausted look in his eyes. "And if we can't talk them down?" he asked.

"Failure is just not an option Neil," Wiremu coldly stated. "Because as you just insinuated, Plan B is to just kill them all."

"Right..." Neil acknowledged grimly.

"What about the kill switch?" In-Su asked.

"Ironic again isn't it?" Wiremu observed, "that I would insist on having one in the first place, only to now have it be a threat to me personally?" Wiremu couldn't help but acknowledge the humour in it, even in their current situation.

"What kill switch?" Armina asked. Another bright and loud explosion from out of one of the walls momentarily startled them all again. They were becoming somewhat numb to the continuous weapons fire, but the occasional electrical explosion still considerably alarmed them if only momentarily.

"I had a simulant kill switch installed on the bridge," Wiremu explained. "Well the original me did. I, he... *we* had a bad experience with a sim once and was reluctant to have sims onboard without a kill switch for my safety. His safety. Whatever."

"You're right, that is ironic. Why didn't I know about it?" she asked.

"Only the captain, matriarch, and patriarch were ever supposed to know," Wiremu answered.

"So what do we do about it?" Armina asked.

"Well, we just hope that they're sufficiently disoriented by your grenade, and that we get a clear shot on them before they realize what's going on and think to make a move for the switch. That's why we need your Dougie here and can't just try to scroll flash them unconscious; we couldn't reach the guys on the bridge with it and they'd be tipped off to hit the kill switch." There was a function on their scrolls which allowed the device under the right conditions to rapidly flash in such a way that it overwhelmed a person's visual cortex and knocked them unconscious.

"Does the kill switch permanently disable you guys?" Armina asked with understandable concern.

"No, it basically just switches us off until somebody is kind enough to reactivate us." Wiremu answered.

"Would it affect Sadhika down on the planet too?"

"No, it's localized to the ship."

"Well shit," Armina replied, not sure what else to say.

"Like I said, we've got a lot of hoping to do," Wiremu acknowledged. "You two ready?" he asked of Neil and Armina, who nodded their heads in response. "Alright, move out."

Neil and Armina retreated back down the hall the way all four had originally arrived, and then turned left down an adjacent corridor. Just as they'd disappeared, a comm request came through Wiremu's wrist scroll. He flicked it open and saw Sadhika's face on the screen.

"Little busy here Sadhika," Wiremu hurryingly said.

"They're alive!" she exclaimed with excitement.

"What? Who's alive?" Wiremu asked, completely distracted from her in his current situation on the ship.

"The... *they're alive*! Well some, only *some* of them are alive, but I thought they were *all dead*! They're *not* though! They were just knocked out by them somehow; we think that they may have the ability to secrete a toxin or something through their skin that immediately knocks humans out!"

"Who does?" Wiremu asked, now trying to catch up with her.

"The... the indigenous, the squiddies!"

"Okay well *that's* kinda fucked up, but we'll have to deal with that later... Exactly how many are still alive down there?" he asked.

"First it was just Søren, but now there are thirty-one more! There's almost a hundred dead on the planet in total..." she reported with a significant drop in her mood, "but not all of them, not *all* of them!" she reiterated. "It's *enough* Wii, do you understand? Especially with the seventeen still at the alpha site!"

"Yes... yes I do." He was quiet for a moment. What she meant was two things. For one, if everything turned out as well as it possibly could from here on out, there were enough people down there to raise the children left in the dining hall into adulthood as well as to have and raise their own children as well. Secondly, forty-nine people alive and already on the planet also meant that thanks to their careful genetic diligence en route, if the New Horizon blew up that very moment, there were more than enough people with enough genetic diversity on the surface to theoretically parent a whole civilization if they could survive long enough.

"Well that's great, now all we have to do is save the ship," Wiremu remarked as though that were the easy part. "Please stand by Sadhika. Neil and Armina are on their way to confront Halley; I have a feeling this information will help them talk him down."

Sadhika nodded and was flicked off the screen by Wiremu as he retracted his wrist scroll screen.

Wiremu turned back to look at In-Su. "Well, you ready?"

"No," he replied in a hurt and scared voice. "Not at all!" It sounded like he was crying out to Wiremu.

The leader looked back and saw In-Su holding his gun exceptionally uncomfortably. He wasn't even holding it by its grip. "I don't want to hurt *anybody*! I've never hurt anyone or... or any*thing* in my *life*! This is *madness*! How could this have ever happened Wii? How could it all have ever gone so wrong?"

"In-Su..." Given the situation, Wiremu was sympathetic, but only to a point. "There'll be plenty of time to worry about figuring all that out later. Someday, when this is all long over, there will be plenty of time for analysis, but right now... right now we *have* to put an *end* to this conflict. We can't let either side win here, neither side can have what they've done be validated. Frankly at this point I'd rather the whole mission be a total failure than to have it succeed by one side winning outright. They've both been so radicalized..." he said, looking out at the continuing chaos again. "If either side wins... the resulting colony will be far darker than even the other G.S.S. missions were."

"I know Wii, I know all that! I'm just..."

"Yeah, you're scared. I know... So am I."

In-Su nodded timidly.

"It's a good thing..." Wiremu offered, trying to be comforting. He put his hand on In-Su's shoulder. "I'd be really worried about you if you *weren't* scared, it's... it's only human," Wiremu remarked with a playfully raised eyebrow.

In-Su smiled despite himself and shook his head. "Okay... let's go."

"Ready?" Neil asked Armina from behind Halley and his two friends as they kept shooting down the hall towards the bridge. They could now see that they had two large boxes of ammunition on the floor, and were only now almost through the first box.

"You kidding?" She asked with a quiet but confident laugh. "I've literally been training my *entire* life for this."

"Don't be *too* enthusiastic," Neil scolded her, then eyed her a little harder than he had before. "I'm still hoping *we* won't have to kill anybody today. I need you to have the same attitude."

"Yes, of course... I'm sorry." She almost seemed ashamed of her previous enthusiasm.

"We're in position Wii," Neil reported through his EAR. "We have line of sight on Halley and his two friends. We're good to go."

"We're ready here too," Wiremu answered back in his ear. "One last thing Neil, Sadhika reports that thirty-two people survived the battle," Armina, who was listening in on their channel through her own EAR squeezed Neil's arm in response to the unexpected good news, "including Søren."

"That could be very useful," Neil observed.

"Yeah, I figured."

Neil thought about it for a moment, and then said: "Alright, Wii. We're ready."

"Good. Go."

Chapter 35

Confusion and chaos erupted as Neil and Armina emerged from their hiding spot around the corner and began shouting loudly at Halley and his people. To be sure their seriousness was relayed, they did indeed find it necessary to fire a few warning shots around them. Halley and company began to turn around with their laser rifle and shotguns, but both Neil and Armina were already standing square with their weapons trained on them. While Neil covered the other two with his shotgun, Armina had the handgun she'd taken from Aset's body pointed at Halley's head, and he knew as well as anyone that there was no way she'd ever miss.

"Don't." Neil demanded in a voice that was more pleading than anything else. "*Please* don't make us kill you. We just want to talk, but we *will* fire if you *make* us." He stated with increasing conviction and authority. There was a tense moment when all five people were pointing their weapons at each other with conviction in Armina's eyes and pleading in Neil's, but still only burning hatred in Halley's. In his companions' eyes all that was to be found was panicked darting glances as they sought cues from their captain as to how they should respond.

"It's too late now." Halley said in a cold, flat, and even voice.

"*No* Halley... that's where you're *wrong*." Neil was trying to sound as soothing as possible while simultaneously being mortally threatening, and mortally threatened. "It's *never* too late to do the right thing... *never* too late to *stop* killing. It's *never* too late for peace... It may already be too late for the mission, but if we start shoo-ting at each other, it'll *definitely* be. Either way though... it's never too late to stop fighting, never too late to stop *destroying*. It's never too late to start *building* instead."

"Alright, we're up." Wiremu said to In-Su. "Remember, we can't let anyone get to the captain's chair. We have to shoot down anyone who makes a move towards it or we're done for. If one of them gets to the kill switch and activates it, then… well as you know, all is lost. When the flash bang goes off, press your hands against your ears and close your eyes tightly. Your simulant body will otherwise simulate the shock whether the blast actually affects you or not."

Wiremu bent down and gently rolled the cylinder shaped grenade down the hallway towards the bridge door. The air was noticeably smoky, and occasional sparks would fly off of the walls from the systems embedded within them, damaged as they were by all of the weapons fire. There was an eerie silence after the weapons fire halted altogether. When Halley and his people were distracted by Neil and Armina, they'd stopped firing and in response Asari and *his* people had likewise stopped firing out of cautious curiosity as to what was going on.

The grenade's detonator was thought controlled, and silently with his fingers, Wiremu counted down to In-Su, three… two… one…

Brilliant light and concussive sound erupted from the grenade just inside the bridge and immediately after the detonation while everyone there was presumably horribly disoriented, Wiremu and In-Su sprinted past a merely confused Halley who had not suffered the full effects of the grenade. He seemed to understand that they were making for the bridge and not for him and accordingly, he kept their weapons pointed at Neil and Armina.

Once they were inside the bridge, they took cover behind a work station and popped their weapons over top of it to have a clear shot at all four people on the bridge. Realizing what was happening as the disorientation was beginning to wear off, one of Asari's people immediately lunged for the kill switch, and Wiremu shot him dead before he could make it.

Before any of the others could bring their weapons on Wiremu or In-Su, *or* make a similarly foolish attempt for the kill switch, Wiremu yelled: "*Don't*!! Don't even mess around, just don't even think about it. Any of you shoot or move and you *all* die; I'm not *fucking around*!"

Asari's eyes were opened wide, as though his body were trying to extract as much information as possible to process his newfound situation.

"Asari? Neil and Armina are out there trying to talk Halley down," In-Su cautiously offered. "We're only here to try to do the same with you. We just want to bring an end to all of this."

"You have a funny way of making peace," Asari coldly stated, gesturing to the body of his fallen comrade.

"You're really not one to talk," Wiremu replied, equally as coldly.

"He... cannot win. I... I cannot allow it. He... doesn't *deserve* to." Asari asserted in a thin and steady voice which chilled In-Su.

"Asari..." Wiremu said with a shaking head. "Take a good look around. Take a step back and reassess, man! We're way, *way* past the point of anybody *winning* here. Winning left the table and went home a *long* time ago. Now it's just a question of how grim the prospects of survival are for the poor bastards left around to pick up the pieces when this is all over. Now, in these few minutes, this is the time when we're all going to find out if any of us deserve to *survive*... not win. We're already all *huge* losers here Asari, *he* can't win any more than *you* could at this point. We're *all* losers already."

"My son..." Aset despondent uttered.

"*His* wife." In-Su reminded him.

"*MY* wife*!!*" Asari roared in an explosion of rage.

"*His* wife *too* now, Asari! *Everybody's* wife, *everybody*'s son!!" Wiremu yelled, reflexively matching his tone and intensity. "Don't you *get* it? At this point *everybody*'s already lost *several* somebodies as dear to *them*, as your wife and son were to *you*! *Dammit* man, there's a whole *dining hall* of children out there who've all already lost *their parents*! You really want to suffer them having to figure out how to get on alone and what to do without *any* adults left??"

"Hey, I didn't *start* this Wiremu!!"

"*Neither did he!!*" Wiremu yelled, gesturing to the door and down the hallways towards Halley. "Not alone, anyway. You both helped each *other* create this colossal fucking catastrophe! We even played *our* part too in setting the stage for you, we acknowledge that ourselves too, and without any reservation at all! Don't you see? *Nobody's* innocent here Asari, nobody! *Everybody's* guilty, everybody! We're *all* to blame in our *own way*... and we're all gonna die together right now, *or* we're all going to find a way to be brave enough to live… brave enough to face what we've all done *together,* and the horror that we've *all* created… together."

"It's never too late to start *building,* Halley." Neil told him.

"Building *what*!?" Halley roared. "What's *left* to *build* with!? *Everybody's* already *dead*! All I have *left* is my revenge!"

"That's where you're *wrong* Halley," Neil answered.

"What do you mean?" he asked angrily with narrowing eyes.

"Call Søren." Neil gently suggested.

"Søren is *dead*!!" Halley snarled.

"*Call* him." Neil implored. Halley studied Neil's eyes suspiciously, but he could detect no subterfuge. With a though command, Halley's wrist pad processed a comm request to Søren down on the surface. Holding his shotgun as he was, his left wrist was already right in front of his face so that when his scroll deployed Halley didn't have to look away from Neil or move his weapon in any way to be able to see the screen. Much to his surprise, Søren did indeed answer, and over his shoulder he could see Sadhika's face.

"*Søren*! Wha… I thought you were dead!" Halley's demeanor, his whole way of being somehow collapsed in relief, he seemed completely overwhelmed to find that at the very least, his dear friend was still alive.

"So did I," he answered with a chuckle.

"What… what happened then?" he asked.

"The squiddies, after they jumped me I just blacked out." He looked back at Sadhika. "We think that maybe they secrete a neurotoxin through their skin that knocked us out. After a while though… we just woke up!" Søren answered with a shrug of his shoulders.

Halley paused. He was afraid to ask. "Ishtar?" he asked timidly, afraid of the answer. Søren looked down and to the right, and then shook his head. Neil could see the anger and hatred growing in Halley again, but so could Søren.

"But there are thirty-one other survivors here besides myself, Halley," Søren informed him. *"Thirty-one."*

"Thirty-one of ours?" Halley asked with a renewed brightness in his eyes. He obviously wasn't thinking straight; otherwise he'd have understood immediately that thirty-one was much more than his own twenty people who he previously believed he'd gotten killed.

"No... no, Halley" Søren answered. "Just... just thirty-one *people*. There is no *ours* and *theirs* anymore. Not down here... not now." Halley looked down thoughtfully.

"Halley," Sadhika said, taking the wrist scroll from Søren, and gently shaking her head. "I know the history of the clones. I know that from the same fundamental genome, you have expressed those genes in wildly different ways based on wildly different life experiences. From what I understand that was the whole point of your first progenitor initiating the cloning program in the first place.

"From what I understand, Markus Bowland wanted to see how differently he could have turned out if he'd lived different lives, how he himself might have turned out if he'd instead been raised as he'd wished he had. And you know what? He was right, we are as much the world we're brought into as we are our inherent nature, and we're ultimately much better informed... for what we can ultimately learn from the cloning program he initiated.

"But we've also learned something else too though, haven't we Halley? We've learned the *limits* of that variability, haven't we?" Halley was quiet, and looking off into space. He wasn't just listening; he was really *hearing* her.

"As wildly different characters as you and all your progenitors may have been from each other, in some ways you're really not all that different from each other at all, are you? You all have the same *flaw*... don't you Halley?"

"What's that?" he asked. He really didn't have any idea, but she seemed confident in having gleaned some insight which might be of value to him.

"I think deep down you really know already... but I'll tell you anyways. You're impulsive... you have trouble changing your mind. Once you get an idea in your head... whether it be boarding New Horizon in the first place or breaking protocol to create clones... murdering your abuser and redirecting the ship to another colony planet... Johannes killing Tycho and deciding to resume the cloning program once it had been exposed and condemned, both Johannes *and* your... your father. And you... you committing to putting *everything* at risk to create a second colony instead of working out your differences with Asari and Aset. You all *always* stuck to your bad ideas and bad decisions no matter how bad the consequences got.

"You, and all of your kind, always refuse to change your course once your decisions have been revealed as *bad* ones. You're all terrible at coming back from that place where you are now, consumed by toxic emotions. You stay there too long, you make too many bad choices in that place and then stick to them… don't you see?"

"Yes." he answered. "I see." He closed his eyes and repeated it. "I see."

"But it's not too late, Halley… you still have a choice. You have it in you to learn from this, to learn that last hard lesson. You right now can still take this under-standing of your own experience and the experience of your previous incarnations, and allow yourself to make a change in the present, to make a *different* choice in *this* moment, for the first time. You are only a slave to your nature if you *allow* yourself to be. Do you understand?"

Halley turned to Neil, who had long since stopped pointing his shotgun at him. Looking at him now, he let out a little laugh which Neil didn't understand. "We've been here before you and I, haven't we… though, neither of us were quite ourselves then, were we?"

Neil didn't say anything. He really didn't have any idea at all what Halley was referring to or what he was getting at, but whatever the reason he was greatly pleased to sense a de-escalation in the man's heart.

"Maybe it *doesn't* have to go down the same way this time…"

"Why couldn't you let him go?" In-Su asked Aset. "Halley I mean, why couldn't you just let it be when he broke away and went on his own. Sure it was stupid and irresponsible, but you had to know that anything other than just letting him go was going to be riskier than doing nothing. Why send your son to spy on him in the first place? Why launch the incursion later on?"

"Because what he did was *wrong*," Asari emphatically answered. "It was *wrong* to let him get away with it."

"And you think that responding to his bad behaviour with further bad behaviour was appropriate?"

"It wasn't about what was appropriate," Asari said through

gritted teeth. "It was about what was *right*; it was about *justice*."

His eyes betrayed only a small touch of it, but deeper within himself Wiremu unleashed the most colossal eye roll of either his own *or* his progenitor's existence. In his time he'd found that justice was one of those buzz words like freedom, which nobody ever meant except to vapidly justify their own hypocritical behaviour. They were words which everybody feigned reverent respect for but never genuinely honoured in their beliefs, opinions, or behaviour, as evidenced by Asari's invocation of the notion of justice to justify his actions.

"Is it right, or just, to allow the mission to be a failure?" In-Su asked. The human didn't answer. "Tell me Asari... why do you hate him so much?"

"Because of what he's done." he answered.

"But you hated him long before that, didn't you? You hated him long before the arrival, long before waking us up... why?"

"Because he never should have existed in the first place," Asari answered quickly and angrily.

"Is that his fault?" In-Su asked.

"That's not the point." Asari snapped.

"I think it is... Can't you see it from his perspective? He had to grow up watching your parents never accept his father-"

"Clone," Asari angrily corrected him.

"Clone-father, then. Your parents took every opportunity to marginalize him... despite his doing everything he possibly could to justify himself and to establish the essential goodness of his existence. No matter what he did though, he could only ever be in their eyes... something that never should have existed in the first place. Does that sound familiar to you?" Asari said nothing. He appeared to be considering what In-Su had just said.

"And what came of it Asari?" In-Su pressed. "Halley did. Halley came of it. Halley and all of his contempt and anger over how he saw his clone-father treated no matter how hard he worked to be accepted. He learned that hatred awaited him no matter how he behaved, so he learned to hate back. Hatred... always begets hatred, Asari."

"That's..." Asari sighed as he shook his head, and then whispered: "an oversimplification."

"I don't think it is. But I also don't think that's all there is to it. You have a *particular* hatred for Halley. Why?" Asari just shook his head.

"Could it be, because you are yourself a descendent of a clone?" The man shot an angry and hurt look at In-Su. "Asari, by being taught to hate the clones, you were subtly taught by proxy to hate yourself in kind, and from day one. Everything you were taught about how bad the clones were, about how unjust and intolerable their existence was… a part of you had to know that it reflected back onto you as well. Maybe your hatred of Halley is so fervent because you deflect and impart on him, in addition to all that he is rightly due, all of the hatred some part of you feels that you deserve as well, if he deserves any at all." Asari again, said nothing and just listened. He was looking at the ground, lost in deep reflection of the words he was hearing.

"You had the luxury of knowing from the very beginning what your origins were," In-Su continued. "Imagine what your grandmother Bianca and *her* children had to go through, to have it thrust upon *them* all at once that their origins were anything other than what was ordinary for the ship, as they'd always believed. They had to find out by surprise that their father and grandfather were both clones, and what's worse publicly and in front of everyone else.

"They must have developed a biting hatred of the subsequent clones as a way of *overcompensating* for how much this unsettled them, and to as definitively as possible draw a clear and unambiguous division be-tween the clones and themselves when in all the ways that really mattered, none really existed at all.

"They must have felt that the best way they could distance themselves from any association with the cloning program, was to become the most vocal opponents of it. Their shock and… and existential disruption at the revelation, was turned into hate propagated through time, getting magnified and focused onto each new generation… and finally onto you and your wife. You were both condemned from the day you were born, taught to carry a burden that was never your own. You were taught to hate yourself, but to project that hate onto *them*. How unfair that was…"

Asari completely slumped and dissolved. He collapsed into the station chair behind him and began sobbing. In-Su instinctively moved towards him to console and comfort him.

"In-Su!" Wiremu called out in a moderate panic, still firmly aware of the danger of their situation, but In-Su waved him off. In response to their leader collapsing, and In-Su's fearless gesture, Asari's two remaining loyalist on the bridge lowered their weapons as well and aimed them at the floor. Cautiously, reservedly, Wiremu likewise lowered his own weapon and pointed it at the ground, but also likewise he didn't completely let go of it either.

In-Su reached Asari, and held him in his arms. He stroked his dark black hair as tears welled up in his own eyes as well. "It's not your fault Asari... It's not your fault," he whispered as they rocked back and forth, crying together.

Chapter 36

"Am I interrupting?" In-Su asked after the door to Bao's office slid open. It was a week later, and negotiations were taking place between Asari and Halley. Although they still quite clearly hated each other, they'd at least both committed to the peace process, and to a negotiated settlement between them which addressed all of the grievances they both had.

Bao had been chosen to mediate between them. She served a role which was at times moderator and at others judge. Both sides respected her fundamental neutrality in the issue and had mutually and bindingly agreed to abide by her final judgements. A makeshift office had been set up for her near the dining hall where the public portions of the negotiations were taking place; the public element to the proceedings allowed all of the mission's survivors to get a sense of the progress which was being made, as well as a chance to voice their own ideas and opinions.

When In-Su entered, Bao had been speaking privately with Asari which was in no way inappropriate. Al-though there was a public element to the discussions, it was not a trial. Bao needed to be able to speak privately with both parties in order to respect their confidentiality in addition to hosting the joint meetings between them in the dining hall. Though they found they could stand to be in the same room together, Asari and Halley found it impossible to bring themselves to speak to each other directly. In the public meetings they spoke through intermediaries or to Bao directly. When the public mee-tings were out of session, both also found it helpful to speak privately with Bao when they found it necessary to do so.

"Not really," Asari answered In-Su. "Actually I'd like your input on this. We've been talking about the possibility of setting up some kind of human breeding farm on the ship."

"Well it certainly *sounds* grotesque." In-Su answered with a wrinkled nose but an open mind. "But tell me more."

"It's an idea some of us have been kicking around," Bao answered. "With the obvious exception of the personnel landers, all of our other drones are still intact. Many of us think that this means our mission can still ultimately succeed if we're lucky. If it indeed can though, our greatest challenge at this point is of course our severely reduced population. Yes we have around fifty healthy adults of reproductive age, and yes together with the elderly they can all pull together to raise the children who have been left orphaned, but that can only get us so far."

"You want to use the artificial wombs," In-Su surmised as he came to understand.

"Yes." Bao confirmed.

"Since we never used any en route there's still the original four installed in the bio-lab and eight more still in back up storage," Asari elaborated. "If we set up the backups as well and ran all twelve continuously, then in a span of only five years we could produce eighty babies. It would be a tremendous burden on the adults left around to raise them all at the same time, but... it could be done. Combined with maximized concurrent natural breeding, we could completely replenish most of our losses... if only numerically."

"So much for mission protocol..." In-Su lamented.

Asari shrugged. "Of course we couldn't raise, educate, and train them as meticulously as we did on the ship, but we might just have to live with that."

"Well in reality," In-Su added, "those protocols were really only enacted for use during the trip here in the first place anyways. The careful genetic management and high level educational curriculum were never really intended to be continued in full once the colony was established and everyone was living on the planet. We understood all along that the new reality would create a new culture and a new way of life, even if we hoped that our careful efforts would greatly inform that new civilization, we knew that things would change in unforeseen ways."

"Right," Bao acknowledged. "Well we'd leave most of the elderly and some of the younger adults on the ship to take care of the babies. Our schmilk producers were always designed to be able to produce human breast milk as easily as bovine. We'd essentially turn the ship into a giant orbital nursery, and send the children down when they were old enough. We wouldn't even have to wait until they were fully mature. In fact the earlier they can be sent down and raised by adopted parents on the surface the better. They'd adapt to life down there faster that way and be able to help out on the surface from an earlier age as well."

"It's a good idea," In-Su agreed. "And you're right, the adults down there who are going to be asked to take on raising adopted children, I'm sure they'd want to be able to start parenting them as early in their development as possible."

"I'm aware of that," Bao said, "but it would be too much to drop on them too soon and all at once, especially while they're still trying to set up the colony sites in the first place."

"Sites?" In-Su asked.

"Yes... sites." Asari acknowledged with some frustration. "To his credit... Halley has made a lot of concessions about it, but he does still insist on having his own alternate colony site."

In-Su shook his head in dismay. "Unbelievable... Well, what concessions *has* he made?" he asked.

"Well," Bao answered. "For starters, Asari and Halley have both agreed to relinquish their leadership roles after the negotiations have concluded," she stated with an appreciative nod to Asari. "In fact they've both suggested that leadership of each colony be assumed by one of you simulants In-Su, and that you should decide amongst yourselves who will lead each one if you are indeed willing. Whichever two are chosen, they will also be the official representatives and liaisons between the two colonies."

"Interesting..." In-Su acknowledged without making any kind of commitment to the idea. "What else."

"Halley has also agreed so far that the two colonies should not be adversarial. He agrees that they should exist in close proximity to one another, and should have normalized communications. Instead of two colonies in opposition to each other as he'd originally had in mind, all parties now agree to a model of two nearby sister colonies working together co-operatively. The premise we are currently working with is that instead of being clear across the planet where Halley originally landed, the second colony site should be no more than a day's walk away from the primary site and that there should be no restrictions whatsoever on any movement between the two."

"Since the only drone they currently have at their existing site is one of the two paving drones, that shouldn't be a problem," Asari noted. "We'll just have the one we already have at the primary site create the twenty kilometer or so road to the new place they choose and do whatever clearing and paving they need done."

"That's another thing," Bao remembered, "as a further show of good faith to secure his second colony site, Halley has agreed to forgo the creation of his own independent landing strip, as well as any kind of claim to primary ownership of either shuttle. This is an added insurance which means that they'll have to maintain good relations in order to have any kind of access to either the shuttles *or* the New Horizon."

"The blimp though," Asari reminded her.

"Oh, yes. He's agreed to all that on the condition that the second site can have primary access to one of the two airships which have far more limited capabilities."

"I find that all very reassuring," In-Su offered. "It seems to indicate that he really does want to make this work and that he wants to do his part to maintain the peace. He's given up a lot though hasn't he? What have you given up to get him to agree to all of these conditions Asari?" he asked the man.

Asari looked up at him from his chair with a somewhat quizzical look on his face. "My consent to there being a second colony site at all," he answered rather defensively.

"Right." In-Su replied, not realizing how big a concession that really was for him.

"And my continuing commitment to share resources and technology," Asari further elaborated. "I've agreed to the principle of there being two sister colonies as part of the same mission, and for the two sites to amicably collaborate. I've agreed to the *peace*." Asari added in sharper defensiveness.

"Of course," In-Su acknowledged. "Asari, I'd like to speak to Bao alone for a moment, is that alright?"

"Sure," Asari agreed as he stood up out of his chair which faced

Bao behind her desk. "I need to prepare for the next session anyways."

"Actually if you could just wait outside for a moment, I'd like to speak privately with you as well. This will only take a moment."

"Alright." With that, the door opened as Asari moved towards it, and once through it closed behind him again.

"You're making wonderful progress Bao," In-Su congratulated her. "I'm very impressed. I'm proud of you." The old woman got up from behind her desk and came around to give In-Su a hug.

"I'm proud of you too old man," she pulled away and looked at him funny, "or young man, however you want to look at it," she laughed.

"It's been nice to meet you. I hope to get to know you much better as time goes by," In-Su offered with a smile.

"Likewise," she agreed.

In-Su found Asari outside the door where he'd asked him to wait for him. He was sitting on the ground with his back against the wall beside the door to Bao's office, with his arms hugging his raised knees. Idly fiddling with his fingernails, he seemed incredibly distant and somehow distinctly grey.

"How are you doing?" the simulated man asked the human as he sat down beside him.

"I hurt... every minute, of every day..." he answered despondently. "I lost my whole family In-Su... my whole family."

"I know..." In-Su replied with a heavy hearted sigh.

"I see their faces every day... I keep expecting to see them again. I keep thinking of things I'd like to talk to Aset about, or things I think Nekheny would find funny, and then I remember that they're dead... that I can't ever share those things with them, and that I'll never have another casual moment like that with them ever again..."

In-Su didn't say anything. There was nothing to say.

"How do you get over something like that In-Su?" Asari asked. "How does it ever stop hurting? I don't know if I even want it to. Part of me feels like I'd be betraying their memory if I ever *did* get over it or, or let it stop hurting me..."

"It never stops hurting Asari; you never get over something like that..." In-Su reassured him. "Sure every day it hurts just a little tiny bit less than it did the day before, but it never goes away. Eventually it becomes a constant dull throb which you get used to and eventually find you can live with, but it never stops altogether. Someday you'll remember that they loved you enough that they wouldn't want you to live a life of misery on their account and not be able to get on with your life because of them, but that day is a long, long ways away, don't worry."

Asari nodded his head. He understood.

"Thank you In-Su." Asari gravely stated. It seemed a more general gratitude, than for anything he had just told him.

"For what?"

"For reaching me... for helping me see something I'd been ignoring and suppressing my whole life. For being compassionate when I needed it, and... and for helping me feel brave enough to live with the consequences of everything that's happened... with everything I've done and been a part of... It would have been so much easier to have just let Wiremu kill me."

"Yes. Death is easy," In-Su agreed, "but living is hard. I'm glad you were willing to take on the challenge though. Yes you've done bad Asari, but you were misguided. You believed that you were doing the right thing, and that makes all the difference. It means that you're not a bad person at heart. It means that the more you learn, and the better you understand yourself and your place in the world, the more accurate you'll be in your judgements of what the right thing to do is in any given situation. You're a work in progress Asari; we all are..."

Chapter 37

"Alright Bridge, we're ready down here. Go ahead and depressurize."

"VEEEERRRPP!! VEEEERRRPP!! VEEEERRRPP!!" sounded the alarm as the entire section's atmosphere was reabsorbed into the ship's reservoirs. Earlier space ships might have merely vented air out to space in order to depressurize, but New Horizon could afford no such wastefulness. They only had enough reserve gasses to completely re-atmosphere the ship a few times over in the event of catastrophe, but had so far been fortunate enough to never need to dip into the backup reserves. In situations such as this where for whatever reason a section of the ship needed to be depressurized, most of the atmosphere could be captured back into storage for reuse instead of wastefully venting it out into the vacuum which the ship sailed through.

Wiremu could tell that they were increasingly in vacuum by the gradual quieting of the alarm, which continued until he couldn't hear it anymore. Without any significant air left to transmit the sounds of the siren through his space suit, the flashing yellow warning lights were the only observable indications of the danger. Although as a simulant it was technically possible for Wiremu to operate in a vacuum, to preserve his simulation as a human he was programmed to simulate death if he ever encountered the situation, but unlike a real human he could then be revived if returned to normal atmospheric conditions. It was kind of cheating, but no feature of simulation authenticity was ever thought important enough to permanently damage or disable a simulant. They were instead only incapacitated, and remained inactive until revived again under proper conditions. In any case, a pressurized helmet made it much easier for him to communicate while he worked, since either way he'd be unable to be heard speaking without air to transmit the sound vibrations of his voice.

The suit was contemporary technology when they left Earth; it was form fitting and relied on mechanical elastic force to maintain pressure on the skin against a vacuum. The helmet was likewise narrow and compact with a forward facing window in front of one's face, and was equipped with a heads up display like in the front windows of the shuttles. Breathable air was provided to the wearer by a backpack air tank, and a tight magnetic seal kept the helmet airtight against the fabric of the suit. The design allowed far greater mobility than the personal spaceship suits which had been used exclusively in the early days of human spaceflight. Both varieties of suits still had their own strengths and weaknesses though, and as such several of each kind were kept in storage on the ship. Since they were staying inside and would only need them for a short amount of time though, they'd opted for the suits which were easier to get around in once they'd struggled into the tight garments in the first place.

"Alright, we're good to go," Wiremu said to Armina. "Hand me the drill would you?" The two had volunteered to fix the shuttle hatch which Halley had damaged when he'd cut through it to gain access to the ship. With its airlock damaged, the shuttle's air was sucked out along with the rest of the section, which was a necessary step either way for the work that needed to be done.

The original Wiremu had had a great many hours in space suits over his career, all of which the simulant Wiremu could remember and draw on as experience. He hadn't volunteer for the task as much as he'd just assumed that he'd be the one doing the job. Armina however, had volunteered for her very first spacesuit operation in part because she'd always been curious to do so but had never had a good enough reason, but also because it was an excuse to spend some more time with Wiremu.

Although when they'd first woken up she'd found herself immediately attracted to the Neil Sagan simulant, ever since their ascent back to the ship to stop Halley and bring everything back under control, she'd found herself increasingly interested in Wiremu instead. Neil was a lot of fun and she still enjoyed his company immensely, but that seemed to be as far as her emotions ever became invested in him.

Wiremu was different though; he was a warrior like her. They had much more in common, and they got each other in that effortless kind of way which was hard to come by. Although no formal overtures had been made or anyone's intentions openly declared, they'd been spending more and more time together. Armina was finding as many reasons to be around him as possible, which is why she'd immediately volunteered for this task when the opportunity arose.

"Shostak?" he had to ask again over the helmet to helmet comm channel.

"Oh yes, sorry… here you go," she said with a little embarrassment as she handed him the tool. Instead of the messy operation it would have been to try to repair the mechanism within the door and then weld over the hole in the hatch in a zero gravity vacuum, they instead just fabricated an entire new hatch assembly. It wasn't hard, and most of the raw materials involved would be replenished anyways when they recycled the damaged assembly back down into its base elements.

Every single component from the large metal hatch casing itself, to all of the locking mechanisms within it, and all of the internal electronics which made it go, were all individually manufactured in the ship's industrial printers, and then hand assembled by a technician. As a result, all Wiremu and Armina had to do now was just swap one unit for another.

Bracing himself against the wall to avoid his body spinning around due to the rotational forces of the drill instead of the bolts he was trying to undo, one by one Wiremu undid all of the bolts which held the bulky hatch in place. He painstakingly placed each bolt into the mesh bag he'd magnetically attached to the adjacent bulkhead in order to prevent them from floating away, and so he could re-use them again when he went to install the new hatch.

"Have you heard about their baby farm idea?" Armina casually asked him.

"Sure, yeah I heard. Sounds a little morbid but it's a good idea if we're still going to pull the mission off in any kind of meaningful way."

"Yeah, that's what I was thinking..." she agreed. Some time passed as he worked before she spoke up again. "You know... they'll be expecting me to um... you know, to be a mom. I'll need to adopt some of the existing children who've been orphaned as well as some of the new ones they make... *and* birth a few of my own."

Wiremu stopped working for a moment and turned to face her. "How do you feel about that?" He asked himself if she seemed the mom type and without further consideration he honestly couldn't say either way.

"Well, I always knew the day would come and I certainly did always look forward to it in principle, it's just... it's just a lot more to take on than I had in mind, you know? I always thought it would be *just* the having a couple kids myself part... Although it's certainly better than the alternative of being one of the ones stuck up here on the ship nursing the infants I think."

"Right," Wiremu affirmed as he returned to his work. He decided that he thought she would in fact be a good mom. She could be tough, but not recklessly or unnecessarily so, and he felt that perfectly appropriate. It's how he perceived his own mother to have raised him himself, and he figured *he* turned out okay.

He undid the last bolt, methodically placed it in the mesh bag, and then pulled on its drawstring to close it. He then pulled the entire hatch off of its hinged bases. "It's almost too bad the shuttle's still mounted here," Wiremu commented. "Otherwise we'd sure have a great view..." He attached one side of a large two sided magnet onto the damaged hatch, and then attached the other side to the wall safely out of the way a few meters back down the access tube. He then grabbed the new hatch and set about seating it into place where the old one had been.

"Wii, did the original you have any kids back on Earth?" Armina asked.

"Oh no, no, no.... None of us four did." Again he stopped working to turn back around to face her. Wearing the space suit didn't accommodate casually looking back over his shoulder at her; it required turning his entire body around to do so. "Now that I think about it... I wonder if that was part of the problem in the first place."

"What do you mean?" she asked.

"Our oversights in setting up the mission… we were all hyper-ambitious overachievers without any children. Maybe that was why we so utterly failed to think about how growing up on the ship would affect children the way it did, and the adults those children grew up into. Maybe it was because none of us were parents, that there were a number of things we never thought about that we really probably should've." He shrugged, and turned back around to his work. After properly seating the new hatch in place, he re-opened his bolt bag and began fishing them out and drilling them back into place again, one by one.

"Now that you bring it up, I did look into what descendants I had here on the ship. All of our genomes were used for breeding once we were underway. It turns out that the real me had a son and grandson, and that his grandson actually grew up to replace him as captain. He died though… in fact right in the middle of the Midway incident while saving one of the clones." he recalled with a raised eyebrow.

"That sounds like you," Armina warmly offered. He didn't turn around to let her see, but her comment made him smile. "Yes I'd heard about Anaru Tynes' sacrifice…" she added.

"He died without having had his replacement child, and after that it doesn't look like anybody ever used my genome again." A few moments of silence passed before he spoke up again. "You know, I always did have a vision in my head of having children someday though… I had a great childhood Armina, our house backed onto the woods and more than anything I loved going out to explore them alone with my dog… It's what ultimately made me want to be a space explorer. I'm not surprised that the other Wiremu had a family once the ship was underway and he finally had the chance."

"What's a dog?" Armina asked after a pause.

"A pet, a wonderful loyal pet… four legs, furry, panting at your knee... terrific."

"Oh right." Now she vaguely remembered hearing about such a thing. "You know... I think you'd make a wonderful father Wii," Armina sincerely offered.

"Thank you my dear, but unfortunately I'm not really constituted for anything like that anymore," he surmised.

It took Armina some time to work up the courage to make the

suggestion which was on her mind. "You know..." she offered, "your genome is certainly still on file. It's not too late to do it all over again." The simulated man stopped working again to turn around and scrutinize her. "Down there on the planet there'll be plenty of space to build a house which backs onto the jungle... We could even make a dog for you and the kids if you really wanted one!" she nervously laughed.

Wiremu smiled in a way that seemed to signify pleasant surprise. "But I'm ancient!" he exclaimed with laughter. He laughed because he'd only meant the age he was constructed to appear, but he remembered as he was saying it that technically he was actually much older than he'd even meant. Strictly speaking, he was also the additional hundred and sixty years he'd been in storage as well. "And you're so young," he concluded. Whether he was nearing two hun-dred years old or only a few weeks old, the age he was built to simulate had nearly thirty years on the young woman who seemed to be propositioning him.

"I'll catch up with you," she pointed out.

"You'll *pass* me," he furthered.

"Well that'd really be more your problem than mine wouldn't it?"

"How do you figure?"

"Well if *you* survive, then on my deathbed you'll appear to me then as you do today. *You're* the one who'd have to watch *me* grow old and die. You'd have to watch our children die, maybe even our grandchildren and *great* grandchildren, and beyond... But you'd also get to see them all grow up and live. I guess it'd be a blessing *and* a curse."

"Oh Armina..." he teased, "why can't you just find yourself a nice *human* boy?"

"Wii..." she sighed, "I already *know* all the boys, and *none* of them have ever interested me. I was so intrigued by you sims in part because you were the first *new* men I'd ever met! You're interesting, you're... you're unique. Life with you would be... a road less traveled. Life on the planet will be an adventure either way sure, but... it's a particularly special adventure for you because you were around from the very beginning. For *us* this will all just be our new lives, our... just our new existence. For you it'll always be about something much bigger though, about something much grander... I want to be a part of that. I want that added dimension to my life; I want to share the adventure with you and... and see it through *your* eyes."

Although he was smiling, Wiremu didn't say anything. Instead he turned around and finished screwing in the few remaining bolts. When he was finished he handed the drill back to Armina and closed the hatch. "Bridge, try the lock." Before they'd come down to replace the hatch, another technician had already been by to repair the mechanism which allowed the hatch to be operated by remote control, the system which Neil had disabled during the height of the troubles.

Wiremu held his hand to the door to feel for the vibrations which indicated mechanisms within the hatch to be operating, since he was still unable to directly hear anything in the vacuum. When he felt the activity cease, he heard the bridge report through his helmet that it seemed to be operating correctly. "Alright, then let's test the seal. Go ahead and disengage the shuttle. Hold it steady just a few meters off of the ship, and try re-pressurizing this section. Go slowly though, if there's a problem we want to lose as little air as possible."

"Understood." After a few moments both of them heard the bridge sound off the pressure even though their helmet's HUDs displayed it for them at the same time. "... twenty percent... ...thirty percent..." Wiremu began to be able to hear the sirens again through his helmet. "...fifty percent, everything's looking good... ...sixty percent..."

Once the atmosphere had been brought back up to a hundred percent with what as far as any readings could tell was a perfect seal, Wiremu confidently removed his helmet with satisfaction. The sirens and flashing lights had shut off completely now that the atmosphere in the section was completely restored. "Alright Bridge, re-dock the shuttle and pressurize it. Let me know when I can try the hatch."

"Understood."

"Armina?" Wiremu asked as he turned back around to face her again. She seemed nervous after having been left hanging over her proposition, but she looked back up at him in response. "How bout you buy me dinner first?" he suggested with a chuckle.

Chapter 38

"Ello, what's this then?" Sadhika asked herself as she slowly and carefully extracted a parasite from the squiddy brain she was studying.

"What is it?" Neil asked. "It looks like a giant neuron..." He was right. It had a primary central body, with multiple projections which significantly branched out into smaller and smaller projections. The central body was only a couple centimeters wide, but end to end the tendrils which seemed to project into multiple brain areas were easily six centimeters across.

Sadhika carefully placed it into a specimen dish and turned to Neil. "It's a brain parasite..." she answered with incredulity. "And it might explain a lot about what happened to the squiddies... I mean if we're right that they were once capable of building those catacombs."

"How so?" Neil asked.

"Well, I'd have to examine many more to be sure, but if all the squiddies have a similar parasite... well, it could explain a regression. While their brains are very different from ours or even any cephalopods back on Earth, we can assume that they developed in a similar way, in that from more primordial and basic brain structures, progressively more complex brain systems were built on top of older ones. From what I can tell this parasite was embedded in the most recently evolved part of their brain, which for humans is the frontal lobe, the higher reasoning part that that makes us so different from the other great apes."

"I'm still not getting what you're driving at." Neil had apparently finally given up on correcting the other sims about not being human.

"If it disrupts function in the most sophisticated brain region it would make them dumber than they otherwise would be."

"Ahhh... so they were once capable of sophisticated engineering, but then they get infected with this parasite and whammo! Suddenly they're much dumber."

"Basically, yeah." She wasn't thrilled with how he put it but it was accurate enough. "It's a theory anyways..."

The two were in a clean and brightly lit auxiliary laboratory on the New Horizon with the specimens they'd collected from the planet's surface. After repairing the shuttle hatch, Wiremu had sent down one of the shuttles to Sadhika so she could return and join them on the ship.

First she had to wait for the shuttle to refuel its hanging auxiliary fuel tanks so she could transport all of the people left alive after the Battle of the Airstrip (as it would come to be known), over to the primary site to join up with the personnel the sims had brought down. While waiting for the shuttle tanks to fill, Søren helped her load one of the bodies of the squiddies into the flight deck so she could take it back up to the ship for study after dropping off the crew.

Soon after they'd done so though, a mass of squiddies returned to the battle field and retrieved all of their other dead bodies. So far they had no idea where they'd taken them or what they'd done with them, but it seemed fair to assume that they had some kind of ritual grieving process. A few people thought that maybe they'd only retrieved the bodies so that they could eat them, but for now there was really no way to know for sure, and as a result there were general misgivings in retrospect about having taken for study the one corpse they did. But it was already in the shuttle, and the squiddies didn't give any indication that they felt they were missing anything. They decided to keep the one they already had, but to acknowledge that going forward it would be inappropriate to ever do the same again.

Once Sadhika had dropped off the crew she was transporting, Søren was again kind enough to help her awkwardly stuff the corpse of the 'pandino' which had killed Blair (as the panda patterned dinosaur looking animals had come to be referred to) into the flight deck beside the squiddy while she was waiting for the supercharger to fuel up the shuttle for her return to orbit.

Now back on the ship, Sadhika finally had the chance to conduct the detailed analysis of the specimens they'd collected, of which there were many. This was the work she'd been most anxious to do since she'd woken up in the first place; biological analysis and comparison was her wheelhouse and the real reason why she was here. Despite all of the chaos which wound up erupting, before and after it, she and her team had managed to collect dozens of small creatures from the rich and lively jungle, as well as some of the larger animals such as the squiddy, quatropus, and pandino. Although she hadn't yet gotten around to studying the latter two, she was also already anxious to have a good look at both the reptilian looking birds they'd seen and the tree dwelling reptilian looking creature they'd observed chasing the quatropus' through the jungle. So far, her preliminary genetic ana-lysis of all the samples they'd collected had revealed that they all had the same different Haven specific DNA base pair elements, meaning that like on Earth all local life shared the same genetic alphabet, but was different *between* the two planet's biospheres.

She suspected that this may have been the reason why the toxin secreted by the squiddies was less effective on humans than it was on the indigenous life. Sadhika had found a network of glands under the skin of the squiddy body she was studying which contained a chemical which could be secreted through their skin as she and Søren had suspected. Chemical analysis of the toxin and tissue experiments with the other animal bodies she had to work with revealed that it was indeed most likely quite lethal to the pandino as well as the quatropus.

"If I were to wildly speculate... based on my years of experience with genetics and evolution..." Sadhika thought as she looked up towards the ceiling and rubbed the back of her neck. "I would guess that all of them were infected with these parasites a long time ago, and that they were all at once compromised before they were able to figure out what was happening or what to do about it. By the time they realized they were in trouble it was probably too late already. If it's in their environ-ment, then their young would've all picked it up too, and probably before the bulk of their brain development occurred."

"What's the significance of that?" Neil asked.

"Well, if that were indeed the case then it could fundamentally affect how their brains developed. It could have dumbed them down structurally in such a way that just removing the parasite from an adult probably wouldn't magically increase their intelligence or anything."

"Oh, I see..." Neil said. "What about their young though? What if a new generation was raised without the parasite?"

"I don't know..." Sadhika admitted. "They might bounce right back... or there might be irreparable damage after tens of thousands of years of aggressive co-evolution. There's no way to know without running the experiment."

"If they co-evolved... maybe it took the parasite a long time to figure out how to make them dumber? Neil asked. "Maybe until it was able to do that the squiddies were smart enough to be able to treat themselves or figure out how to avoid becoming infected in the first place."

"I also wonder," Sadhika said, "if maybe the parasite is what makes them attack loud noises at night too... there's no reason to positively think it's the case, but imagine if something which made loud sounds at night preyed on the organism back in its history before it ever became a parasite in the first place? And then once they figured out how to affect the brain of another creature they compelled it to attack anything loud at night out of preternatural spite or something?"

Neil nodded and Sadhika chuckled to herself. "It's like Søren said, if true it certainly wouldn't be the *strangest* thing about this planet."

"Speaking of the humans, do you think this parasite poses a threat to them?" Neil asked.

"Could be," Sadhika answered with a shrug. "If they *are* susceptible to it though, it'd be easy to come up with a treatment protocol for it. We'll have to run regular scans on everybody on the surface for a while. Like I was alluding to, we could probably treat the squiddies too; we could eradicate it from their entire population if we really wanted to."

"Would that be ethical?"

"Not my department." Sadhika laughed, which made Neil laugh along with her. "I don't know Neil. We certainly *could* help them regain some of their former glory. Personally I'm certainly inclined to try, in fact I could see that being In-Su's new project as well!" she said with another laugh. "I'm sure he'll stop at nothing to develop effective communication with them; I have no doubt he'll find some way."

"There's always the playing god issue though... as you know many people think that however things naturally are without human intervention, is the way they should stay."

"Or sim," Sadhika corrected him.

"What?"

"You said without human intervention, you should have said without human or simulant intervention."

Neil laughed out loud. "Aw fuck it. I've finally given up on trying to maintain that distinction."

"Good for you," she said with a smile. "Anyways, I think we should help them if we can. I mean, it's not like we're trying to artificially turn them into something they're not, it's more like we'd be trying to help them become again what they once were; we'd just be helping them to reclaim what was once theirs."

"I'm inclined to agree." Neil admitted. "Of course there's always the risk that they'll turn out to be incredibly violent and xenophobic, and that they'll wind up killing and enslaving all the humans..." he casually mentioned with an entirely deadpan delivery. Sadhika gave him a smile which indicated that she recognized the humour in what he was saying, but also that she understood it was not entirely beyond the realm of possibility and that perhaps this was why it was funny at all. The dread of humanity creating its own destroyer was a fear in the human psyche as old as human storytelling itself, and yet it'd never happened. For anything that ever does happen though, there does always have to be a first time...

"It's the least we can do... after all it's *their* planet and I still feel rather guilty about dropping in on them the way we did. We specifically meant to avoid any chance of landing on a planet that already had beings with anything resembling intelligence as we understand it."

"Yeah but here we are, and we still haven't even explored the catacombs any further. There's a whole lot more to discover about these guys; there's still so much to learn about them."

"There's so much to learn in general... that's what makes this all so exciting, that it's a brand new data point to explore, a whole new world waiting to be discovered and understood. We have to start from square one with everything!"

"Indeed..." Neil agreed with a profound reverence for all which they had yet to learn about this planet and the star system it resided in. "The unknown can be very scary Sadhika, but... damn is it ever exciting to turn it into the known, piece by piece by piece..." Sadhika nod-ded her head in agreement with the comment. "So, now that I think about it I've got all kinds of questions about the possibility of curing the squiddies," Neil stated.

"Shoot."

"Well what if there are squiddies all over the planet, but we've only just met the one population?"

"If we cure these guys, then... we'll just commit to curing any populations we eventually come across."

"Okay... but what if a population we cure gets to an uncured population before we do, and now the smarter ones we've created enslave or annihilate the dumber ones?"

Sadhika laughed. "I don't know Neil. There's no reason to think they'll necessarily act the way humans tend to."

"An even better point," Neil realized. "What if we cure the squiddies and they wind up just smart enough to become the perfect slaves for future humans and are then kept from becoming any smarter so that they remain contented as slaves?"

The simulated woman shook her head. "I don't know Neil... you're right. There's a chance it could all go down that way. I guess we just have to have faith that our descendants will know better." Sadhika chewed on the thought for a few moments. "It could go the other way too though, you know. In a couple thousand years after they've all recovered and been amply educated, maybe even genetically modified to be even smarter, there could be a beautiful future of peaceful collaboration between human and squiddy. Maybe someday there will be a *new* New Horizon mission, jointly orchestra-ted and peopled by human *and* squiddy kind alike in a collaborative effort."

Neil shrugged his shoulders. "There are people who never thought that humans on Earth could ever get their act together enough to collaborate that thoroughly and effectively... but *eventually* they did."

"Yes. Eventually they did..."

Chapter 39

It had been a few days since negotiations on the ship had concluded, and most of the people who intended to live down on the planet had already been ferried down in the shuttles. Ever since the end of the conflict though, Halley had been distant in a way which made those who still cared about him worry. Søren in particular, as his closest friend, could tell that there was something which was still bothering him beyond the self-evident. He'd asked him a few times what it was but Halley only ever waved him off without explanation. Knowing his friend as well as he did, Søren understood that he would talk only when he was ready, and that pressing him about it would only serve to push him further away.

Halley had angered and frustrated Sadhika, but she was intrigued by him nonetheless. Although she could never condone what he'd done, she did on some level understand his motivations and the deeper dilemma of his existence. While their respective situations were in some ways entirely different, in other respects she figured that they were actually rather similar. Both of them had to reconcile being reincarnations of a sort; both of them were in their own way different kinds of copies of an original. He was of the same stuff but an altogether different person, whereas she was of different stuff but essentially the same person. His ingredients were the same but his manifestation was different, while her ingredients were different but her manifestation essentially the same, at least by comparison.

She found him sitting on the cliff which Sadhika and the other sims had come across when they'd made their way to the ocean. It was mid-morning and he sat with his legs hanging over the edge of the cliff, staring out into the deep infinitudes of the ocean and the distant horizon. As she approached, Halley picked up a small stone and rolled it around in his hand thoughtfully for a few moments before lobbing it out in front of him and watching it fall all the way down to the water below.

She didn't ask if she could join him, instead she just sat down beside him without saying a word. Instead of hanging her legs over the edge as he had, she instead sat cross-legged and wrapped her arms around her legs. The two sat in silence for quite some time, long enough for Sadhika to watch several clouds roll in overhead and create an overcast effect, not across the entire sky but quite significantly in the area above where they were. The clouds looked heavy, and she found herself wondering if it might rain.

Sadhika was waiting patiently for Halley to feel the need to break the silence. She was hoping that if she sat there long enough he would open up to her about what, beyond the obvious given the past few weeks, was still bothering him so much.

"I've never seen clouds before…" he finally said. "I mean, I guess I must have seen them when I was preoccupied with my mission, but I never took the time to really notice or appreciate them. I'd only ever seen pictures on the ship before we landed."

"Pictures can never really tell the whole story can they? Not even your PANEs on full immersion can, there's something about really being here isn't there…"

"Yeah…" he said with a sigh as he studied the sky. "It's beautiful." The simulated woman sitting beside him nodded her agreement.

"Sadhika I've been meaning to, um…" Halley started without looking at her and instead still holding his gaze out towards the horizon, "I wanted to thank you for talking me down that day…" he finally said.

"You're welcome," she softly replied.

Halley sighed heavily, as though a tremendous weight on him made the act of sighing particularly laborious. "I think I *wanted* to die…" Another heavy sigh. "I think in that moment… I think that was the whole point for me. I guess I wanted to do the whole… blaze of glory thing. I wanted my star to burn brighter and hotter than anybody else's. As a clone I had something to prove… but when I realized I wasn't going to get my way I guess in response I just resolved to burn even brighter and hotter. But the hotter and brighter a star burns though, the sooner it burns out… a part of me knew that maxing out the intensity meant that I had to die for it. I think that was the whole point at the time… I knew it would be so much easier than… god, than going through all this." Halley started to tear up at this point. "It would have been so much easier than facing the world I helped to create and… and the people that I hurt. It's killing me to face what I did and all the people who were lost as a result… people like Ishtar."

"I know." These were the things which she could have imagined would be bothering him. She figured that maybe he had to work through these things out loud before he could get to what was bothering him beyond this.

"And you were trying to warn me all along weren't you?" Halley said through tearful eyes as he finally looked directly at her. "Beyond trying to save everyone else… you were also trying to spare me all *this* weren't you?"

"Yeah…" Sadhika agreed with a heavy sigh.

"Well," Halley said with a morbid chuckle as he wiped tears away from his eyes, "I certainly appreciate the effort."

"You know, there's no way I could have reached you if there wasn't some part of you that *wanted* to be reached, if on some level… you didn't *want* to be stopped."

"I suppose so…"

"So are you going to tell me what's really bothering you *beyond* all that?" Sadhika finally felt she had to ask directly. "Søren and I are worried about you," she gently added.

Halley hesitated for what seemed like a long time, but then finally answered: "I don't want to be the last."

"The last?" Sadhika asked, not quite understanding at first.

"The last clone."

"Oh I see." She now understood completely, but she didn't know what to make of him saying it. She found herself immediately and deeply troubled by the prospect of Halley taking it upon himself to create yet another clone; it was a prospect she'd never considered before.

"I'm not saying that the experiment should go on forever, but… I don't want to be the last one. I don't want *me* and everything *I've* done to be the… you know, the definitive version. I don't want *my* actions to be what we are *all* ultimately and collectively remembered as being."

Sadhika felt that she had to handle the situation very delicately. She was absolutely opposed to the idea of course, but she was wise enough to know that her outright forbidding him at this point might only serve to totally commit him to the idea. "Why do you feel that way?" she hesitantly asked.

It was at this point that Halley bolted up to his feet, and in the process almost launched himself off of the cliff in the process. He turned away and walked into the tall grass which lay between the cliff edge and the jungle which separated them from the primary colony site. As Sadhika stood to follow him, he stopped and stood still with his back to her. "Because I'm a failure." he quietly answered. "Not just because of the mess I caused *here,* but… but because I proved to be just as flawed as any of the others. After my… after my father I can only be thought of a step backwards, as a… as a regression. I am error."

"You're looking at it all wrong Halley," Sadhika said as she approached him from behind, and then came around to stand in front of him. "I think *your* error… was only the original error in the first place of thinking that anybody can clone their way to self-actualization. It just… it just doesn't *work* that way.

"For one thing, it was a fundamental error from the outset, to believe that there is some ultimate standard by which you can measure yourself as a human being, some definitive standard which you can progress towards and judge yourself by how closely you mirror it. In the end there is no 'correct' way of being human Halley, any more than there is an incorrect way. There are only… *different* ways of being human. The only meaningful metric of one's way of being is whether or not it is counterproductive to one's own goals and values.

"You and the other clones have successfully and definitively demonstrated that from any given genome vastly different kinds of people can arise given different lived experiences. As we've discussed though, there are also deep fundamental traits which seem to be constant throughout and which seem to fundamentally anchor all of that vast variability. I think as a result that is enough to call the experiments a success on their face and… and to let it be at that. Any scientific justifications which may have existed for the experiments have been satisfied and now no longer exist. The idea that's been developed throughout though, of continual improvement towards some ethereal ideal incarnation which you have to keep replicating until you achieve… I think that is not only an unjustifiable idea, I think it's a dangerous one.

"It's too much pressure to lay at the feet of any new being… and you know that as well as anyone, don't you? What makes it so insidious is that it's an impossible ideal because there can never be any agreement on what the idealized human being would be. It is different for every whole being, every being who is both their genetics and the life they've lived. There can be no ideal expression of a genome because the life it is subjected to is as integral to its ideal expression as the genome is. Ask a million different people, hell ask a million different clones of Markus Bowland what the correct way of being human is and you'll get as many different answers. *That's* the problem."

"The point is not to strive to live any particular life…" Halley said as he came to understand, "the point is to enjoy and live well the life you get isn't it… to learn acceptance of who we are and to make the most of the life we're given."

"Precisely," Sadhika agreed, "not in a fatalistic acceptance of some kind of destiny, but in a deterministic appreciation of how our futures are shaped by the decisions we make in the present and the lessons which we draw from the mistakes we've made in the past. The key is to never stop learning and recalibrating our understanding of who we are, what we really want out of our lives, and how best to pursue what really matters to us so we don't waste a single moment of our ever so brief moment on the stage. That's the process which led me and the others to throw ourselves into the mission which got us all here in the first place. It's what you did on some level when you chose to recalibrate what you really wanted in that moment on the bridge… when you chose to *live*."

"Tycho didn't choose to live," Halley observed, "he wasn't able to… but I could. We were all different, not different degrees of separation from the ideal, just… just different."

"Exactly. Each one of you had to figure it all out from scratch for yourself just like every other human being. To learn about oneself and about the universe we're born into... is the birthright of every human child. It's the only kind of betterment and self-actualization any hu-man being has any genuine access to, the individual kind. The whole point of a human life is for it to be *lived* Halley, to be dis-cover day by day. You can't cheat your way to self-discovery through cloning. It's cheating the game of life, and if you're cheating... you're not really playing the game are you?"

Halley nodded that he understood, but he didn't say anything. The clouds were rolling in more thickly now; it was definitely threatening to rain.

Sadhika thoughtfully added: "If you're always preoccupied with who you've been, and who you might become in the future, you'll miss the most important part of your life – who you Halley Bowland are right now, singularly here with me as an individual being, in this moment of time. There is only now. There is only your own life, as you live it, right now. It is one's *existence*... and it's easy to miss if you exist somewhere else."

"You know... I was going to ask you to be my mother, I mean... mother to the new clone. I always believed that my father was the most developed of us and that it was because he was raised by your granddaughter Dhika. I remember my grandmother, and I remember her being a lot like you. I have to think that she was what made all the difference for Herschel.

"But now... now I think that maybe you're right. Maybe it really is finally time to put it all to rest. You know, Ishtar always agreed in principle to us raising a new clone together. I believed that in the right environment, in our own community and with loving parents, that together we could produce a truly idealized clone... but you know, we also planned on having our own naturally conceived children as well as the mission outlined."

"You could still have a child with her you know... certainly her genome is on file; it wouldn't be very difficult at all."

Halley nodded. "Have you sims agreed to who is going to lead the different colony sites?" he asked.

"Not yet, no." she answered.

"I want you, Sadhika. I want you to be the one to lead us. I trust you. I... I respect you. I'd accept any of the others as I agreed of course, but… you're the one I'd choose."

Truth be told, Sadhika hadn't given much thought to who would live where when it was all said and done. But it was also true that she didn't have any immediate aversion to it being her to live with and lead Halley's camp. After all she'd be able to communicate with anyone wherever she wanted, and it was a pretty short trip between the two colony sites so on some level it really didn't matter in which site she lived.

Plus, she had a certain sympathy for Halley which she couldn't entirely explain. Perhaps it was her empathy over their shared burden of both being new incarnations of former beings, and the constant pressure to live up to a predecessor which went along with it.

"If I agree to lead you," she offered as gently as she could, "would you agree to commit to ending the cloning program?"

Halley spent several moments in silence, presumably considering the proposition. Instead of answering her question directly, he answered with another question. "If I instead have a novel child using Ishtar's genome… would you agree to be its mother?"

He asked it so casually, as though he were asking her to stir the pot while he used the bathroom so the sauce didn't burn. She was taken aback, but she didn't find herself settling on declining right away. She was actually rather surprised by the degree to which her heart called out to ascent. There was a part of her which had always been sad to not have had children back on Earth when she was human. She never regretted her path and she'd made her life choices with her eyes wide open, but it also made her appreciate the offer which had now been so casually made; she in fact found it quite flattering. She was also acutely aware that as a simulant her procreational options were limited to say the least.

After a bit of awkward silence, Halley started: "I'm not suggesting we be lovers or a couple or anything-"

"I know," she acknowledged with a muted nervous laugh. In truth she was surprised to discover she wasn't sure that in the very long term she'd always be opposed to such a thing anyways. In her head she was already speculating about the possibility of their next child being a blending between both of their respective progenitors.

"I mean, I haven't even begun to process losing Ishtar," Halley nervously clarified, "and-"

"I know, Halley," she said as she put her hand on his shoulder. "I know. I'm just... I'm just thinking."

"I wouldn't want to do it alone and, and you remind me so much of my grandmother..."

"I know," she offered as reassuringly as she could. "So is that your settlement offer then? No more clones if I be the leader of your town and the mother of your child? Is that everything?" she asked in jest, trying to lighten the mood.

"If you want to call it that..." he replied, still a little too serious for her comfort. "I'd call it offering you to be more generally enshrinement as our matriarch."

"Right..."

"We've got a lot of work to do..." Halley observed, "raising families, taming a wild planet... hell, building a whole civilization."

"I look forward to it," Sadhika said with an eager smile.

"Me too..." Halley agreed with a gentle chuckle. "I didn't before though. It used to feel like a burden, but now... now it's exciting. Now I look forward to the challenge."

It was at that moment, that if finally started to rain. It started with a moderate shower, but quickly escalated to quite a significant downpour. Neither of them felt the need to run for cover or lament their lack of anything to cover themselves up with. Halley looked up into the sky, and put his arms out with his palms up to feel the drops falling down on him. He started to laugh in delight and Sadhika could understand why. He'd never seen the rain before.

Epilogue

"We did it… we really did it."

The madness had finally settled. It had now been a few weeks since the terms upon which the two colony sites would co-exist had finally been agreed to, and so far the peace was holding without any indication that old conflicts would re-emerge. Some were inclined to think that the hard part was over, but it could also be said that the truly hard part was still what lay ahead of them. The suffering and hardship of the long journey was over; the conflict which erupted as a result, was likewise now over. Now all that was left was the work. It wasn't glamorous, and it wasn't exciting, but it was what they were here to do, what all the rest was ultimately in service of, the ability to work hard towards a goal. Now all that was left for them to do was build a civilization.

Now it was just the work, constructing buildings, establishing industry, cultivating science and art. The nature of the mission had shifted again, no longer about enduring, no longer about winning; now it was only about building. Now was the time for work which one could be proud of, which one could step back from and appreciate as the products of one's efforts. Now was the time for accomplishments which were one's own, instead of having to concentrate on fulfilling the wishes and instructions of long dead figures.

The four simulants were taking a full day off for the first time in their entire existence. Now that all of the humans had a sense of their tasks and were feeling somewhat situated, all four felt the need to take a long moment to breathe, process, and appreciate everything that had happened. There was also a tacit understanding that going forward they would likely see less and less of each other as they moved on to their long term positions.

They'd settled on a lunchtime picnic by the sea in the same spot from which they had first seen the ocean, beyond the jungle where the tall grass gave way to some rockier terrain. They'd lain down a blanket and unpacked the lunch they'd prepared for themselves. Included with their lunch were a few select bottles of wine from a small reserve the original Neil Sagan had stashed onboard for just such an occasion.

"So how many wound up staying on the ship?" Wiremu asked.

"A hundred and forty-five," Neil answered as he popped the cork on the bottle and smelled it. "Sixty-three seniors, seventy-one children, and the eleven adults we were able recruit to stay on the ship and help out with running the breeding lab and parenting the children."

"That leaves us only fifty-nine humans on the surface," In-Su lamented. "It's not much… especially with them split between the two different colonies. It's a pretty silly situation, isn't it?"

"Of course it's silly!" Sadhika answered. "It's utterly ridiculous!" she further affirmed. "But… it's what was necessary to keep and maintain the peace," she shrugged, "so it's what had to be done."

"It's enough," Wiremu offered as he held out his glass for Neil to fill. "It'll make development slow going at first, but within a couple decades the adult population will more than double, and it'll triple again at least just a few decades after that. It'll work… as long as we can keep up with our food and water supply, and keep up with infrastructure construction. We supremely lucked out with the near zero failure rate bringing down the rest of the drone landers."

"We have a fighting chance." Neil stated as he finished pouring Sadhika's glass and then moved the bottle to fill In-Su's. "That's all we ever really asked for in the first place, isn't it?" The others nodded. "There's a way, there's a chance… it's *possible.* It's not guaranteed, it could still all go horribly wrong, but… there's a chance. I'll take a *chance* over the alternative any day of the week."

"Well at least we shouldn't have any more political problems now that everyone finally seems to be content with having us lead them," Wiremu observed. The simulants had collectively decided that it would be best for Wiremu to lead Asari's camp after Sadhika had volunteered to lead Halley's.

"Unless *we* have to go to war," Sadhika dryly stated with a feigned sternness which made the others laugh. She held up her glass and offered a toast. "To the end of one journey... and to the beginning of another."

"To the journey," Wiremu agreed.

"To all journeys," In-Su added.

Neil smiled and held up his glass. "To success," he said, "and to the opportunity to *further* succeed."

All four clinked each other's glasses and took a drink. They savoured the moment. All four had the strong sense of being at a crossroads. There was a strong sense that today and at this moment, one story was finally concluding, just as a new one was dawning. All of human history on Earth had narrated them to this point in space and time, and now human history on Haven was beginning on the very first page. It was a new beginning; they had reached the horizon, and they had found a new one to strive for. All four reflected on this as they listened to the waves crashing against the cliffs not too far away, and relished the sunshine on their face and the salty smell of the seaside air.

"We really owe a debt to those adults who volunteered to stay up on the ship long term," In-Su noted. "After all that time stuck on the ship, only to now volunteer to stay on it forever..." he added while sha-king his head at the thought.

"They all volunteered," Neil said with a shrug. "I think they were the ones who to varying degrees were afraid to come down in the first place. It may be hard for *us* to imagine, but after spending their whole lives within the confines of the ship, the idea of a planet surface's wide openness could easily scare the hell out of some people. It's like a... reverse claustrophobia."

"It's kind of sad..." Sadhika thought out loud.

"I agree, but it is what it is," Neil replied with another shrug. "We should be happy for them that we now have an essential role for them up there. We should just be happy that they are indeed so willing to be there as opposed to anyone being resentful of *having* to be."

"What will become of the ship long-term?" In-Su asked. "I mean, when we've done all the artificial birthing we intended to and there's no reason to keep anyone up there any longer."

"Well that raises an interesting question..." Sadhika answered. "Do we really *want* to completely abandon the ship at some point in the future? It's certainly capable of sustaining a small population as long as the hydrogen fuel holds out for the fusion core... but long term the systems will inevitably have to break down one by one no matter how well they're built."

"Well at a certain point there's not much left we can do with it," Wiremu answered. "You're the ones who tell me there's essentially no chance of us developing our own space flight level of technological sophistication before the shuttles finally become unusable. That means that if we keep a permanent presence on the ship then at some point they'll inevitably be stranded up there. And like Sadhika said, if we try to use the ship indefinitely it *will* finally break down at some point."

"Boy, it breaks my heart to think of us losing space capability..." Neil commented. "Given the probability though... as much as it does break my heart, I think that once we don't need New Horizon's facilities anymore the only responsible thing to do would be to abandon it. We should put everything into a safe powered down mode and boost it up into a high enough orbit that it can last up there on its own for millennia. It would be... our lasting monument, to ourselves, to our progenitors, and to all of the humans who got us here and helped us establish a presence on the surface."

"A monument," In-Su repeated, "I like that."

"And maybe most importantly," Neil added, "it'll always be the brightest object in the night sky. It would always forbid every future generation from forgetting where they came from, and why it's so important to find their way back. It'd be an invaluable reminder for them of... some very important things."

"I'm sure you're right, *and* that it'll inspire distant members of the new astronomical society you're founding," Sadhika said with a smile.

The satellites in their orbital network could function as remotely operated astronomical observatories, but their capabilities were limited and the system was usually preoccupied with its primary intended functions. Also available to him as long as the system held up, was remote operation of the New Horizons' four telescope interferometric array, but someday that system too would inevitably go offline. As a result, Neil had al-ready drawn up plans to build a series of different terrestrial astronomical observatories in order to capture all of the light which penetrated Haven's atmosphere. He was anxious to study the new alien star system he found himself in and was sometimes positively giddy at the thought of everything that was out there just waiting to be discovered. So far he was only discovering that planning was the easy part, and that the *hard* part was going to be figuring out how to build from scratch all of the high precision technology and equipment he would need.

In-Su had already begun work on what would become the Squiddy Research Institute, a program fo-cused on studying all aspects of the seemingly quite intelligent animals they'd run into. The primary focus was to unearth as much of their history as possible, and to definitively determine what caused their apparent civilizational collapse. Although Sadhika had suggested that it was due to the brain parasite she had discovered, a lot of work still had to be done to confirm her hypothesis. In-Su was also still convinced that he would be able to develop some kind of rudimentary communication with the squiddies, but all of the sims found themselves curious about what could happen if the creatures were cured of their parasites, and what aid they might be able to provide them in being restored to their previous capabilities using the sophisticated genetic technologies they'd brought with them to Haven.

Fortunately, all parties readily agreed that whether they were able to help them or not, the squiddies were there first and that needed to be respected. Everyone agreed that an active effort should be made to avoid displacing the squiddies from where they already lived. Detailed analysis of the planet using the orbiting satellite network's ground penetrating radar system had revealed that the underground caverns which suggested their presence were extensive in a neighboring continent where they seemed to be centred, but were less extensive on adjacent continents such as the one the simulants were currently lunching on. It meant that there was a lot of the planet's territory declared off limits for colonization, but it also left a lot of territory still open for future human expansion. Either way, it would be a long time before anyone was thinking about expanding beyond the existing two colony sites, which were already overextending them as it was.

"You know, I remember Kim In-Su..." In-Su observed, "and I'm not him. But I couldn't tell you... if it's because I'm a simulant, or because I've lived through things which he never did. Is it being a simulant that makes me not him, or is it just the same way in which... none of us are really the same person from one day to the next, the way each moment of experience changes us and updates who we are in some infinitesimal yet not insignificant way?"

"Yeah... we're ultimately nothing more than the sum of our experiences are we?" Wiremu offered. "Every-thing else aside, different experiences... different person I guess," he concluded with a shrug.

"In some ways we're always the same person," Neil offered, "but in other ways we're continually changing into somebody different aren't we?"

"It's almost like at one point," Sadhika observed, "we made way too big a deal of our physical form changing, and attributed to it *all* of the change we observed in ourselves... but now we're realizing more and more that it's just the kind of perpetual change that *any* being goes through as it is continually changed by its experiences."

"So if it's more our different experiences which make us distinct from our progenitors in essence, as opposed to our physical nature..." Neil asked with a subtly pained expression on his face, "then how is anyone *ever* really the same person over time?" he asked the others. "What is... what is the actual *self* which seems to under-write every successive incarnation over time?"

"Maybe there isn't one..." Sadhika distantly re-marked. "I mean, the clones demonstrated pretty definitively that the genome certainly can't be thought of as the source of that deeper self you're talking about."

"No, I think you got it exactly right Sadhika," In-Su commented, "whether you really meant to or not. The idea that there is no self centering it all is in fact an ancient one, and an idea I take very seriously. Every-thing about our experience of the world is calibrated to create the *illusion* that there is a 'self', that there is a 'there' there, somewhere in our heads. But I believe it is just an artifact which arises as a result of the way the human brain processes sensory information. The sense of self, the sense that we are some kind of eternal spiritual being which resides in the centre of our heads, and which listens through our ears, sees through our eyes, smells through our nose, and feels through our skin, is just an illusion. It's an illusion which is the product of the brain unifying all of those senses together so that they can be processed simultaneously and compared against each other. It's the same system which gives rise to phenomenological consciousness itself, as a kind of… operating system which allows integrated simultaneous processing of multiple streams of information; a system which is also used to recall memories, and allows humans to project different possible future outcomes of present situations."

"If I recall correctly, through cell division humans continually recycle most of their physical material over time…" Neil reflected. "So it can't even be said that the continuation of *physical* self is a self which is preserved over time… so if it's not the physical that's ever preserved, and the mind is continually changing and evolving… you must be right In-Su, there's really nothing left is there?"

"It is only identity which is preserved…" In-Su offered.

"What do you mean?" Sadhika asked.

"Multiple incarnations of the same identity," he answered. "Kim In-Su is a shared identity, not any particular embodiment of it. Kim In-Su is not any particular instance of me, nor of my human progenitor. Instead, there are an infinite number of both of us, which exist at every single indivisible point in time of both of our existences; each is a discrete entity which all collectively contribute to a global and incorporated entity which is Kim In-Su. There is the idea of Kim In-Su, and an infinite number of different incarnations of him, each of which are distinct, but which all share an equal claim on the identity."

"That's what makes the now so important…" Sadhika responded in reflection on a conversation she'd had with Halley a while ago. "The now is characterized by our embodiment of just one of those incarnations amongst an infinite number of variations. The passage of time could be thought of as the perpetual shift from a past incarnation of Sadhika Sengupta into the next, into the one which exists in the present. Now is when we have the power to change who we become in every successive incarnation."

"I'd have to agree." In-Su said.

"It's quite a thought…" Neil offered as he processed the metaphysical suggestion.

"Oh, the vast emptiness!" Wiremu exclaimed, not really following the conversation and instead quoting something nobody had seen or heard in hundreds of years, and entirely for his own amusement's sake. He'd overdramatically held up his hands to the sky as he said it, and then slyly shook his empty wine glass at Neil, thus completing the reference. Obligingly, Neil picked up the wine bottle and filled his captain's glass before doing the same for his other two friends and then himself.

CPSIA information can be obtained at www.ICGtesting.com
Printed in the USA
LVOW10s1447160615

442682LV00015B/617/P

9 780994 026545